PRAI
WICKED AS ~~YOU~~

★ "Chupeco...has brought readers a truly original novel. A deftly executed melding of folklore and reality grounded in contemporary issues."
—*Kirkus Reviews*

★ "An enchanting story that is both a feast for the senses and a unique spin on the hero's journey."
—*Publishers Weekly*

"Rin Chupeco's marvelously magical *Wicked As You Wish* is a great read for fans of fairy tales, myths, and legends. In fact, avid fans will want to read it two, three, or four times just to catch all the twists, updates, and Easter eggs, as nearly every chapter is loaded with delights. Come for the adventure; stay for the sassy jerkwad firebird."
—Kendare Blake, #1 *New York Times* bestselling author of the Three Dark Crowns series

"Readers looking for a vibrant, Harry Potter–esque fantasy full of secrets, spies, magic, monsters, and mayhem need look no further."
—*Booklist*

"Wildly creative, with myriad references to folklore and fairy tales, this alternate-reality adventure will surely appeal to modern fantasy fans who can keep up with a complex plot that unfolds at a breakneck pace."
—*Horn Book*

PRAISE FOR
AN UNRELIABLE MAGIC

"Cultural deviations add wit, and chapter titles bestow particular joy. The cast is authentically diverse, their youthful uncertainty and determined courage engaging readerly affection... Come along for the utter delight of young folk using energy and magic for good."

—*Aurealis*

"A whirlwind adventure that balances the fantastic with dreams of how real-world problems might be solved."

—*Kirkus Reviews*

"A fabulistic alternate history with friendship at its heart, *An Unreliable Magic* is an enthralling fantasy novel."

—*Foreword*

"Chupeco's second installment in the Hundred Names for Magic series combines the quip-filled vibe of a contemporary teen rom-com, the breadth of an epic fantasy, and the irreverent verve of a punk rock mix tape blaring out of a speeding hot rod."

—*Booklist*

"Pure fun with a Filipino-inspired flair."

—*School Library Journal*

PRAISE FOR
THE BONE WITCH
TRILOGY

★ "*The Bone Witch* is fantasy world-building at its best, and Rin Chupeco has created a strong and colorful cast of characters to inhabit that realm."

—*Shelf Awareness*

★ "Mesmerizing. Chupeco does a magnificent job of balancing an intimate narrative perspective with sweeping world-building, crafting their tale within a multicultural melting pot of influences as they presses toward a powerful cliff-hanger."

—*Publishers Weekly*

"*The Bone Witch* is a fantasy lover's fantasy, with a rich history and hierarchy of its own. The secrets and workings of its magic are revealed slowly in a suspenseful novel that is sure to appeal to those with a love of serious, dark fairy tales."

—*Foreword* on *The Bone Witch*

"Chupeco craftily weaves magic, intrigue, and mystery into a captivating tale that will leave readers begging for the promised sequel."

—*School Library Journal*

"Readers who enjoy immersing themselves in detail will revel in Chupeco's finely wrought tale. *Game of Thrones* fans may see shades of Daenerys Targaryen in Tea, as she gathers a daeva army to unleash upon the world. Whether she is in the right remains a question unanswered, but the ending makes it clear her story is only beginning."

—*Booklist*

"A high-fantasy *Memoirs of a Geisha*, Chupeco's latest excels in originality… Chupeco is a writer to watch."

—*Kirkus Reviews*

"In this sweeping high fantasy, Chupeco concocts a grim world of magic, both light and dark."

—*Bulletin of the Center for Children's Books*

★ "Rin's beautifully crafted world from *The Bone Witch* (2017) expands in this sequel, which joins dark asha Tea on her crusade of revenge… Dark and entrancing with a third volume to come."

—*Booklist* on *The Heart Forger*

★ "In this spectacular follow-up to the rich *The Bone Witch*, Tea's quest draws the reader further in, setting them on a more dangerous yet intriguing adventure."

—*Foreword* on *The Heart Forger*

★ "Chupeco has crafted a glorious world for her twisting, turning plot, rich with magic, exotic beasts, romance, and treachery. The alternating narratives are masterfully designed, drawing readers ever closer to their inevitable convergence. A mesmerizing tale, this sequel is even stronger than its precursor."

—*Shelf Awareness* on *The Heart Forger*

"A wonderfully original tale—even better than the first… Readers will be pleased with the satisfying direction that Chupeco decides to go in regard to Tea's love interests. The ending is equally explosive and delightfully romantic, and the conclusion really sets up events for the next title. These books have loads of potential to become a phenomenal fantasy series."

—RT Book Reviews on *The Heart Forger*

"A worthy conclusion to a story that is, at its core, about love and letting go."

"Required reading for fans of the first two novels, whose many questions will finally be answered."

"Head-over-heels romance, terrifying curses, political intrigue, and epic magical battles will appeal to fantasy enthusiasts… A must-purchase."

ALSO BY RIN CHUPECO

THE
WORLD'S
END

THE
WORLD'S
END

RIN CHUPECO

sourcebooks
fire

Published by Sourcebooks Fire, an imprint of Sourcebooks
P.O. Box 4410, Naperville, Illinois 60567-4410
(630) 961-3900
sourcebooks.com

Cataloging-in-Publication Data is on file with the Library of Congress.

Printed and bound in the United States of America.
VP 10 9 8 7 6 5 4 3 2 1

For Ezio and Altair, my wishes come true

In Which the Adarna Is the World's Most Wanted Bird

The adarna had done nothing wrong. Quite frankly, it was rather offended by all the people trying to murder it at the moment.

The Piedra Platas was not a forest conducive to human habitation. Mining and deforestation had taken its toll, but Filipinos in general were a superstitious lot. Even the greedy rich avoided magical places that were known for their implacable, centuries-old curses, even if they had beautiful trees and unexplored mountains ripe for the pillaging.

But the people chasing after the adarna were not interested in the forest. They were made of ice. They were made of shadows.

The adarna had done nothing wrong, but it fled all the same.

More projectiles whizzed past its head, streaming the air in its wake. One nearly punctured through its talon. The woods were thick enough to serve as rudimentary protection, and the interlopers were missing their aim so far, but they also showed no signs of giving up despite all the obstacles in their path.

A sudden barrage of sharp icicles made the adarna cry out in pain; one had found its left wing. It plunged down toward the unforgiving forest floor, only managing to curve up at the last minute to swing itself onto a branch, ducking beneath a heavy canopy of leaves.

Huddled underneath the foliage, the ice shard still buried in its skin, the adarna waited.

It could hear the crunching sounds of feet treading on the dried leaves littering the ground. Voices drew closer.

"You shouldn't have done that," one of its pursuers snapped, angry. "If you kill it, the queen will turn us *both* into ornamental Popsicles."

"I have hunted for Her Majesty far longer than you have ever been alive," came the response in a voice that made the adarna imagine cold winters and lifeless tundras. "And I have obliterated those who have questioned my authority for far lesser transgressions."

"Well, *this* isn't supposed to be an obliteration. We need to bring it back alive. How hard is it to get that into your thick inhuman skull?"

"The queen favors you now, though you have yet to swear your complete obedience. But her mood changes with the seasons. Do well to remember that." The sounds of more footsteps, closer this time. "It is hiding nearby. I can smell it."

The adarna remained perfectly still, not wanting the whisper of leaves against its feathers to give away its hiding spot. It swallowed a whimper.

A gust of wind whipped through the tiny clearing. There were gasps, the scraping of more ice, and then another new voice, angry and full of heat.

"You are trespassers to the Piedras Platas. Surrender yourselves now, mga hijas."

A low hiss from one of the ice people. "Corazon Makiling. What a pleasant surprise."

The adarna dared to poke its head out, just far enough to witness the scene unfolding before it. It saw a short, slender old Filipina with a scowl on her face and a bayonet over half her height strapped to her back. In her hands was an abanico, the fan carefully folded between her fingers, held like a throwing knife.

With her were others with her dark skin and black hair, all similarly armed. They scowled at their opponents—the first a young woman with a short bob, wielding a large banana leaf with a sureness that was at odds with the uncertainty on her face; the second, by all appearances, an ice sculpture with a human shape, one that moved with a woman's grace but spoke in a chillingly inhuman voice.

"An ice maiden," the old woman called Corazon Makiling stated grimly. "And you—I've seen you before, hija. You are the one they call Vivien Fey."

"You are one of the Makilings," the young woman replied, eyes narrowing.

"Now that we have been properly introduced, let us make this quick. You are both under arrest for attempted theft, trespassing, attempted *murder*, and conspiring with known terrorists."

The ice maiden laughed, and the air turned colder from the sound alone. "You know as well as I that this is no theft. The adarna has always been Buyan property. We have simply come to reclaim what *you* have stolen from *us* all these centuries ago. You cannot win. Her Majesty shall rule these lands."

"You will not take the adarna."

"Then try and stop us."

The adarna ducked out of view again when more ice shards filled the air, aimed at Corazon and her soldiers. With a deft flick of the old woman's wrist, the cold arrow melted midflight before it could reach them. Another flick, and the fan she was holding snapped to its full width. A further twist of her arm sent a fresh gale of wind rushing toward the ice maiden and her companion, the former disappearing and reappearing some meters back, the latter dodging behind a tree to avoid the blow.

The Filipinos strode forward, their bayonets out. The ice maiden growled and struck at the ground this time, turning it into ice in an instant. There were startled cries as the group fought for balance, but the old woman remained unperturbed. The cold around her feet simply thawed away, leaving a path for her to move through, bearing down on the two interlopers.

"You have a chance to renounce all this, Vivien Fey," Corazon Makiling said. "It has only been three months since you left with the accursed Snow Queen. You have not yet given up your soul, and that is good. But the longer you remain in her control, the more likely you are to end up like her." She swept her fan toward the ice maiden, clear contempt on her face. "Is that what you want? Is that what your sister would have wanted for you?"

For a moment, Vivien Fey wavered, a look of anguish on her

face. But her expression hardened quickly enough. "You are one of the reasons why my sister is no longer here," she said and raised the banana leaf.

The resulting wind was at least ten times stronger than what the old woman had been able to produce with her abanico fan. The adarna ducked for cover as powerful hurricanes screamed through the trees, the world wobbling sideways, and then it continued to cartwheel over until it was tumbling toward the ground, head over tail. The tree it had tried to conceal itself in could not withstand the force of the attack and had toppled over with a resounding crash, sending the adarna down along with it. Discombobulated, it lay splayed out on the ground, surrounded by dead leaves, but not for long. Someone grabbed it by the scruff of its neck, yanked it up.

"I got it!" came Vivien Fey's triumphant cry. "Let's go!"

A portal shimmered into life behind them, and the sight was enough for the adarna to begin struggling again, trying its best to squirm out of the woman's grasp. It did not want to leave the woods it had lived in for most of its life. And it knew instinctively that if it was made to go into the portal, it would not be alive for very long.

"Stop them!" another voice shouted, and something invisible in the air shifted, barreled past the adarna and its would-be kidnapper, straight into the glowing portal. The ice maiden swore.

"Kill them!" she screeched. "They're altering our port back into Beira!"

Still keeping a firm grip on the adarna, Vivien Fey lifted the banana leaf toward the Filipinos only to lower it again, suddenly hesitant.

"What are you waiting for, Fey?" her companion screamed. "You knew this would happen. Finish them off!"

One of the other Filipinos had been stealthily approaching the two from the right, keeping out of view. Now, with a victorious shout, he rushed forward, striking with his bayonet. Vivien turned to block his move with the leaf, but the momentum sent her barreling right into the portal, taking the adarna along with her.

With a snarl, the ice maiden turned to leap in after them, making it just in time. The hole closed behind her.

Corazon Makiling stood before the empty space where the Beirans and the adarna had once been, breathing hard. "Masyado na akong matanda para dito," she muttered.

"Lola." Miguel approached her, also switching to speaking Tagalog. "You altered the coordinates. Where did you send them?"

"Not to Beira. Somewhere we still have a chance to bring the adarna back."

Miguel was quick to understand. "I don't think they'll want to see us again, Lola."

"It doesn't matter what they think. Ambrosio, send word to King Alexei as soon as you can. The adarna is loose in Avalon." The old woman let out a slow, resigned sigh. "We," she said, "are in trouble."

1

IN WHICH KEN STILL
CAN'T SWIM

Kensington Inoue, latest wielder of the Nameless Sword, heir to the famed Yawarakai-Te and Juuchi Yosamu swords, and current public face *and* hero of the kingdom of Avalon, was drowning in six feet of water.

Nya was trying her best, though to little avail. Her boyfriend had his arms wrapped tightly around her neck, clinging as she fought to keep them both afloat. Nya was technically a mermaid and therefore not in any danger, but Ken seemed to have sprouted eight arms all at once in his bid not to sink underwater, and his panic was dragging her down along with him.

"It would be a lot more comfortable," Nya was saying with all the patience of a saint, "if you would just relax and let yourself float."

"I don't float," came the warbled, strangled answer. Ken also had his feet locked around her waist at the junction where her flesh ended and her scales began. Nya's large purple-blue mermaid tail stirred just beneath the surface, the only thing keeping them buoyant. "I never float. That's the problem. And will you stop laughing at me, you ungrateful melt? You're the whole bloody reason I'm afraid of water!"

That last bit was directed at Ken's kelpie, with the unfortunate name of Horse. The creature was swimming circles around them, pausing at intervals to neigh cheerfully at Ken's plight.

"Don't think about Horse," Nya said encouragingly. "Think about floating."

Tala and the other members of the Order of the Bandersnatch were congregated around the water's edge. They were watching Nya's attempt at teaching swimming lessons, occasionally shouting their encouragement at Ken, pretending that the hundred or so guards unobtrusively stationed around the area weren't there for their protection. Whatever her threats the last time they'd seen her, the Snow Queen had been keeping a low profile for the past three months. Tala had enjoyed the respite, though the niggling feeling lingered at the back of her head, knowing the woman was only biding her time before attacking again.

They wouldn't be able to do this much longer. The winter months were approaching, and Alex said winter always came earlier in Avalon than it did in most other kingdoms, though the trade-off was an even earlier spring. In a couple of weeks, it would be too cold for Nya to teach Ken how to swim, far too chilly for them to stay by the lake like they were doing now.

A lot had happened in the last three months. After CEO Ruggedo Nome's death, OzCorp had fought to rebrand itself, distancing the company from the dubious projects of its late founder and committing itself to various philanthropic activities in a bid to rework its image. Activists remained suspicious, noting that very few executives had been fired or replaced. "Sounds like par for the course to me when it comes to dealing with corporations," Alex had told Tala wearily, and he had since responded by reinforcing stricter conditions on the company regarding the spelltech they could manufacture and sell on Avalon soil.

Alex was more forgiving of OzCorp's attempts to kill him than the Royal States' media were of OzCorp's failure at doing so. Nome's role in the whole fiasco had been minimized to the point where news pundits called Alex equally at fault for being a foreign tyrant, an immature king unable to control the spells he himself had set loose on his lands. Tita Teejay had reported, troubled, that resentment toward Avalon was brewing and that Alex was being blamed for surviving his own assassination attempt.

A movement calling to depose King John had been started among several American groups but was finding resistance from the Royal States Council, many of whom had been friendly with Nome. Tala would have thought being caught literally brainwashing people against their will into attacking another kingdom would have ended King John's reign, but apparently not. "More people than you expect want only what they are accustomed to so that things can stay the same," Lola Urduja had told Tala grimly. "Not always what they think is right."

Three months since, and Ryker Cadfael still hadn't woken. Tala visited him at Whitesnake General Hospital every day, watched him sleep while IV drips pumped nutrients into his body. The icicle he'd been stabbed with had somehow managed to miss vital organs, the doctors had assured Alex, and Ryker was expected to make a full recovery. He would wake up when he chose to wake up.

Three months since, and her father was still in a maximum security prison in Norway. Kay Warnock voluntarily turning himself in to the authorities had made the headlines for several days, and his trial was to begin in a matter of weeks. Tala was reassured upon learning that Norway had no death penalty, but several other countries had also been vying for his extradition. Belgium, a nation that *did* have capital punishment, was at the top of that list, and it didn't matter that Kay had once murdered one of their kings because of his horrible abuse and genocide of the Congolese. As Zoe had put it, "If either you or I kill someone, it's murder. But if a head of state does it, it's the law."

Tala and her mother were given an hour every Saturday to talk remotely to Kay, and Tala was looking forward to this week's session. Lumina Makiling Warnock was not often one to be emotional, but their meetings often left her teary-eyed, and Tala was inclined to be the same. It wasn't likely for her father to ever be released from prison, but Kay handled it with a quiet, unperturbed calm, far better than Tala or Lumina were. The press had been hounding him for an interview, though only one had ever been successful—someone had thrust a microphone into his face when he was being moved from the Norwegian courthouse to the jail.

"Sir Warnock," the determined reporter had shouted. "Any other crimes you've done that the courts have yet to charge you with?"

Her father had flashed the lady a bright grin and said, "Punched J. Edgar Hoover in the face on at least three occasions. And I'd do it again."

All things considered, her father was dealing pretty well.

Three months since, and Tala's agimat was still embarrassingly weak. It was to be expected, said the Filipino albularyo Tala had been seeing for her weekly therapy. She'd nearly drained her agimat to counteract the Nine Maidens and save her best friend from a likely painful death. Recovery required patience. But Tala, who had been patient nearly all her life for so many other things, was sick of waiting to be stronger, to be better, to be more useful.

She could now manifest her agimat in smaller ways, could deflect some spelltech. But it wasn't enough, and it always felt like she was constantly being left behind while her friends were coming even further into their own abilities.

Not so very long ago, she had given up the chance to wield the Nameless Sword herself, had forfeited it to Ken. Her friends had been kind ever since learning what she'd done, as friends were often wont to do. But despite their reassurances, knowing she was the weakest in the group was a harsh, constant thorn at her side. She wanted to be worthy of being a Bandersnatcher. She didn't want to be a charity case.

As a distraction, Tala had thrown herself wholeheartedly behind Three Wishes, Zoe's nonprofit dedicated to bringing much needed spelltech to war-ravaged or poverty-stricken areas around the world, which was a lot more complicated than it sounded.

The Gallaghers had created a faster, more efficient way to detect the millions of still-undetected land mines dropped into Laos by the Royal States of America's army decades ago, successfully cutting down fatalities by nearly fifty percent. Local chapters supervised the handling of the equipment; Zoe had been adamant that they only supplied the tech, that the local people were capable of saving themselves. Ensuring that no one misused the tech was their priority.

Avalonian engineers, for instance, had to add low-level fail-safe curses to the cornucopias they distributed to areas below the poverty line, from small villages in Ghana to remote Philippine barangays to refugee camps, after one enterprising warlord had literally tried to seize their means of production.

Alex had approved of Zoe's endeavors. He'd taken it one step further, had announced that one of the prerequisites for membership in the Order of the Bandersnatch included a year's work with Three Wishes, and Ken had declared his own support of the organization, giving it the promotional boost needed for more donations to roll in. It worked. Segen-wielding youths of Avalonian immigrants—and quite a few adults who'd been unable or had chosen not to pass their weapons on—had shown up at Lyonesse, happily swearing their allegiance to Alex for the opportunity, many opting to join the rangers afterward, like Loki had.

It wasn't out of character for Zoe to organize such an initiative, but Tala hadn't expected Cole to be as involved with it as he was, even with Zoe as his main motivation. She'd been less surprised to discover that he and Zoe had started dating, despite all their previous bickering. The media had been hard on the couple as well.

Alex had scoured the world to the best of his capability and with all the spelltech he had on hand, but Abigail Fey's disappearance remained a mystery, even as her dubious legacy remained. Fortunately, the curse she'd placed had apparently been a one-time endeavor, effective only at the moment of her disappearance. No other male pregnancies had been reported in the months since.

But without Abigail around to blame, most of the resentment had been redirected toward Zoe. The girl had taken the hate calmly, had announced that Three Wishes was working with health facilities all around the world to provide people with the tools needed to manage their conditions however they thought best for themselves, despite the Royal States' abrupt announcement afterward that it was illegal for anyone to accept any help from Avalon and that offenders would be arrested. It could not have been easy, but Zoe seemed to have accepted the consequences of her role in it.

Things were better now. Tala hadn't seen Zoe look this happy since she'd been cursed never to cry. Or Cole, for that matter. The Nottingham boy's arm was around Zoe's shoulder, and she was snuggled up against him, smiling as they gazed out onto the lake.

West had shifted into a large tortoise, drifting easily along the water nearby, an alternate flotation device for Ken to opt for should he need it. Loki, who was already an excellent swimmer, was treading sedately beside the boy, offering practical suggestions and instructions that Ken was intent on ignoring in favor of clinging to Nya, who looked to be nearing her limits.

"I'm giving it another half hour before she gives up and drags Ken back to shore again," Alex said. His presence was the reason for the armed security currently around Lake Nimue, but Tala was glad he'd taken the time to get out of Maidenkeep to accompany them. The Avalon king had been swamped with work the last few months, bouncing from important meetings to high priority briefings to public addresses, and she'd been worried that he wasn't eating or sleeping right.

It didn't help that during one of his first official public statements after the OzCorp incident, Alex had calmly come out not only to his citizens but to the rest of the world. Tala was proud of him regardless.

She'd been especially worried after she saw the latest entertainment gossip yesterday. Alex had come down to breakfast with dark shadows underneath his eyes, with a slightly hungover air about him and an insistence that despite his haggard appearance, everything was, in fact, all right.

Tala knew him well enough to know that it was, in fact, not all right.

The firebird—one of Avalon's greatest weapons, one that had singlehandedly saved Avalon many times in the past, and the magical creature that the Snow Queen had spent millennia trying to obtain—was napping on top of Alex's head. It made for a rather comical sight, if Tala and the others hadn't grown used to it by now. It appeared to be catching up on the sleep that Alex didn't get; its behavior so very often demonstrated what Alex was really feeling, as much as the latter tried to hide it.

The young royal glanced at Cole and Zoe and managed a wry grin. Despite the hot sun, he had insisted on wearing the long-sleeved robes he often used for important functions. "At least they've got time for a social life."

"You'd have one too," Tala said, well aware that she was about to tread on prickly territory but was fairly certain she could dare do so on account of being his best friend, "if you'd like to talk about what happened yesterday."

Alex's smile faded into a scowl. "Not really sure I have anything to say about that."

"I'm pretty sure you have a lot of things to say and that they might involve chucking things into the lake or punching something to feel better."

Out in the water, Ken was finally floating. His eyes were squeezed shut, and he didn't seem to notice that Nya had relinquished her hold on him and was now several feet away, watching her boyfriend with a pleased smile on her face.

"What's there to talk about?" Alex stared off into the distance at the glittering waters before them. "There's nothing left to say. He's engaged. His parents are finally pleased with him, which was what he always wanted. I don't need him calling me up to explain when everything's this crystal clear."

Tala blinked. "Are you telling me that Tristan called you last night?"

"Fifteen times, until I got tired and turned off my phone. Several more this morning when I bothered to check. Like I said, I'm not interested in his apologies or his explanations. Announcing his engagement to the princess of Luxembourg tells me all I need to know."

A yell from the lake. Ken had belatedly realized Nya's betrayal and had sunk down again. Nya dove in effortlessly, the scales on her tail glinting under the sunlight, and brought a sputtering Ken back up two seconds later.

"Uh-oh," Tala said.

Alex glared at her. "What's that supposed to mean?"

"So the only thing you saw last night was Tristan's engagement to Princess Esmeralda?"

"I wasn't in the mood to watch anything else, so I went to bed right after."

"And you were so busy this morning that you never even bothered to look at the gossip papers today. Uh-oh."

"Tala, if you're going to *uh-oh* me one more time without explaining yourself, I'm gonna—"

"Tristan isn't engaged. Well…not anymore. I think."

"What are you talking about? They only just announced the—"

"Yeah, they announced his engagement, and then Tristan went and got himself wasted at some crowded bar in Differdange, and then picked a fight. With several people, all at the same time. Some reports were saying he took on the whole room, but I think that was an exaggeration."

Alex froze. "What?"

"Apparently someone there may or may not have been, um, making prejudiced comments about your, um, romantic preferences."

"Sure," Alex said impatiently, "but what did Tristan do?"

"You're acting awfully interested for someone who just said they had nothing to talk about with—"

"Tala!"

"Tristan punched the dude, okay? It wasn't the only scumbag he punched. He defended your honor, and he wound up taking on a whole bar full of drunken assholes as a result. I think they threw everyone in jail, and it wasn't till later that the police realized who he was. He's out now, and I think his parents were hoping to keep things quiet, but word leaked."

"Is…is he all right?"

"He bailed himself out at six this morning, and he's been missing ever since. The princess's parents are balking at continuing with the engagement, though Tristan's are fighting to keep it. Dammit, Alex, I thought you knew."

Alex had his phone out, typing a number rapidly into it and hitting the call button. The prerecorded voice that wafted out through the speakers did not inspire confidence. "The number you have dialed," it intoned, "is either out of the coverage area or..."

"You have his number memorized?"

"Shut up, Tala." Alex ended the call and tried again, and then seven more times. "Where could he be? If he'd been calling me since... I didn't know—"

There was a splash nearby. Loki had paddled back to shore, shaking the water out from their hair and grinning. "Want a go in the lake?" they asked. "Water's nice."

"It's a lot more amusing to watch Ken." Loki was her closest friend after Alex nowadays. Soon after they'd been granted official ranger status, they'd both spent some time hiking and camping together, and Tala could almost forget about all her troubles when she was with them.

"Something wrong?" Loki asked Alex.

"Loki, do you know any way to track someone through their cell phone?"

"I'm sure Lord Gallagher does, but wouldn't there be some privacy issues?"

"I know. I want to track him anyway."

Loki blinked. "Your Majesty—"

An unexpected scream cut them off, and it didn't sound like Ken. There was a flash of bright light, followed promptly by what sounded like a small explosion from somewhere within the Sleeping Woods, only a short distance away from the lake.

The guards around them kicked into action. A swarm of rangers surrounded Alex, their guns already out, scanning the area for enemies. Most of the soldiers were already running toward the forest in practiced formation. Nya had grabbed Ken and, over the sound of his protests, dragged him back to shore, covering the several hundred meters' distance in only a few seconds. West followed soon after.

"We must evacuate, Your Majesty," one of the ranger leaders, a stout, no-nonsense woman named Maggie, told Alex. "There's no telling what it could be, and it would be safer for you back in Maidenkeep."

Alex paused, nodded resignedly. "Tala—"

"You want us to head in with the rangers and investigate," Tala guessed.

"This should help dry everyone out," Nya said, fishing into the pouch she'd entrusted to Zoe for safekeeping while she'd been out in the lake, tossing small vials of a pink-colored potion to the swimmers. "It's faster than towels."

"Wish it could dry me out from the inside," Ken grumbled, shoving himself into his pants. "I think I've drunk half the lake by now."

"I don't think that's accurate, Ken," Loki said, who wouldn't know what a metaphor was if it kicked them in the head. "There's still a lot out of water there."

"I don't need to learn to swim," Ken grumbled. "If I ever need to negotiate peace treaties on behalf of Avalon while on a ship, I'll just wear a rubber ducky life preserver around my waist."

Tala kept her silence, as did Nya and the others while they put their clothing back on. They all knew why Ken was doing this, for all his complaints. Ken wielded the Nameless Sword. He now called it Kusanagi as was his right as its wielder, after a famous Japanese segen that had once belonged to Yamato Takeru, a legendary Japanese prince. But the fame and notoriety came with knowing that its owners always died young and often violently. The seeress of Tintagel had once told Ken to learn how to swim. They had all taken the innocuous suggestion seriously since then.

The firebird warked out a question. Alex paused to consider it. "Yes, stay with them," he decided. "There won't be much for you to do back at the castle anyway."

The firebird let out a pleased coo, then hopped onto Tala's head. "Thanks," Tala said.

A portal shimmered behind Maggie. "Be careful," Alex said, still sounding reluctant to leave. "Dex should be opening a comm link to you from Maidenkeep."

"Don't be such a worrywart," Tala said confidently. "If we find anything weird, you'll be the first to know."

"Well," Tala conceded exactly twelve minutes later. "It's *weird* all right."

"Dexter said we should have some visuals in a few seconds," Alex's voice said in her ear. "What are you looking at exactly?"

"Um," Tala said. "You ever heard those stories about those magically cursed geese that could, you know, lay golden eggs and some such?"

"Of course I have. Some of my ancestors owned a considerable number of those geese, which is probably the reason I'm a king right now. What does that have to do with the explosion we heard?"

"What do you call the opposite of birds that can poop gold? Like, a bird that just, um, poops poop?"

"What kind of question is—" There was a faint beeping noise and then a low hum as Dexter activated the display screen, enabling everyone back at Maidenkeep command to view what Tala was seeing at the moment.

"Oh," Alex said. "Oh, crap."

It was a rather stunning bird, and it was sitting on one of the higher branches above Tala. It had a long delicate tail that curled up behind it, reminding her of a rather oversize feather duster. But what was truly stunning about the scene were the rangers who had encountered it before Tala and the other Bandersnatchers arrived. Those men and women were now frozen in place in a semicircle around the strange creature, unable to so much as move. As Tala watched, the bird shivered slightly, then proceeded to poop on one of the newly immobilized soldiers, the white goo slowly materializing into something that looked as strong as steel around the man's figure, forming a transparent shield.

"A bird that uses poop as a weapon," Ken said. "A creature after my own heart."

"Are we going to capture it?" Loki asked softly. "Because it very clearly wants to be left alone."

"Is it a nightwalker?" West asked. "Maybe Cole can wave his doo-hickey sword and control its mind."

"My doohickey sword can't do much," Cole said, "since it's not a nightwalker."

"There is no such creature known to have ever existed in Avalon," Alex said. "That I know of anyway. I wouldn't be surprised that we're still finding new species, but…"

"That's because it's not native to Avalon." From Tala's view screen, she saw her mother move to stand beside Alex and Dexter. "It's called the ibong adarna," Lumina Makiling Warnock said, staring hard at the bird. "And it's the only one of its kind. It purportedly lived in the forests of the Reino de los Cristales kingdom within the Philippines, several hundred years ago."

"Then what's it doing here?" Zoe asked.

"I'm not too sure. Loki, can you maneuver yourself behind it, just in case it tries to flee?"

"I can try."

"I'll help," West volunteered, already shifting into a small barn owl, flying off to the side with Loki close behind.

"What can the rest of us do?" Nya asked.

"Stay alert and gauge its reactions," Zoe decided. "I definitely do not want to have it pooping on me."

"Let me try," Tala said.

"Are you sure?"

"Positive." Surely her agimat could handle bird feces, even as weak as she'd become. "I want it on record, though," Tala added, "that this is the first time I ever have to use my abilities to negate literal crap. If it turns me into a statue, at least put me in the gardens facing Alex's window so I can moon him every time he looks out."

"Gosh, thanks," Alex said. "What did I ever do to deserve such a gift?"

"Maybe talk to Tristan once this is over, you big galoot." Warily, Tala approached the adarna, which shrank away from her. "Hey, buddy," she coaxed. "No one's trying to hurt you here. We're all friends. You're all right."

Still on her head, the firebird, who'd been uncharacteristically silent since they'd arrived, chirped lightly, almost cheerfully, in a tone pitched a couple of octaves higher than its usual baritone.

The adarna craned its head to look at it.

The firebird sang again.

"What are you doing?" Tala asked, suspicious. "You're not acting like your usual grumpy self."

The firebird let out a low hiss of a warning that clearly told her to *back off, you're killing my mojo*, and then cooed sweetly again at the adarna.

"Are you flirting with it?" Tala asked incredulously, and the firebird responded by thumping its butt briskly against the top of her head in a bid to shut her up.

"It's *blushing*," Ken said, amazed.

But it was working. The adarna hesitated and took a small tentative step toward Tala. The firebird immediately puffed out its chest and started to squawk out a brief refrain of melody.

And the adarna responded. It had a beautiful, melodic voice with a strange hypnotic quality to its timbre, and Tala suddenly felt a lot lighter, a lot less worried about Alex and Ryker and her father and her agimat and everything else.

"That's it," Lumina encouraged. "If it's singing, that means it's calming down."

"Your Majesty?" Dexter interrupted nervously. "You've got an emergency call coming from the Philippines. From their Department of Spelltech."

"That would be Mother," Lumina muttered.

"We're a little bit busy at the moment," Alex said. "Can it wait?"

"She wants you to be on the lookout for an ibong adarna that she might have redirected to Avalon for good reason, and she is offering coordinates as to where she ported it into."

"We're way ahead of her at this point, Dex."

Something bright flickered at the corner of Tala's eye, and gut instinct told her to duck.

The icicle whizzed past where her head should have been, embedding itself in a tree trunk behind her.

"She also wants to let you know that a couple of ice maidens might have gone in after the adarna, but that you'll have to keep them from getting their hands on it."

"Great," Alex said. "Thank Lady Corazon for us, but I think we're way ahead of her on that one too."

2

IN WHICH THE ADARNA MAKES A POOP REFERENCE

The ice maiden didn't look like she wanted to be there. There were leaves and small twigs stuck to her person, and they were already turning brittle from contact with the substance that passed for her skin. Unlike others Tala had encountered in the past, this one didn't bother with any taunts or japes. She simply bared her teeth at them and struck at the ground with both hands, and Tala had to jump out of the way when a series of stalagmites jutted out from the forest floor, barely avoiding getting skewered by the sharp points.

"Rangers, stay back!" Tala could hear Alex yelling through their link.

"That's an order!" This one from Maggie. "Holster your guns! At this range, you're more likely to hit another ranger than the target! Stay back and give the Banders the space they need!"

Ken was already rushing in, Kusanagi at the ready. The ice maiden avoided his first swipe, manifesting a fresh shield made of ice to brace against his second. The adarna had fled, the firebird hightailing immediately after it.

"Loki, West!" Zoe shouted, and the two immediately gave

chase after the birds. The girl whipped out her own segen; Ogmios whipped through the air, the tail end sending volts of electricity in the air before the ice maiden when she attempted to follow the duo.

"You will never have it," the ice maiden hissed. "I will die and take you all with me before I ever let you have the adarna!"

"Lady, I didn't even know what an adarna was until, like, ten minutes ago," Ken said. Kusanagi glowed, split apart, and Ken was now holding twin swords—one a stark, shining silver and the other an impenetrable dark. Yawarakai-Te cut through the shield with ease, shattering it within moments. The black-bladed Juuchi Yosamu followed shortly afterward, loping through one of the ice maiden's arms. The ice maiden didn't bleed, but she shrieked and sent another barrage of shards at him with her remaining good arm.

Tala jumped to Ken's side with her agimat, the magic-negating shield expanding to shelter him as well.

It almost worked. Most of the shards melted when they reached her defenses, but a few made it through all the same, and Tala winced when one grazed her arm. Ken's swords flashed, slicing through the rest of the projectiles, and then he leaped to protect her in turn.

The ice maiden shrieked again when Ken cut down her other arm, leaving herself wide open for the kill. But with his blades already pointed at her, about to deliver the final blow, Ken paused. "What's the adarna to you?" he asked. "And why are you so keen on finding it?"

The ice maiden smiled up at him, her eyes turning opaque. "Oh, but wouldn't you like to know?" she purred.

Just as quickly, more icicles erupted, this time right out of her chest, hurtling straight toward Ken, but they melted abruptly before they could reach him. The ice maiden gasped, mouth falling open as water streamed out her lips. Behind her stood Cole, grim and hunched over her frame. Gravekeeper's blade protruded out from in between her breasts.

"Answer him," Cole growled, sweat dripping from his face.

Even dying, the ice maiden continued to resist. "Wonders," she panted. "The seven... No...I will not... I must not!"

More icicles materialized, growing out of her legs, body, face, until she no longer had a woman's shape. There were loud cracks of ice, the sounds reverberating from deep within her, and both Cole and Ken stepped back in alarm, the former withdrawing his blade.

"She's gonna explode!" Zoe shouted. "Everyone, get clear!"

Tala managed to dive into the bushes just as the ice maiden exploded, bits and pieces of her flying outward in all directions, each one just as deadly as the shards she used as weapons. When the woods stopped ringing with the echoes of her dying screams, Tala peered out. There was nothing left of the ice maiden beyond a few puddles, and even those evaporated quickly, turning into fog in the warm air.

"She was loyal to her mistress till the very end," Nya muttered.

"But she did give us something to work with." Zoe moved to stand beside Cole, who was getting back to his feet, wincing. "You okay?" she asked softly, rising up on tiptoes so she could pick the leaves out from his hair.

"I'll live," the boy said, his normally expressionless face softening just a smidgen when he looked down at her.

"Wonders? What did she mean by that?"

Ken watched Cole and Zoe, looking a little envious, then cast a sidelong glance back at Nya. "I got a blister on my thumb," he whined. "Would really like it if someone took a look for me."

Nya rolled her eyes. "You're so annoying," she said as she took his arm, but in a voice warmer than the words suggested.

"You like me better when I'm annoying."

"We've caught up to the adarna," Tala heard Loki report through their shared comm link. "I'm...I don't really know how it does it, but the firebird's succeeding better than we are."

"Bastard just wants to make a move, more like," Alex muttered. "Any chance you can retrieve it?"

"Not very likely. It's calm enough with the firebird, but it starts acting skittish whenever West and I try to get any nearer. I think it can recognize West as human even when he shifts."

"I can try again," Tala said promptly. "It wasn't too nervous when I was trying to approach it."

"You sure you're up for it, Tala? I know using your agimat takes a huge chunk out of you nowadays."

"I said I'll do it. Give me a chance before you start judging what I can and can't do."

She hadn't meant to sound snippy, but Alex backed off all the same. "All right. Whenever you're ready."

It was easy enough to find the coordinates Loki had provided. Tala and Nya set out while the others remained behind to help transport the immobilized rangers back to Maidenkeep. Tala's attempts to undo the magic on them had not been successful, and she couldn't help but feel despondent.

"Here," Nya said quietly, pressing a small tonic into Tala's hand. "Keeps your strength up. I take it a lot too. It hasn't been easy since Ken drew the sword out."

"Thanks," Tala said, grateful.

The adarna was on another branch again, a little higher up than the one it was on before. The firebird had settled itself on another from an adjacent tree, still singing sweet nothings. The adarna was listening avidly but was doing little to close the distance between them. It turned when it heard them approaching and visibly tensed.

"We're not having much luck," Loki said.

West had already shifted back into human form and was in the act of putting on his pants. "It knows I'm not a real bird," the younger boy confessed sheepishly.

The adarna shifted nervously, raised its wings.

"Don't," Tala called out, trying to make her own voice sound as soft and as harmless as possible. "We don't want to hurt you. My friends dealt with the ice maiden that's been chasing you. You're safe now."

The adarna seemed to understand. It relaxed slightly but remained watchful.

The firebird cooed and then flew back to Tala. She winced as it settled itself once more on her head. "Can you stop using me as your nesting place just because Alex isn't available?" she muttered.

The firebird only sniffed.

Tala took a step forward. The adarna didn't stiffen up or try to fly away again, so she took another.

"I know we've only just met," Tala said, "but I think there might be other people after you for your, uh, *unique* abilities. We think it would be best if you stayed with us in the meantime. I don't know how to make you trust us, but I promise to do my best to see you safely back to your home, wherever that is. I'm not as—"

The adarna leaped—not away but toward her. There was a muffled squawk as the firebird lost its position on her head and flailed awkwardly, managing to land upright on the ground at the last second, looking startled.

Tala stared down at it. Slowly, she reached up to feel warm feathers and heard soft sweet chirping from above her.

"Well, what do you know?" West sounded impressed. "The adarna wasn't acting coy toward the firebird because it was the firebird. It wanted your head."

"What?"

"It looks mighty comfortable," Loki said, trying to sound reassuring. "I think it likes you."

The adarna responded with a flurry of songs, as if in agreement.

Nya was already biting her lip in an attempt not to giggle, though she was slowly losing the battle.

"Somebody please get it off my head before Alex sees," Tala pleaded faintly.

The firebird, not happy with this fresh turn of events, flounced on the ground and sulked.

The others had been diplomatic about it so far, but Alex could not stop laughing. The adarna was smaller than the firebird, but it was also so much more…decorative. Its tail had the scale and size of a tiny male peacock's and, as far as Tala was concerned, the weight to match. It was like she was wearing the world's most oversize, ostentatious hat.

The other Bandersnatchers were present, as was the Duke of Suddene, a young man who'd inherited a family curse in the form of a great shaggy beast. Lola Urduja and the Katipuneros were also in attendance, as was Captain Mairead of the Neverland pirates, who had accepted Alex's offer to make Avalon their semipermanent abode. She patrolled the kingdom's waters in exchange for good wages for her and her crewmates on the *Jolly Roger*, a spelltech ship that was second only in magical might to Maidenkeep's Nine Maidens. All were most definitely doing their best not to look directly at Tala and the bird taking up residence on top of her head.

"I would really appreciate it if someone found a way to get it off me," Tala said, liking her role as the adarna's favorite perch less and less as time went by. The stares she'd garnered walking into Maidenkeep had been humiliating enough. Two interns had already run themselves into walls gawking at her. "It poops, remember? I don't want that in my hair!"

"You'll have to bear with it just a little longer, I'm afraid," her mother said with the kind of straight face that told Tala she would be laughing herself the moment she found somewhere private to be.

"Sure." Tala glared at Loki.

"I didn't say anything."

"You don't have to. If you dare laugh—"

"I won't," the ranger said sincerely. "I think it looks really nice on you. Like—like a really fancy headpiece."

That would have been a joke had it come from Alex or Ken, but not from them. Tala turned red, then focused her glare downward instead.

That Lola Corazon had returned to Avalon and was there with them at Maidenkeep's briefing room had not diminished Lumina's good humor. Even the normally cranky Makiling matriarch was doing her best to look everywhere but at Tala.

The firebird was once more safely ensconced on Alex's head, though it arguably looked less ridiculous on the king compared to the adarna on hers.

"The good news," Alex said, "is that the magical, uh, excrement doesn't last for more than a couple of hours, and the rangers who were hit with it managed to recover with no other injuries beyond a faint headache. Which brings me to Lola Corazon. What possessed you to send an ibong adarna here to Avalon and with an ice maiden on its tail?"

"Filipino spelltech, unfortunately, is not on the same level as Avalon's," Lola Corazon said calmly. "The ice maidens were escaping with the ibong adarna, and there was very little we could do to stop them. So we used our own agimat to disrupt their portals and redirect them to a place we knew could deal with them more effectively."

"Thank you for volunteering Avalon, Nay," Lumina said, more brusquely now. She had not parted on good terms with Lola Corazon, although Tala's mother had never been on good terms with the old woman to begin with. "Tell us how the ibong adarna came to be in your possession in the first place, since it's been reported missing since the fifteenth century."

Lola Corazon stared stonily down at the table before her. "That was a necessary lie of course," she said.

"Nay!"

"Perhaps if you had been more enthusiastic in working with me than going off and getting married to that…that man, then I would have been inclined to share such secrets with you." Lola Corazon squared her shoulders. "The Makilings and the Ma-i tribe have been protecting the adarna for far longer than you even know. Other cultures would have called it a firebird as well, though we opted to make a distinction for it. Neither the datu nor the Philippine government is aware of its existence, which was why I had to use back channels to reach out instead of our official communication. I will not apologize for keeping the rest of you in the dark. The fewer who knew about its existence, the more protection we could provide it."

"Such good protection," said Lola Urduja, whose own history with Lola Corazon had been turbulent at best, and the world's longest and slowest catfight at its very worst, "that not only have the Snow Queen's minions discovered its location and tried to take it by force, but you had to come to us in the end so we could fight your battles."

"What I need to know first," Alex said hurriedly, because Lola Corazon was already rising from her seat, and he wasn't all that eager to witness the two duking it out again, "is why the Snow Queen is interested in the ibong adarna. Is it a weapon she intends to use, like my firebird?"

"The adarna is more than just a weapon to her," the duke said, moving to stand himself. "It is, in a way, also a means to resurrect her father and open Buyan."

Everyone stared at Tala. The adarna, perhaps because of exhaustion, was already asleep on her head.

"You mean this is the Snow Queen's father?" West asked blankly. "Was Koschei the Deathless reincarnated as a bird with magical... magical, um...?"

"Turds," Ken supplied.

"The adarna may be one of seven you will need to open Buyan and revive Koschei," the Beast of Suddene said. "He was a woefully paranoid man, convinced that his own allies and subordinates would turn on him at any second. He allegedly kept part of his soul within the Alatyr, knowing that none of his people nor the Avalonians would ever choose to destroy it. Within that spelltech lies the means to reconstitute himself, I believe."

"And how do you know this, milord?"

"I have found more of my father's notes. As you know, Buyan and its miraculous tech were something of an obsession of his, and he was the foremost expert in the world on it before he and I were trapped in the frost. I am inclined to put my trust in his theories."

"What's an Alatyr again?" West spoke up.

"It's similar to the Nine Maidens," Loki reminded him, "but much more powerful."

"And at a terrible cost," the duke agreed. "During the war between Avalon and Buyan, Koschei gathered the seven most powerful magical artifacts in his keeping and divided parts of his soul among them, placing the remaining portion in the Alatyr. The fighting was turning badly in his favor then, for the Avalonians were stronger than even he thought."

"But that would require someone he could trust to help him, wouldn't it?" Zoe guessed shrewdly. "He wouldn't have been able to reconstitute himself on his own. Was he relying on his daughter to do that?"

"Yes," Lumina said quietly. "Except he wasn't expecting the Snow Queen to fall in love with the enemy and to eventually side with Kay against him."

"But she turned against Avalon eventually," Loki pointed out.

"Ah," the duke said triumphantly. "When we talk about history, we tend to be so much more favorable toward our own nations, and sometimes it distorts what really happened. Avalon historians would say that the Snow Queen was in the wrong, naturally. Even in your father's time, this was considered fact, Your Majesty. The shock I felt, to reach out to some of my father's old contemporaries only to find the absolute schmuck now occupying the top position in their Department of Educa—"

"Lord Suddene," Alex said very patiently, "I'm afraid we're deviating from the original discussion."

"Ah yes, my apologies again. According to my father's research, the Snow Queen had claimed that it was King Arthur himself and Merlin who had reneged on their alliance with her and had actively tried to kill her."

"Arthur and Merlin?" Alex looked stunned. "But why?"

"They were always worried that she would grow powerful enough to wrest Avalon from them the way her father tried. They plotted to have her killed and then to frame Kay as her murderer."

"Dad?" Tala burst out, shocked. "They were going to blame her death on Dad?"

"Two birds, one stone. Arthur was no longer certain of Kay's allegiance and believed he would side with his lover should the time come. Far easier to get rid of two challengers to his authority and claim they deserved it. But as you know, history, when viewed through the lens of the victors, tends to be less truthful than the reality. And so it is that both the Snow Queen and Sir Kay, formerly of Camelot, became traitors instead."

"Did you know about this, Lady Makiling?" Captain Mairead asked. "You're married to him after all."

"It wasn't something he wanted to talk about often," Lumina said quietly. "He always told me it was old history and that nothing could be done about it now."

Alex had gone silent. Tala's heart went out to him. "Why didn't you tell me earlier?" he finally asked.

The duke shifted uncomfortably from one hairy foot to the other. "Your father was adamant about not releasing details of my father's research, Your Majesty. My father was, of course, opposed to the decision. It's partly why Avalon academia turned its back on him, branded him a recluse and a conspiracy theorist. And I wasn't sure that you wouldn't follow in your father's footsteps and do the same. I didn't know you as well back then to know how you would react."

Alex nodded. "Thank you for telling me now. I am sorry about the treatment your sire suffered."

"Oh, that's all right, Your Majesty," the duke said, much more cheerfully now. "Father had always been an old bastard, regardless. Few people could stand him, even without his unconventional theories."

"And that changes nothing," Lola Urduja reaffirmed. "Whatever claims the Snow Queen made in the past, it does not condone her actions. So Koschei split his soul into eight parts, hid one in the Alatyr, and hid the rest all over the world. One lies within the ibong adarna apparently. What then must we do to ensure that the Snow Queen does not lay her hands on the others to successfully revive him?"

"It is not just to revive him," Lola Corazon said tersely. "Only Koschei knows the way back to Buyan. That, I believe, and not his resurrection is the Snow Queen's main goal."

Tala remembered the quiet longing in the Snow Queen's voice as she talked about returning to her home, the way she had pleaded for Kay to abandon them and leave with her. Tala could understand wanting to find a place to belong when so many people had made it so you couldn't.

"How does she intend to do that?" Zoe asked.

The duke shrugged. "The Snow Queen is in possession of a mirror that allows her to control the hearts and minds of others through its shards, to do her bidding. It was also the mirror that Koschei used to split his soul into several pieces, allegedly a part of the Alatyr she was able to take away. She can't use that to get back to Buyan, but my father believes gathering the rest of Koschei's soul supposedly unlocks the way."

"She's never been able to find any all this time?" Ken asked.

"Father believed it was something of a last resort, as she had not been inclined to want to revive him either."

"I've been going over the emails we retrieved from OzCorp

servers," Loki added quietly. "I think they've been researching what those seven items were. The Seven Magical Wonders of the world. The Snow Queen must have told them."

"No one can actually say to a degree of certainty what those wonders are," the duke confirmed, "though my father has made several educated guesses."

"What were your father's choices?" Alex asked curiously.

The duke typed rapidly at his computer, and a fresh display popped up on the large screen before them, containing at least four dozen or so items. "I combined both my father's suggestions and a list of artifacts we found during our investigation of OzCorp's documents."

"That's a lot of possibilities," Nya said, alarmed. "Are you telling us that we'll have to hunt down every one of these to find out?"

"Unfortunately so. We can only rely on conjecture for the most part. These ones my father singled out. We've pinpointed the current locations of the others." The display called up more places and countries, linking them to the artifacts' names. "Most of these kingdoms may not be aware of the significance of these relics and only consider them important cultural artifacts."

"We're going to need a lot of diplomacy," Tala murmured, "to ask them all for permission, not knowing if we'd even be able to give them back afterward."

"Your Majesty!" Dexter called out, alarmed. "I'm getting some fresh reports regarding the Snow Queen."

Heads swiveled in his direction, and Alex visibly tensed up. "What's happened?"

"There's been an explosion at the Halden maximum-security prison in Norway, Your Majesty."

Lumina shot up from her seat. So did Tala. "That's where Dad is," she whispered. "Dex, don't tell me..."

"I'm sorry, Tala. I'm not hearing any confirmation yet from the Norwegian authorities, but it appears that several ice maidens have attacked the facility. Your father is the only one missing from the premises so far."

3

IN WHICH SEVEN IS A LUCKY NUMBER

Tala passed the next few hours in a fog. She was aware of the flurry of activity around her; of Alex issuing curt orders to open communication channels directly with the Norwegian prime minister herself; of the Fianna leader, Lord Bharat Keer, preparing to teleport a team of rangers into Norway with the kingdom's permission for a joint investigation into the break-in; of the rest of the Bandersnatchers who now surrounded her, saying relatively little but intent on offering their support.

Nya had pressed another potion into Tala's hands and insisted she drink it. Zoe sat on her right, monitoring the news grimly on her phone for any new developments. West, who had only just learned what an emotional support animal was and had discovered that sloths were in fact one of Tala's favorite animals, had shifted accordingly and was now lying on her lap, a long furry arm draped over her waist. The firebird hovered close by, though it was more concerned with making pretty eyes at the adarna than with actually comforting her.

Loki was on Tala's left and hadn't left her side since the news came. Their hand was on hers, and Tala appreciated the warmth it brought her.

The adarna had slept all throughout the mayhem, still a dead-weight atop her head. Tala no longer had the heart to protest.

Her father was missing. He would not have gone willingly. His past relationship with the Snow Queen did not mean she wouldn't harm him. She'd said as much before. *Let him be all right*, Tala prayed silently. *Please don't let anything happen to him.*

More reports came filtering in, many opinion pieces highlighting the link between Kay Warnock and the Snow Queen, suggesting that they'd resumed their infamous relationship.

"Your king was *literally* using ice shard spelltech," Ken snapped at the screen. "Like, *literally* using it to enslave people for fun and sport. Isn't there anyone else of American royal blood with a shot at deposing him? He can't be the only one in the running to be the ruler."

"Well…" Zoe accessed her phone again, and a small display screen popped up in the air before them. "The next in line to be the king—well, queen in this case—just happens to be…"

A face popped up. They all took a good long look at the photo of a smiling Black woman in a smart business suit and collectively sighed.

"Yeah," Ken said, "they'll prop up that old arsehole for more decades if they can."

"Tala." Her mother looked exhausted.

Tala stood to face her, heart pounding. "Is he…?"

"The bad news," Lumina said, "is that Kay really is gone. There are no reports of any deaths at the prison, and he was the only one unaccounted for. The good news—the only part I can think of—is that if the Snow Queen had intended to kill Kay, she would have done so there. The chance that he's still alive, somewhere, is likely. Alex has been in talks with the other generals, trying to see if infiltrating Beira for a retrieval mission would be feasible. It's the most likely place she's keeping him captive."

Tala's shoulders slumped. "I'm so worried, Mom."

"I know. But let's not jump to any conclusions until we know for sure what's going on. There's a possibility that she may demand the adarna in exchange for him."

"Dad would never allow that to happen."

"I know. Until Alex finds anything more, we can only hope."

"Except I haven't found anything new regarding your father's disappearance," the king said grimly, striding back into the room. "Yet. Nothing from Beira so far. No ransoms, no threats. I think she's taken your father to convince him to join her cause one last time."

"I can make a good guess as to what she's planning," came a familiar but weak-sounding voice from behind Alex. "But you're not gonna like it."

"Ryker?" Tala asked disbelievingly as the boy stumbled into view, leaning heavily against Cole for support.

He looked like hell, like something more than his strength had been taken away from him. He was noticeably thinner, his clothes loosely gathered on his person, and there were faint circles underneath his eyes, like the months he'd spent asleep had done little for his rest.

"Cadfael was awake when His Majesty asked me to check up on

him," Cole said, sounding apologetic. "The doctors wanted him to rest, but he insisted on coming with me."

"I asked them for the rejuvenating spell the wonderful people from Ikpe concocted so I could use my legs without needing the therapy, but I was prepared to crawl if I had to," Ryker said faintly. "Hullo, Tala. What the hell is that thing on your head?"

"You should have stayed at the hospital!" Tala exclaimed.

"How does that saying go? I'll rest when I'm dead." Ryker grinned. "Seems like I woke just when things started getting interesting. Has it been really four months?"

"Three since you've stumbled into Tala's quarters with an icicle through your back," Zoe said dryly.

"Three months late for an explanation, then. How much in hospital fees do I owe?"

"None," Alex said. "As your country's media likes to say, we're all just dirty commies over here."

Ryker grinned widely. "Then let me repay you some other way. Telling you everything I know about the Snow Queen should cover much of that, don't you think?"

"Are you sure you're up to this?" Nya asked as Alex gave the order to clear out the rest of the room, leaving only the Banders, Lumina, and Captain Mairead.

"I may not look it, but I'm healthy, thanks to your doctors. Just need a bit more time to get my toes back into circulation." Ryker looked around at the sea of faces before him and winced. "I understand," he said, "that given everything that's happened, you all have good reason to still be suspicious of me."

"You weren't very forthcoming about the Snow Queen a few months ago," Zoe pointed out. "What's changed now?"

"What's changed is that I've done the unthinkable and betrayed Mothe—the Snow Queen, and she's decided that I am now an official liability to her. Hence trying to murder me with an icicle." Ryker settled into a seat with a huff of relief. "The last time we met, Alex, I told you that I couldn't take you up on your offer to stay in Avalon and cut my ties with the Snow Queen. That's because I owed it to the other kids I'd rescued over the years not to leave."

"The ones you'd rescued from those facilities in the Royal States?" Tala asked.

Ryker nodded. "Among other places. The Royal States doesn't have the monopoly on cruelty. The Snow Queen promised me that anyone who wanted to be reunited with their parents would be allowed to do so. It was when she was working with OzCorp that I discovered she'd been lying to me. She'd been keeping them against their will. Just like the facilities I've been trying to save them from."

Loki inhaled sharply. "That's vile."

"The last few months—the ones I was conscious for anyway—were spent spiriting out all the kids I could get to as many safe houses as I could. The Neverland pirates helped me make sure I could get them out safely, find their families again."

"You told us nothing about this," Alex said reprovingly to Mairead.

The captain shrugged. "I promised him, knew it wasn't my place to say. Would have if he hadn't made it. Figured he'd be up to tell you himself."

"I haven't completely given my soul over yet, but the ice maidens considered me one of them, however grudgingly," Ryker said. "The Snow Queen was too busy with OzCorp to realize what I was doing until after Nome's death."

"We can figure something out with Captain Mairead," Zoe said. "Coordinate with her to see the rest of those kids back with their families."

"We'll get them all out this time, mate," the pirate leader agreed.

Ryker smiled his thanks. "Didn't want to see them abused. Turns out I was siding with an abuser myself. I know it might sound incredulous to you, but she was so kind when she first found me. Whatever else she's done, I stayed because I believed she really was helping them. I never intended…"

The sloth left Tala's lap, snatched up a discarded shirt to cover itself up, and shimmered back into West. "Sometimes people can be kind if they think they can benefit from it," he said philosophically, "and then cruel to others. It isn't your fault not knowing, but it's about how you own up when you finally do."

Everyone stared at him.

West shrugged. "I was an animal celebrity for a couple of months. I've learned a lot since then."

"I can tell you more," Ryker said, nodding at the display screen listing the numerous magical artifacts from the Duke of Suddene's research. "I know what you're searching for. She never liked her father, you know. He was even worse to her than he was to his subjects. It was why she was so eager to take Avalon's side during the war against Buyan. She would have stayed with Arthur and Merlin if she hadn't been betrayed in turn. In fact, I can do you one better: I know the seven you'll be needing."

"You would save us a large amount of time if you do," Lumina said slowly. "But why didn't the Snow Queen use her knowledge of them to open a path into Buyan before?"

"Because it's a complicated process, even for her. I'm not too well versed in the details myself, but I do know that for it to succeed, a life must beget a life. To revive Koschei means sacrificing another in his place—someone with the same immense magical ability as the person being revived. Law of magical equivalence still applies there. It was the only reason Koschei imparted that kind of knowledge to Moth—the Snow Queen in the first place."

Zoe gasped. "Are you telling me that Koschei was expecting his own daughter to give up her life for his?"

"He'd raised her to be the perfect obedient child, and she would have no doubt done so if it weren't for Kay Warnock's influence." Ryker colored a little. "I'm so sorry, ma'am."

"Don't be," Lumina said sadly.

"I don't think she's all that interested in reviving him anyway. She only wants to go back to Buyan. I wasn't supposed to know either. But I like to snoop, and it's saved my ass before. I can tell you what the seven are, and maybe you can retrieve those artifacts before she can."

"We intend exactly that." Alex gestured at the screen again. "Any of it here?"

Ryker scrutinized the display. "You got a lot of them right, but there's a couple ones you're still missing. May I?"

Alex let him take over, and Ryker typed hastily, deleting items and adding new ones. Finally, only seven remained on screen:

The Singing Bone

The Hamelin Flute

The Tamatebako

The Lotus Lantern

The Raskovnik

The Adarna

The Wonderland Tree

"I don't even know what some of these are," Ken said wonderingly. "A singing bone? A raskovnik?"

Zoe had gone slightly pale. "The singing bone was a horn of the Wild Hunt," she said. "You know that spectral army that's supposed to be haunting a forest in Germany?"

"Weren't people supposedly missing because they witnessed the Wild Hunt?" Loki asked.

"Yes. You can probably see why I have concerns."

"That's another thing with these seven," Ryker said. "Supposedly only those with segen can survive retrieving them."

"We can't ask the rangers to do it, then," Ken said, looking far too eager than he should be.

Ryker coughed. "Specifically, the Nameless Sword and the segen of its owner's companions. There's a reason the Snow Queen had been trying to find the Nameless Sword all this time. She'd never met a wielder she wasn't trying to woo to her side."

Ken's smile was almost beatific. "Well," he said. "Well, well, well."

"Ken," Nya sighed.

"I'm getting sick of being steamrolled by American media as the bad guy just because they don't want to put the blame on their very petty king, Rapunzel. Way I see it, this fight isn't going to remain between just us and the Snow Queen. If she intends to take all those other artifacts by force, then a bunch of other kingdoms are going to be rising up in arms against her soon enough."

"I don't think you have very long to wait," Lumina said quietly. "I am hearing reports of ice maiden activity in Germany. There's already been at least one skirmish between their army and nightwalkers appearing in the area."

"What?" Tala exclaimed. "Alex!"

"I didn't want to alarm the rest of you," the king defended himself. "I can't even give you any updates regarding Uncle Kay's whereabouts yet. Dexter's been reporting strange new anomalies on our own borders. Ruggedo Nome was a greedy son of a bitch, but he knew his spelltech. He'd found a way to infiltrate the shields we set up around the kingdoms using the jabberwock, and it's likely that the Snow Queen has access to that."

"She did," Ryker confirmed wearily.

"Which means we're going to have to do everything we can to take those seven artifacts and destroy them if we have to *while* defending Avalon from incoming attacks."

"Destroy them?" Tala was appalled. "Alex, you forget that one of those artifacts also happens to be a living, breathing bird that is currently sitting on my head."

The adarna chirped sleepily.

"That's what Koschei had been hoping for when he chose them as his vessels," Ryker said. "He knew their innate magic would come to be prized. Enough for kingdoms to not want to destroy them."

"We can decide what to do once we actually have them in our hands," Alex said. "Right now, it's only a matter of time before—"

The starkly black portal that materialized out of thin air behind him took everyone by surprise. The shades that came crawling out of it even more so.

Despite his condition, Ryker was the quickest to react. A ball of ice formed in the palm of his hand, which he lobbed with speedy accuracy at the first few who'd come slithering through, turning them quickly into frozen, grotesque sculptures.

"Sound the alert!" Lumina shouted. A flick of her wrist caused the frozen shadows to shatter, but more were still climbing out. "Get more rangers in here!"

Ken was already standing in front of Alex, his sword at the ready. The king wasn't unarmed for long. In a blink of an eye, the firebird had soared to his side, transforming into a fiery bow when it did. The blazing arrows ripped into the shadows even as Ken slashed and stabbed, cutting them into ribbons.

Zoe had jumped to Ken's side, as did Cole. Zoe's Ogmios sent shock waves through some of the shades headed their way, visible electricity jolting through their bodies as they sank to the floor, overwhelmed. Cole's Gravekeeper had already sunk into three of the nightwalkers in succession, causing them to turn on their fellow shadows, ripping eagerly through the tangible void that substituted as their flesh. Loki was fighting with their Ruyi Jingu Bang; the staff hurtled through the air of its own accord, shoving its way into their opponents' chests using nothing but brute force, then stilling so the ranger novice could snatch it and deliver their own deadly blows. West, being West, remained in sloth form by Tala's side, haunches raised, and snarling and swiping at anything that drew close to them with his long curved claws.

Tala raised her hands and concentrated. Her vision blurred slightly, and her head spun, but she could feel her agimat, weak as it was, slowly expand. The shade caught within its range shrieked as it shredded and dissolved, and the exertion from that alone was enough to send her to her knees in pain. Taking out a second shadow made her nauseous, ready to throw up.

And then Loki was by her side again. They swung their staff, and the other shades broke apart from the fury of their blows.

The adarna, who had been quiet this whole time, threw its head back and sang.

Its soft, syrupy voice sent a strange peace through Tala again, making her almost forget that they were in the thick of battle. But the melody had an even more profound effect on the shades. They stopped, remaining motionless as if entranced, listening to the adarna's song.

And then Ryker was planting himself between Tala and the shadows, and the creatures were transformed into unmoving icicles in a heartbeat.

Lumina had rushed toward the portal, sweat standing out against her forehead as her own agimat began to destabilize the glowing hole above her, slowly forcing it shut. A sudden thrumming sound blistered the air, much like audio feedback, and Tala recognized it as an added layer of security from Maidenkeep's defense protocols finally kicking in. The portal wobbled and wavered like a desert mirage, the energy flowing out of it weakening.

That was all the help her mother needed; with one last superhuman effort, she snapped it closed with another cutting gesture and then sagged down.

"What the hell was that?" Alex demanded. "What's going on? How did anything get past Maidenkeep's—"

"Your Majesty!" Dexter was not a fighter, but he had been brave enough to stay by the workstation to use the console. "I'm sorry," the boy panted. "It took a while to activate the additional security."

"You did great, Dex. Thank you." Alex turned to the adarna, who had stopped singing the instant the portal closed and all the remaining shades had been dealt with, settling back on Tala's head and nodding itself back to sleep. The king's fire bow had shifted back into the firebird, and it was staring at Tala's head with a look of undisguised adoration.

"I can see why the Snow Queen might be after it," Ken said. "Koschei's soul or not, it's pretty powerful in its own right."

"My question is how they got through our defenses in the first place." Alex scowled. "They'd never been able to before. Not even OzCorp could—" and here Alex stopped, faltered. "No," he said. "They *did*, didn't they? They overrode our defenses and teleported into the Nine Maidens, the most secure place in this palace. And the Snow Queen has their spelltech."

"There's also a chance that OzCorp executives are still working with her, still supplying her with their inventions," Lola Urduja said grimly, striding back in with General Luna and Tito Boy flanking her sides. "Our apologies for the delay, Your Majesty. There were shades outside as well."

"There was more than one portal?"

"Five that we detected. When Dexter activated the additional defenses, they started to wane, and we were able to close them with the anti-magic spelltech we had on hand."

"Corazon Makiling and her colleagues shut two of them down," Tito Boy signed.

"They did the bare minimum, considering that we now have to take on their responsibilities," the old woman said stubbornly. "I would suggest doing another roundup of the OzCorp management and subject them to more questioning as to the amount of spelltech they have sold or given to the Snow Queen."

Alex nodded. "In the meantime, maintain these added defenses. I don't want them to succeed next time."

"There's a possibility that we could wind up overloading our overall security if it stays up for too long," Dexter said nervously. "It wasn't made to enforce this much magic indefinitely."

"I'll take care of it."

The matter-of-fact way Alex said the words immediately made Tala suspicious. "Care to explain what you mean by that?"

"Don't worry about it," Alex said dismissively. "I'll have things under control soon enough."

"What he means," a new voice broke in, "is that he's hiding

something else from you, because he think it's only going to make you worry."

Of all the unexpected visits they'd had this day alone, Tristan Locksley walking into the room was the least surprising. Gone was the calm, charismatic boy from their last meeting. He was clearly hungover and needed a shave, and the few bruises that marred his handsome face indicated that the reports of his involvement at the bar fight had not been inaccurate.

"How did you get in here?" Tala asked.

Alex had been stunned into speechlessness at the sight of his ex, gaping dazedly at the newcomer like he'd just been decked. The other Banders hesitated, looking at each other as if not quite sure how to proceed.

A cough was Tala's answer, as both Tita Chedeng and Tita Teejay strolled nonchalantly back out of the room, as obvious as the day was long.

"I wasn't expecting to have to fight my way through a crowd of nightwalkers when I arrived," Tristan said, "but that's still not an excuse either. We need to talk, Alex."

The king set his jaw firmly and crossed his arms, but since Tristan was standing in between him and the exit, he had no choice.

"And even if you think we have nothing to talk about, you owe your friends an explanation of why you've been trying to expand your control over the Nine Maidens without any of them knowing."

Alex's mouth fell open. "How—" he began, then thought better of it. "I don't need to explain anything."

But it was too late. "And what exactly does Tristan mean by this, Alex?" Tala asked dangerously.

"It really is not as bad as he's making it out to be."

"I disagree," Tristan said. "They need to know about what you're hiding underneath all those robes you've been constantly wearing. Clearly you no longer bear any goodwill toward me, so I suppose I shouldn't give a crap if you hate me worse for telling them."

He took a step forward toward the king, and Alex froze. "It's really nothing at all," he muttered and shoved his sleeves back to reveal a pair of bracers on either arm, both a bright shining silver.

"Alex," Zoe said, her voice just as grim as Tala's had been. "Explain."

"I had these commissioned by the Gallaghers," Alex said. "They'll allow me access to the Nine Maidens at a moment's notice, grant me use of its spelltech wherever I am should we be attacked again. It will keep Avalon safe."

"At the cost of draining your life force from constant use," Nya said, saying what they'd all been thinking.

Alex sighed, like that was nothing more than an unfortunate but mild side effect. "Yes. Yes, I suppose it does also do that."

4

In Which Ken and Tala Bond Over Infamous Swords

I love you, Alex," Tala said, "and I know you're only trying to do what's best, but for like the eight hundredth time since this all started, *why would you want to risk your life for this?*" She raised her hand when Alex looked ready to protest. "And yes, we've been arguing about this long enough that I know what you're going to say. You feel like you're living on borrowed time anyway. The Baba Yaga said you were supposed to have died and her predecessor only intervened out of the goodness of her heart, blah blah blah. Well, screw destiny. They've changed the fates for you before, and I know they can sure as hell do it again. There's a reason the old Baba Yaga saved you, and it's definitely not to put yourself in danger again at a moment's whim!"

"I haven't even used it yet," Alex protested. "Look at my self-control, having shades invade our command center and not even so much as activating a spell with it in retaliation."

"Doesn't make it right," Tristan said, "that you never bothered to tell them."

"You're going to call me out on dishonesty now?" Alex rounded on him, red with anger. "After everything *you've* done?"

"Yes," the boy said wearily. "Even after everything I've done. Because I'm trying to change, and you still think you can take on the world on your own. I realized that my family drama was going to make it worse. It was a mistake to tell you that what we had didn't mean anything, and I've regretted it ever since."

"Uh," Nya said delicately. "If we're sure that no other shades can get past Maidenkeep's defenses now, I think we should, um, leave and give you two the privacy you need while we discuss what we ought to do next regarding those six other artifacts that are still out there."

"You're right," Zoe said. Even so, as they slowly filed out of the room, Tala saw her cast a quick rueful glance back at Tristan. She'd dated the Locksley boy before she realized he was Alex's ex, and while they had broken up and she seemed happy with Cole, Tala couldn't help but think that Tristan's admission to the king still stung.

"Wait," Alex said when Tala made to follow the other Banders out. "I want you here with me."

"Are you sure?" Tala asked doubtfully. "This sounds like a personal matter that you two should—"

"Since you've been the one constantly telling me I should hear him out, you can at least stay and see this through with me."

"You did?" Tristan asked gratefully. "Thank you, Lady Makiling Warnock."

Tala, who understood that Alex wasn't comfortable enough to be alone in the same room with his ex, only nodded. "I'll be standing guard by the door."

"Are you sure?" Loki asked, lingering behind.

"I'm sure. I'll be okay."

The ranger nodded. "I'm going to keep an eye on Cadfael," they said. "I still don't trust that guy, whatever he claims."

Tala tried very hard not to listen in on the conversation, but their voices were loud enough for her to hear regardless. The adarna had already gone back to sleep on top of her. The firebird, who was probably even more protective of Alex now that it was no longer under the Snow Queen's influence, was swaggering along one side of the room, trying its best to look intimidating but failing miserably. From time to time, it would cast a stealthy look in Tala's direction, only to look disappointed upon seeing the adarna still asleep.

"How did you even know I was wearing these bracers?" Alex demanded. "Dexter and Lord Gallagher were both sworn to secrecy."

"Nobody needed to tell me," Tristan said, droll. "In almost every public appearance you've made, you've been wearing those hideous robes. You told me you've always hated them and that if you ever had the chance to get Avalon back, that was one policy you were going to abolish. Maybe you had to wear them for official addresses, but there was no need to all the damn time. I knew you were hiding something, and it was likely spelltech wear. And the last time I spoke to you, when you were so convinced that it was your duty to sacrifice yourself for the kingdom, it wasn't hard to make the connection."

"You still think you know me," Alex said sourly.

"I don't know you as well as I ought to. But I'm trying. You don't have to like me, but I can't just stand around and watch you..." Tristan looked away. "I told Princess Esmeralda that I couldn't go through with the engagement," he finally said.

Alex glanced down.

"I don't even know why I let it go as far as it did," Tristan continued. "She wasn't interested either, but she was willing to let the engagement stand because, like me, she wanted to please her parents. When it was announced, I realized I was making the biggest mistake of my life. I went out, got myself drunk. I was trying to psych myself up to go back and tell my parents I was going to refuse. But at the bar, I heard some asshole talking about you…" He shifted. "I was on him, driving my fists into his face before I even knew what I was doing."

"Oh," Alex said.

"When I got arrested, I thought, *Well, that's that.* But then my parents tried to bail me out, told me I had to be on my best behavior from then on so they could still salvage the engagement." Tristan shrugged, grinned. "So I told them to fuck off, got a friend to bail me out instead. And now here I am."

As far as Tala was concerned, this was an unexpectedly romantic turn of events. Even the bar fight. *Especially* the bar fight. But Alex looked like he needed more convincing, and the other boy seemed to understand.

"I am not interested in anything more from you," Tristan said. "This is my problem and not yours. But let me stay and fight with you. I'm handy with the bow. This is the best way I can think of to apologize for putting up with my shit these last few months."

"You'll need to be part of the Order of the Bandersnatch then,"

Tala said cheerfully, unable to help herself. "You'll need to work with the Three Wishes during your probationary status."

"Three Wishes?"

"It's a nonprofit that Zoe founded."

Tristan winced. "She's another person who I need to ask for forgiveness."

"You're free to do whatever you want," Alex said. "Given the recent attacks, more hands would be good, and the rangers can only do so much. They're already spread far too thinly for my liking. If helping Avalon is all that you're expecting from me, then fine. I accept. Report to General Urduja after we finish this briefing. She should have something for you to do."

Tristan nodded, looking like a burden had been lifted from his shoulders. "I will. And, Alex, don't push yourself either. I've said it far too many times already, but I'll say it again. You can't do all this on your own." He gave Tala a quick bow and exited the room quickly.

The adarna's neck craned forward, watching the boy leave with interest. "You've been shamming being asleep, haven't you?" Tala murmured. The adarna gave a quick toss of its head to indicate that it regretted nothing.

"I hope you're happy," Alex said. He didn't sound resentful as he had that morning, which Tala took as a good sign.

"Seeing firsthand how destructive OzCorp could be and how much damage the Nine Maidens could bring on you is making him scared for your safety. If my opinion means anything, I think he's being sincere about the help at least."

"Your opinion means a lot to me." Alex rubbed at his temples. "I just—I feel guilty. About you most of all. You blew out your agimat to protect me. I don't know what would have happened if you hadn't."

Tala grinned. "And I'll do it again if you keep on being this stubborn. I understand why you need those bracers. Just don't use the Nine Maidens except as a last resort, okay? You don't seem to understand how important you are to Avalon or the chaos that's going to break out if anything happens to you."

"I know, and I will." Alex turned to his firebird. "And you were of no help at all."

But the firebird, who still only had eyes for the adarna, could only let out a long, infatuated-sounding sigh.

By the time they returned to the command center, some of the tension following both Ryker's and Tristan's arrivals had abated, though not completely. Tristan was talking to Zoe, both looking distinctly uncomfortable. "I had no right to ask you out while on a rebound," the Locksley boy was saying. "And to ask you to pretend you were still with me while my parents were in Avalon, that wasn't right either. It didn't matter if you agreed to it or not, because I put you on the spot all the same. I don't know how to make it up to you. His Majesty mentioned that you were working on a nonprofit, and if you need any more volunteers for that..."

"Thank you," Zoe said, looking like she'd opened a box expecting something gross and wasn't sure about finding a delicious cake instead. "That's very kind of you to offer."

"It's not really. But it's a start." Tristan turned to Cole, who was very good at pretending not to listen to their conversation. "Looks like we'll be working together for a while, Nottingham," he said gruffly. "Hope that's all right with you."

"Seems like you have far more to lose than I have, staying here in Avalon," the other boy said dryly.

"True. But it's worth it." Tristan held out his hand.

After a moment, Cole took it. "Suppose we could use the help," he said in just as rough a tone as Tristan's had been.

"Amazing," Nya said softly after Tala took the seat beside her. "Never thought I'd see the day. If Tristan wasn't trying his best to get himself disinherited at this point, this would cinch it. The Locksleys despise the Nottinghams."

"You know what they say," West said, his voice also pitched low so no one else could hear. "You don't always know the truth until you're punched in the face with it. Or you don't know how much willpower you have in you to forgive until you want to get with their exes."

"West," Nya said, swallowing her laughter, "never change."

"Now that we're all settled," Lumina said briskly. "Alex has given me charge of this meeting. We've received confirmation from Germany, Japan, and China that there have been attempts to infiltrate their respective kingdoms by what they believe to be the Snow Queen's forces. They've been successful at pushing back, but it's only a matter of time before they try again, which makes this our priority. Germany and Japan have graciously allowed us access to their respective magical relics. China has given us permission to enter their territory despite their closed borders policy, given their ongoing dispute with the other Asian kingdoms. However, they're not as keen on providing us with their artifact, though they say they are willing to discuss matters."

"They have no intentions of delivering any of their artifacts to us," Lola Corazon said stubbornly. "I have dealt with them enough times to know it is likely a trap set for us."

"Are they allied with the Snow Queen?"

"They have been neutral regarding our situation, but I would not be surprised. Easier to sneak into the mountain and return it afterward. The negotiations they want are clearly delays."

"That would be very unfortunate," Lord Suddene rumbled. "The lotus lantern is one of the artifacts Sir Ryker kindly pointed out and the relic we must procure first."

"And why is that?" Ken asked.

"Because the lantern is said to light the way and show its owner the safest paths to take. It can detect hidden traps and magical snares. It would be the most useful to us starting out. I've taken the liberty of establishing the order in which you must find these items to ensure the least danger for all involved."

"Sounds like this is all going to be dangerous regardless," Tala said.

"Which begs the question," Alex said. "Who do I send? I would like the Katipuneros ready, of course, but I'm not sure we have many other people to spare. The rangers have their hands full patrolling the rest of Avalon to ensure no other breaches take place, and—"

"You've gotta be kidding me, Alex," Ken broke in. "We're literally sitting right here."

Alex frowned. "It's too risky, Ken. I can't guarantee to your parents that you'll—"

"I've got this, don't I?" Ken held up Kusanagi. "I can't be brandishing this about if I balk at a little danger. I'm sure previous owners of this thing never had to ask their mums and dads permission to save the world, right? There's a reason it chose me." He grinned when he saw the king's worried expression. "I know you're trying to be extra cautious on my behalf. But what will be will be. Besides, I just had my birthday last month. I'm good and legal."

"So am I," Loki volunteered.

"I'm *technically* legal," Nya admitted.

"I've got special dispensation from the French government to act for both Avalon and French interests if that's what you need from me," Zoe offered.

"My parents are cool with it," West said.

Cole, being Cole, only shrugged.

"I know most of the Snow Queen's tricks," Ryker said, "and am decidedly free of any parental supervision whatsoever. I can help too."

"How are we to believe that you are not working as a spy for her?" Lola Urduja asked suspiciously. "Just because she stabbed you doesn't mean you aren't."

"Lola," Lumina protested.

"No, she's right. I do have to prove it. It wasn't all that long ago that I was fighting for her. You can start by talking to Captain Mairead, who would be more than willing to vouch that I only planned to stay with the queen long enough to get the rest of the kids out. But if that's not enough…" Ryker paused, thinking. "Do your techmages have more of those thrall collars lying around?"

"Oh, we do," Dexter spoke up enthusiastically. "Dad actually reverse engineered the process, and he was able to modify it to a point where you don't actually have to use it on people anymore. He took out the mind control spells and the pain switches, and reconfigured it mainly as a tracking device that would help animals like dolphins—" He broke off. "You're not suggesting that we have you wear one, are you?"

"That's exactly what I was about to suggest. In fact, I'd like for you to keep the mind control and pain spells on mine."

"What exactly are you trying to do?" Tala gasped.

"Lola Urduja doesn't trust me. I'm sure a lot of you feel the same way and are just being too polite to say it out loud. This way, I can take part in the search, keep an eye out for any ambushes. And if I happen to step out of line or if you think I'm about to betray you, then it would be easy to keep me docile."

"We're not going to do that!" Alex exploded. "We aren't like her!"

"That you aren't like her is exactly why I'm asking. I know none of you would ever choose to take it out on me unless I'm an active threat, no matter the harm I've caused you in the past. And I *know* I have no intentions of going against any of you, so the chances of ever having to use the collar are practically nil." Ryker shrugged. "It's the best compromise I can think of."

"His guidance may be important," Lord Suddene concurred. "He would have the most experience combating the Beiran queen, barring perhaps Kay Warnock himself."

Alex scowled at Ryker. "Dex, get me a collar according to the specs he wants," he said.

"Alex!" Tala protested.

"I don't intend to use it on him. But a war is brewing, and I want every precaution necessary to safeguard Avalon."

"Good to see we're on the same page, then," Ryker said. "Incidentally, the adarna has to come with us."

"And why's that?"

"You really don't understand the extent of its abilities yet, do you?"

"It can magically turn people into stone with its poop," Ken said.

"If there are any nightwalkers waiting for us, it should prove handy. It might not turn an ice maiden with its song, but it can stop her minions long enough to gain an advantage."

Alex nodded. "I highly suspect that the adarna isn't going to want to leave Tala—Tala's head anyway. You think you're up to it?"

"Yes," Tala said immediately.

"Tala," her mother said. "You're not up to your full strength. You'll need to wait a bit more before you can—"

"I can do it," Tala insisted. "I'm not going to stay in Maidenkeep while they're off fighting. I can handle it."

"You don't have to keep proving yourself. We're just concerned about your—"

"I said I can do it! The sword chose me first, remember? Why are you so intent on treating me like a child ever since you found that out?" She was shouting. She didn't realize it until she saw the startled looks. "Sorry," she muttered, embarrassed, pushing her chair back. "I'm going to go get some fresh air."

No one stopped her from leaving. Tala marched on, down the corridor and the very busy command hub, past Lord Keer directing orders to the other rangers out on the field, past Lord Severon Gallagher, Dexter's father, planning a kingdom-wide scale of spelltech defenses with his team, and onward until she found herself out of the palace and at the castle courtyard, which was currently deserted. The adarna on her head had remained silent all throughout the walk, making no sound, as if sensing her distress.

The stone that had once housed the Nameless Sword was still there. Without its famous weapon counterpart, it had been mostly forgotten by the press and the tourists. Tala stared at it, remembered pulling the sword out herself, the strength and power that filled her when she did—and the fear that assailed her when she discovered she could be, in fact, quite deadly with it—could be quite merciless.

"Penny for your thoughts?"

The Cheshire lounged on a branch above her, smiling down. It gathered itself and leaped, but before it hit the ground, it had already transformed into a smartly dressed man with an old-fashioned top hat on his head. He stood beside her, studying the anvil with quiet gravity. The adarna raised its head and chirped at him.

Once upon a time, the Cheshire, too, had pulled out the sword from its stone and had promptly rejected it out of fear, much like she had. His love, Alice, had taken up the sword herself to finish their war against the Snow Queen and had paid for it with her life.

"You told me once," Tala said, "that there was a reason I rejected the sword, why it chose Ken in my stead. But what if there isn't any? What if thinking that prophecies and destiny know what's best for us is just our way of forgiving ourselves for not doing more? Why are we simply relying on the Nameless Sword, or the firebird, or the Nine Maidens, when it puts more of the burden on other people while taking the responsibility away from ourselves?"

"Do you speak of King Alexei? Or of Kensington?"

"Alex is going to kill himself using the Nine Maidens to save Avalon, and I'm afraid we may not have much choice but to let him do it. And the same goes for Ken and Kusanagi. And I..." Tala looked down at her hands. "And I feel like I'm the reason they're both in this predicament. And I can't do anything about it. My own agimat isn't even working properly to be of much use."

"And with the sudden reports of the Snow Queen's attacks, you are worried that you might not be able to help them the way you want to?"

Tala nodded.

Quietly, the adarna began to sing. Just as before, the melody washed over her, a soothing sound.

A warm hand touched her shoulder. "That has always been the problem with prophecies, I think," the Cheshire said. "Being told of something that will happen before it actually happens makes you feel that you ought to do more when it does. But the problem with being forewarned is that trying to effect change can sometimes make the outcome worse. There are reasons why many people choose not to be told their own dooms. Practical people, for the most part."

"The Baba Yaga said Alex was supposed to die when the Snow Queen attacked Avalon all those years ago."

"I was supposed to die in Alice's place all those centuries ago," the man said. "I am alive now thanks to the Snow Queen, though it no doubt aggrieves her to know that she is to blame for my longevity. Have I ever told you that? We were so close, Wonderland and Alice and I, to taking Beira and destroying the queen's mirror, the source of all her abilities. My Alice—she shattered it. It's why the Snow Queen can only use bits and pieces of it, you see, to enthrall her victims. But

Alice lost her life in the process, and the backlash transferred some of that mirror's magic onto me, cursing me with my very long life. All these years, I've wondered, as someone who is only waiting to die, what my purpose is without her. Perhaps one of them was to meet you. Perhaps one of them was to tell you this."

"I don't know what to do," Tala said.

"Not even the best seers are immune to wanting to change things for the better." The Cheshire smiled. "It would help to remember that you are more than just your agimat. That your Makiling lineage is not the only reason you are here. Don't let that limit you."

Staring at the anvil, Tala nodded again.

"Did that help?" the Cheshire asked.

"It did," Tala said. "It really did."

"Tala?" It was Ken. "Loki wanted to see if you were okay, but I told them there were a few things I wanted to talk to you about in private first." He bowed low to the Cheshire.

"I'm sorry for running out," Tala muttered. She noticed the Cheshire take a few steps back to give them privacy.

"Nah, I understand. You're taking it a lot better than I would have." He, too, gazed at the anvil. "You're not still feeling bad about the sword, are you?"

"No. Maybe. Things could have been different if I'd just...just..."

"I'm a complete melt most of the time," Ken said cheerfully. "Nya forgives me a lot for it. And when I first heard of what the sword could do, all I and every knucklehead like me could think of was the fame and the glory associated with bringing it out. Destiny? Death? Hah! That's only true for someone else who isn't me!"

Ken set the tip of Kusanagi against the anvil and pushed down. It slid into the stone easily.

"Know what I've thought ever since I pulled it out? That it's also brave to take this sword, to realize the strength it can give you, along with all the harm you can possibly do under its power, and choose to put it back." He drew it out again.

"You told me you'd felt that too," Tala said. "That sudden surge of energy, that malevolence."

"Yeah. And it's a good thing I'm not bright enough for any malevolence to take advantage. Just ask Juuchi Yosamu. Even then, it's hard not to listen to its call, you know? But me deciding to use it anyway doesn't make it any better or worse just because you decided not to. I could have refused it too. If I had half your brains or Nya's, I would have." Ken sighed and slid the sword back into the scabbard on his side. "I don't regret it, though. Thank you for giving me the opportunity, even if that damn thing only chose me as a backup. And I'm going to keep saying it till you get sick of me and agree. Lord Suddene's about ready to finish the briefing, so we ought to head back soon. You know how I am with those. I'm likely gonna sit there and blink and nod a lot and forget everything we discussed once it's done."

"Thanks, Ken," Tala said with a small smile.

"No problem. That's what friends are for."

Tala's mother was waiting for her outside the command center when they returned. She looked surprised to see the Cheshire accompanying Tala and curtsied gracefully at him.

"Oh please, Lumina," the Cheshire scoffed, though he was laughing all the same. "There is no need for such formalities. If anything, it is I who owe you, for keeping His Majesty safe." He doffed his hat to her and then to Tala and strode past them down the hall, whistling noisily.

"Tala," Lumina said. "I am sorry. It wasn't my place to make that decision for you and especially not in front of everyone else."

"I know you're worried, Mom," Tala mumbled. "But you can't ask me to stay here and do nothing while everyone's putting their lives on the line. My agimat's full strength might return, or it might not, ever. But that can't stop me from wanting to help. I can't stay on the sidelines forever."

Her mother nodded. "And I agree. I won't stop you if that's what you want." She paused, looking at the adarna. "And I don't suppose it's going to leave your side anyway," she added.

The adarna purred, completely in agreement.

5

IN WHICH THE GANG ATTEMPTS TO JOURNEY TO THE WEST

It's not too bad," Ryker said, running his fingers through the collar secured around his neck. "I bet some social media influencers can turn this into some fashion statement if they squint hard enough."

"Given what it stands for, I wouldn't actively recommend it," Tala said. "You know you don't have to do this."

"I do have to. This coat Alex loaned me hides it just fine."

"I trust you. Thought you ought to know that."

Ryker smiled at her, that dazzling, confident grin that had bowled her over nearly two years ago. "Thanks. That makes all the difference to me." He turned to Loki, who was slouched against the doorframe and frowning at him. "I *am* being sincere about helping, you know."

"I'm sure you are," Loki said in a tone that suggested they found that hard to believe.

Following the duke's advice, they had agreed to strike for the lotus lantern first, with the other rangers on standby. Lola Urduja was swift to express her disapproval.

"Lord Suddene and Ryker were pretty clear about segen being a prerequisite," Alex pointed out. "We'll be monitoring them through the comm links every step of the way. We need you here, Lola. The Esopian borders are barely manned as it is."

The old woman scowled. "It does not feel right to be sending so many younglings in on their own, my dear."

"Have a little faith in us," Ken drawled.

"I agree with Lola Urduja," Lumina said. "We do have faith, but all the same…"

"Oh, we'll go with them, Urduja," Tita Baby spoke up. "We're not too busy."

Lola Urduja harrumphed but said nothing else.

"Your first priority is making sure Alex is safe," Tala told her mother fiercely. *And finding out where Dad is and what the Snow Queen has done to him.* She let it go unspoken, but the older woman's expression told her she understood. "We'll handle everything else."

"Every source I have on the lantern says it's located somewhere within the Kunlun Mountains," the duke told them. "The Chinese government has some heavy security defenses in place, but Lord Gallagher believes we can override enough of them to keep track of your locations. He's less sure on whether they can pull you out immediately should trouble arise once you're within their borders. Not very many have actually explored Kunlun. There's been a ban against entering the mountains for several hundred years now, even among the Chinese. From the little I've heard, every investigation the authorities have made there failed. It leads me to believe that—" He paused.

"Believe what?" Zoe asked.

"Well, it makes me believe that they've never located the lotus lantern either. If they had, more likely they'd have taken it out, housed it in a much more secure facility they would have more control over."

"Maybe they just wanted to keep their sacred item in a similarly sacred place?" West suggested.

But the duke shook his head. "I think it's far too valuable to them to leave it just like that. The lotus lantern is tied to two popular heroes in their history—Chenxiang and the Buddhist monk Sanzo. The documents China has made public don't provide a lot of details, but it was Chenxiang who took the lantern from a supposed god named Erlang Shen—an equivalent to what Koschei was to Avalon—and purified it. It was later guarded by Sanzo and then by one of his companions inside Kunlun after his death."

"That's a lot of alarming information to heap on us just before heading in," Nya said.

"It's the best I can do, given the circumstances and the short time we have," the duke said apologetically. "Kunlun is sacred. It's why they're resistant to granting Avalon access."

"How are we going to get in if they don't want us there?" Ken asked.

Lola Corazon coughed. "There are ways to get past their security defenses if you know where exactly to hit."

"And how do you propose we do that?" Lola Urduja asked warily.

"The solution is simple. But first we make a slight detour."

The slight detour turned out to be a short trip to Manila. Tala had never been to the Philippines before, and the busy rush of jeepneys and wooden carts and noisy hawkers and vendors shouting their wares was a shock. She jumped to give way to several men striding past, weighed down with sacks on their backs, followed by several others pushing small wooden carts piled high with a stunning mishmash of kitchen appliances and fresh vegetables.

The streets were narrow and flanked on both sides by makeshift stalls selling bolts of cloth and ornaments. Aging buildings that looked to be part warehouse and part wet market loomed over them. The cheerful noise was a stark contrast to the quieter streets of Invierno, but she liked the liveliness.

"This is Divisoria," Lola Corazon said, accustomed to all the chaos. "One of the busiest places in the city. If we had more time together, hija, I would have delighted in showing you many more places like this. It is not good to have been so long away from the motherland like you have been."

And maybe if you hadn't been so dismissive of Alex just because I don't want to marry into the Tsarevich lineage, Tala thought sourly, *I would have accepted.*

A street food vendor had set up shop nearby, deep-frying large pieces of calamares in a large wok, and Lola Corazon directed them toward him. "Have as many as you'd like," she said. "My treat. I will be right back."

"Take this barbecue stick here and this plastic cup," Tita Chedeng instructed them as the older woman left, "and pick out the pieces you would like. Here is the vinegar."

"Can everyone hear me?" Alex's voice crackled in Tala's ear.

"Loud and clear," Ken pronounced, his mouth already full.

Even the firebird, safely hidden inside his jacket, had gotten in on the action, happily wolfing down a strip of seafood. The adarna had grudgingly relinquished its perch on Tala's head to find anonymity inside her hoodie, though its sighs made its displeasure known.

"Where exactly are you in Manila?"

"I believe we are in the district of Tondo," Zoe said, "eating fried calamares while we wait for Lola Corazon's return. These are delicious, by the way."

"Oh." Tala heard her mother's voice next, sounding envious. "I haven't had it in so long…"

"Tangina," General Luna said contentedly, scarfing down his share.

The firebird took another piece, almost shyly pushed it in the adarna's direction. The adarna chirped a question, and the firebird responded with a hoot. The adarna poked its head out briefly to eat the offering, and the firebird beamed, then blushed again.

Lola Corazon was back ten minutes later. "Everything's ready," she told them. "There's a side door on the next street. Go in twos and threes. There may be people watching."

"Why all the secrecy?" Ken muttered after they were finally standing in what looked to be another empty warehouse.

"This place is not, technically, recognized as government property," Lola Corazon admitted.

"Keeping secrets from your own superiors now?" Lola Urduja asked with a smirk.

"We cannot all have the same noble rulers as Avalon. Or do you not remember living under the horrors of a dictatorship, Urduja? The Makilings cannot be protected by anyone else but the Makilings.

We have learned that lesson the hard way many times before." Lola Corazon made a gesture, and half a dozen more people emerged from the darkness. Three carried a looking glass. "A few Chinese nationals were resourceful enough to configure a port that allows them to bring products in from China without going through our customs," the old woman said while they set about activating the portal. "We have since taken possession of it. Kunlun magic is unpredictable. Be as quick as you can about it, find the lantern, and get out without arousing attention. My clansmen here can negate enough of the Chinese government's security to port you inside and also to port you out when needed."

"Be careful, all of you," Alex said, sounding grim.

"Of course," Ken said with a grin. "We're always careful," and Nya rolled her eyes.

The looking glass flared to life, the bright light illuminating the whole room. "Game na, madam," said one of Lola Corazon's men.

"Ready?" Zoe asked and received nods all around. "Right. Thank you for helping us get this far, Lola Corazon."

"Think nothing of it. Return safely, and protect my granddaughter."

Traveling within this looking glass was very different from others Tala had been in before. It actually resisted her as she went through, like she was forcing her way through a sea of very thick molasses. "Must be the security defenses your grandma was talking about," Loki said, landing beside Tala with a grunt as they finally made it out the other side. "Can't even begin to think of the exertion it would take to get past official..."

They trailed off when it became apparent that the Banders and the Katipuneros were not the only people in the clearing.

The first thing Tala saw was the Kunlun Mountains: a majestic view, their peaks hidden by a thick froth of white clouds. Even with her faulty agimat, she could taste the powerful spells emanating from within, heavy with incense and burnt wood.

The second thing she saw was the group of officious-looking people standing on the same narrow stone path they were on, gaping at their unexpected arrival. They were military, likely government soldiers judging from the state of their uniforms—two dozen in total, all armed.

The third was Vivien Fey, standing with the men and looking just as gobsmacked to see them.

"You," she hissed.

"Oh," Ken said. "Oh no."

"Run!" Ryker grabbed Tala's arm and dragged her away, toward the mountains. "We need to get inside before they catch us!"

The Banders and the Katipuneros had come to the same conclusion. The adarna had hunched itself over, clinging to the back of Tala's head. There were yells behind them and then a sudden surge of wind.

"Crap," Ryker said. "Crap, crap." He paused long enough to lob a tire-sized ice sphere over his back, and the subsequent explosion resulted in loud curses in angry Mandarin Chinese.

The firebird lingered at their rear, but Tala didn't need to turn to see what it was doing. She could feel the sudden intense heat behind her and hear more swearing.

"No!" Vivien shouted. "Don't let them escape!"

She followed that with a stream of Chinese that Tala didn't understand but that no longer mattered. They were close to the base of the mountain; she could spot a cave entrance up ahead, and she followed the others as they raced through the opening.

Loki held Ruyi Jingu Bang aloft. The staff spun in the air.

The other soldiers recognized the weapon and skidded to a halt. Only Vivien and who Tala presumed was the general in charge of the troops continued running, the latter shouting commands at his men, urging them to continue the charge.

"Why are you doing this, Fey?" Loki shouted.

"Are you still asking me that question, Wagner?" Vivien yelled back fiercely. "You know exactly why I'm doing this!"

"The Snow Queen will turn on you!"

"You're wrong. She's the only one left who can help me!" Vivien turned to Ryker, standing just beside Loki. "We thought you were dead."

"Sorry to disappoint. This isn't going to end the way you want it to, Fey. You're not so coldhearted as the others to survive this."

Vivien looked fearful for a second and then rallied. "I'm not here to talk to traitors," she said and raised the banana leaf fan she was holding over her head. She swooped her arm down, sending a powerful whirlwind hurtling toward them.

Loki spun Ruyi Jingu Bang, and the dangerous gusts of wind dissipated once they made contact with the spinning staff. Titas Teejay and Chedeng were giving them further cover. Their abanico fans were not as powerful as Vivien Fey's, but they were knocking soldiers off their feet before they could get too close, and General Luna was successfully warding the rest off with his shiv right up until Ryker gestured. A thick wall of ice promptly shielded them from the soldiers' view, obscuring the entrance of the cave.

"They were never going to let us borrow the lantern," West said. "Lady Corazon was right."

"So what now?" Nya asked. "We just walk farther inside Kunlun and see if we can get out the other side?"

"Pretty much," Tala said with a sigh.

"All I see is darkness," Ken said. The firebird glowed. "Okay, I see...well, still nothing."

"I hear a river," Zoe said. "It sounds like it is coming from somewhere nearby."

"Is that a good thing or a bad thing?" West asked.

"I may have a few suggestions," a voice through Tala's earpiece said—the Duke of Suddene's reassuring timbre. "My father had a Chinese colleague who was willing to put up with some of his odder quirks. I've only just found letters they exchanged. He told my father about a poem attributed to Sanzo in the fifth century. Its translation isn't as pretty to the ears as the original, but the gist of it is this: *Follow the ways of the Red River, and repent at the Rushing Sands, for nothing there is your enemy. Only when you win without defeating your opponent will you behold the true beauty of Chenxiang's light.*"

"A riddle?" Tala asked.

"If it is," Cole said quietly, "I don't think anyone knows the answer."

"There's a first for everything, eh?" Ken drew out Kusanagi. "If the prophecies or whatever say this sword is gonna help us find it, then I'll go with it."

"If everyone's putting him in charge, I'm not sure how practical that actually is," Nya grumbled.

Ken grinned at her. "Love you too, Rapunzel. Let's get going before they find us."

"Tangina," General Luna said and sighed.

It didn't take long for them to locate the river and confirm Sanzo's poem. The waters were three feet wide and wound even deeper into the mountain, seemingly with no end in sight. They were also the color of blood.

"Poisonous?" Ken asked.

"I don't think so," Loki said doubtfully. "Tala?"

Tala shook her head.

"Best not fall in anyway." Zoe pointed. "The passageway's large enough for us to walk beside it one at a time."

"What was that thing Fey was using?" West asked. "That oversize fan?"

"A banana leaf," Tita Baby said. "Another of China's treasured artifacts. It was once owned by one of their royal nobles, Princess Iron Fan. It's said to put out forest fires with just a swipe."

Zoe crouched down tentatively beside the embankment and slowly pulled out something from her boot that resembled a thermometer.

"Zoe," Nya warned.

"It's all right. Dex showed me how it works. It'll take a reading of the water's composition. Maybe we can figure out what this river's made of."

"You're a bloody Girl Scout is what you are," Ken said. "Do you have emergency kits on you too? Needle and thread? A toolbox?"

"First, your girlfriend's got a medical bag on her too. That's a pro. Second, I *did* bring my trusty sleeping needle to fall back on. I don't think I should be using Ogmios too close to this much water. Dexter? Are you there?" Zoe scowled. "Is anyone getting anything back from Avalon?"

"I'd be surprised if you could," Ryker said dryly. "Not even your best spelltech can get past a whole mountain chock-full of ancient magic."

"We'll keep trying to reach Avalon and see if we can get a signal," Tita Baby said. "Can you reach out to Alex, little firebird?"

From its position on Loki's shoulder, the firebird folded a wing over its eyes and then spun around in a circle, stopping to point deeper into the caves with a flourish.

"Thanks," Ken said. "That's a lot of help."

They resumed walking. Loki kept glancing over their shoulder as if they were expecting the government soldiers to pop out of thin air at any second.

"I'd tell you she's a lost cause if that means anything," Ryker said quietly to Tala. "She wants to be an ice maiden, but she'll need to prove her loyalty to the queen in horrifying ways before she can. Take it from me."

"You aren't an ice maiden. Or an..." Loki paused. "An ice dude?"

"Not a lot of dudes who choose this, I'm told. Guys angry at the world tend to also be angry at women, so they don't last long being subordinate to one. She had no plans of turning me anyway—I was more useful recruiting people to her cause. Foolish me just thought I was saving them." Ryker gazed ahead. "She'll offer you a taste of her powers," he said, "if you'll do something for her. Help build up her army maybe, or steal some important spelltech she has her eyes on. Something easy enough to accomplish with her support. For a good cause, she'll say. That's the first step. Next she'll ask you to do something incredibly cruel to prove your devotion, bind you to her. Finally, she'll ask you to kill for her, and then she'll strip you of your humanity and mold you into her image. I didn't know that was what she asked of those who wanted to be her ice maidens until before she stabbed me. She—" His hands curled into fists. "She boasted to me about it."

"I'm sorry," West said sympathetically.

"There isn't anything here that could turn the river red," Nya said, sounding bewildered. "The rocks aren't the type for it. It's almost like it's just red because it's red."

"I can try and drink it," Ken offered.

"You absolutely will not."

"The redness of the water might be the least of our problems now," Zoe said. "Take a look at what's up ahead."

They looked. And then looked again.

"Is that *more* water?" Tito Boy asked presently. "Is it normal to have this much inside mountains?"

"It's not water," Loki confirmed. "It's some kind of transparent sand."

There was a large stone arch over the river, unadorned, though its near-perfect symmetry and smooth ridges suggested that it was man-made. The color of the river as it passed underneath the arch changed remarkably, from scarlet to an odd opaque color. And while the red river had gushed forth and burbled and flowed, this new stream was strangely placid, without even a ripple on its surface.

"The riddle's starting to look very literal instead of metaphorical," Zoe said. She took out the measuring spelltech again, gingerly dipped a part of it into the still water. There was a very decided *gloop* as the metal tool touched the odd liquid—and then remained there. Startled, Zoe took it with both hands and tried to push it down but couldn't. "You're not gonna believe this," she said. "But the water's so dense that it's not letting anything in it sink. I can't even get an inch past the surface."

"But why?" Nya asked. "What purpose does this have?"

"You're forgetting about what the duke said about this place and how it's the same as Wonderland," Tita Teejay said sagely. "There weren't any real good reasons for some of the magic in Wonderland to be the way it was. Shrinking teacups and stairs that go nowhere and flowers dripping paint and all that. I think it's the same here."

"Not quite," Tita Chedeng demurred. "There was some purpose to Wonderland magic—as a good defense against outside forces. Maybe it's the same here."

Ken spun, Kusanagi in his hands leveled at the ceiling above them.

"What's wrong?" Nya asked.

"Something's bloody following us. I don't know if it's Fey or the soldiers or something else, but it looked like a shade to me. I keep seeing it out of the corner of my eye, but it isn't attacking."

The others immediately formed a circle, standing shoulder to shoulder with their backs to each other as they all gazed around. "I don't see anything," Loki said presently.

"I know what I saw," Ken growled.

"One shade, Ken?" Zoe asked. "They usually attack in groups, so one shade doesn't sound like—"

"*I know what I saw. Hey, firebird. Did you see it too? Nottingham?*"

The firebird blinked at him and then shook its head.

"I don't sense anything," Cole confirmed.

"I didn't sense anything either," Tita Baby confirmed. "Maybe Kunlun magic?"

"Tangina," said General Luna.

"Stay alert," Zoe instructed. "Call out if you see anything else that's strange."

"We've just seen a bloodred river and water so dense nothing can sink in it," Tala said.

"Anything else that's *stranger.*"

They headed deeper in, and to Tala, it seemed like they'd been traveling for hours. Their cell phones were useless, with neither reception nor even a working internal clock. The passageway had widened enough to fit two people at a time. She was all too aware of the adarna alert on her head, silent, and of Ryker, who was beside her.

"I would volunteer to take the weight off," Ryker said, "but I'm not sure the adarna is as fond of me. Would you like to sit on my head instead, little bird?"

The adarna looked at him and then, very emphatically, shook its head.

"It reminds me of the firebird in a lot of ways," Tala said. "Mostly its entitlement issues."

There was a squawk up ahead from somewhere along Loki's shoulder as if to say, *I heard that.*

"I think it's acting that way toward you in the same way the firebird acts toward Alex," Ryker chuckled. "It just wants to look out for you."

"Easy for you to say when you don't have a bowling ball on your head," Tala grumbled and received a light peck on her ear for her efforts. "Hey!"

Ryker laughed softly again, making her laugh with him. She stopped abruptly. So did he.

"Sorry," Tala said. "It just reminded me of the way things used to be back at Elsmore High. You and me and Alex."

"I'm sorry too," Ryker said quietly. "For ever having put you in danger, even when I said I would never harm you and meant it. If I could have just—"

"Oh hell," said Ken, who had just stepped through a smaller entrance. He'd disappeared from view, but Tala could still hear his voice, awed and very much worried. "Oh hell, oh hell, oh hell."

"Is it safe to assume this isn't anything good, Ken?" Zoe asked warily.

And then it was their turn to enter, their turn to gape.

Before them was a large cavern the size of ten football fields, and there was sand *everywhere*. It poured down from above, though where it was streaming from was obscured by more sand spilling from even higher ledges.

Tala pressed her foot against the uneven ground, her boot sinking a couple of inches lower when she put her full weight on it. The sand swirled around her, pulled along by some unseen current.

"This sand is acting more like water than the water we just left," West said.

"Now what?" Ken asked. "I don't see any other exits beyond the one we came out from."

Several hundred meters in front of him, something rustled from deep within the endlessly shifting sands. He jumped back when it burst through the surface.

It was a demon. Its skin was reddish in color, a bushy, bristly beard starting from its chin and reaching its knees—a considerable achievement, given that it was about eight feet tall. It had bulging eyes and wore a necklace of skulls around its neck, possibly a testament to other intrepid explorers who had gone before them, because even as the sands stirred and settled, Tala spotted skeletal remains lying haphazardly within the cavern, the bones scrubbed clean from the grit.

The demon settled its lidless eyes on them, its mouth pulling back into a horrifying grin to reveal at least three rows of jagged brown teeth, and roared.

"Uh," West said. "I guess that's what."

6

IN WHICH LOKI DOESN'T WIN

It's not charging at us," Zoe said cautiously. "I guess that's a pro. It's just standing there, staring at us with its creepy eyes."

"I'm pretty sure the con about this whole situation is everything else," Ken said. "You think I should go over there and give it a whack with Kusanagi or something? The Beast of Suddene never said anything about what to do in that poem of his."

"It's in here for a reason," Tala pointed out. "Maybe it's the lantern's guardian, and someone needs to beat it to win? Is it some kind of nightwalker?"

"No," Cole said, staring back at the strange demon with a frown. "I don't know what it is, but it's not that."

"It's trembling," Loki said.

"Everything in this place is trembling," Ken groused. "It's hard to keep your balance when the ground is constantly spilling out underneath you, and it's going to make fighting this dude especially hard."

"No," Loki said. "I mean Ruyi Jingu Bang is trembling. I don't know how to explain, but it recognizes that creature."

"Recognizes?" Nya echoed.

"That necklace of skulls…I've heard about that before." Loki's forehead unwrinkled. "Right. My fathers always felt bad they couldn't tell me much about my biological parents. Most adoption records from China are sealed. So they helped me learn as much as I could about my culture. And when I first got the staff, they showed me this old historical book called *Journey to the West*, which listed Sanzo's encounters with demonic creatures. Ruyi Jingu Bang was the weapon used by Sun Wukong, one of the monk's companions. Kunlun was one of the places they traveled to."

"Do any history books say how they were able to beat this guy?" Nya asked.

"Not really. Just that they did."

"Great."

"But I know I have to be the one to fight it."

"Have you *seen* how many dead people it's wearing, Loki?" Ken yelped. "With Kusanagi and your staff, we'd *both* have a better chance at—"

But Loki shook their head. Their gaze was trained on the scarlet-skinned creature, and the beast was, disconcertingly enough, staring right back at them. "I think—I think I know what I'm supposed to do."

"You're not expecting us to let you fight it alone, are you?" Tala asked anxiously.

"I won't die. Probably. Trust me."

The others had their own segen out. "At the least sign of trouble," Tita Baby said, "we're all rushing in. There's no helping that."

The red demon stuck its scaled, clawed hand into the sand and slowly drew out a large weapon, far taller than even Ken or Cole.

There was a series of sharp hooks on one end, much like an oversize rake that no sane person would ever use for gardening. The monster swung it through the air, and Tala didn't like the grating sound it made.

Loki carried the staff loosely in one hand, and Tala finally understood what they meant when they said it was trembling. The staff was practically radiating with eagerness, nearly jumping out of Loki's hand in anticipation.

The creature didn't wait for Loki to draw any nearer. With a roar that sent more sand spilling down on them from everywhere, it lashed out with its weapon.

Ruyi Jingu Bang immediately lengthened to several times its size and struck at the base of the rake, where all the sharp hooks lay joined together, nearly knocking it out of the red ogre's hand.

"Clever," Zoe said. "Now I know why they insisted on fighting it alone. With the staff, they'd never need to draw close to the creature to get hit."

In vain did the monster try nonetheless. Loki was an expert at gauging the distance between them and reacting accordingly, quick to dodge out of the way and keep out of the ogre's range. Despite the instability of the sand underneath their feet, their movements never faltered, snatching their staff out of midair and delivering sharp, jabbing attacks with it.

"What are they doing, though?" Ken asked. "Loki's more intent on attacking that thing's weapon but not the thing itself."

"I'm sure they've got a plan," Zoe said, sounding worried all the same.

Loki showed no signs of tiring, though Tala knew the longer the fight was, the more it was to their disadvantage. They were content with heaping most of the damage at the monstrous rake, landing no blows to the monster itself.

Until there was a very loud and very deliberate crack. The heavy rake broke in half. The upper part of the weapon with the dangerous-looking spikes and hooks crashed into the sand before them, leaving the creature holding on to the broken end of a long rod.

"They kept hitting it at almost the exact same spot," Ryker said, reluctantly impressed. "Pretty good way to disarm an opponent."

But Loki didn't press their advantage. Their staff shrunk back into a toothpick's size, which they then stuck behind their ear.

"Loki, what are you doing?" Ken called out. "Finish it off already!"

Loki did nothing of the sort. They began walking toward the creature, hands raised.

"What are you doing?" Tala gasped. "Loki!"

"I have a theory!" the ranger called back.

"Is it possible for you to work on that theory somewhere farther away from it?!"

The creature watched Loki approach and did the strangest thing. It cast away its broken staff and raised its own hands, mimicking their overtures.

"I have no idea what's going on," Zoe muttered, gripping her whip, "but my anxiety is through the roof."

Both ranger and creature stopped within a few feet of each other, hands still up. Slowly, Loki lowered theirs, and the demon followed their movements. Loki then dropped to the ground, rearranging themselves into a sitting position with their legs crossed before them, and the monster did the same.

"Are they going to have a picnic now?" Ken asked.

Neither of the former combatants spoke. They gazed steadily at each other for a few moments. And then Loki got back on their feet, walking back to them. "All right," they said. "It'll give us the lantern."

"How?" Ken asked. "Were you guys conversing on some higher astral plane or what? Because it didn't say a word to you."

"It didn't need to. Sanzo and Sun Wukong fought this creature—they called it the Sha Gojyo—and it wound up becoming one of their companions. Ruyi Jingu Bang recognized it as a friend. I can't explain how I know, but when I took out the staff, I thought I could see the memories of some of its previous owners. And maybe a bit of their fighting abilities too. I did a few things back there I didn't even know I was capable of."

"I could see that." Tala threw her arms around them. "You worried me! Please don't do that ever again!"

Loki looked down at her, stunned. And then, a bit awkwardly, they patted her on the head. "I'll try my best not to."

"Your ears are red," West noted.

"Quiet, West. I realized what the riddle meant," Loki continued. "Win without defeating your opponent. He must have meant a stalemate. Sha Gojyo isn't our enemy."

"I'm impressed, my dear," Tita Chedeng said. "I would never have gotten that."

Ryker was glaring at Loki, inching closer to them and Tala. "So is it going to show us where the lantern is?" he asked abruptly.

"Yeah. Its task is to guard this place until someone worthy comes along. In the past, that was Sanzo." Loki grinned self-consciously. "Today, it's us."

"Then what are we standing around for? You should go and get it."

"What's gotten into you?" Tala asked, surprised by his sudden shift in mood.

Ryker shot Loki one last glower. "It's nothing. But we need to leave."

"Why?" West asked.

"Because I can feel nightwalkers in the area. Either Fey's found a way here, or it's the Snow Queen herself, and I'm not liking either option."

The creature raised its hands higher, over its head. As if in response to that silent command, the sands around them began to recede, the grit underneath Tala's boots slowly leaching away until she was once more standing on flat, solid ground.

And as the sands flowed away, they revealed a small locked box previously hidden underneath, tucked at one corner of the cavern.

Loki gently peeled Tala off them, then raced toward the newly unearthed box. They slowly lifted the lid.

"I think this is it," they said, not bothering to hide their excitement, and lifted the lantern out. It was a particularly common-looking paper lantern, one that would have been easily overlooked elsewhere. Loki held it reverently all the same, turning it sideways. "I'm not entirely sure how to use this," they said, "but it can't be anything else but what we came for, right?"

"It absolutely is," Vivien said, "and thank you for finding it."

Loki turned, startled, in the direction of her voice, but Ruyi Jingu Bang reacted immediately, lengthening and putting itself in front of Loki. It spun rapidly, once more dispelling the powerful slice of wind that Vivien's fan had aimed their way.

Tala heard Ken mutter a curse, and then Kusanagi was swinging. Vivien had not come alone; with her were the same soldiers as before and the same general commanding them. But now there were shades and ice wolves along their flank, the latter baring their sharp teeth and growling. They leaped, making a beeline toward Loki.

It was Cole's turn to throw himself in front of the ranger. With a swipe of his Gravekeeper, he impaled the nearest ice wolf, dark thornlike lines appearing all over the creature's body as he fought to gain control over it. The ice wolf's eyes glowed, the red from them fading. It turned to attack an approaching shade, tearing it to pieces with its fangs. Cole struck again, this time impaling a shadow, which turned on its own brethren as well.

There was a sizzle of electricity, and Ogmios whipped across, sending bolts of electricity at another ice wolf as Zoe stepped up to Cole's side, protecting her boyfriend.

The last few months had helped Nya gain even better proficiency with her broom, keeping the shades at bay while West shifted into a large dog, tearing through the rest of the shadows. Tala focused on the nearest ice wolf, felt a quick rush of both relief and triumph as her agimat took hold and the beast started to fracture, her curse wreaking havoc on whatever inherently magical physiology her opponent was made of. But it was taking so much longer than what she could do in the past, and already three other ice wolves had turned toward her, marking her as a new target.

Stop relying constantly on your agimat, Tala! She switched to her arnis sticks instead, beating back the first ice wolf to reach her, then other shades that fell within attacking range.

The adarna on her head rose to its feet and sang. Its voice carried into the air, echoing throughout the cavernous chamber, and once again the shades and ice wolves froze as if spellbound.

It took off and flew above their heads. Tala was expecting more music from it, only to hear the far-from-melodic sounds of the adarna's other secret weapon, splattering noisily on the soldiers' heads. Their cries of disgust ceased abruptly as the magic took hold, the poop the adarna had dropped on them swiftly transforming them into immobile statues.

Ryker had rushed to her side, sweating as he held out his hands toward the ice wolves, slowly closing them into fists as the ice wolves shattered inward. Tala crushed the first wolf and then tackled one of the others Ryker was keeping at bay, though she was already tired.

She dodged a sudden volley of fire as the general and his remaining soldiers turned their guns skyward, the adarna in their sights.

It was the wrong move to make.

With a screech of fury, the firebird was upon them. From the terrified yelps and the crackle of flames, it was clear that the bird was taking no prisoners.

Ken was bypassing all the other nightwalkers, leaping immediately for Vivien. She flung another heavy gust of wind at him, but he simply slashed at it with his sword, dispelling the wave. Tala actually saw the incoming air visibly split, both sections spinning away from him.

"Interesting," Vivien noted coldly. "The Nameless Sword has fused with your original twin swords. One capable of cutting through anything that isn't alive, another that does the exact opposite, amplifying both. It would be interesting to see you deal with the contradictions inherent within the swords."

"Lady," Ken said, "I'm not the one who sold her soul to the Snow Queen. Philosophizing on the moral ethics of my swords is the height of some damn hypocrisy right there."

"Where did you get Princess Iron Fan's fan?" Loki snapped. Their staff cartwheeled freely around them, a shield against incoming assaults.

"On loan from my friend here, General Cao. He agrees with me that the lotus lantern should never come into possession of one who has forsaken the lands of their birth to side with a rogue kingdom seeking to gain power with ancient relics."

"Do you even hear yourself, you absolute wombat?" Ken took down another blast of wind, every word emphasized with a deliberate upswing. "*You're* the one siding with the rogue kingdom!"

The general called out something Tala didn't understand, and then fired his gun. His shot wasn't aimed at the Banders but instead at the demon, who had not moved since sitting down with Loki. It raised its large fist and calmly swatted the resulting bullet away like it was no more than a bothersome fly.

"My Mandarin's a bit rusty," Loki said, "but I'm pretty sure the general's telling us that the lantern belongs to the Chinese people and not to *invaders* like us." They turned back to Vivien. "The queen hasn't given you any abilities yet. That's why you're still using that iron fan. That means you're still hesitating."

The winds ceased. Vivien faltered before the anger in her eyes returned. "You don't know anything about me. You're just some little lost child who doesn't know what they're doing." She raised the fan again to send cutting whirlwinds of air, this time at the Sha Gojyo.

With its weapon broken, there was nothing it could do to stop the attack. The creature lifted its arms wide above its head and allowed the sharp slices of air to cut into its body. It toppled and then sank down into a large mound of sand that had grown underneath it.

The cave shook. The sands that had temporarily receded were now back in full force, and they were pouring in three times faster than they had receded. Tala stumbled, the ground once more uneven, making it difficult to keep her balance.

"Fall back!" Zoe shouted.

"Fall back to where?" West shouted back, shifting briefly into human form. "They're the ones covering the exit!"

The shades, which had no problems keeping upright despite the shifting sands, were gunning for Loki again. The ranger raised their staff, the other hand with a firm grasp on the lantern, which promptly emitted a powerful burst of light that illuminated the cavern. Something bright and dazzling streamed out, directed in a straight beam toward the farthest wall.

"That's your answer, West!" they shouted. "Everyone, move!"

The Banders were already scrambling before they'd finished speaking, with both Cole and Ken taking up the rear and keeping most of the nightwalkers from following. Nya was the first to reach the wall, her hands gliding over the uneven stone surface, searching for anything that would suggest a hidden entrance. "Here!" she shouted as her fingers found some invisible recess. With a low groan, part of the wall swung back.

Everyone dashed into the new exit. Ryker had joined the other two boys, ice shooting out from the ground as barriers to keep the soldiers from getting close, while Cole was using half a dozen shades and ice wolves to keep their fellows at bay, the firebird aiding him by promptly burning those still too close for its comfort. The last thing Tala saw as they all finally scrambled in and Nya found the inner switch to pull the wall closed behind her was the look of furious frustration on Vivien's face as she stared futilely at them.

The firebird glowed and found its way back to Loki's shoulder. They now stood at another longer passageway extending farther into more darkness. Tala could hear heavy blows from the other side of the wall they'd just burst through—no doubt Vivien unleashing her fury there, or perhaps the soldiers firing more shots. For the moment, the stone held.

"When they said the lantern would help show us the way," Zoe said, "they meant that literally too."

Loki gave the lantern another quick search, frowning. "I'm not sure what I did to activate it."

"We'll have all the time to inspect it more closely as soon as we return to Avalon and the Gallaghers can run tests on it." Zoe peered out into the dark. "The lantern says this is the way out, although we don't really have much choice now, do we? I can see a fork in the path up ahead."

"Well, the lantern's gone dark, and I'm not sure how to get it working again."

The adarna sang a quick snatch of melody. The lotus lantern glowed again as if in reply. Another stream of light, smaller than the previous blaze, shot down the stone corridor, showing them the path.

"And we're gonna have to do this with five more artifacts, huh?" West said, trying not to sound miserable and failing.

7

In Which Avalon Is a Popular Target

Finding their way out of the Kunlun Mountains had been anticlimactic. The lotus lantern was just as accurate as Sanzo's poem had said it would be, painstakingly guiding them through the often-confusing tunnels and unerringly pointing out the right way at every break in the path, past passageways that looked identical to the ones they had just emerged from. When they finally stepped out onto what appeared to be the other side of the mountain, blinking at the now-unfamiliar daylight, there had been no soldiers or nightwalkers waiting for them. Their comm link back to Avalon started working soon after.

"Where have you guys been?" Alex groaned, sounding relieved. "We've been trying to track you for the last two hours, and we couldn't get through anything. The Chinese government claimed they hadn't even detected anyone porting in."

"It's a long story," Zoe said wearily, "but we got what we came for, thanks to Loki. Get us out of here as soon as you can, before anything else comes chasing after us."

Now that they were safely back in Avalon by way of Manila, the

Gallaghers and their team had gathered around the lotus lantern like it was the most fascinating thing in the world, running scans over it and conversing excitedly with each other using technological jargon that made not one whit of sense to Tala. She sat wearily on one of the command center's comfortable couches, all now occupied by the rest of the Banders. The adarna stirred on her head and yawned.

The bird had been looking after her, Tala realized. Its song had paralyzed most of the nightwalkers, giving her enough time to recover. She looked up to see the adarna gazing sleepily back down on her. It seemed…inquisitive, and also reassuring. "Are you sitting on me," she asked, "because you want to protect me?"

The adarna let out a short ditty of a song, then bobbed its head enthusiastically.

"Why?"

It shrugged.

"You're just as exasperating as the firebird, you know that?"

"Maybe it just likes you," Ryker offered quietly, plopping down beside her. "People and magical creatures have the right to like you, you know."

"Funny." Tala continued to scowl up at it. "My agimat still isn't up to par," she said. "But I know there's another reason you're singling me out beyond that, and I would like to know why."

Much to her surprise, the adarna craned its neck downward and then, very lightly, pecked her affectionately on the cheek.

"Told you," Ryker chuckled.

Tala lifted a hand to touch the side of her face. "I… Thanks?"

The adarna cooed.

The place where it had kissed her felt warm on her face, soothing. "Do you think I might be putting the rest of you at risk? Am I being stubborn, wanting to join the group when I could put them all in danger just by coming along?"

"I assume the weakening of your agimat was directly caused by what happened with the Nine Maidens," Ryker surmised.

"Yup."

"Then think about it another way. Maybe you still having the use of your agimat means you're stronger than you think you are. I've heard enough stories about the Nine Maidens to know that most people who tried what you did lost more than just their abilities."

"That's not gonna be much help if nightwalkers can overwhelm me easily just because I'm weaker now."

"The Snow Queen...well." Ryker shifted uneasily. "I know a lot about the agimat only through her experiences with encountering it, from her stories of fighting some of your Makiling ancestors. You need to be constantly using the agimat to enhance it further, right? Have you been using it much the last few months?"

"Mom's been putting me through exercises," Tala admitted.

"That other girl, Nya—she doesn't seem to have any magical abilities or segen of her own, but she's still pretty good at fighting, right?"

It wasn't Tala's place to tell him that Nya was technically a magical creature in her own right, which made *her whole self* a segen, so she nodded instead.

"Well, there you go. Besides, I don't think they'll feel the same going into missions without you there."

"Thanks. It just feels like there's a part of me that's gone, you know? It's not easy. How would you feel, had you been in my place?"

"I'd be a better person, to start," Ryker said dryly. "But that's all my fault."

He looked like he had more to say, so Tala remained quiet, waiting.

"I meant it when I told Fey back there that the Snow Queen's intention is to corrupt her, make her another ice maiden," he finally said. "And also when I said that the Snow Queen will ask all her novitiates to prove their loyalty by killing for her. I'm not proud of what I've done for her, even if I thought the end justified the means."

He looked down at his hand, formed a tiny ball of ice barely bigger than a thimble on his palm. Tala saw Zoe look curiously their way but didn't comment.

"I guess Fey's gonna tell her I'm still alive," he said. "If she wants to take these abilities away from me, she's gonna have to come over and forcibly take them herself."

"And part of your abilities is being able to sense any nightwalkers nearby?"

"Gotta know where your expendable army is, right? Just never thought she considered me that too."

"It's okay to forgive yourself for being fooled by her," Tala said sternly. "You were vulnerable, and she took advantage of you. That you even managed to get away from her influence says a lot."

"I probably wouldn't have if I hadn't met you and Alex. I've always been jealous of your friendship, because as grateful as I was to her, I've never had that with the queen or with anyone. She was the closest thing I ever had to a parent after my mom, so I held on to her for years, even when she was distant. Always thought it was my fault, that I had to work harder to make her proud of me. And seeing you with the other Bandersnatchers…I've never had that either. I can at least make amends now by fighting with Alex." He looked down, deliberately avoiding her gaze. "And this isn't a ploy just to ask you out again, or anything like that," he added roughly. "I am—that isn't to say that I'm not interested. I just need to pull my shit together before doing anything else."

"I understand," Tala said, and she was surprised at how this no longer bothered her. Her old puppy-dog crush on him felt like it had happened to someone else lifetimes ago, now that she had fallen out of it and a new solid, more grounded affection had taken its place. "I don't understand why you were so rude to Loki, though."

Ryker looked back at her for a moment and then sighed, putting a hand over his eyes. "I'm not going to tell you."

"Why not?"

"Guy's still gotta have some secrets."

The Gallaghers were still busily conducting their analysis of the lantern, a visibly enthusiastic Lord Suddene at their elbows. The rest of the command center was a flurry of voices, Lord Keer, the Wake of the Fianna, still on hand directing his people spread out all over Avalon. It looked like the ranger leader hadn't even stopped for a break since Tala and the others had left for Manila. On-screen, Tala could see a group of rangers patrolling one of the designated outposts, their magic-infused weapons at the ready. There were at least three regiments within the Fianna comprised primarily of segen wielders now;

a few months before, Tala would never have imagined there would be so many of them, much less pledged to fight for their cause.

Alex was looking a bit harried himself, though she was sure it wasn't solely because of the constant stream of reports coming in. Tristan was still sticking stubbornly to the king like he was his official bodyguard, and the look on the young Locksley's face told Tala that he intended to keep doing so for the indefinite future.

"We don't have much time," Alex finally said, and heads turned his way. "The Fifth Honor are reporting strange activity along the Burn, and Lord Keer has sent both the Second and Third to shore up their numbers there. I've issued a kingdom-wide alert for everyone to remain alert but calm. We're triple-checking every port in the kingdom, building fail-safes at vulnerable areas. We don't know where the Snow Queen intends to strike, but I don't intend to be caught defenseless this time. Severon?"

"Nothing in our scanners is telling us this lantern has even a shred of magical ability, Your Majesty," Lord Gallagher reported.

"How is that possible?" Ken asked. "We literally saw it shoot beams of light while it was getting us out to safety."

"That may be so, Lord Inoue," the man acknowledged, "but that doesn't mean it contradicts our findings. If this was modified using the Alatyr, then it would have been created using some of the purest concentrations of magic known to humanity. Our most advanced spelltech would not even begin to detect it."

"Do we really *want* to use the Alatyr?" Lord Suddene asked. "I admit that it is tempting to study, but the Alatyr is a crueler spell than the Nine Maidens. The latter requires a sacrifice from a royal of the

Avalon lineage to prevent it from falling into the wrong hands, but the Alatyr consumed any sacrifice it found, used their life forces as batteries to power the next massacre. Koschei offered up so many people this way, killing them and strengthening it without any loss to himself. Nome adopted a similar mechanic in his prototype when he used the jabberwocks."

"I'm surprised," Lola Urduja said. "I would have thought you of all people would have wanted the opportunity."

"I'm not my father, Lola. I won't forsake the possible consequences just to further my research."

"We can discuss all that once we have the actual coordinates to Buyan." Lord Gallagher scowled. "It does nothing for us to speculate on controlling the Alatyr if we cannot make much sense of its artifacts."

"I'm guessing you haven't found a way to recreate what we saw it do in Kunlun?" Loki asked.

"Unfortunately, no. There's a possibility that it can only be triggered in the presence of some real and immediate danger and also by a worthy owner."

"Loki, superglue yourself to the lantern from now on," West ordered.

"The only thing I'm sure of," Lord Gallagher continued, "is that it seems to be forged from the same kind of concentrated magic as your staff, Loki. I asked a few Chinese colleagues of my father still with the profession, and they confirmed that weapons like Ruyi Jingu Bang can come back stronger after they're destroyed, although no one's quite sure how."

Loki nodded thoughtfully, playing with the toothpick behind their ear. "It broke in Sun Wukong's hands numerous times. And I broke it that one time too, fighting the jabberwock."

"Whether or not it can be reforged depends on its owner's willpower—whether or not the magic finds them worthy to be remade for them. That is a quote often ascribed to Sun Wukong," Lord Suddene said. "Let us hope that we will be just as fortunate with the other artifacts."

"Tala," Lola Urduja said crisply, "did Corazon accompany you and the others back here to Avalon?"

"Yes. They're with the Fianna right now. They're patrolling alongside the group guarding the Burn."

The old woman scowled. "Now why would she be so interested in the Burn?"

"Is it really all that important, Lola?" Tita Baby asked. She and the other Katipuneros were guarding the command center, their abanicos (and in General Luna's case, his favorite shiv) at the ready in case another unauthorized port opened.

"I can't trust her as far as I can spit. If she shows interest in something, I know there's some scheme she's involved in that she's refusing to tell us."

"There are far more things to worry about than Corazon, Urduja," Tita Baby chided gently. "With the attack on Alex and with the other relics still to be found, I wouldn't think that—"

"Wait," Tala interrupted. "What's this about an attack on Alex?"

"It's nothing," Alex said, glowering at Tita Baby, who pressed her hands against her mouth and only looked a little guilty.

"That you say it's nothing is the biggest warning sign that there is something."

"They do need to know, Alex," her mother reminded him. "It's not like you can hide this for long when it's already in the news."

"In what news?" Tala demanded.

"There've been reports of certain areas in the Royal States being hit by unknown ports. No details on the specifics of those attacks—no one's covering those details just yet—but King John has gone on record accusing Alex of the attacks. Everyone's bracing for him to declare war on Avalon at this point. There's still a lot of anger from the Abigail Fey incident, especially from the men, and he's using it to stir up even more hatred."

"Oh great," Zoe groaned. "Just what we need right now."

"That's not your problem," Alex said brusquely. "What you need to concern yourselves with right now is finding the rest of the artifacts. If Vivien Fey was already on-site when you were, then we need to step up before they can get to the next one. And if she's getting other countries involved, whether they be the actual authorities or rogue government agents, then we may already be in trouble. Lord Suddene, what's the next item on the agenda?"

"That would be the tamatebako, Your Majesty." The monstrous lord took command of the display screen once more, the world map shifting to concentrate on the Japanese empire. "We might be on surer footing with this one, since their government has been on much more friendlier terms with Avalon, especially now that Kensington has taken control of the sword. After you all left for Kunlun, Ken, we received word from some officials of the emperor himself wishing you well. It sounds like they were rather pleased you'd chosen to name your sword after Kusanagi."

"Well," Ken said, flushing a little, "that's real bloody high praise, isn't it? And from the emperor!"

"One of the emperor's own attendants has very kindly agreed to be here with us today, once we've made our wishes known. They can tell you more about it than I can. We are also reaching out to the other nations whose relics we may have to, uh, *borrow*. Most have been welcoming so far and willing to listen to what we have to say, though understandably cautious."

The woman shown in was clad in a resplendent kimono, dark blue with the emperor's current showa year written on one side underneath her obi. She bowed low toward them, and everyone did the same. "My name is Motoyama Chiaki," she said softly. "Lord Suddene tells me you are interested in locating one of our more mysterious artifacts—the tamatebako, isn't it?"

"Yes," Alex said. "Please extend my gratitude to Emperor Hirohito for giving us permission to use it."

Chiaki chuckled. "You may not be as pleased when you hear where it is located. We have been fortunate in Japan to have preserved many of own revered relics. Some of our precious artifacts have even been showcased in famous museums without issue, but the tamatebako is not one that we have current possession of."

West groaned. "Please don't tell me we gotta go into another mountain."

"Behave, hijo," Tito Boy chided with a reproving flick of his hands.

Chiaki shook her head. "It is not located inside a mountain. It might be easier to retrieve if it was. I do not know if any of you are aware of the legend behind it. We have many Japanese heroes often associated with powerful segen. Inoue-sama here has inherited Muramasa's and Masamune's swords, for instance, and his father has distinguished himself with their use in the past.

"The tamatebako in particular is often associated with one of our most popular heroes, Urashima Taro, who was said to possess extraordinary longevity because of his ownership of it. By keeping his life's essence within the tamatebako, he was able to survive numerous attempts on his life, lead his people to victory, and fight for our emperors against those who sought to overthrow their rule. Many of his opponents who thought they had killed him in battle, even at times going so far as to desecrate the body to make sure—against our code of honor—would often be astounded to learn, days later, that Urashima had once again turned up, alive and without a mark on him."

"Do you know the specifics of how he was able to return to life?" Dexter asked eagerly.

"Accounts of it vary. Every time the tamatebako was opened and his soul released, he would reappear, alive and whole, in some nearby village, sometimes within days of his death, others a few months more."

"Will your country not come under fire for helping us?"

"Officially, the emperor has nothing to do with Koschei or with the Beirans," Chiaki said cheerfully, "and Japan maintains a neutral stance. I am here simply because Lord Suddene has very kindly asked me for information about the tamatebako, and we are more than happy to oblige."

Alex grinned slightly. "Acknowledged, Lady Motoyama. But why do you not safeguard the tamatebako like your other artifacts?"

"Urashima threw the tamatebako back into the ocean after the war, choosing to grow old and die peacefully. He himself couldn't carry it on his person at all times. His enemies could have simply killed him and taken it from his body. Often he would entrust it to someone loyal to him, though even that has its own dangers."

"I suppose that could pose a problem," Zoe acknowledged. "May we know where it is?"

"It is said to be located beneath the waves at the Ryugu-jo, the Dragon Palace, which lies underneath our seas."

But Ken was already out of his seat before the woman finished, folding his arms and looking like there were no levers in the world large enough to move him. "No," he said. "No, no, no. Absolutely not. And if you need me to spell it out in Japanese too, that's iie, *dame*, and k'so!"

"I don't understand?" Chiaki asked, confused.

"Avalon's hero has an averse reaction to large bodies of water," Nya said dryly. "You did manage to float the last time, Ken."

"If I'm going to take *beneath the waves* literally, then I will not be, in fact, floating!"

"If it is the fear of drowning that concerns you," Chiaki said, "then we have spelltech that will allow you to breathe underwater for several hours if need be. I believe Avalon also has their own versions of it. I do recommend ours, which has been perfected by some of our most esteemed deep-sea divers. The Dragon Palace is not for tourists or even for the Japanese. Many artifacts are stored within its walls, most that we do not know much of ourselves. Curses within it make it dangerous to travel to."

"Any specifics?" Nya asked.

"There is a strange time-lapse spell that lingers within the palace. It is similar to the frost that you have endured in your kingdom— *the Avalon year*, as they have now called it? Where over a decade has passed outside Avalon and yet only twelve months for its inhabitants?"

"I was one of those inhabitants, and yes, they *do* call it the Avalon year now," Nya said sourly.

"It is the same with the Dragon Palace but for far longer. There were records in the early 1300s of an explorer who chose to enter the Dragon Palace, disappearing without a trace, only to reemerge in the 1920s, disoriented but claiming to be the very same person. As he was of a noble clan, many records had been kept of his ancestry. His DNA proved his claims true."

"There were no chances at all of him being a con artist?" Loki asked.

"None at all, because I, too, was descended from that very clan and had the chance to talk to him in his later years. As it turned out, he was my many times great-uncle, whom my own family had written off as an eccentric who'd been lost at sea."

"I hate water," Ken said. "I really do."

"You can sit this one out, Ken," Zoe said reassuringly. "We can retrieve it ourselves."

"Horse can take your place," West chimed in.

"There is no way we are going to force you into doing this if you don't want to," Nya said sternly. "You've got good reason, and while I appreciate you trying to overcome it, it needs time to—"

"I wasn't trying to overcome it," Ken said. "I was just trying to overcome it a *little* bit, because my very hot girlfriend is a goddamn sea goddess, and I can't impress her if I'm terrified of her favorite place to be."

A blush grew on Nya's cheeks. "You don't have to. I'm not asking—"

"I know. But the problem is that I'm asking *me* to do it, and I'm kind of an arse." Ken groaned again. "Fine. I'll do it. I'll do it, but I want a pack of that bloody breathable spelltech you've got, and then three more."

"Our scholars believe the Nameless Sword is required to gain access to the Ryugu-jo," Chiaki said. "The only one successful at opening its doors in the past was Musashi, another warrior who had known ownership of the Nameless Sword."

"How did he get out of the palace?" Zoe asked eagerly.

"He never told anyone else how he was able to overcome the curse for fear that others would take advantage. But he said that all it took for him was his strength of mind."

"Well, there you go," Ken said sourly. "I don't need to swim; I just need brain muscles."

"That doesn't answer the question of the time-lapse spell still within the Ryugu-jo," Zoe pointed out. "I don't suppose the Japanese have found a way to fix that either?"

Chiaki shook her head. "Dabbling in time-lapse spells tends to be more disadvantageous than not. We have, in our foolishness, made many of those attempts in the past—with unfortunate results. In a very odd way, we look to the Ryugu-jo to protect and preserve our history and are content to leave it be. We revere it as a historical landmark but take steps to prevent anyone from entering its territory. The artifacts that remain within are not intended for use."

"But your emperor was kind enough to make an exception for us," Alex said.

"We understand the uniqueness of your position, Your Majesty. And of course, should your business with the tamatebako be done, then we would be grateful to see it returned to Japan, where it will be protected."

Alex laughed. "I can't guarantee you what state it will be in when we return it, but we do hope to keep it in one piece. Thank you again, Lady Motoyama."

"I can speak with your other generals. It is necessary for me to explain what you would require for protection."

"No one's telling me how we're going to overcome the time-lapse spell," Ken complained after the woman left with Lord Suddene. "I don't want to get in there and come out five hundred years later. Six months in the Avalon frost was bad enough."

"You don't have to worry about that." Alex held out his bracers. "I'll need all the strength I can get to hold on to any spells I can find at the palace."

"No!" Tristan exploded.

"I told you I wasn't going to use it unless we had no other choice. Time-lapse spells are something that not even the Gallaghers can control. OzCorp didn't even bother making spelltech with them, knowing their unpredictability. Or shall we abandon searching for all the artifacts altogether?"

"That's exactly what I'm saying. Nothing inside that palace is worth your life. That place ought to be safe from even the Snow Queen. If she can't access it, then she won't be able to cobble together what she needs to revive Koschei. In fact, we should let her try. If she disappears for several centuries, that would solve a lot of problems."

"You're forgetting that the Snow Queen has her mirror," Zoe spoke up. "Broken as it might be, it still has some of the Alatyr in it. That's the prototype the Nine Maidens was based on. What are the chances of her using time-lapse spells there too?"

Tristan shot her a stony glare. "You're not helping, Zoe."

"Your Majesty?" This from Dexter, who looked scared out of his wits.

"Dex, I insisted on shorter shifts for a reason. I don't remember seeing you taking a break—"

"I'm a-all right, Your Majesty," the boy stammered. "It's just—I think this is something that Miss Motoyama should know immediately."

"What?"

But the young Gallagher was already switching the display over to video. "Miss Motoyama said their people were monitoring the Ryugu-jo," he said. "She gave me permission to access the body cam from one of her soldiers on-site."

It was difficult to make anything out at first; the waters were churning heavily, like some kind of fight was in progress. And then a familiar dark shape slid into view before it was promptly gutted with a harpoon.

"Shades," Ryker snarled.

Other fighters came into view, most of them firing at another person who, unlike the Japanese warriors decked out in scuba gear, was bare chested and clad only in a dark latex outfit. He was clearly not Japanese and was wielding a heavy ax that his opponents were keeping their distance from.

Tala stared at the invader as he slowly drew nearer to the camera.

She recognized that wild wave of hair, the scraggly beard that she liked to tug, the heavily muscled arms that had taught her arnis.

"Dad," she whispered.

8

IN WHICH THE DRAGON PALACE IS THE WORLD'S WORST ATTRACTION

The officials waiting for them at Osaka were friendlier than the ones they ran into at Kunlun; Tala recognized one of them as the kingdom's prime minister. They were inside the National Diet Building, one of the major seats of Japanese government, but right now it was strangely deserted.

Horse had gone with them. If any of the officials had registered surprise at the sight of the powerful kelpie, stomping his hooves and looking about with eagerness, they were careful to keep their expressions neutral. They were more visibly awed at the sight of the firebird, who was showing off by surrounding itself in a halo of small flames, and at the adarna on Tala's head, who was sleeping again.

Prime Minister Hamada was remarkably calm considering the battle currently going on underneath their waters. "Thank you for receiving us on such short notice," he said through a translator, bowing.

"Thank you for not declaring war on Avalon when you discovered who your attacker was," Lumina said, not bothering to mask her anxiety. "Bring us to where my husband is, and we will do our best to keep him from causing more harm."

"You are Lumina Makiling Warnock-san, yes? We are aware of the circumstances involving Kay Warnock. Even if we were not, Avalon has been kind to us. Our kingdoms were once bitter rivals, and yet in the aftermath of war, your rulers showed us compassion. We hope to offer our support in turn, though many obstacles prevent us from saying so along official lines." The man gestured at an ornately designed looking glass. "This should bring you to the Ryugu-jo. I have ordered our samurai to maintain their distance, to engage only when necessary, but your husband, Makiling Warnock-san, is a rather stubborn man."

"Believe me, I intend to knock some sense into him."

"My warriors have reported something unusual with regard to his person. They have caused him injuries, but the man shrugs it off like they are nothing. On the other hand, he has already put several of my soldiers out of action, though he is but one against many."

Tala had a bad feeling in the pit of her stomach. Beside her, Ryker slowly squeezed her hand just as Loki moved silently to stand beside her.

"I also must caution you about the Ryugu-jo," the prime minister went on. "We cannot guarantee your safety inside. I cannot promise that you may even be able to leave the palace nor confirm the time period you emerge into. Even with your Nine Maidens on standby."

"That's a chance we're all ready to take, Minister," Lumina said shortly. "Unfortunately, we have little choice but to see it through."

"I might pose a problem," Zoe muttered. "My segen works using lightning. I doubt I'd be able to harm anyone given how vast the sea is, but…"

"You can always use your needle," Cole said with a straight face.

"You are just full of ideas today."

The firebird landed lightly on her shoulder and then squawked importantly.

"It says it'll protect you," Alex said drolly over the comm link.

"I am surrounded by gentlemen."

One of the other officials posed a question to the minister. "He wants to know if this odd firebird will be accompanying them," the translator said.

"The one on my daughter's head is called the adarna," Lumina said. "A similar species, though it is somewhat native to the Philippines."

"It saddens me that we know so little about those outside our own kingdom," the man who had originally asked said. "I hope that things can change in the future."

The looking glass glowed. Everything beyond it was underwater. The connecting mirror appeared to have been installed at the bottom of the sea.

"We use looking glasses strong enough to withstand the pressure of our oceans," the prime minister said with a grin. "We use them to analyze and predict incoming tsunamis and earthquakes, and also to guard against thrill seekers who come to search for our treasures."

"All right," Nya said, "pop in your breathables, guys. Even you, West, just in case. Not only will it help us breathe, but the additional pressure spells in there ought to prevent barotrauma."

The spelltech tasted, oddly enough, like fresh mint. As Tala chewed, it felt like she could actually feel her lungs contracting, that weirdly refreshing sensation spreading throughout her chest.

"Don't worry," Nya said to Ken. "I'll be with you every step of the way."

"There are no steps," Loki said. "It might be easier for Ken to use the sea bottom to walk."

"God bloody dammit, Sun-Wagner," Ken growled.

Horse whinnied.

"Alex?" Lumina asked through her comm link. "How are things over there?"

"We're about ready," came the prompt response. "Japan's Department of Spelltech has been monitoring the Ryugu-jo for close to a century, apparently. They can lock on to the time-lapse spells seeping out of the palace even if they can't modify them. I can use those as a conduit to burrow in and slow it down. With the Nine Maidens and my enhancers, the Gallaghers are positive it will work."

"All while it drains more strength from you," Tala heard Tristan's voice grumble. "I still think there has to be another way—"

"You had all the time to complain a couple of hours ago while we were hammering out the logistics. Now there's nothing else for you to do but shut up so I can focus."

Some more faint mutterings, but Tristan wisely kept his mouth shut.

Tala was completely in agreement with the Locksley boy. "You aren't to exert yourself, Alex," she snapped, taking up the fight in his stead. "The instant anything goes wrong, give us warning to retreat, whether or not we've found the tamatebako. Tristan, don't leave his side, and make sure he does exactly that."

"Yes, ma'am," Tristan said, sounding pleased. Alex merely grunted.

West was the first to take the lead, already shifting into dolphin form before he was halfway through the portal. Zoe and Cole promptly followed suit, and then Loki. Ken stood before the shining portal, visibly hesitating.

"You don't have to do this," Nya said again, worried.

"Bollocks," Ken said, taking a deep breath. "If I went and backed out of anything that threatened me with a watery death where the air is sucked out of your lungs and you die choking and fishes come and feast on your eyes while you—what was I saying? The point is, I can't claim to be worthy enough to hold this sword if I chicken out, right?" And then, summoning up his courage and making Tala so proud of him, he threw himself through the portal. With a sigh, Nya dove in after him.

"Ready?" Lumina asked.

Tala nodded. "Let's go get Dad."

"We will keep the port open indefinitely," Prime Minister Hamada said. "May the gods give you victory."

"Victory, my butt," Tala heard her mother grumble just before she leaped into the looking glass. "I am going to kick Kay's ass."

Even knowing she could breathe underwater, Tala's first thought was that she was going to drown. The faint shock of liquid filling her lungs and yet finding that she was still capable of letting out breaths felt like a contradiction. She should have felt cold this deep down, but there was a warm field around them, keeping her from hypothermia.

It was her mother's hand on her elbow, a steady presence, that helped her calm down. The older woman directed her attention toward something in the distance, and Tala gasped.

The underwater palace was a stunning sight. She had been expecting something that was covered in barnacles and other sea debris, much like the pictures she'd seen of shipwrecks. The Ryugu-jo gleamed a pearly white, bright even in the gloom of the sea depths. It was beautiful in a strange, unearthly way.

"How?" she asked, and then realized she could also talk.

"The government hires specialized cleaners to fix it up every now and then," her mother said. "It isn't uncharacteristic of the Japanese to keep things tidy."

More figures swam into view. The rest of the Bandersnatchers looked awestruck at the sight as well, but soon their attention was directed toward their left, where an army of Japanese soldiers were engaged in battle.

Tala saw him. His long hair was loose and he was still bare chested, sporting no other armor or weapons but the large battle-ax that he was swinging at the soldiers. Harpoons whizzed at him, but he simply cut them down without fail.

Around him were shades who glided through the water the same way they glided through air, and the Japanese had their hands full fighting them off.

"Kay," Lumina breathed.

There was a whinny behind them. Horse cantered into view, Ken already clinging for his life on top of it. The boy's face was a little pale, but he was holding up a lot better than Tala had expected. Beside them was Nya, resplendent with her tail, and beside *her* was West as a dolphin, greeting them with a faint screech.

"Hang on to Horse," Nya told them. "It'll get us there quicker. Or you can hang on to me, and I'll get us there just as fast."

She was true to her word. Horse sped on while the others clung tightly to its neck, astride its back, or anywhere else they could cling. Nya was right beside it, tail kicking out behind her as she propelled both Tala and Ryker to where the fight was at its thickest.

Lumina was the first to disembark and the first to throw herself in between the wall of soldiers and her husband. "Kay!" she shouted.

Kay showed no signs that he recognized her and continued to batter away at the shields. Lumina swam closer, lashing out with her arnis sticks. It was not a strike intended to injure, though it was more than just a glancing blow; Kay's head whipped back from the force of it.

"What are you doing?" Tala's mother shouted. "Snap out of it!"

Slowly, the man paused and then turned toward them.

Tala cried out. Her father's eyes, normally warm and brown and kind, were now blank and colorless .

"She actually went and did it," Ryker said beside her, sounding stunned himself. "She turned him into a Deathless."

Lumina appeared frozen in disbelief, gaping at her husband, who was now slowly raising his ax.

Tala lunged forward, grabbing her mother and pulling her out of the way as her father swung, missing them completely. He moved toward them again but was shoved back by Loki's staff, which had come spinning out of the air to block his blade.

"The sooner we can get into the palace, the better," Zoe said.

"I don't know if I can go in and leave my mom to face him alone," Tala whispered. Her father was a Deathless. The Snow Queen had claimed that she was no longer interested in pursuing Kay, that she intended to have him pay like the rest of Avalon. And she had.

And the anger that had been slowly building up since learning that her father had been taken and now in a condition that had no cure—

Tala took it out on the shades who were approaching. She hadn't been able to use salamanca since their fight with Nome and the Snow Queen, but Tala shoved out with her agimat all the same, forgetting everything in her rage.

The shade exploded. One minute, it was reaching for her in its uncanny humanlike form, and the next, it had erupted into nothingness like a slow-acting firework. The blast took out a couple of other shades who had strayed too close. Tala turned, pointed her finger at another, and shattered it as well.

The Snow Queen had won. She would never have her father back.

A sudden roar broke through the waters. It was a familiar, terrifying one.

"Again?" Zoe groaned as an ogre appeared out of the darkness. It strode across the seafloor, horrifyingly fast on its feet. One unfortunate soldier was caught in its grip and then slammed hard against the rocky ground.

Another roar, this time from Ryker. The water around him was slowly solidifying, a by-product of his anger. "She didn't," he rasped. "She wouldn't."

Tala looked, saw that her father was no longer alone. More people emerged from the darkness to flank him, most teens their own age. All had the listless blank stare of the Deathless, and all were armed.

"She *turned* them," Ryker snarled. "The kids I couldn't get out yet. She—she—"

"Surprised, Cadfael?" a voice purred. An ice maiden drifted into view, smiling cruelly. Sharp icicles formed to encircle her like a barrier.

"Jessika," Ryker hissed. "What a surprise to see the Snow Queen's most devout follower sent on such a trivial mission."

"I obey Her Majesty always, though I agree. Anything that concerns you does not deserve my attention." The ice maiden's voice sounded like it was made entirely of chimes, a soft tinkling echo accompanying her cruel voice. "You were foolish enough to betray her."

"I betrayed no one!" Ryker shouted. "She said she would pro-tect them!"

"You promised her your fidelity. And yet here you are." The woman patted one of the Deathless teenagers affectionately on their head like they were her pet dog. "She gave them a warm place to stay, food, and affection. And you responded to her generosity by conspir-ing with her enemies."

"She broke her oath! She was to bring them back to their families!"

"To be neglected and abused again? To suffer through the system like you once suffered? You of all people know how cruel the world can be, Cadfael. They would have been safe with her. But your defection compromised them, and they can no longer be trusted. *You are the reason Her Majesty had no choice but to turn them. Behold the consequences of your own selfishness."*

Ryker fired straight into the group of Deathless, turning the water around them into blocks of ice that trapped their legs and prevented them from moving. Several sank down, but the ice maiden only laughed and swept at the spaces before her, dispelling his magic with ease. Her icicles shot out toward him in retaliation, but the barricade he hastily erected took the brunt of her attacks.

Kay avoided the blast radius easily. Another of the Japanese soldiers shot a harpoon his way, this time tipped with a blazing fire enchanted to keep it aflame. Tala's father reached up and caught it in his hand before it could hit him.

West was battling the ogre, making high-pitched shrill noises as he slammed a snout hard against the side of the ogre's face, then nimbly swimming away when the ogre tried to snatch him. Ken was still riding Horse while all the others had relinquished their hold, and he seemed to forget that he was underwater. The kelpie neighed gleefully as it zipped around the monster, moving far too quickly for it to do anything beyond reaching with its mighty fists to grab at the space they were already gone from.

Kusanagi flashed, outshining even the Ryugu-jo's gleam. One quick swipe cut deeply into the ogre's shin, and its vile black blood came dribbling out, creating a small miasma around it.

"Wait, Ken!" Zoe was hurtling forward, her face strained. She lashed out with her Ogmios, and the whip wrapped itself around the creature's wound.

There was a sharp spark of electricity, and Tala felt a strange tingling sensation that seemed to have come from everywhere. The monster roared, but the dark blood around it dissipated, slowly mixing with the water. It sank down.

Zoe was already swimming back toward them as fast as she could, but the girl looked strangely wan. The immense volume of the sea had protected them from getting shocked, Tala realized, but not completely for Zoe. Nya swam out toward the girl, grabbing her and bringing them both speedily back to where Cole was waiting, his own face stricken when he caught sight of Zoe.

"We need to get her back," he said tersely.

"No, we don't," Zoe said immediately, letting go of Nya and drifting backward. "We need a way into the palace while everyone else is—"

Cole grabbed Zoe and yanked her away as a burning harpoon sailed past, only narrowly missing her. Horse blurred into view, Ken on its back. The boy's left hand, white-knuckled, gripped at the kelpie's mane while the other batted away the second fire-bespelled harpoon Kay threw at them. Cole grabbed at Ogmios, which was still wrapped around the wounded ogre, and black tendrils of smoke swarmed up its length toward the beast. The ogre hollered and then stood stock-still as the Nottingham segen did its work.

"That harpoon could have gotten me," Zoe said shakily. "If you hadn't moved, it would have—"

"I can't control it for long," Cole said brusquely, like she'd never spoken. "I can stall it for a few minutes at most, but that's it. What do we do next?"

"I have a suggestion." Loki held up the lotus lantern, which was glowing brightly. Light shot out of it, cutting through the darkness and into the Ryugu-jo. "If that's not an invitation, then I don't know what is."

But Kay, too, was turning toward the palace, intent on following the light's path for himself.

"No, you don't!" Lumina blocked his way, and a well-placed kick to his shins sent her husband doubling over with a grunt. "Tala, you and the others need to get in the palace immediately."

"But—"

"Trust me. I've sparred with Kay far longer than you ever have. I'll keep him at bay, Deathless or not." Her mother parried, ducked, delivered a quick swipe with her arnis that knocked Kay's ax out of his grasp. "Hurry!"

"She's right," Nya whispered, tugging hard at the hem of Tala's shirt. "We need to go before they beat us to the entrance."

Swallowing, Tala nodded. Ryker was still exchanging projectiles with the ice maiden, but despite his initial anger, he seemed to sense that it was time to retreat. With a deep breath, he balled his fists and pushed them together.

The waters around him solidified into even thicker ice and expanded farther out. The ice maiden let out a small squeak of surprise when she realized she was no longer swimming but was instead frozen, trapped inside a giant ball of nearly solid ice that was at least half a mile wide. The other Deathless and many more nightwalkers were also caught within its confines, all struggling to move.

Ryker sagged down. Tala caught him by the collar and dragged him along while she fought to keep up with the other Bandersnatchers, all swimming briskly toward the path the lotus lantern had illuminated for them. "Let me help," she heard, and then she herself was being dragged up, only to be deposited onto Horse's back behind Ken. "Thank you," she whispered.

"No problemo." Ken still had a death grip on his kelpie's mane like it was his lifeline. Nya swam beside them, her large tail lifting up and down behind her as she kept pace with them despite the speed of Ken's mount.

Loki reached their destination first—the palace's massive main doors. "Now what?" they asked once the rest had caught up.

"Didn't one of the prophecies about this place say that it will need Avalon's sword wielder to get in?" Ken asked. "Do I just wave Kusanagi and yell, 'Open sesame!' or something?"

"Wait," Alex said, his voice unexpectedly loud and clear. "Give me another minute. I can feel the spells leaking out from the place through my firebird. I can use the Nine Maidens to grab hold of it and keep it locked down to within a year's time frame."

"Within a *year's* time frame?" Tala asked.

"It's a better alternative than throwing you a hundred years into the future, don't you think? No, Tristan." Alex's voice faded slightly, like he had turned away from the comm to address someone beside him. "I didn't test any of this beforehand because there wasn't any way to. Now will you shut up and let me concentrate? Ken, are there any changes to Kusanagi that you can sense?"

"Nothing so far. Do I have to get closer to check?" Horse whinnied and inched closer so that Ken could reach out and take hold of the door knockers if he wanted. He touched the tip of the sword against the wood, then waited. "I guess that's not it. What if we just kicked our way in? Would anyone inside take offense?"

"Whatever it is, Ken, we need to hurry." Nya pointed. The ice maiden had broken down the sphere, and now she and the rest of the Deathless were streaking toward them rapidly. Tala could see her mother still locked in battle with her father, holding her own. "Because I don't think they're going to be as polite about it as you are."

"Can't Lord Suddene find any clues as to how we're supposed to access the palace?" Cole asked as he, Loki, and West lined up to face the approaching threat, the first two with their weapons at the ready and West shifting into a larger, teeth-heavy great white shark.

"Nothing yet," the duke's voice rumbled in response. "The only mention of the residents of the Ryugu-jo was that they were hospitable and courteous, known for their good manners and sense of propriety. Most Japanese are the same, so it's not an unexpected—"

Ken lifted his hand and knocked at the wood with Kusanagi. "Ojama shimasu!" he shouted.

The doors opened inward without warning.

Everything turned strange after that.

9

IN WHICH A SHADE
DECIDES TO BE HELPFUL

"D ammit!" Tala burst out in frustration, rubbing at the side of her head where her mother had scored with one of her arnis sticks.

Far from being apologetic, Lumina only laughed. "You keep thinking your weapons are enough to deflect a move you see coming. I can attack you in so many other ways, and you must be prepared to anticipate every one of them."

"Easy for you to say," Tala grumbled. The ringing in her ears had finally ceased, and the pain was letting up. Her pride had taken a harder blow than anything else. "I don't have as long a reach as you do."

"Your mom's got far shorter arms than I have," her father rumbled cheerfully, extending one long brawny arm for emphasis before pulling it back to flip over a burger sizzling on the grill before him, "and she still kicks my ass on a weekly basis. It's not about what you've got, it's about knowing how to *use* what you've already got."

"It's not like I can even use arnis in my daily life," Tala grouched.

"Are your classmates bothering you again?" Lumina asked immediately, a scowl forming on her face. "Because I told your principal that if he's going to blame you again for beating up some bully—"

"No," Tala said hurriedly. "What I mean is that—I don't know, Mom. This is Invierno. Nothing ever happens here."

"We can help you compete for the Olympics if that's something you're interested in," her father offered.

Tala wrinkled her nose. "If I can't even beat Mom, what makes you think I'd be good enough for that? I don't think I have anything I'm really good at."

"You are not allowed to have an existential crisis before lunch," her father ordered, "and definitely not before you have a bite of one of my special burgers and secret sauce."

He had a point. The smell was making Tala's mouth water.

"Sesame hoisin and sriracha isn't that hard to make," her mother said, grinning.

"Hey!" Kay protested.

"We'll take a break to eat," her mother allowed. "I think you would be exceptional at anything you put your mind to, anak. You just have to figure out what that is first, but you've just had your seventeenth birthday. You have all the time in the world to find that out."

"Four months on, and doctors are still at a loss explaining this phenomenon."

Tala stopped. She hadn't noticed the television set on their lawn. This one had a nearly transparent screen, the news reporter sitting in the air like some kind of hologram. This was Avalon tech, but in a place like Invierno, spelltech almost never worked.

Avalon tech? But she'd never even been to Avalon. Avalon had been frozen in ice for almost—

The reporter's image shifted to that of a harried-looking doctor.

"It's not possible for many of those who have been assigned male at birth to undergo pregnancy," he said. "The amount of magic necessary to rework the human anatomy is more than remarkable. It's going to change the medical industry. So many things we know about our bodies have now become obsolete almost overnight."

The news reporter took over. "While some view this as nothing short of a miracle, others have condemned those responsible— among them Zoe Carlisle, niece to King Philip XXII of France. Hundreds of death threats have been sent to the rue la Farge since the news broke, along with bomb warnings—"

"It wasn't her fault!" Tala burst out without thinking. "She's being blamed for something she never even—"

"Are you all right, lass?" her father asked. "Who's Zoe?"

"I—" What was she doing? She'd never even met this Zoe Carlisle. But why did the name sound so familiar?

"If you ask me," her mother said with a sigh, "they should normalize treating pregnancies like any other medical condition. I would have hoped this would lead to a better discourse to make pregnancy safer for all, but alas."

"You mean Dad can get pregnant now?"

"I'm a bit too old for that to be a real possibility," her father said, laughing, "but I'd give it a try if your mom's still hankering for a another kid."

"Tala is more than enough for me," Lumina said. "But I wouldn't say no to a puppy or a kitten."

"Riselle Gardner's golden retriever, Daisy, just had a litter. We could ask for one if you'd like. Apparently Daisy took a shine to their next-door neighbor's dog, Picard, and no one knew until she was already—"

"Picard?" Tala broke in.

"That's the name of their neighbor's dog. Odd choice, but—"

"He said he wanted to have a dog so he could name him Picard," Tala said, her head spinning. "*Star Trek*. Picard always called Riker Number One. He hoped that he could be that to any dog he had. Because he'd never had anyone to care enough for him to be their number one. This is wrong. This is all wrong. This isn't real."

"Tala, what are you talking about?" Lumina sounded alarmed. "What's—"

Tala rounded on her. "This isn't real!" she cried. "This is an illusion! I need to break it! Where—?"

An agimat. She was still so annoyingly weak, but at least she remembered that. She seized it now, felt the familiar surge around her after all her years honing it at Invierno—the *real* Invierno with all its ugliness and bigotry, and not this attempt at keeping her complacent and trapped forever in wherever the Dragon Palace had thrown her into.

Her parents leaped back as she pushed her agimat forward. It caught on to some strange, complex magic that was absolutely staggering in the waves she could feel emanating from it.

Whoever had placed the barrier clearly meant to prevent her

from getting out. Trying to match its strength would only exhaust her, so she switched to the salamanca technique Lola Corazon had taught her, allowing the magic to bounce back onto itself, letting its own momentum be the catalyst to its destruction. There was a sudden give, and Tala found herself looking at the surface of a mirror.

"Wait!" Lumina shouted. She and her father were walking toward Tala. "Don't leave!"

She had no time to ponder what lay beyond the other side of the looking glass. Tala took a deep breath and plunged through—

—and stumbled into a darkened hallway. The looking glass from where she'd emerged gleamed brightly, but the light soon faded away.

Tala's first instinct was to examine it, taking care not to touch the surface lest she fall in again. Her reflection stared back.

This was not the only mirror there. More fanned out on either side of the passageway. Some were shining, others dark.

She looked through one and saw everything.

Some mirrors were of the past and gleamed gold; she saw armies mobilizing, flags waving in the air as opposing forces clashed together. She saw lances and horses, both simmering with ancient magic, shifting into cannons and fire, guns and bullets as the centuries rolled on. She saw Avalon's banner flapping in the wind, saw a king sitting at a round table full of knights. It crossed her mind that her father might have been one of them, but it was too late, and another scene, another war, had already flitted past.

She tore her gaze away and took a step back, proceeded farther down the hallway. The mirrors here were now silvery by design, and as she looked into them, Tala realized they documented the present.

No, not the present—the *possibilities* of the present. Those that *could* happen, *might* happen. Because Tala saw the Snow Queen triumphant in one, the ruins of Maidenkeep a smoking background behind her victory cries. And yet she also saw Avalon standing in another, their armies pouring into Beira. It was similar to the dream she'd had a couple of years ago at Tintagel Castle—dreams of smoke and nightwalkers and her friends.

She gazed into another looking glass and saw nothing but fire. It obscured her vision, preventing her from seeing anything but soot-filled skies. She leaned closer, straining to see past the smoke, shaken at how similar this looked to what she had dreamt, and reared back when the heat blazed out at her, the fires just as hot as if she'd been standing within them.

"Coo," something said.

The adarna had been lurking behind one of the silver-gilded mirrors. It poked its head from around the frame and managed a curious, nervous tweet.

"Are you real this time?"

The adarna looked relieved. It stepped out and chirped happily.

"Can we at least find the others, retrieve the tamatebako, and make our way out of here before you decide to—"

The colorful bird flew straight toward her, landing with practiced assurance on top of her head.

"—use me as a perch again," Tala finished. "Do you know where everyone else is?"

It shook its head.

"Do you have an idea of where we should go next?"

The adarna bobbed its head up and down.

"Lead the way, then."

The bird leaned forward, jabbed its beak at one of the mirrors farther along the hallway.

The mirror showed her another war, one between Buyan and Avalon. It was easy to spot the red and gold flags of Avalon dotting half of the battlefield, slowly but steadily gaining ground over the armored troops bearing the matte-black flag of Buyan.

This must be the final war between the two kingdoms, with Koschei defeated and presumed killed, the Snow Queen siding with King Arthur and his knights. But the mirror kept switching scenes too rapidly for her to process the details, and she realized that she was seeing through the eyes of many of the battle's combatants. She moved closer.

The adarna trilled out a warning. Tala felt wings flap down on her face, slapping her lightly on the cheeks and forcing her to retreat. Was it her imagination, or did the mirror's light recede ever so slightly?

"Is it trying to pull me inside?"

The coo from her head told Tala she'd guessed right.

"So everything is a trap designed to keep us all here forever." And the other Banders didn't have her agimat to fall back on to negate the magic.

The mirror changed again. Tala stared into a throne room that seemed to be made of nothing but ice. She could see a tall warrior in elaborate heavy armor, face heavily concealed beneath a black visor, shouting in a language she didn't understand. He slashed angrily at everything he could reach with his broadsword, sending shrapnel flying. Before him was a pretty girl, ashen-faced and trembling, wrapped up in a long robe that surely could not keep her warm given their surroundings, though she showed no signs of being cold. Her face was familiar. The Snow Queen, though she was only called Gerda then, before she'd called herself Anneliese in a bid to disguise her true identity in the years since.

And the man in armor must be Koschei.

There was a gleaming mirror on the wall behind him. It was shining, but neither Koschei nor Gerda seemed to notice.

There was another man on the ground, his gray armor streaked with blood. He wasn't moving.

Tala watched as the man in black turned his wrath on his daughter, roaring curses at her face. Gerda shrank back, but her hands clasped at a strange black dagger, its blade more like it was made of a shard of glass than from steel. When he moved toward her again, his sword raised, she sprang.

Tala had thought that the armor would be enough to deflect the blow, but the knife sank into the man's side like he wore no protection at all. Koschei stared down at the dagger in shock before raising his head to stare at the girl. He managed to utter a few more words before he staggered backward, trying to get the blade out, but the girl shook her head, tears streaming down her face, and forced it in even deeper.

Even from the other side of the mirror, the magic coursing through the dagger and spiraling outward hit Tala like a thunderclap.

With a cry, the man tore his helmet off. Tala had thought Koschei would look cruel, as if the evilness of his soul was great enough to stamp itself across his physical features. But the man underneath the visor looked ordinary enough—bearded with a scar across one cheek. He looked like he could have lived in Invierno his whole life and never stood out from the crowd.

Koschei turned to stare at the mirror, and Tala saw what he finally did—a small part of the glass was gone, the missing piece shaped like the dagger Gerda had plunged into him.

A fine mist rose around the man, obscuring him from view. When it dissipated, only the girl was left, staring blankly at the blade now in her hand, a strange steam rising from it.

She turned to the other fallen figure. She plunged the dagger into him too, but it appeared to do the opposite. The figure in gray wheezed as his chest took in air, and the girl wrenched the visor off his face. He was young—so, so young—but Tala recognized her father in the youth's face. He smiled faintly at the girl as she sobbed, clinging tightly to him. The dagger clattered to the floor, magic still swirling in its depths.

The Snow Queen had been telling the truth. It was she who had killed her father, not King Arthur and his men, but she had never been lucky enough to write history.

The dagger. Did the Snow Queen still have it? That must have been the magic she'd used to resurrect Tala's father, bind him to her side as a fellow immortal. The mirror had been a part of the Alatyr, Lord Suddene had said. If the Snow Queen was already immortal in that vision, then it must mean that she had already been bound to the Alatyr by her father as well. It helped explain why she despised Koschei.

Tala watched the young Kay's face for several long moments, the look of concern and love there as he held his lady in his arms, letting her cry while he murmured soothing words of assurance.

A sudden loud crash brought her back into the present. She spun, heart pounding, the adarna on her head already squeaking out nervous threats.

The shade was frozen in motion, one hand stretched out toward one of the mirrors that it had accidentally toppled. The glass didn't shatter; the shadow was attempting to right it, a puzzling thing for a nightwalker to do, given the little care they had for lives, much less property. The shade itself managed to look almost embarrassed despite its lack of a face. It would have been almost comical if it wasn't for everything else.

"Wait!" Tala shouted, but it was already springing away, scuttling across the floor and then scampering up one side of the wall. She raced after it, the adarna clinging to her head for dear life.

The shade ducked behind another row of mirrors, and Tala spotted the closed door up ahead—no doubt locked, though that had never stopped shadows before.

A sudden shower of magic rained down on them. The shade was thrown back violently as the door refused it, sending its form to the floor, its skinny arms flailing.

"Ha!" Tala cried as she reached it. She stomped one foot down on its side, keeping it in place to prevent it from fleeing again. "What the hell are you? You aren't like any of the other nightwalkers I've fought before."

The shade looked up at her, limbs still splayed wide on the ground. Tala saw its shoulders move up and down as if in a shrug.

Most would have attacked mindlessly, but this one appeared to have a working brain.

"Why are you following me? How did you manage to sneak in?"

A second shrug. The shade pointed toward the closed door again.

She didn't have much choice. It looked to be the only way out of this corridor. "Are you going to run again when I take my foot away?"

It shook its head earnestly.

Tala slowly lifted her leg. It hopped up, danced a little jig to discern that it still had all its body parts, and then pointed at the door again.

"If you couldn't get past it, what makes you think I can?"

The shade pointed at her and then gestured widely, and Tala realized it was referring to her agimat.

"Fine. But if this is some kind of trick…" She focused on the door. Something was fusing it shut, that much she could determine. She concentrated on her agimat once more, trying to overload the defensive wards like she had done inside the mirror.

It was much more difficult this time. She was still drained from her last bout, and that had been fueled by adrenaline and panic.

The adarna sang. Its melody filled the room, and Tala saw the mirrors flickering in and out, the magic within them waning and ebbing to the rhythm. At the same time, she felt some of her old strength returning. She pushed back harder against the spell, and the adarna sang louder in response.

The door folded into itself and crumbled down noisily, the wood splintering like it had been made of paper, pulverizing into dust. The open doorway now stood before them, dark and threatening.

The shade scampered through before she could stop it.

"Dammit," Tala growled, shaking off the strange high the adarna's song had given her, and followed.

She wasn't expecting to find *more* mirrors in this room. She groaned.

The adarna was a flurry of chirps and squawks, its wings agitated. Something was making it nervous, but Tala wasn't sure what it was until she realized that the looking glasses weren't the only things in the room.

There was a wooden table. On it were several jeweled boxes, all a dazzling display of colors and gems. No wonder there were treasure hunters eager to get into the palace—one box alone must have cost a fortune. Tamatebako, she realized.

Were they all just different variations? She didn't recall Chiaki describing what it looked like, and she presumed it was because none of them knew. Neither had they been told that there was more than one.

She picked a jeweled box up at random. It didn't look like it required a key—there were no unlocking mechanisms that she could spot—but nothing seemed to suggest how it could be opened.

"Any ideas?"

The adarna shook its head. Tala felt the bird dip down, poking cautiously at another box. It let out a curious sound.

"Is this it?" Tala asked, picking it up. She admired the craftsmanship; it was simpler than the others, but the turquoise color interspersed with the small gems dotting its exterior was nice to look at.

The lid slid back without warning.

And then she was falling yet somehow still on her feet. It felt like a part of her was slowly being dragged into the box, and she could hear the frantic chirping of the adarna as it, too, was slowly being pulled down in to the depths of the—

The lid was slammed shut abruptly by a shadowy hand, and the box spun away from her grasp. It hit the floor with a loud thud, and the shade chittered admonishingly at her.

"What was *that*?" For a moment, Tala was afraid that she was already *inside* the box. Everything was disorienting, the world strange and alien all of a sudden. But as her anxiety dissipated, her sense of normalcy returned. "What did I do?"

The shade made a noise that sounded suspiciously like a sigh.

"I only touched it! How are we supposed to bring the tamatebako out of here if it starts sucking in our souls whenever we pick it up?"

The faceless shade gave her a look as if to say, *That's not my problem.*

"It destroys no souls," someone said from behind her. "It does quite the opposite."

Tala spun, arming herself with her agimat.

The woman staring back only looked amused. She was entrancingly beautiful, her bangs arranged in an even, almost severe cut across her forehead. Her hair was so long that it all but brushed the floor as she moved to take the turquoise jeweled box off the floor, cradling it lovingly in her hands. She wore robes of an ancient style that Tala recognized from long-ago Japanese dynasties in history textbooks, and her eyebrows were drawn in an odd teardrop shape.

But the woman showed no anger that they had entered her home without permission. "You must be one of them," she said.

"One of them?"

The woman gestured at a row of smaller mirrors lined up beside the table of jeweled boxes.

"Oh no," Tala said once she caught sight of what lay within those surfaces. She could only see flashes of scenes, but it was enough.

She saw glimpses of Loki in the first one, scaling up the trees toward a large tree house, laughing with their parents. She saw Zoe in a large stage production of a ballet, beautiful in her tutu as she pirouetted and jetéed to wondrous applause, and Ken riding Horse across the plains, singing into the wind. She saw West in shifter form with the rest of his family, the pack chasing each other with gleeful howls. She saw Nya in her village, dancing and laughing as fireflies gleaming with bright magic fluttered around her, and Cole stalking through the snow with other hunters, rooting out nightwalkers. Every mirror was configured to offer each Bandersnatcher pieces of the happiest moments in their lives, even if they were lies. And Ryker's—

It hurt to look at Ryker's mirror. She saw a younger version of him lying in a narrow cot in a small room, and a woman with long dark hair and eyes and a smile so much like his own reading him a bedtime story. He was snuggled in her lap, eyes drifting closed.

"I apologize for our trespassing," Tala said, fighting to keep her voice even, sensing that the woman was stronger than she looked and attempting to take her on in a fight would be harder than it appeared. "But would you please release my friends from their prisons?"

"Is it really a prison if they are happy within it?" The woman sounded far too calm. She had taken to rearranging the other jeweled containers, fingers lingering affectionately over each one.

"It is if they don't know their lives are a lie."

"I do not command the Ryugu-jo," the strange woman said. "I only live within its walls. There is nothing I can do for them if they cannot do it themselves. There is only one way to break through the illusions. Only then can they prove themselves worthy."

Tala's gaze drifted back toward the table. "To take one of these as a reward?"

The woman's lips curled. "As it had always been with Urashima Taro and those who came after him. The tamatebako tucks a part of your soul away to bring out when all else seems lost. But only if their souls can find their way back, if they trust in themselves enough to withstand temptation for truth. Such has always been the price, and so it shall ever be."

10

IN WHICH THERE ARE FAR TOO MANY CURSED BOXES

The woman made no move to stop her when Tala approached Loki's looking glass. Tala ruminated for a few minutes and then looked up at the adarna. "Do you think I can pull another song from you?"

The adarna chirped its agreement and puffed out its chest. As before, its music lifted Tala's mood, and she felt some of her waning strength return. But nothing within the mirrors changed to reflect what it had done. The bird cut itself off after it came to the same realization and grumbled for a bit.

Tala eyed the shade next. It lurked in one corner, looking at the Japanese woman with obvious misgivings. It hadn't attempted to flee or steal anything. If the shade was a nightwalker, it wasn't any of the Snow Queen's minions. Possibly something that had been stuck in the palace far longer than they had been and had gained independence after so long. "You seem to know more about this than any of us," she said. "What do you propose we do?"

The shade skulked out of its dark alcove and drifted toward Loki's mirror.

"Oh. Of course. Loki still has the lotus lantern, right? Adarna, could you do that thing you did to activate it like when we were in Kunlun?"

The bird brightened. Its response was to sing its heart out, the lovely melody echoing throughout the room. Tala focused her agimat, channeled all of it that she could into the looking glass, hoping it would be enough to offset whatever wards were keeping them spellbound.

From inside the mirror, Tala saw Loki turn, frowning. "Yes," she muttered under her breath. "*Yes*. Come on, Loki. I know you can hear it."

Loki glowed. Or rather, their ear glowed. They blinked, reached up, and stared open mouthed at Ruyi Jingu Bang and then down at the lotus lantern that had suddenly appeared in their hands.

Tala could see their not-real parents moving toward them, sensing the shift in magic. "No, Loki!" she hollered into the looking glass. "Don't listen to them! Focus on the staff! This is all a lie! You need to—"

Loki was already a step ahead. They twirled the staff expertly and then swung the lantern about, looking for a way out…and finding it when the lantern glowed and shot a beam right onto where Tala was standing. Loki began running straight toward her, leaping into the air—

—and narrowly missing her as they hit the ground rolling, up on their feet in seconds, looking alert. "That wasn't real," they gasped. "I thought I was at the tree house I built with my parents when I was ten."

"Yes, and we're still inside the Ryugu-jo!" Tala grabbed them by the shoulders, waiting for them to breathe slower, to calm down. "The others are still trapped."

"I saw something, some kind of vision, before I was able to jump out. I—" They shuddered. "Never mind."

Tala turned toward the shade and stilled. It was gone. "Oh no," she muttered. "Did you happen to see a shade somewhere around?"

"A shade? No. Is the ice maiden here too?"

"No, I don't think it's under the Snow Queen's control. It was trying to help." Tala spun around to no avail. Whatever the shade was, it had obviously decided that its services were no longer required.

Getting the rest out was easier than Tala expected now that they had possession of the lantern. With the adarna's added support, all the Bandersnatchers shook free of the spell entrapping them and made their way out of their respective mirrors until everyone was gathered around the hallway, all visibly shaken. Ryker was the last one out, and the look of pain and regret on his face was hard to see.

"Well," Ken said sourly. "That was fun." He'd been muttering, "Two twenty-five," over and over again when they finally pulled him out, though he had refused to elaborate on what he meant. Now he turned to glare at the strange woman, who had watched everything without a word. "And now that we're out, are you going to let us go, or do we have to fight our way out of here too?"

"I will do nothing to stop you," she said placidly. "You have paid the toll, and the mirrors have found you worthy. Take what you need and leave. But be warned. Sacrifice and pain always follow those who choose the tamatebako, as Urashima-san and Musashi-san learned."

Zoe surveyed the table. "How are we gonna know which one houses Koschei's, uh, soul or body part or whatever?"

A chirp from the adarna, who had temporarily abandoned Tala's head to sit on top of a black box without any carvings or gemstones.

"I guess it'll be that one." Zoe gingerly picked it up.

"Does this mean we can grab more boxes if we want to?" Nya asked.

"I think so." Tala rubbed at her head. "What does she mean when she said we were found worthy?"

"I think it was because we saw the future," West said.

"What?"

But Nya was nodding, her face troubled. "When I was jumping back into the looking glass to get here, I saw...I saw myself with a jeweled box in my hand, and I was..."

"This black box?"

"No. Another." Nya pointed. "That red one."

"So we can take more than just Koschei's box. Did everyone have visions?" Zoe asked, and only Tala shook her head. "Well, does anyone want to speak up about what they saw?"

Nobody volunteered either.

Zoe sighed. "Thought so."

"Was I not able to see anything because of my agimat and my family's penchant for negating prophecies?" Tala asked. "How bad were yours? If seeing the future can give us an advantage over the Snow Queen, then I think you all should—"

"It's not that," Ken broke in tersely. "In my case, I don't think knowing what's going to happen in advance is going to help matters. If anything..." He paused again. "If anything," he said again, much more quietly, "I think the reason we saw it was to ensure that we actually make it happen."

"I can share a bit of what mine was," West said hesitantly. "We were standing in front of some grassy hill somewhere in Avalon, looking down at a village at its bottom. I don't know where it is exactly, but I remember feeling at peace about everything. Except... except some of us were there, but some of us weren't. I—I won't say who."

"So some of us didn't make it." Ryker was still looking a little weak, still not quite recovered from his fight with the Deathless outside the Ryugu-jo.

"I don't know," West said, miserable. "Maybe they just didn't come with us to that valley."

"I was surrounded by the dead," Zoe said slowly. "They weren't Deathless or nightwalkers. I wasn't fighting them. I was fighting *with* them somehow. I remember feeling desperate, like we were losing. But everything went blurry after that."

"I was fighting too," Loki said shakily. "But I was fighting with the Neverland pirates. Something hit their ship, and then I don't remember anything else."

"Seems like most of us received visions of ourselves fighting," Ken said. "Not surprising."

But Nya was already looking suspicious. "What exactly did *you* see?"

"Is it really that important?" Ken asked airily. "I saw me sticking Kusanagi into various body parts of numerous nightwalkers and generally kicking ass, like I always do. I can give you the director's cut later, but right now, we gotta get moving, or Alex will be a very old man by the time we're out."

Zoe looked at the table again. "This isn't some kind of test where our faces melt off if we pick more than what we're supposed to, right?"

The lady only smiled.

"Get the one with the rubies," Nya said immediately.

"Are you sure?" Ken asked doubtfully. "I don't know if there's a difference, but if we pick the wrong one—"

"Just do it, Ken. Trust me."

The boy shrugged and obediently took the container Nya was pointing at.

"You, too, must take your prize," the lady told Tala.

"My prize?" Tala saw the turquoise box she'd inadvertently opened. "You mean this one?"

"It is rare enough for an owner to be chosen," the woman said. "It opened for you and will no longer do so for another."

"And how do we open this one?" Ken asked, holding up the ruby box.

"Only light and shadow can conspire to reveal its contents, sword wielder. Only pain and hope. It can only capture the darkness that can be seen in the light. You must guard it well, else all shall be lost."

"That is the worst user's manual I've ever heard of in my life, lady, and I had to build a cabinet from IKEA for my mum with instructions in Swedish."

"Ken!" Nya barked, but the lady was fading from view, her whole body becoming translucent.

"There is another in the palace," she whispered. "You must leave immediately." And then she was gone.

"Was she a ghost?" West whispered. "Is this place haunted?"

"It doesn't matter because we're taking her advice and getting out of here—as soon as we figure out how to contact Alex."

"—here," something crackled through the comm, and they all jumped.

"Alex?" Tala shouted.

"—here—can't—enough time—portal—"

"I'm only hearing about every third word coming from you, Your Majesty!" Ken yelled. "We got the tamatebako! If you can hear us, open up a port whenever you're ready!"

A loud bang against the wall made them start a second time.

"The lady ghost said there was someone else here," West said hopefully. "Maybe it's Aunt Lumina?"

Ice began to form along the edges of one wall.

"I guess not."

Brittle icicles sprouted along the floor, then shifted and reformed into the ice maiden, smiling cruelly. "I must thank your king for finally providing us with the means to enter the Ryugu-jo," she purred. "His manipulation of the Nine Maidens anchors you here in the present but also allows a new pathway for me to enter."

"You're one to talk about manipulation, Jessika," Ryker growled.

"Her Majesty strives to revive the Alatyr, the purest magic in all the land. How dare you use a poor imitation against her."

A sudden sizzle went through the air, and a portal opened up behind them.

"Thank you, Alex," Ken said, drawing out Kusanagi anyway. "I'll bring up the rear."

"No!" Zoe said sharply, already realizing what Ken hadn't. "We can't leave as long as she's here! No telling how many of these tamatebako she'll take with her when we do!"

"Smart as always, Carlisle. But can you really stop me?" The ice maiden moved toward the table, but Loki blocked her path. "You broke your little staff once before," the ice maiden drawled, the icicle in her hand sharpening into an even deadlier point. "It would be a pity to see it destroyed again."

The woman swiped and Loki ducked. Ruyi Jingu Bang jumped out of their grasp and batted at her, but a blow sent it spinning away. Zoe's Ogmios wrapped around her wrist, but the ice maiden only smiled. Her arm melted away but reformed after the whip slipped out of her grasp.

It was Cole's turn to attack, the thorns rising out from Gravekeeper a defense just as much as it was an offense, keeping the maiden's icicle from reaching it. But the woman reached out with a finger, and one of the tendrils she touched promptly turned into ice, extending out and starting to wrap around the blade. Cole jumped back before it could completely freeze his sword, keeping out of reach.

Ken barreled into the fight next, and his Kusanagi matched the ice maiden's weapon blow for ringing blow, neither giving ground. But however hard he swung, the icicle never shattered, though every attempt by the maiden to freeze his blade failed, the ice sloughing off just as quickly as it began to manifest.

"Yawarakai-Te merged within your sword is capable of cutting through everything," Jessika said. "Including my ice. How creative."

"Everything but human flesh, and I'm willing to bet you've lost yours ages ago." Ken moved out of the way as her icicle came down where his head had been half a second ago, then crouched to jab his sword toward her abdomen. It grazed her side, water spilling out from where blood should have. The ice maiden hissed, the wound slowing her down not a whit, and her next slash took Kusanagi's blow. Steam rose between them, and parts of Ken's sword began to whiten, ice creeping toward the hilt.

Ken jerked his sword forward, and the ice that clung to his blade shattered, spraying back at the ice maiden's face. She stumbled backward and he lunged, attempting to plant the tip of his blade in the center of her stomach, only for her to dissolve unexpectedly into water, the puddle at his feet moving away and then reshaping itself back into her previous form.

"Hurry!" Tala heard through the comm. "Too—can't hold—"

"Ken, it's either we go now, or the portal fails and we're stuck here for God knows how long," Zoe yelled. "Get your butts moving!"

"Give me a sec!" Ken began giving wary ground.

Taking it as a sign that he was weakening, the ice maiden surged forward, smiling coldly. "With these jewels, we can create as many immortal souls as we would like," she gloated.

"It ain't over till the adarna sings, lady." Ken relaxed his grip on Kusanagi.

The ice maiden leaped forward, icicle ready to stab him through the heart.

"Ken!" Nya shrieked.

But rather than counter the incoming attack, Ken simply dove to the floor and rolled toward the ice maiden, tripping her in the process. In her surprise, the ice woman stumbled forward—straight into one of the mirrors. And went right through it. Her startled face disappeared into the reflective surface, followed by the rest of her. The mirror glowed brightly once she was all the way through, then returned to its normal hue afterward.

Tala couldn't help herself. She glanced in and saw someone laughing, running through a meadow—no longer the ice maiden but just a young girl enjoying the summer day.

"Yeah," West breathed, looking in beside her. "She's never gonna get out."

"Tala!" Zoe shouted. "We have to go, *now*!"

"I—but—"

"At least she'll be happy in there," Ryker said, grabbing her elbow. "Come on."

With her hand in his, they raced toward the portal that was already shrinking, throwing themselves through and bursting back into the cold waters of the Sea of Japan. Behind them, the whole of the Ryugu-jo glowed with the same unearthly brightness as one of the many mirrors within it before falling back into darkness.

Her mother was still there, still fighting her father. Both had taken a pause, acknowledging their stalemate.

There was a gurgle beside her. Ken was flailing again. Nya hurriedly swam over to his side, her tail reappearing. Horse reached them both, neighing disapprovingly about being shut out of the adventure again.

"I'm going to stop you, Kay," Lumina said, though her eyes were shining with unshed tears. "If you still had your mind, you know you'd tell me to stop you, and I will. We've both worked too hard to see her demolish everything. If you can hear me, Kay, please. I love you. Tala loves you. Please fight it."

This time, Kay hesitated.

Tala's hopes grew. He could hear them. Somewhere inside the curse the Snow Queen had inflicted on him, her father was struggling, fighting to break free for their sake.

But then the big man shook himself again, face hardening, and raised his ax.

A shrill scream ripped through the water like a sonic wave, the force of it sending Kay and many of the nightwalkers back. Tala's eyes widened.

They were mermaids. Dark-skinned mermaids were swimming toward them, their mouths open as more screams burst from their throats, aimed with precision at the shades and at the ogre that the Japanese soldiers were still engaging with. The monstrous brute clasped its hands against its head and howled, but the mermaids were unrelenting.

Grinning, Nya helped Ken back on Horse and then swam forward to join her fellow villagers, toward where her grandmother was leading the fight, the latter's tail the exact shade of purple as hers.

Their arrival was more than enough to turn the tide. West had shifted into a great white shark, and Tala and the other Banders swam to his side, latching on to his fin and clinging while he propelled them forward, back into the thick of battle. Zoe slashed at every shade that dared draw close, now more able to control the sizzle of her whip. A swipe of Gravekeeper turned several shades in an instant, all of whom now surged forward to aid the soldiers in combating the ogre.

Loki hopped onto West's back, riding him like a bronco as their staff lengthened at will, taking out nightwalkers despite the distance. Tala still felt drained from everything that had happened inside the Ryugu-jo and remained on standby, taking out the rest of the shades within her agimat's range while at the same time keeping a firm grip on Ryker, who was also lobbing ice projectiles at nightwalkers despite his own exhaustion.

Some unspoken signal passed between Kay and what remained of the Snow Queen's horde. A portal opened nearby, and they all began a hasty retreat, slithering through the opening.

"Wait, Kay!" Lumina shouted before her husband could step through. "Fight it! We'll find some way to cure you, I swear—"

Kay Warnock turned and regarded her with cold white eyes. "It is too late for us, mahal," he rasped in a voice that sounded like Tala's father's yet like a stranger's at the same time before turning away. The portal swallowed him up, disappearing before any of the soldiers or West could reach it.

11

In Which a Lot of
Yelling Takes Place

The briefing afterward was subdued, mostly because Alex had remained upright only long enough to welcome them back before promptly collapsing, the firebird following suit and tumbling to the floor.

A team of physicians was on hand to rush both to a private room—Tristan had insisted that medical personnel be present while they were at the Ryugu-jo. The doctors soon ascertained that Alex and the firebird were exhausted more than they were injured, and everyone breathed easier after that.

Koschei's tamatebako had been duly turned over to Severon Gallagher, who had donned latex gloves, a lab coat, and a heavy-duty visor like he was about to handle an explosive device before disappearing back into the recesses of his lab with it.

Tala had handed over her turquoise box as well, still unsure why the palace woman had let her leave with it. Nya had decided to keep hers for now, promising to do the same after she'd consulted with her grandmother.

"The tamatebako functions like, well, a backup server almost, if I can be a bit more technical." Dexter was trying to explain it to them. "I've talked about Peter Schlemihl before, I think. He's the techmage who studied shade magic, used his own shadow for experiments. Captain Mairead and the Neverland pirates use similar magic, but they're very simple spells compared to this. Schlemihl's theory about the tamatebako was that it's possible to use it to house part of a person's soul to revive them after death, but only Buyan technology has ever been successful at it. The problem is that we don't know how to activate the box."

"I don't think we want to," Tala said nervously, "if they're right and there's a part of Koschei inside it."

The situation remained grim. No other unauthorized portals had appeared in Avalon, but Alex could not afford to pull out the soldiers stationed in other key parts of the kingdom. The brunt of the sightings was still at the Burn, where the Katipuneros, the pirates, and Lola Corazon's Filipino forces remained. Every attack they were able to repel only seemed to sprout a fresh new horde an hour later, and while Lord Keer was adamant about letting each soldier take shifts to replenish their energy, Tala knew they couldn't keep that pace up for long.

Even now, they were still fighting. Through the screen, Tala saw the twins Tita Teejay and Tita Chedeng between them conjuring up a horrifying powerful vortex of wind that was cutting through the one ogre who had dared to show up. General Luna was in fine form as always, preferring to fight up close with his trusty shiv, with Tita Baby and Tito Boy backing him up. Lola Urduja delivered a stunning blow with her abanico fan that cut several shades back into nothingness, and with her, surprisingly, was Lola Corazon. The women had always been like two cats fighting whenever they were in the same room, so seeing them work together was the biggest indication to Tala that the situation there was dire.

At the moment, all nonessential parts of the kingdom had been shut down, including Simeli Mountain. The mountain pass was closed now, its staff staying at Maidenkeep for the meantime. The nice old lady who worked there had taken to sweeping the palace courtyards and corridors with the same enthusiasm she had when she was collecting unsuccessful participants inflicted by Simeli's fowl curse.

The Banders had taken over the multiple couches and armchairs within the command center, more interested in looking everywhere else—the ceiling, the walls, the floor, at the techmages scurrying back and forth, at the Wake still giving orders to his people out on the field—than in meeting one another's gaze. The adarna was, as always, fast asleep on Tala's head.

"Are we going to talk about it?" West finally asked, breaking the silence. "Because we really ought to talk about it."

"Speak for yourself," Ken grumbled. "All you saw in your future was a hilltop and a sunrise."

"It was a sunset."

"We do need to talk about it," Zoe said, "and I know just who to start with." She swiveled in her chair and glared at Cole, who was skulking by a nearby window. "You never said anything about what *you* saw."

"I saw myself fighting, the same as nearly everyone else," Cole said calmly.

"I know you're not usually one to share, Nottingham, but I know when you're evading. What happened?"

"Don't you think there's more to worry about in the present than in the future?"

Zoe's eyes narrowed. "And what do you mean by that?"

"You nearly died today, Carlisle. If I'd been any second slower, that harpoon would have…" He trailed off.

Tala had never heard Cole sound so furious before.

Zoe brightened. "Then that's a good thing, isn't it?"

"Are you bloody kidding me, Zoe?" Ken asked. He'd thrown himself facedown onto the couch earlier on, but his muffled voice was otherwise still audible. "It's a good thing that you nearly got shish kebabbed?"

"I meant that this is another tick off the list in the prophecy Nottingham and I share, and it must be a sign that we're doing what we're supposed to do. His doom says he'll save me from frogs and fire and winter, and I'll save him from poison and sword and madness. He already saved me from that horrid oversize toad in the swamps the first time we entered Avalon, and now this must be the fire. So all we need to do is watch out for the winter one—obviously the Snow Queen—"

"That's not it!" Cole shouted, and everyone jumped. Even Ken made a little flop with his stomach, just as startled as the rest. "I don't care one goddamn whit about the prophecy! You could have been killed!" He hunched over, rubbed at his eyes. "I don't want to treat this as a game, Carlisle," he said roughly. "Or as one of those riddles that you like to solve, or even a pros and cons list. Just because we know what's going to happen doesn't mean we can prevent it. We can't be complacent. I don't know what I'm going to do if you—"

Zoe looked so soft, about ready to cry if she hadn't been cursed not to. "I'm sorry. I'm trying to deal with it with logic so I don't freak out myself, but I didn't think about how you felt." She rose from her couch and moved to where he was standing, taking him by the hand. "So you do like me that much, huh?"

"Yes, Carlisle." Cole's voice was rough. "I do."

"We have to believe that everything's going to pay off," Ken said quietly, turning his face away from the cushion he was sprawled on to face them. "Why would fate or destiny or whatever go through all this trouble to warn us of what's to come if the outcome means everything's going to suck anyway? We gotta go into this thinking— *knowing*—that we're going to win." He grinned faintly. "But hey, don't worry. With me in charge, you're all going to be all right. We're going to be optimistic about this even if it kills us. Except not literally, because, you know, that's the whole point."

"We are going to win this," Loki said firmly. "But that doesn't mean we don't have questions." They stared down at their hands, one idly flipping their toothpick over their knuckles. "The Dame of Tintagel said I was going to break a scepter and deliver it into Neverland's mercy. I had a vision of myself fighting with the pirates. Does that mean something?"

"We won't know until we go through with it." Alex still sounded weary.

Tala was up on her feet in an instant, taking in the harried-looking doctor who had scurried in after the young king, clearly against Alex being up and about so soon. At his heels was Tristan, who looked mad for the same reason.

"I won't take too long," Alex said hastily before his self-appointed bodyguard could open his mouth. "I'll say my piece, and I promise to go back to bed."

"You'd better, or I'm helping them drag you back there myself," Tala growled.

"I know." Alex's lips thinned. "Our hunt for the rest of the artifacts resumes early tomorrow. We are still trying to negotiate with the German government for clearance to enter their country, and they have been reluctant for good reason. They currently have their hands full with nightwalkers who've been trying to gain entry into Löwenberg forest."

"Technically," West said, "if they let us into Löwenberg to retrieve the singing bone those nightwalkers are after, then they'd solve that problem too."

"It's not that easy, West. They have reason to be wary on their end."

"What if we promised to take really good care of it? And offer them a chance to come here and fight some of these nightwalkers themselves?"

"That's the other thing I wanted to talk to you all about. We're not going to be receiving reinforcements from the other kingdoms."

"What do you mean?" Zoe asked warily. "The attacks at the Burn have been all over the news. We've had mutual support agreements in place with other nations."

"Except those agreements aren't quite set in stone, my love." Zoe's mother flounced into view, stunning in a red business suit and dark cape. She smiled at her startled daughter and slipped her gloves off her hands. "Surprised to see me, darling?"

"I thought you were at King Philip's court!"

"And most of my business there has finally been concluded. Your uncle has been watching all the current goings-on in Avalon with keen interest, Zoe. He thought it would be best to send me here to keep an eye on things. Not only do I still hold Avalon citizenship, but you are my best reason for being here."

"And he's not going to help us?"

"Avalon is not the only kingdom his court maintains an alliance with. The Royal States has been a powerful ally for so long, and even he hesitates at stepping out of bounds and incurring their wrath."

"Their king is literally unhinged," Ken said, lifting his face off the couch, balancing on his elbows. "They literally tried to send Zoe off to prison!"

"An alliance is more than with just the person in charge of a kingdom. *Unofficially*, we will do our best to offer support, but that must be done behind the scenes, without any official acknowledgment. And that is why I am here—I and about two dozen of France's best spies. We know a thing or two about revolution, ma chérie. Our people's magnanimity is why the rulers of old still kept their heads and agreed to spread their wealth around and be kinder about it like my brother."

"And what exactly do you propose to do, Felicity?" Lumina asked warily. She'd been loitering at the edges of the group, keeping an eye on any fresh updates coming in from the Burn as well as the breaking headlines flashing across the command center's display screens.

Nightwalkers sighted in Germany. Ogre put down in Iceland. Even more stringent tightening of security within the Royal States as anger from extremist groups began spilling out into violence. Asylum seekers, Tala was sorry to see, were still being herded into containment camps along the borders. Not even the revelation of King John's treachery had done anything to slow those arrests down or to make things any easier for those who'd been detained.

"There are many things I would be glad to discuss with your king away from wandering ears. But I can offer some bit of news now." Felicity Fairfax leaned forward, her eyes grave. "We have our own share of extremists within France," she said. "We have just arrested several terrorists caught planning Philip's assassination. They had planned to make a show of it with a kidnapping and a live execution—with a guillotine even."

"What?" Zoe exclaimed.

"I suppose it is a French custom, to attempt to cut off our lieges' heads every turn of the century or so. But these men we caught, they have ties to some of the more dangerous groups within the Royal States. They claim an alliance with the Snow Queen, and all that we could extract from them during their interrogation tells me that Avalon is their next target."

"Do you have any details?" Alex said, once more on the alert.

"You promised to rest," Tristan reminded him pointedly.

"That's before I learned that nightwalkers aren't the only things I have to worry about."

"We have discovered spelltech from their hideouts that they could not have gotten through normal means," Felicity said. "It's not anything that is even available in the black market. I suspect they are getting some of their more powerful weapons from Beira. We can talk more about this when there are less people around, Alexei. The fewer people who know, the better."

There was little else to do after that. Alex had expressly forbidden them from doing anything more for today and had commanded them all to retire and prepare for tomorrow. Tristan had then informed him, rather coldly, that he was to do the same once his meeting with Felicity Fairfax was concluded. Tala still didn't know him all that well, but she liked his penchant for pestering Alex into getting some needed rest.

Soon enough, the Locksley boy announced that Alex would be leaving for his private chamber and that he was not to be disturbed. Everyone at the command center knew how things stood between him and their king by then, and none chose to protest.

Ryker was currently being subjected to a series of tests by Dexter and his father to ensure that the thrall collar had no adverse effects on his person. Loki was beside Tala and could not stop glaring at the other boy.

"He's not all that bad," she said mildly.

Loki folded their arms. "Whether or not he should be trusted, he's still too involved with the Snow Queen for my peace of mind."

"I can look out for myself, you know."

Tala wasn't angry—she knew the ranger was only looking out for her—but Loki reddened unexpectedly. "I know that. Of course you can. It's just… I don't like that he… I would much rather it was me that… Ah, hell."

"Disgustingly healthy," Ryker reported cheerfully, trotting back toward them. "They want me to get some more shut-eye, though. Despite all my protests that I was asleep for nearly three months."

"I'll accompany you back to your quarters," Loki said abruptly.

Tala blinked. "What? You will?" This seemed like an abrupt one-eighty from the conversation they'd just had.

"There's something I have to talk to him about."

"That there is," Ryker agreed with a grim smile.

Tala sighed. Something odd was going on between the two, but she was too tired herself to bother. "No fighting," she warned.

"We won't." Ryker bowed to Loki. "Shall we get going, then?"

Tala's mother was busy as well, so she decided not to bother her. With Alex needing rest, it had fallen on Lumina's shoulders to make many of the decisions at Maidenkeep command, but Tala knew she was hurting too. Best to wait until they both found a quieter time together to process everything.

She didn't want to think about her father again. Not yet. She might break down if she did, and she didn't want that now.

Instead, Tala headed for the Gallaghers' lab. Nya apparently had the same idea, because she was already there. And she wasn't alone either. It looked like every woman in her village had come along, and they crowded the table where the tamatebako took center stage.

"It's difficult to analyze what kind of m-magic was used for it, even with our advanced t-tech," Severon Gallagher said, clearly flustered by all the female attention and stuttering as badly as his son sometimes did. They were not the only personnel within the lab, but the other scientists had very discreetly drifted away from the immediate radius of the tamatebako to find more immediate concerns to work on farther away, leaving the Gallaghers to fend for themselves. "There are fail-safe systems built into modern spelltech that would have made the production of these spells illegal if they were attempted today. The requirements would be unethical by modern—"

"Are you saying, Lord Gallagher," Nya's grandmother interrupted him, brown eyes ablaze with interest, "that the spell used to fashion this tamatebako is a sovereign spell?"

"What's a sovereign spell?" Tala asked.

Dexter smiled nervously in greeting. None of the women looked surprised to see her. Nya smiled, too, though a hint of worry remained along the curves of her mouth.

"A sovereign spell," Nya's grandmother said. "An extreme sacrifice on the part of its caster to gain something they would consider far more beneficial. Such magic is banned today, but most people wouldn't be able to conjure such spells even if they wanted to. It requires immense willpower and great strength. But the consequences can be grave. You saw it in the poor girl's attempt to seek revenge against her abuser not so long ago."

"Abigail Fey," Tala said.

"I am here at your labs to ensure that my granddaughter shall not suffer that same fate. And to do that, I must know all that you know of shade magic, sovereign spells—everything of the other artifacts."

"What?" Tala asked, looking back at Nya.

"I saw myself holding the box," the girl said in a small voice. "I don't want to make a mistake that I can't fix. Not when so much is at stake."

"Isn't it best to destroy it? Without Koschei's soul, the Snow Queen won't be able to get into Buyan."

"Lady Motoyama mentioned that those who tried to destroy Urashima's soul died while the tamatebako remained intact. The box must first be opened to be vulnerable, and that is the real riddle in all this."

"It is difficult to quantify s-such magic," Severon said, gaining back some of his confidence. "It's not something that can be easily reproduced. Equivalent exchange dictates magical law. For something like a tamatebako to prolong life, then a life must have been sacrificed in its creation."

"But there were so many of those jeweled boxes inside the palace," Tala burst out, stunned.

"How that process goes, I don't know myself. I don't *want* to know, I should say." Lord Gallagher pointed at the ruby box. "But what I can confirm is that there *is* a mechanism holding this tamatebako shut, and some prerequisites must be fulfilled before it can be opened. This turquoise container, on the other hand, has already been used—"

"Wait," Tala cried out again, not wanting to interrupt the man but unable to help herself, startling the adarna on her head awake to boot. "What do you mean by *already been used*?"

"Unlike the ruby box, the magical signature from the turquoise chest is low," Dexter said timidly. "Which means it's been diverted to protect whatever is within it. We can't exactly determine what it has, but it exhibits heat signatures like something's alive inside."

"And I did that?"

"Yeah. I think it would be best that you keep possession of the b-box after we're done analyzing it, Tala. Might be best to keep it close to you at all times, j-just in case."

"But nothing happened when I opened it!" Tala froze. "No, wait. It did feel like something was trying to pull me into the box when I did. If the shade hadn't slammed the lid shut and stopped it, then I could have—"

"Child." It was the seeress's turn to interrupt. "Did you say a shade?"

"Well, yes, but it didn't act like any other shade I've ever encountered. I thought it must have been trapped inside the Ryugu-jo for far longer than we had and gained self-awareness—"

But that was about as far as Tala got before immediately being surrounded by a circle of women.

"Was it able to convey to you where it came from and what it was?" one of the elders asked.

"Did it say anything about why it chose to help you?" another inquired.

"What did it do specifically to aid you?" a third piped up.

"Aunties!" Nya said sharply. "Give her some time to answer all your questions!"

Tala took a deep breath. "It didn't tell me anything about itself. It didn't explain why it was helping me, and I thought it just wanted to find a way out. I don't even know if it escaped with us, because it disappeared just as quickly. And it was the one to remind me that Loki had the lotus lantern. It helped me bring the others out from the mirrors they were trapped in."

"But if it had been stuck in the palace for ages," Nya asked shrewdly, "how would it have known that Loki had a lotus lantern?"

Tala hadn't thought about that.

But the villagers were already switching targets, resuming their study of the ruby and turquoise boxes on the table. "It looks like our hunch is right after all," Nya's grandmother said. "The key lies within this box. And we will not leave this laboratory until we have uncovered the means to unlock it."

Dexter and his father shot quick, horrified looks at each other.

"Milord," one of the laboratory scientists called out, switching the lab's screen display to the news. Tala turned and gaped at the sight of Ken Inoue, Kusanagi in his hand flashing against the light, laughing as he fought his way through a swarm of shades. The bright flames of the Burn that separated the inaccessible territories of Esopia from the rest of the kingdom served as a magnificent backdrop, and the chyron underneath that flashed Avalon Sword-Wielder Defeats Nightwalkers only made it all the more impressive.

Not so to Nya. "I," she said with the icy confidence of a commander knowing they were about to put the fear of God into a lowly officer for his insubordination, "am going to kill that man."

Tala had looked in on Ryker to see if he was sleeping but wasn't at all surprised to find his bed empty. She should have expected it, of course.

It was easy enough to find him. He was at the courtyard, looking at the empty anvil that had housed the Nameless Sword, now Ken's Kusanagi.

"You're supposed to be sleeping."

Ryker didn't look back to see her, but Tala could see the small smile on his lips as she moved to stand beside him. "If Ken could sneak away to the Burn against His Majesty's orders, then me playing hooky within castle grounds shouldn't be cause for scolding."

"Ken's not getting away with anything. Nya's prepared to give him what for as soon as he returns." It was hard not to look at the anvil and think about all the what-ifs. "What did you and Loki talk about?"

"We've come to an understanding about something."

"I didn't know you disliked them that much."

"I don't. I think they're a good person. It's just that there's one specific thing I disagree with them about, and it's unlikely that we can be friends because of it."

"And what would that be?"

"I'd rather not say."

"Fine, but I want it on record that you're both being very weird about this." Tala paused. "You doing okay?"

"Yeah. No. I'm mad. Furious. And ashamed." Ryker stared hard at the stone. "None of this would have happened if I hadn't brought those kids to her. And now they're under her power forever. I failed them." His voice broke and he dashed an arm angrily against his eyes. "And now there's nothing else I can do."

"Now is not the time to be giving up. You said the Snow Queen wants her hands on the Alatyr to open the path leading into Buyan. If the Alatyr can do that, then surely there's a way to reverse her spell and bring them back."

Ryker nodded. "I'm just angry—at her and at myself, that I never got wise to what she was really doing."

Tala tore her gaze away from the anvil. "You know, you never told us what you saw in the mirror before we got you out."

Ryker fell silent. "It's not that important," he said after a long pause.

"Do you really think I'm buying that?"

He laughed. "No. I should have known better. Like everyone else, I was fighting. You're right. I saw it."

"Saw what?"

"The Alatyr. It didn't look like anything they say it is. It didn't look like anything much, in fact. I reached out and touched it, and things got a little hazy after that because I think you all managed to pull me out before I could take a second look, but—" He took a deep breath. "I think we can win this, Tala. I really think we can."

The portal that popped out from nowhere came as a shock. It opened up between them and the anvil, but it wasn't a shade that came tumbling out.

It was the Baba Yaga they had met at the Avalon festival a few months back—far less put together now than they had been then. Their hair was dirty and tangled, clothes torn and messy like they'd been wearing them for days. Their face sported a black eye, and there were several deep cuts on the rest of their body, some of which they were still bleeding from.

"Oh good," they said breathlessly. "I'm sorry to spoil the moment, but I was wondering if you would be so kind as to grant my request for sanctuary, because there is a very annoying group of pus sacks from the Royal States that are trying to hunt me for sport at the moment."

12

IN WHICH PEOPLE KEEP ATTACKING AVALON

I knew they were coming, of course," the Baba Yaga said calmly, like they hadn't just escaped by the skin of their teeth. "I knew I would make it here in time. But it was pretty damn close."

"If you knew they were coming," West said, "then why didn't you just leave earlier and avoided them completely?"

The Baba Yaga gave him a baleful stare. "And have my own predictions turn out false? It's not like that would make much of a difference. If that's how I see it, then that's how it's going to be, regardless of what I actually do."

"You have bullet wounds," Tala said, horrified.

"Wounds *grazed* by bullets. There's a difference. No vital organs affected. I would have predicted that too."

"Minor injuries aside," Alex said soberly, "you're telling me that people from the Royal States were *hunting* you?"

"Quite a few groups there have now dedicated themselves to stamping out what they call heretical magic. Specifically the toxic ones who thought Abigail Fey demeaned their masculinities."

"You didn't sound this angry about the Royal States the last time we met," Loki noted.

"I've just been shot by the worst of their lot, Sun-Wagner. Bear with me." The Baba Yaga scowled at the bandages Nya was busily wrapping around their arm. They had refused to be admitted into the hospital and had remained at the courtyard, asking only that their wounds be seen to. "Do you really need this much?"

"If you can see the future, then you probably know the answer," the girl said calmly.

"I've come here more than just to ask for sanctuary, Your Majesty. I'm here to warn the rest of you that things are going to get worse."

"I thought it was against a Baba Yaga's policies to try and change the future?" Alex asked.

They smiled grimly. "I'm not sure my being here would even change matters. I only saw myself here at the forefront of the upcoming battle. Don't know why, because you can bet your ass I don't want to be here. But if the fates have decreed it, then here I will be."

"The upcoming battle? If you haven't been watching the news, that battle has already been waging the last couple of days. Are you telling me this doesn't even constitute a—"

"My lips are sealed on that one," the Baba Yaga said. "And while I'm here, I ought to look up an old friend of mine. There's a few things he needs to know too."

"I'm here, Ilyena," the Cheshire said, once again popping out from nowhere. He still kept to his human form instead of the cat shape he often preferred, smiling sadly at the seer.

"You look the same as always, Ches," the Baba Yaga said calmly. "Almost twenty years, it's been?"

"I wish I'd reached out sooner, but when you're wanted in several kingdoms, sometimes the matter is taken out of your hands. What are you doing here, Ilyena?"

"Like I said, to ask for sanctuary and warn them about—"

"That's bullshit and you know it."

The Baba Yaga sighed loudly. "All right. I have three reasons for being here. One, sanctuary. Two—look, you all know that I didn't agree with my predecessor about changing the future. That seeing it unfold doesn't mean we should do anything about it. But this one—I can understand now why she saved you as a child, Your Majesty. If the future happens the way I saw it, then I don't know if there's much hope."

"Is it that bleak?" Ken asked.

"Nuh-uh. You won't try to pry the answers out of me again. The Baba Yaga I took over from was fine with sacrificing her powers, but I'm a much more selfish person to give all this up. But I want to be on hand just to—just in case something changes and I can warn you faster."

"If this is your attempt at pacifying us, then it's not working."

"Tough." The Baba Yaga looked at the Cheshire again. "Are *you* ready?" they asked.

"I've been ready for a very long time. What will be will be."

"Wait," Zoe said. "You said you had three reasons."

"Right." The Baba Yaga checked her watch. "In five minutes' time," they said, "a band of those same assholes chasing me will open a portal directly into the Burn. It will cause another international incident."

"What?" Alex turned toward Tristan and Lumina, who also

looked stunned at the news. "Send word to Keer immediately!" he yelled. "Tell his people to brace themselves. They don't have to pull their punches, but I want them all taken in alive, do you understand?" He turned back to the Baba Yaga. "You've been here close to an hour, and *now's* when you choose to spring this on us?"

"I thought it was the perfect time to say it." The Baba Yaga grinned. Their gaze drifted over to the swordless anvil, ignored it to look further afield—and then froze. "Oh," they whispered. "Oh."

"Don't tell me there's more," Tala said warily. Alex had already rushed back inside, Tristan and her mother following. Ken, Zoe, and Nya were following suit.

"No," the Baba Yaga said. "I think I just realized why I was supposed to be here."

Tala turned to look around the courtyard, trying to see what the Baba Yaga had. But all she saw was the cleaning staff bustling about and the gardeners working at the hedges.

The men came tearing out of the portal, just as the Baba Yaga had predicted. They were all dressed up in camo gear and night vision goggles despite the daytime and despite the Burn being an open stretch of land where there was nowhere to hide. They sported guns with more personality than they had, and several of them were already firing haphazardly the instant they stepped out.

"Fuck Avalon!" one of them crowed, possibly the gang leader. "Get them all!"

The rest took up the chant, but their bullets did little. A few of the shades were caught in the spray and dissolved, but more avoided the shots. Having been given the few minutes' heads-up by Alex, the rangers simply parked their shields in front of them and calmly withstood the hail of gunfire.

Back in Avalon command, Alex was swearing. "Those dumbasses are going to get themselves killed, and we're going to get blamed for it."

"Let us fight them," Ken spoke up.

Alex glared at him. "You aren't even done being in trouble for sneaking off the last time."

"The news is gonna get wind of it whether we want them to or not. And you know that as soon as Lola Urduja gets their hands on them, she's gonna be spanking their whiny little asses on live television, and that's going to be worse than anything we can do."

"He does have a point," Zoe conceded.

"You too?"

"They're going to sensationalize this regardless of what you decide, so we may as well adopt a hard stance," Loki said. "I agree with Ken. If we don't, then we're going to be seeing more of these groups show up unannounced and compromise our operations here."

Alex considered that. "Very well. Go and beat the crap out of them whenever you're ready, but please make it quick. Let's not give the media any more ammunition than they already have."

They were true to their word. All the Banders had been eager to suit up and port, and only Ryker had been left behind, sulking, because his presence might bring up questions no one had the time to answer.

The men stood no chance against the group of teenagers. Ken simply took Horse and ran rings around them. Their guns were cleanly sliced in half with a few swings of his sword before they had time to respond.

"The Baba Yaga made it sound more serious than it was," West noted, watching the group of men be carted off into an official Avalon portal, screaming obscenities at them. The rest of the Banders had aided the rangers and the Katipuneros against the nightwalkers, defeating the last wave soon after.

"The Baba Yaga knows it will be more than just this fight," Loki said. "The Royal States will want compensation from this. They'll raise a fuss even if they were the attacking party. And with their king still in charge, there's no telling what he'll do to retaliate."

"We'll be here when they do, then," Captain Mairead said cheerfully.

Tala turned toward the Burn, which looked even higher now than when she'd been there last. She summoned her agimat again, weaving it once more into a salamanca spell. The results were the same; she could encourage part of the fire to overload itself, letting its powerful magic short itself out, but she wasn't strong enough to subdue the wall of flames completely. Even the small hole she'd managed to puncture was soon swept away as the rest of the conflagration consumed it.

Above her, the adarna sighed, sensing her frustration.

"I see that your agimat has been growing stronger, hija," Lola Corazon said gravely, stopping beside her.

"Are you gauging to see if I'm well enough to arrange my marriage with some other noble now that you've realized Alex is gay?"

She was expecting her grandmother to be angered by her temerity. Instead, the old woman chuckled. "I would not have forced you if the idea so repelled you, hija. But it would have been the best match for you, objectively speaking."

It wasn't an *objective* assertion if her lola could benefit from having Alex as a grandson-in-law, but Tala decided not to argue further. She felt Lola Corazon summon her own agimat, but it had just as little effect on the Burn as hers had.

Lola Corazon gestured at the adarna. "It is neither male nor female, like the firebird," she said. "It simply is. We told you nothing about it because we wanted to protect you a little longer. This may sound like lies and schemes to Urduja, who only follows orders and thinks nothing about planning ahead, but the Makilings have survived all these centuries because of our contingency plans. If it sounds mercenary to you, to scheme to ensure that future generations will continue to thrive long after I am gone, then yes. Perhaps that is not the way the young minds of today work, but I will not apologize for doing what I believe is best. Unfortunately, your mother has raised you to become too much like her."

"Mom raised me well."

"Yes. Didn't I already say that?" Lola Corazon took a step farther toward the Burn, frowned into its depths. "Why?" she asked it. "Why focus on these fires when it would be much more to their advantage to attack Maidenkeep itself? Hinahanap ba nila ang—"

"Your Majesty!" It was Zoe, shouting into her comm link. "We've got trouble!"

A few of the techmages were already on the scene, going through the bags the terrorist group had brought with them. They were slowly backing away from a complicated-looking device they'd just found in one of the packs.

"The retrieval team isn't sure what it is yet, but they're ninety percent certain it's not an explosive device. They're requesting Lord Gallagher's scanner, but we're going to keep our distance in the meantime."

"Can you aim your camera and give me an idea of what it looks like?" Dexter asked through Tala's earpiece. "Yup, just like that. Running it through the sensors here and—oh. Oh crap!"

"Is it going to blow up?"

"No, but it is an electromagnetic pulse that looks like it's been designed to wipe out any defense barriers within a three-mile radius. Zoe, you have to destroy it as soon as you—"

Zoe was already whipping out her Ogmios before he was done talking, and Tala was already running toward her, pushing her agimat out toward the device, hoping it would absorb any damage it might let out.

But she was still a few seconds too late as the spelltech blitzed into life with some kind of sonic wave that shoved them both backward. Zoe's whip drove down into the middle of the device, breaking it into two, but the damage was already done. All around them, Tala could hear a sharp high-pitched noise as the magic protecting the place petered out and fell silent.

The command center now sounded like a madhouse coming through her ears. "Get as many of our techs there this instant!" she heard Alex shout. "I want more rangers on hand and everyone they can spare to set up a secondary system—"

There were more crackles around them, this time not from Avalon magic.

Five new portals opened almost simultaneously.

"Shit," Ken said.

The things that staggered out weren't shades or even an ogre. They were of a new breed that Tala had never seen before—a hodgepodge of both and more. Some of the creatures had human body parts like hands or legs, but they were attached to something that looked like the shadows of strange beasts. Some actually had faces— creatures' heads that would not have looked out of place in some medieval bestiary, like carved statues of gargoyles and other fantastical beasts given life.

The last monster to storm out of the portals was an ice dragon.

"Not this one again!" Tala heard Ken say, but he was the first to charge forward, Horse whinnying. The dragon flapped its brittle wings and roared, and a hailstorm erupted from its mouth, covering the ground in ice. Tala heard more shouts through the comm; despite the danger, there were more techmages appearing through Avalon's own port, carrying or dragging heavy pieces of equipment to restart the barriers and close the rest of the ports. But these new nightwalkers weren't making things any easier.

Zoe's whip lashed out again, this time taking hold of one of the strange shadow-human hybrids. Electricity churned through the lash, and the creature seized up as the bolts rebounded into it again and again. The shadows dissolved. Not so much the human parts, which thumped onto the ground sans owner, and the look of horrified revulsion on Zoe's face said it all.

West was in black hound form, shaking his head back and forth as he ripped through one of them with his teeth, but it was proving much harder to tear through. It was taking more blows from Loki's staff before they could successfully puncture through the shadows, and Tala was realizing the same thing with her agimat. It took more focus, more strength to force the strange hybrids to implode on themselves with her curse, and she already didn't have much to spare, even with the adarna singing its heart out.

A group of rangers moved in, clearly from the segen regiment. One soldier punched at the ground with a gloved fist, and spikes rose up, swiftly impaling several shades. Another wielded twin daggers that she used to strike at a different shadow, sending swift jolts of electricity through the latter much like Zoe's Ogmios could.

Cole and Ken were still actively engaging the ice dragon, as did the Katipuneros, the pirates, and Lola Corazon's team. Several rangers joined them, fire licking out of their respective weapons as they tried to burn the horrid creature before them. "We need time to power up the *Jolly Roger*," Captain Mairead said tersely. Sparks were flying off her, and Tala realized it was her connection to her pirate ship that was causing those fissures of magic. "One good blast from it should do the trick."

"And how long do we have to wait?" Lola Corazon asked through gritted teeth. The dragon's tail was lashing out at random, but it encountered an invisible wall every time it tried to hit the old woman, parts of it melting with every attempt.

"Lady, we're doing the best we can." Seraphina the pirate still looked as glamorous as ever, and it was impressive to see her run so quickly on her six-inch heels, feathered boa flapping in the wind behind her, to summon her own shadow to deliver a powerful backhand to one of the strange chimera creatures that actually sent it flying.

Horse worried at the dragon's heels, swiftly rounding it when the dragon turned, giving Ken a chance to slash through the beast's flank with Kusanagi. The sword cleaved through its side easily, leaving a large angry gash that on any other animal would have been fatal.

The dragon merely growled. It didn't even seem all that interested in any of them. Its attention returned to the Burn, as if fascinated by its heat. Its icy breath slammed into the fires to no effect. Not even it could douse the flames there.

Cole had snuck up behind it, using its distraction to plunge his own sword into its back. The dragon did rear up at that, forelegs kicking at the air, but Cole persisted. The black opaque smoke that funneled out of Gravekeeper began seeping into the dragon, parts of its scales turning black as it shook its head, befogged, trying to rid itself of its influence.

Cole didn't notice a blue-tinged arm slowly appearing from within one of the hybrid shadows that was creeping nearer toward him, like the creature itself was a portal. An ice maiden emerged, smiling cruelly, and she wielded an icicle sword in her hands. She raised it over her head, aimed at Cole's unprotected back.

Tala shouted, running toward them, but knew she couldn't make it in time.

Not so with Zoe, who threw her Ogmios. It wrapped itself expertly around the ice blade, and the maiden shrieked as more bolts of lightning lanced through her form, forcing her to drop her weapon. Cole had succeeded, if not at taming the dragon completely, at least at keeping it from attacking any further, though the strain was obvious on him.

The ice maiden turned toward Zoe and was hit with an unexpected slap to the face. Another shade—a *regular* shade, without all the unnerving corporeal body parts attached like the others had—punched her again, though it wasn't as effective as it had hoped. The ice maiden snatched it up by the scruff of what should have been its neck, staring down at it in surprise.

"What is—" she began and then yelped when the shadow actually *bit* her. She dropped it, and it scampered away to freedom.

Ken urged Horse faster. The kelpie rode up the dragon's tail and onto its back, ascending the upper part of its mane toward its head. Horse made one last flying leap, so far up in the air that it looked like it was flying, and Ken jumped off like it was a diving board, his hands on the hilt of his sword as it plunged downward, right at the center of the dragon's skull.

Ice dragons could shatter into pieces. Tala had seen that happen months ago, when one had literally crashed into a party being held at Avalon by one of Nome's executives. This one *cracked*; its head was split in two by the force of Ken's blow, and then the sword kept moving downward in a straight line, cutting lengthwise through its face, its neck, its upper body. Cole had already moved out of the way, retrieving Gravekeeper and expertly ducking through the falling ice in the seconds it took for him to get clear. There didn't seem to be anything within the creature but more ice, which splintered into minute fragments as its body toppled, each segment crashing down on either side and breaking into even more pieces when it hit the ground hard.

Horse leaped again and caught Ken on its back before he could fall any farther.

And then Captain Mairead shouted, "Get back! Get back, all of you! We've got a blast heading your way, and you'd best vamoose before it finds you!"

No one even needed to ask where the blast was coming from. Tala could see it coming down at them from the sky like a meteorite. Everyone scrambled to get out of the radius, but Mairead proved to be astonishingly accurate when aiming the *Jolly Roger*. The beam struck at the remains of the ice dragon but also took out most of the hybrids and beast-like monsters nearby, dissolving them under the force of that light. Even the portals had no protection against its force, and Tala watched as four of them folded under its strength, collapsing.

Only one looking glass remained. The ice maiden stared back at them with that same mocking smile before stepping through it, the opening winking out behind her. There was a sudden burst of static and then the hum of familiar magic as Avalon's defense systems started up, surrounding the area with their barriers once more.

"What happened?" Alex's worried voice sounded from over the comm. "Are they gone?"

"Tala?" Ryker's voice came on too. "Are you all right? Is everyone?"

"Another ice dragon." Tala was still shaken. She'd been hoping she'd seen the last of them, given how they were created. "And these other...*things.*"

"The good news is that they're probably not created with living humans, if that's what you're worried about," Ryker said through the link, still sounding grim despite the assurance. "The bad news is that they're cobbled together from corpse parts. It's been done before, when the Snow Queen wanted larger armies. It's darker magic than even she usually uses. That she's resurrected that art again tells me she might be getting desperate too."

"She should be," Zoe said. "We've got a lot of the artifacts she needs." She took a deep breath and accepted Ogmios, which Cole was handing back to her. "Was that it?" she asked him softly. "Once from sword. Was that it?"

Cole looked back down at her, his expression once more unreadable. He pulled her forward slowly until she was wrapped up in his arms. "Thank you," he said quietly.

Captain Mairead had sagged down, and the rest of her crewmates were attending to her. "That was stunning," Ken said, drawing nearer to her. "How are you able to control the *Jolly Roger* like that?"

"The same way your king can control his own version of the *Jolly Roger* back at your castle," the pirate said with a drunken-sounding laugh. "Blasts and some standard defenses are all we use it for, so it won't kill me in the way it'll kill him—just a month or two of my life to sacrifice every time—and lads if it doesn't tire me out. You were pretty impressive yourself, m'boy."

"Was I?" Ken brightened. "Were you impressed too, Rapunzel?"

Another long, annoyed snort from Nya. "I suppose."

"She supposes," Ken said happily. "You heard that?"

"You could do it too, ranger," Captain Mairead said to Loki.

"There's a spark in you, makes you more attuned to the magic. I suspected it, but now I believe it. The *Jolly Roger* sang when I saw you the first time. If the ranger life isn't for you, you could always join us."

"I don't know." Loki's expression was troubled.

"They used a jabberwock to summon an ice dragon the last time," Nya said. "Are you telling me they've gotten hold of another to experiment with?"

"If they did, they didn't get it from Avalon's woods," Tala's mother volunteered, holstering her arnis sticks behind her. "Every one we've found has been sent to the sanctuaries in Iceland and Australia, and all the forests here are tracked to make sure we don't have another one loose again."

"Then how did the Snow Queen get her hands on another one of those?"

"She has more OzCorp tech we are still in the dark about," Lola Corazon muttered, folding her abanico. "The one they made to house the jabberwock was a prototype, remember?"

Lola Urduja glared at her. "You sound far too confident. Why then would she choose to reveal it now? What do you know that we don't?"

"There are so many things that you are unaware of that it would be difficult to list them all today." Lola Corazon looked back at the Burn, the same furrowed look on her face. "She wanted to test if she could weaken the barriers around the Burn," she said. "First it is the device that the foolish men carried with them, and then the ice dragon, but again, why? What lies beyond the Burn that she seems to so desperately want?"

13

In Which Everyone Is Mad at Everyone Else

It took until the next morning for Alex to reach an agreement with the German government permitting them to enter their kingdom and borrow their artifacts, which allowed Tala and the others several hours' sleep. She had tossed and turned, caught up in between fits of dreaming and nightmares, searching desperately for her father in one, fighting an ice maiden through a hallway of mirrors in another, surrounded by fire in the next.

She woke up briefly when she felt her mother's presence. Lumina had climbed into bed with her. Tala had burrowed into her warmth without thinking, welcoming her familiar scent. Not too far away, sitting atop a small mound of pillows it had set up like a nest, the adarna began to sing, sweetly and softly. Tala sank back into unconsciousness and dreamed about nothing else for the rest of the night.

King John of the Royal States of America had declared war on Alex for the eighth time while they'd been asleep, and the headlines were filled with quotes of his ranting rather than his terrorists' attempts to blow up the Burn, which had been covered like an afterthought.

Her best friend merely received the news with an exasperated grunt when they gathered for their briefing, like he'd heard this all before. "More importantly, Prime Minister Merkel's given us the clearance we need to port in, but you'll need to brace yourselves. They're still fending off nightwalkers around the paths leading into the Hamelin Mountains, so you may have to fight almost as soon as you get through."

"Alex, that toothless royal arsehole just called on his people to bring him your bloody head," Ken said. "Maybe we should talk first about putting more guards around you, reinforcing the wards inside Maidenkeep?"

"I've already given the order," Tristan said roughly from behind the young ruler.

Alex spun, eyes flashing. "And on whose authority?"

"On Lady Lumina Makiling Warnock's. You might think it's fine to risk your life and potentially leave Avalon without a ruler again, but I don't."

The king paused. "I'm not deliberately trying to kill myself."

"Could have fooled me." Tristan leaned forward so he was nose to nose with Alex, the latter's eyes widening. "This is about what's at stake for Avalon. And if you think I'm going to let some overgrown malfeasant sitting on some colonial throne put your life in danger, then I'm going to shoot him myself if I have to, along with every neck-beard with mommy issues he's going to send here after this. Lady Makiling Warnock has ordered increased security wards, and Lord Keer has added half a dozen more rangers in the palace as a precaution. They're sending teams of techmages to every vulnerable spot within the kingdom, armed with the necessary spelltech to keep any ports sealed and the nightwalkers at bay. They'll be more effective than a regiment of Fianna."

Alex stared at him. "That's actually a very good idea," he admitted reluctantly.

"I can do more than just warm your bed while I'm in Avalon, Alex. My father is a diplomat. My great-grandfather and great-grandmother fought in wars like this. Let me be more useful." Tristan took a step back, heedless of Alex's reddening face and the dropped jaws around him. "I have an idea I'd like to ask Lord Keer his opinion of. Don't do anything rash while I'm gone."

"Alex," Tala said after he was gone, trying to hide her smile with a glare. "How dare you. How dare you not tell me any of this. I thought we talked about it the last time you and he boned—"

"Tala!"

"I thought this was what you finally wanted him to do. To take responsibility and fight harder to win you over?"

"Can we not do this right now maybe?" Alex snapped, as bright as a tomato.

"At least you're getting some," Ken said mournfully. "Rapunzel and I've been too exhausted to—"

"Kensington!" It was Nya's turn to hiss.

"Liaisons from the prime minister are already on standby," Alex said, deliberately loud. "Let's not keep them waiting longer than they have to."

"Zoe isn't here yet," West said.

"That's odd. She's usually the first to show up—"

The brunette chose that moment to stumble in, and for once, she was not perfectly turned out. Her hair was a mess, and her clothes were slightly askew. There were smudges around her eyes like she'd applied makeup too haphazardly that morning.

"Sorry," she said, breathless. "I overslept."

Cole sauntered in. His short hair was slicked back, his clothes neat and clean, and yet somehow that gave them both further away.

"At least *some* of us are getting some," Ken muttered, and it was Zoe's turn to redden.

Alex cleared his throat hard. "Lord Suddene, do you have all the information we need?"

"Unfortunately, it isn't much at all." The duke switched on another display, treating them to a view of mountains. "This is Hamelin, allegedly the most haunted place in Germany. It's been warded to prevent anyone from entering, just like Kunlun is, and for similar reasons. People claimed to hear a strange flute playing within the depths of those mountains, and it's been said to turn most mad from the sound alone."

"And this is the infamous Pied Piper flute that we're supposed to retrieve?" Loki asked.

"Exactly, which is a cause for concern. The legends surrounding this fabled pipe contradict each other at points. In one, the man it was named after supposedly lured all the children of a village into a nearby river to drown after he was refused payment for ridding the area of nightwalkers. In another, he instead saved them from turning Deathless and brought them away to safety. Some claim that he, too, wielded the Nameless Sword and that it manifested to him as this very same flute."

"As Ken is the current wielder of that same sword, I'd say it's inaccurate that the flute would still be there if they're one and the same," Loki noted.

"He saved children from becoming Deathless," Lumina said. "Is the flute capable of bringing back those who've been cursed that way?"

Tala leaned forward eagerly in anticipation of the answer and noted that Ryker had done the same.

Her hopes were dashed a little when Lord Suddene said, "There is no proof of that. Only one person has ever been successful at retrieving it."

"And who was that?" Tala asked.

"Another wielder of Avalon's sword, one called Siegfried, though there is little known of him that could be verified. He was said to have a charming way with words, could persuade thousands to join his cause with a rousing speech, and once rescued a Valkyrie from an enchanted sleep. He supposedly brought the flute to the mountain shortly before he died, and while much of his life was unknown, bits of that journey were documented and passed down to historians and scholars. It's a start."

"Dex has upgraded the specs of the comm link you're all using, so it should be possible for us to keep in contact no matter how far inside Hamelin you all are," Alex said. "You are to meet with the prime minister's liaison, Mr. Brandt, who will be accompanying you inside with soldiers to ensure your safety."

"They're going to risk going in with us?" Ken asked.

Alex finally smiled. "They wanted to help, even if they can't state so officially. Incidentally, I want Tito Boy to go with you. Nearly all the soldiers with you also have hearing loss, and they think he would be advantageous to the team."

"But why?"

"An unusual thing about Konisberg is that those who can hear cannot make it into the mountain without succumbing to the voices, and those who cannot get lost despite the instructions Siegfried left behind and cannot find their way. We've tried combinations of both teams before with no success. We hope the Nameless Sword will make all the difference."

The adarna made an oddly discordant sound. And then, to Tala's shock, it hopped off her head, settled itself on the couch, and folded its wings behind it, shaking its head while it did so.

"What's it doing?" West asked.

"It doesn't want to go with us," Tala said, feeling a little stunned.

"Because it's dangerous," Alex asked it, "or because your presence will somehow compromise the team?"

The adarna chittered out a monologue.

"Tala, did you understand that?"

"I think it said the latter."

"Can it go into any more specifics about why?"

But the adarna stubbornly shook its head.

"That doesn't sound very promising, does it?" Loki asked.

"We don't have a choice. If it told Tala that it refused to go because it was dangerous, I would have aborted this mission. I want you all to be careful anyway."

The firebird alighted and seductively wriggled its way toward the adarna's side, who sighed and resigned itself to the inevitable.

The introductions were brief, mostly because of the fighting. The wards the Germans had set up to keep the nightwalkers from drawing nearer were working. There were the sounds of heavy blows from outside the invisible dome as a shade battered uselessly against its surface before it was dispatched by one of the fighters outside.

"I am sorry that you should find us in such circumstances." Leon Brandt was a no-nonsense man with a blond goatee who spoke in unapologetically accented English. He raised his hand and made several gestures at his men, who all immediately stood to attention. "These are the guards who shall watch our backs inside the caverns. I understand that you have a mission to prevent the Snow Queen access to our treasure, but it does not feel seemly to let our guests run into such dangers without claiming our own share in it."

"You're coming with us too, sir?" Ken asked.

"We do not order our people into situations without being willing to do so ourselves. I am an avid spelunker and am as familiar with mountains and caves as anyone else here." The man paused. "I do not know if you have already been briefed, but you may hear some strange things as we go farther in."

"Weird music?" Zoe asked.

"No," another of the soldiers signed—a pretty girl their age named Lilia. "Most people would not call it music. They could not explain it in detail, only that they started acting...strangely soon after. I am just as much in the dark about what you might hear as you." She grinned. "But I am always open to new experiences."

"But if your soldiers can't hear the music, then wouldn't they have a better chance at finding it?" Nya asked.

"We have tried once before to no avail. We believe the Nameless Sword is necessary."

"Close enough," Ken said. "We have a lotus lantern that could show us the way, and if there are any barriers keeping the flute under lock and key, then my Kusanagi can probably do something about that."

"Should the flute be found, we do expect, of course, that you turn it over to us once you are finished with its use," Brandt said.

"I'm not sure we can promise anything at this point," Alex's voice said apologetically. "Our main objective is to keep it away from the Snow Queen. Once that is done, we will gladly return it."

"This is likely the closest we are ever going to get to finding it ourselves," Brandt admitted. "Short of another German taking up Avalon's sword. We shall take the risk now and hope we are lucky." He grinned and whipped out a small display screen. "This describes Siegfried's journey through the mountains, keeping note of the passages he went through, of any multiple branches within the passageway. It is the only map we have in our possession of the inside of Hamelin. Many of our own techmages have tried and have been unsuccessful. Perhaps Avalon's champion shall succeed where we cannot."

"Of course," Ken said. "No pressure at all."

"Are you sure there's nothing we can do to help?" Nya asked, glancing back to where the sounds of fighting were still coming from.

"Everything is under control. The hordes come nearly endlessly, but we are efficient at managing them. It gives my men practice. If we succeed in finding the Pied Piper's flute, then I suspect the attacks will ease. The Snow Queen appears to want our prize almost as badly."

Siegfried's directions had been even less detailed than they'd expected. His notes only made observations of anything unusual that struck his fancy rather than detailing the way in. They were a few miles inside the mountain when they paused to take note of their surroundings. Tito Boy had started a quick friendship with several of the other soldiers, and they spent many minutes debating about which way to go next while the Banders waited for them to come to a majority decision.

"Another mountain," Ken groaned. "At least we're not being chased into it this time. Are you worried, Rapunzel?"

"What?" Nya asked. She kept glancing back behind them to stare suspiciously at the shadows, though Tala couldn't detect anything in them.

"What's up with you? Is there anyone following us? Because you're acting like there is."

"No, I—" Nya sighed. "Forget it."

"Are you sure?"

"Very sure, so I'd rather not talk about it!" Nya marched off, still red-faced and grumbling. Ken hurried after her, looking puzzled.

"I think the last couple of days have been getting to all of us," Ryker murmured.

"You were pretty worn out yesterday," Tala reminded him.

"I was. Hadn't had that good a sleep in a long time. You're not good enough to be here with the rest of them all the same, but maybe

I'll actually take the doctor's advice once we return and try to sleep longer."

"What?" Tala asked, mouth open.

"What?"

"What did you just say?"

"I said I'll try to get some sleep once we get back to Maidenkeep. Why?"

"I—nothing." Had she only imagined him saying that?

But Loki hadn't imagined it either. "What did you say to her?" they snapped, hostile.

"Nothing. What are you going on about—"

Loki had seized Ryker by his collar, and Tala had to step in between them before both could start fighting. "Stop it!" Loki was usually so levelheaded. "This isn't the right time for this!"

Loki glared at Ryker and then stalked off.

"Are they okay?" Tito Boy signed worriedly.

"It's not my fault," West said. Tala wasn't sure who he was arguing with, because it appeared that he was holding a debate against his own shadow. "So what if I didn't have as good a doom compared to everyone else? So what if I can't do anything fancy beyond shifting? I'm just as good a member of this team as any of them! You don't get to tell me whether I should be here, you...you... doodoo-head!"

"West, remind me to teach you some good old insults to use whenever you're raging," Ken said. "But no one's saying that. No one's even thinking it. You all right, mate?"

"What everyone else is thinking," Zoe said icily, "is why you still haven't told anyone about what you saw in the mirror." She wasn't answering Ken. She was directing the statement at Cole. "Every time I ask, you do everything you can to dodge having to answer me," she continued. "And when that doesn't work and I keep on bugging you, you kiss me to try and shut me up, and then we lose hours, and you get to avoid the question until I remember long enough to bring it up again. It's not gonna work this time!"

Cole was leaning against the wall with his arms folded, but despite his defensive stance, he couldn't quite look Zoe in the eye. "It worked, didn't it?" Tala heard him mutter, but that meant his girlfriend did too.

"I am tired of you giving me the runaround! If we're going to be together, opening up to me is something you'll have to get used to!"

"And what if I don't want to get used to it?" Cole asked.

"What are you saying?"

"I'm saying that I don't have to tell you everything. You know far more about me than I've ever told anyone else."

"This isn't something ridiculous like telling me some weird kink or some hidden family secret. If you care about me—"

"And that's just it!" Cole was shouting again, for only the second time since Tala had known him, and the words ricocheted all over the cave. "Just because I don't tell you things doesn't mean that I don't care! And if you're going to judge our relationship solely on what I tell you instead of everything else, then maybe we shouldn't—we shouldn't be in a—"

"Don't say that." Zoe's voice had gone deathly low. "You can't mean that."

Cole's anger had left as quickly as it had appeared. Now he just sounded tired. "I don't know anymore," he said.

"You are all being extremely unprofessional," Brandt snapped, startling them. "It is not enough that we now have our hands full of nightwalkers because the Snow Queen has once more taken up war against your country and we have been shoved into this mess along with you—" He broke off, because Lilia was pulling hard against his sleeve, shaking her head and signing frantically. Brandt listened and then rubbed at the side of his head, bewildered. "I am sorry," he said. "I don't know what came over me."

"I think I do," Nya said. "We're all acting irrationally, and it's not a coincidence." She paused to glare back at Ken. "I said not now!" She snapped.

"What?" Ken asked, confused again, but Nya had already turned to Lilia.

"None of you feel anything odd?" she asked, gesturing with her hands as well. "Tito Boy?"

"You are the only ones acting unusual," Lilia explained.

"She's right, hija," Tito Boy said. "This is not normal for any of you to be this angry. There is something here that is not affecting us simply because we cannot hear it."

"But we're not hearing any music whatsoever," Ken said. "Shouldn't we be?"

"Not quite," Lilia said thoughtfully. "The people I've questioned who have also acted strangely within these mountains never attested to hearing any kind of music. It is why they did not realize their erratic behavior until it was almost too late."

"So this is like one of those dog whistles where dogs can hear it but we can't, except now it's something that we can't hear but we react to?" West asked.

"A good comparison, and possibly the closest answer. Perhaps if we keep that in mind, it will help keep our concentration."

It did not help at all. Tala didn't know what the others were hearing, but what she could *hurt*. Everyone seemed to have something terrible to tell her.

"Maybe if you stopped being useless, Tala, you could actually contribute something to this mission," Loki said as they scanned the dark tunnel up ahead. "Arnis sticks can only do so much, and it's not like you're even any good at them."

"It's her agimat," West said, following at their heels. "Without it, she's nothing. Even *with* it, she's nothing."

This isn't what they're actually saying, Tala thought. *It's not. It can't be.*

"Is it?" Zoe asked loftily. "Or is this what everyone's been thinking all this time, and they've been too cowardly to say it to your face before?"

"What if this is exactly what they believe you to be," Nya added, "and the curse in these mountains has access to their thoughts?"

"You *know* you're useless, Tala," Ryker said. "You've always been. Without the Makiling name, without the agimat, what good are you? Even the so-called Nameless Sword abandoned you. What other proof do you need?"

"Stop it!" Ken shouted, startling her and everyone else. "Just stop it!"

"Ken," Nya began, but Ken was on a roll.

"I have just as much right as anyone to wield Kusanagi! I don't care that you think I'm too young, and I don't care that I don't even have a bloody shadow to show! I especially do not care that I was its second choice! I've beaten back everything so far, haven't I? And I've got the right to be angry, don't I? They take videos of me fighting off nightwalkers and then pretend I'm killing innocents! Who wouldn't be mad?"

"Ken!" Nya shouted, and Ken whirled around, his rage softening once he caught sight of her.

"Sorry," he muttered. "It's getting a little hard not to take the things this bloody mountain is saying personally."

"No," Tala said, staring at Kusanagi. "I think your being here is actually helping us."

"What do you mean?"

"Raise your sword."

Ken did. Kusanagi was black as sin and yet still shining. Tala could see it pulling some odd smokelike tendrils from around them, funneling them into the blade.

"I see!" Nya gasped. "Whatever it is that's making the people violent—it's mitigating some of the effects."

"Juuchi Yosamu is fused inside the sword," Loki said. "Normally it would protect you from all this, Ken. I think it's doing that for the rest of us—not enough to completely shut out the negative energy but just enough to keep us sane."

"Um, hey, Zoe." It was Dexter's voice that came through, and he sounded nervous. "I, uh, moved the equipment we've been using to monitor you to a private room instead, away from the others. Uh, the others are indisposed, so I'll be the one talking to everyone for now."

"What do you mean? Where's Alex?"

"That's the problem. Whatever it is that is making you all snippy with each other is affecting us here too. Not to the same extent, but enough for Aunt Lumina to realize what was happening. Everyone's back to normal since we moved this far enough where the rest can't hear through the comm, but Alex and Tristan are here with me, and they're still arguing, and I don't really know how to make them *not* fight."

"What's that?" Brandt gasped. "All the way to Avalon?"

Tala could hear Alex's voice from a distance with his voice raised, shouting. "You don't get to pin your parents' disappointment with you on me! I didn't ask you to kiss me back then. You thought you could get away with it, and then you blamed me when you couldn't!"

"I didn't see you coming out of the closet back then either!" Tristan shouted back. "You didn't want to let anyone else know just as much as I did! I don't owe you anything to tell! It's my life!"

"He's right," Cole said unexpectedly. Tala wasn't sure he even knew he'd said it out loud.

Zoe glared at him. "Maybe not everything, but there's a give-and-take to a relationship! Any information you hide could affect me too!"

"Affect you?" Cole gripped Gravekeeper so hard it looked like he was actually squeezing the black smoky tendrils out of its hilt. "You want to know what I saw in the mirror, Carlisle? I saw myself dying.

All your fussing about whether we hit some milestone in our shared prophecy that you can check off your pros and cons list means nothing." His voice dropped. "I'm going to die. That's it. There's nothing else to do but wait for it."

Everyone had fallen silent, stunned. Even the terrible voices that the mountain's curse had brought on had gone quiet.

"Cole," Zoe said quietly. "You don't know that yet."

"I've always known that. My doom always said so. The mirror at the Ryugu-jo confirmed it. And that's why it might be better if I do this alone. But I shouldn't have taken it out on you. We shouldn't have gotten into a—"

"If you're going to tell me right now that you regret being with me," Zoe said furiously, "I am going to walk over there and smack you so hard it will echo within these caves for a million years, and this is *me* speaking, not this awful mountain curse. I'm not going to give up. I don't care what any ridiculous mirror is telling you."

"I'm trying," Ken said helplessly, waving Kusanagi around Cole, as if Juuchi Kosamu contained within it could stanch the other boy's emotions. "But I think Cole feels things a lot more strongly than we first thought."

"I am very sorry to interrupt," Tito Boy signed, "and I know this is important to the both of you, but we all ought to do so at a later time. I think we've reached the end of our journey."

He pointed toward the end of the passageway, where an odd light glinted from within.

"Can we talk about this later?" Zoe asked. "Please?"

A quiet inhale from Cole and a nod.

Tito Boy was the first to step through, and the others quickly followed.

It took a moment for Tala to realize they were not the first ones to enter the room.

The attack, when it came, was swift.

14

IN WHICH POSITIVE REINFORCEMENT SAVES THE DAY

The flute didn't look like it possessed any extraordinary abilities. It looked like the kind that Tala saw at a typical store that sold similar musical instruments. It was lying on top of a large slab of stone in the center of the room, and small rays of light from somewhere above the cavern just so happened to be trained on it like a well-placed spotlight.

Across the cave from them stood Vivien Fey. She was still carrying her wind fan, already raised. Another exit to the cave stood behind her, obviously where she had emerged from. With her were the shadows with the now-horrifyingly familiar patchwork of legs and arms, some sporting more than was the human norm.

She moved just as Loki did, both of them racing toward the flute, trying to get there before the other could, but reaching it at nearly the same time.

The flute did not appreciate this.

A sudden explosion threw them both backward. Loki hit the ground and rolled effortlessly, getting back on their feet quickly enough. Vivien took longer, staggering. The flute lay exactly where it had been before.

"Is this another trick?" Vivien hissed. Her clothes were dirty and her face smudged black, hair in tangles. That she had not gone through the mountain's curse unscathed was evident.

"We're not going to let you take the flute, Fey," Loki said angrily.

"I've had to endure this dratted Hamelin mountain insulting my dead sister. I won't be coming out of here empty-handed." She started, turning to address something that wasn't there. "And don't you dare say that about her!"

A sharp gesture from her slashed at the side of the cave, leaving a groove several inches deep in the wall. Another tore toward them, and it was Tito Boy, expertly weaving his own abanico to cut the incoming attack in half, who halted its progress.

And then everything turned to chaos.

The magic was thicker here, Tala realized. She could sense it now when she hadn't during the journey, which meant the effects on them would be much worse. No wonder Brandt had said that there were many cases of people going insane the closer they neared the center.

None of the Banders were at the point yet that they would actually draw weapons against each other, thanks to Kusanagi, but the anger was real.

"I can hold my own just fine!" West yelled, clapping his hands over his head. "My accomplishments are my own and not my family's! I was the antifa dog! I inspired people! You can't tell me I haven't done anything worth talking about!"

"Is that why you've been avoiding me?" Ken asked Nya heatedly.

"Am I boring to you now? Do you think I'm going to ditch you or something just because the world's watching me, waiting for me to mess up?"

"Of course not!" Nya snapped. "What I'm doing right now is protecting *you*!"

"Protecting?" Ken's eyes narrowed. Both seemed to have forgotten that Vivien Fey and her band of shades were even there. "What are you doing behind my back that means you need to protect me, Rapunzel? Because you've been awfully secretive since we returned from the Ryugu-jo."

"I can't tell you right now!"

"*Another* secret? Like you didn't learn from the last time you decided not to tell me that you were, I dunno, a freaking *mermaid*? Do you really want us to go through all that again?"

"No, but I don't have a choice!" Nya's eyes filled with tears. "Someone filmed Grandma and the other villagers fighting at the Sea of Japan. There's talk now of hunters who want to get more illegal ports into Avalon to start hunting us all over again!"

"And I want to help you, but I can't do that if I don't know what you and your grandma are even planning!"

"There's no use talking about it," Cole said, sounding about as gloomy as someone like him could be, his previous rage dissipated. "I've accepted what's going to happen, and so should you."

"And you're going to break up with me because you think you're going to die?" Zoe challenged him.

"It's not like this is going to last, is it?"

"I want to shake you so hard right now! You really think so little of me that you expect me to give up on us?"

Ryker had staggered back. He was leaning against the wall, his face suddenly pale.

"What's wrong?" Tala asked, but he merely shook his head at her, his hand clutching one side of his head like he was in pain.

"I can—I can hear them," he rasped. "Farah, Kari, Ben—so many others." He turned his head. "Are they here?" he asked desperately.

"It's all in your head. You have to fight it."

"But you don't understand. I *want* them to be real. If they're real, then that means they escaped her. They can't—" He let out a quiet sob. "I can't. They can't be gone. I won't let them be gone."

The fight had revolved mainly around Vivien, Loki, and the other soldiers. The woman was blocking most of their blasts with ease, simply using the fan to deflect any projectiles coming her way. It was harder to shake off Loki and their staff, which was also good at warding off the sharp gusts of wind she was tossing in their direction. Even the shades were not immune to the powerful curse, stopping in their tracks to waver briefly whenever Vivien did, and Tala realized they were affected by it because they shared some strange link to the former OzCorp employee.

"Give it up," Vivien snarled. "You fight on the wrong side of history."

"You're the one controlling the nightmare body horrors," Tala snapped. "You tell me if that looks like you're on the right side of history."

She smiled. "Even shades are a finite resource in Beira. It was easier to imbue a part of their essences into corpses. My time at OzCorp taught me to both economize and innovate, even if their executives were greedy fools."

Loki's staff swept through the crowd of corpse shades. Several leaped toward them with a snarl but were immediately waylaid by another shadow—one that possessed none of their human limbs. It punched one hard and then swiveled around for a fistfight with several more.

Tala realized, even as she was focusing all her strength into warding the other shades away from both her and the still-despondent Ryker, that this looked like the same shadow that had been with her at the Ryugu-jo, likely the same one that had fought with them at the Burn as well.

"You think you had it bad?" Vivien's lips twisted into a pained grimace. "At least you have a good family who cares about you. What did I have? Parents who thought I was a good-for-nothing, who spent my whole childhood mocking me for being odd. Who later saw me as nothing but a paycheck to support their lifestyle. All I had was Abigail, and even she was taken away from me. I have *nothing* now. You don't know how good you've got it, and you still think *you've* been wronged?"

"And you believe the Snow Queen's going to do anything about it?" Tala shouted. "You know she's going to bleed you dry just as your parents tried to. Just as OzCorp did."

"Don't you think I know that?" Vivien shouted back and then looked startled that she'd even dared to say it out loud. "I have no other choice," she whispered. "This is the only path I can take. And if I fall, then at least I'll take them down with me!"

Somewhere in all the tumult, Tala was aware of someone else shouting, growing in volume with every second until she realized it was Dexter, shouting through their shared link.

"You are all good people, and you are valid! I appreciate every one of you for being my friend through everything, and I am better for having known you all!"

Tala had no idea how loud the volume on their earpieces could be turned up, but Dexter was hitting the maximum strength, and he was so loud that it was starting to shut out everything else. She could see everyone around her hesitating, finally stopping their arguments long enough to listen.

"Ken!" Dexter hollered. "You were always kind to me, always going out of your way to treat me like I'm a warrior in my own right, even when I can't fight like the rest of you. Thank you for that. Nya! You are the warmest, kindest, nicest person I know, and I like how you always put other people's concerns over your own, although you really shouldn't be doing that too much. But it's so like you to. Zoe! You always understand how to make everyone feel better just by being in the room with them, and you always know how to cheer me up when I'm at my lowest. Loki, you are so strong! So, so strong. You take on so many responsibilities on your own so it would mean fewer duties for your friends, and I think highly of you all the more for it. Cole, I was scared of you at first, but I understand now that it's because you don't like anyone worrying about you, even if they should! And also that one time I was worried about taking on this job, and you sat me down and told me not to worry 'cause I'm good at it and made me feel like I could take on anything, thank you so much! West, you have the purest heart of us all, and I hope you never change. Any pack would be glad to have you as a member. And, Tala—"

Dexter paused to cough, embarrassed.

"I think you're great. You came into this not knowing anything, but you've always risen to the occasion and fought just as hard as everyone else. I think you're the soul of this team and that everyone is better off for having you here with us. And, er, that's all I got. And I really mean all of this! It's not just because I've asked the techmages here to amplify this with all the positive reinforcement spells we have on hand. I really, really like all of you! Please don't fight! Did it work? I'm hoping it worked!"

"If you mean that all the good thoughts you've been shouting our way is enough to break the verbally abusive spells that this place is awash in, then I'd say yeah, it kinda did." Ken grabbed Nya and planted a great big noisy kiss on her lips. Nya made a faint muffle of protest but wrapped her arms around him. "Now that I've got my boost, let's end this and get out of here before something else tells me I'm bad at kissing too."

He rushed to the stone slab where the flute still lay and leaped, Kusanagi catching on to some of the beams of light, making it glint. For a moment, the sword looked like it was made of two completely different kinds of steel juxtaposed over each other—a gleaming bright blade overlapping one of an opaque, matte black.

He sliced the whole rock in half, and something in the air seemed to shift, the sudden fizzle of magic dissipating loud to Tala's ears. The stone crumbled noisily, sending up clouds of dust into the air.

But Vivien, nimble as ever, was already dashing forward, having anticipated the move. She snatched up the flute triumphantly before anyone else could, lifting it frantically to her lips.

The awful clash of melody was horrible. Tala was on her knees before she knew it, trying desperately to keep the sound out of her ears. All around her, everyone was following suit, reeling back from the revolting noise. Even Tito Boy and some of the other soldiers dropped to the ground, looking stunned by the sounds they shouldn't have been able to hear. Vivien herself dropped the flute, hands rising to her head and flinching from the dissonant notes she'd created.

Zoe was the first to shake it off, the first to grab the flute next. She lifted it and Tala cringed, expecting another wave. But a sweet melody flowed out instead, almost as beautiful as what the adarna could make.

Vivien gasped. And then her whole body grew slack, her eyes glazing over. All around her, the shades under her control were doing the same.

"Dexter," Tala whispered raggedly. "Do you see this?"

"And I can hear it too. I didn't know Zoe could play." Alex was back. "I'm opening up a port directly to where your coordinates are. I don't know what's happened, but the magic around the place is gone, though I don't know for how long—I'm guessing until Zoe stops playing. Get out of there!"

Even as he spoke, a looking glass glittered into view before them. Tito Boy gave a signal to the others.

But Nya had other ideas. She was darting toward the other side of the cave, where the hybrid shades were at their thickest.

"Rapunzel!" Ken yelled, but Nya was triumphantly snagging the friendly shade from within a mob of its fellows. Another swipe of her hand scattered a thick cloud of some strange powder over the rest. The shades began to shrivel up, the parts of them that had been human flesh rapidly decaying. Nya reached into her pouch and took out the turquoise-colored box.

There was another flash of bright light. When it was gone, Nya was sitting on the ground, stunned and frustrated. The other shadows were actually backing away from her as if fearful of what they'd witnessed her do. "Dammit," she groaned. "I was so close!"

Zoe continued to play, though from her strained face, she was struggling.

Vivien pushed through the music to begin another attack, lashing out with her fan again. The blow aimed at Zoe was deflected easily when Cole grasped his sword and swung, countering the force. But Vivien was already scrambling toward a portal that had materialized beside her, slipping through and winking out of view.

Zoe sank to the floor, her breaths coming out in exhausted, uneven pants. "It's *fighting* me," she said in between grunts. "No wonder Siegfried decided to leave it here. It's like battling a whole army of shades but in my mind."

"I didn't even know you could play," West said.

"Playing the recorder was a prerequisite in the boarding schools I've had to attend." And then Zoe let out a squeak as Cole scooped her up in his arms. "I can walk!" she protested, but she wrapped her arms around his neck anyway.

"I know," the boy said gruffly. "Carlisle, I didn't mean—I'm sorry—"

"So am I. I think the flute brought out the worst in all of us. You're not going to break up with me?"

"I plan to do everything in my power to stay with you."

"Ken!" There was a second yelp, this time from Nya, when Ken copied Cole's actions with her. "I'm all right!"

"I'm sorry," Ken said hastily. "I know you have good reason to not tell me things sometimes. I run my mouth off a lot, and I wind up blurting out a lot of things I shouldn't even be saying. It was bad of me to demand that, especially when your village is already in danger because they swam all the way to Japan to help us—"

Nya took Ken's face firmly in her hands and then kissed him thoroughly. "You do run your mouth off sometimes," she said. "But I still have to keep you in the dark. Please, please trust that I am doing everything to protect you, even as you're protecting me and everyone else."

Ken paused. "So you're saying everything hinges on my not knowing things?" he asked.

"I'm afraid so."

"Am I doing a good job, not knowing?"

"You're doing an excellent job."

"Well, it's not like I already know what I'm bloody doing anyway. I don't think it's gonna be all that different for me to *not* know more than what I already don't."

"You trust me that much?" Nya's eyes were shining.

"As long as one of us knows what to do, then that's all right. And since that's always been you anyway, it's not like anything's really changed, has it?"

"Can we finish up all the apologies and reconciliations at Maidenkeep before someone steals the flute a second time?" Alex asked testily.

Tala helped Ryker back to his feet. The boy was still pale, and his melancholy had not completely gone away after Zoe stopped playing. "Guess you never needed this collar, Tala," he said with a poor attempt at lighthearted humor. "Seems like my one weakness has always been the past I don't know how to escape from."

"Ryker," Tala said, now gripped with a sudden certainty. "What did you see in the mirror inside the Ryugu-jo?"

"I died," Ryker said, smiling. "That's the best contribution I can make to Avalon's goals, or so the future says. At least you've got one less enemy to worry about now."

15

IN WHICH, BELAY THAT EARLIER STATEMENT, IT'S THE WILD HUNT THAT'S ACTUALLY THE WORLD'S WORST TOURIST ATTRACTION

Ryker had refused to elaborate once they were back in Avalon, and Tala had chosen not to pry. She had no right to demand that he recount what was obviously a traumatic moment to have to relive, but a part of her was stubborn. There had to be some way that the future could be altered. Hadn't the Baba Yaga herself done so by changing Alex's future?

Tala stood in between Ryker and Loki now, who had both decided she needed a bodyguard and were pissed that the other had come to the same conclusion. The adarna was back on her head, fussing over her a little, as if questioning whether she was all right.

Zoe had turned the flute over to Alex and the Gallaghers, though Tala didn't think they would find much more out of it than they had the lotus lantern or the tamatebako.

The mysterious singing bone was next on the list, and it was the one they had the least information about. There were no other nightwalkers reported within the vicinity of Löwenberg forest. "It could be that there's something in the woods itself that repels night-walker activity," Lord Suddene surmised, "or that they are naturally afraid of the Wild Hunt."

"Why would they be?" West asked.

"Every rational person in Germany fears the Wild Hunt for good reason," General Tobias Schreiber explained. He had replaced Brandt as their liaison for the next artifact, the latter having requested some time off to recuperate from the ordeal, and Tala couldn't blame him. Schreiber, fortunately, was just as efficient. He had brought a heavy-looking stained suitcase with him, which looked odd in contrast to his crisp business suit and slightly meticulous air. "It is said that everyone who even sees the hunt is doomed to travel with them for the rest of eternity or until the curse is lifted. Those who have com-mitted wicked deeds, on the other hand, are slain on the spot."

"So whoever leads the hunt is at least someone with a strong sense of justice, even if it's a little overenthusiastic?" Loki asked.

"Quite the opposite. There are many legends surrounding its possible leaders, but none of them were known to be good men."

"Punishment for the crimes they committed in life?" Zoe asked. She couldn't stop holding Cole's hand, and Cole wasn't stopping her either. Everyone had been quick to patch up their differences follow-ing the initial awkwardness. Even Alex and Tristan had managed to sort things out, and they kept sneaking furtive glances when they thought the other wasn't looking. Dexter had been the star of the hour, everyone taking turns to thank him for his quick thinking, and the young techmage had beamed with shy pride.

"No one's fool enough to find out for themselves." Schreiber looked wary. "Ah, excepting current company, of course."

"I'm almost tempted to leave this one well alone," Alex confessed. "The Snow Queen doesn't seem as willing to get her hands on this one if the lack of nightwalkers is an indication."

But Schreiber shook his head. "The queen has been trying to infiltrate Löwenberg for many centuries now, long before Sir Inoue here ever laid hands on the sword. Long before Avalon was encased in ice."

"We didn't know that."

"We try not to make ourselves look weaker on the global stage, Your Majesty. It is often ice maidens she sends out—in twos or threes, never enough to attract attention but enough to do damage. We have lost many soldiers this way, though we have always been successful at repelling their attacks. And what we cannot defend, the Wild Hunt takes themselves. Many of those ice maidens, like many of my fellow countrymen, went missing after their alleged encounters with the Horned One, the hunt's leader."

"Is the Wild Hunt really that dangerous?" Ken asked.

"Some say the devil himself leads the pursuit, Avalon wielder. Even those who have raised the sword before you chose not to involve themselves with the spirits in these woods. Leave them to their pursuit, I like to say."

"Then what changed?" Zoe asked. "You're not happy at the idea of us getting involved, but you also say we have no other choice."

Schreiber lifted the suitcase onto the table. "If I may, Your Majesty."

Tala had been expecting German spelltech, perhaps weapons to combat ice maidens. What she wasn't expecting was a very dead, thoroughly mummified body. Its features were drastically shrunken and withered.

"Meet one of the participants of the Wild Hunt," Schreiber said dryly as everyone clustered around to stare at the macabre sight. "Very rarely do we find these in perfect condition in our woods."

"In perfect condition?" West echoed. "You call this in perfect condition?"

"One that hasn't crumbled completely into dust, yes. Members of the Wild Hunt appear ageless and immortal—as long as they are not knocked off their mounts. But when they are, they shrivel up almost immediately and die, centuries of old age catching up to them. We have already recovered six of these. Please do not touch them, Ranger Sun-Wagner," he added when a faint prod on its leg by Loki caused a part of the mummy's flesh to rapidly evaporate into air. "The satchel contains a special coagulant spell that binds their form in place, but they are easily damaged."

"Sorry," Loki said, jerking back their hand guiltily. "Six, you said?"

"Six in two days, when we would be lucky to find one or two every few years and almost always in body parts. These were frozen before they were killed, which helped preserve them. It also tells me that there are ice maidens—or worse—within the woods, and that the Wild Hunt is not faring as well against them as they have before."

"Sounds like the Snow Queen's trying to use subterfuge to take the bone this time," Ryker said.

Schreiber eyed him warily. "I understand that you are now a close ally of Avalon, Lord Cadfael, but you must forgive me if I say I still have my doubts."

"And I don't blame you. I won't sugarcoat the things I did in the past, and I hope to use what I know of the Snow Queen to help. But I don't know anything about the Wild Hunt. I do know that the Snow Queen has occasionally sent some of her ice maidens there over the years as a way to test their loyalty." He turned away. "They never returned. And I used to be fine with that, because the ice maidens she sent...they were some of the cruelest people I've ever met. I always thought she chose them because their viciousness had a likelier chance of succeeding."

"Did she ever say what it was she was looking for there?" Tala asked.

"She only said that the leader of the hunt had something that belonged to her once."

"It's either this or the raskovnik next," Zoe said. "What do you think, Lord Suddene?"

"The dangers are just as great at World's End, milady," the duke said soberly.

"Why do they call it World's End?" Tala asked.

"One of the last battles between Koschei and the Avalonians was fought there. This place became the graves of whole regiments, though the magic was so strong that there was nothing of them left to bury. They call it World's End because many thought it would *be* the end of the world. Their fight was so destructive that a powerful barrier was erected by Avalon's queen, Talia, to keep it from spilling into other kingdoms, binding it to the area at the cost of her life. The wall that stands now is a testament to her power, continuing to protect us from what lies beyond it."

"So it's like an even worse version of Wonderland," Ken said.

"The same kind of magic that was used to create the Jolly Roger," Captain Mairead said, joining the discussion.

"It has the potential to be that powerful?" Loki asked, aghast.

"Aye. It was a blatant abuse of the powers bestowed on Hook, and Pan was just as much a fool for attempting to wrest it away from the pirate. We are still reviled in many parts of the world for the fear that we may cause another similar cataclysm. It is similar to why many detest Avalon and its Nine Maidens yet at the same time covet its power for their own."

"Is the shadow magic you use tied to the ship too?"

"In a way. Old Neverland lore says we keep our souls in our shadows, and we believe it. Peter Pan could manipulate his, you know. Knew enough to give him his near immortality. Not enough to survive a continent-wide explosion, though. That knowledge's been lost since. We could control ours to punch an ingrate or twelve, but that's about it."

"Can you?" West asked. "Make another explosion like that?"

The pirate leader pursed her lips. "The repercussions of both Pan's and Hook's excesses still linger within my ship's psyche, Sir Eddings. The blast crippled the *Jolly Roger*, took half of its original strength. No longer is it as powerful as it once was under Hook and his crew. Perhaps it is for the better. And what vision do I see before me now?"

The last had been directed at the Baba Yaga, who'd just entered the room. "Your Majesty," the seeress greeted courteously.

"How are you feeling?" Alex asked them courteously.

"Much better, thank you. I have reached out to both the Dame of Tintagel and the Nottingham dowager. There are things I would like to discuss with them."

"Do you all know something that's about to happen that you're refusing to tell us?" Nya asked. "Does my grandmother know too?"

The Baba Yaga only grinned. "Nothing ever gets past your grandmother, Nya. With the exception of the Makilings, of course."

"I fear I can no longer say the same," Captain Mairead said. "Rarely do I let such loveliness escape my notice. You must be new to Maidenkeep, lest I would have taken earlier heed of your presence."

The Baba Yaga shot a startled look at the pirate and then smiled. "Well," they said. "Well, well."

"What are you proposing to discuss with the three other known seers of Avalon, Baba Yaga?" Alex asked suspiciously.

"As I've said before, the battle that is to come." Baba Yaga paused, their eyes looking up at the ceiling, their expression perplexed for a few minutes before their face cleared. "Oh," they said. "So that's what it meant. I understand now."

"Pardon?"

"The burnings around Avalon," the Baba Yaga said. "For so long, I thought they meant that Maidenkeep would falter, that all would be lost, but no. It is simply that Maidenkeep will no longer be where Maidenkeep once stood."

"And what's that supposed to mean? I am getting pretty tired of all these mysterious—"

But the Baba Yaga was already turning around with a flourish. "There will be tragedy of course, and we must mourn what must come to pass. But I see it now. Messinda, you clever, clever woman."

"What?" Alex asked a third time, but the seer had already flounced out, still talking to themselves. As if drawn by some unseen magnet, Captain Mairead followed them out.

"What's the use of having a prophet in Maidenkeep if they're not likely to tell us anything?" Ken asked.

"My grandma's a seeress," Nya said, "and she's still not telling me squat either."

"We can yell at them all later," Alex grumbled. "We have a decision to make. We can't afford to leave those last three artifacts alone. The Snow Queen has turned far too many people into Deathless. If there's a chance we can turn them back with those last three…"

"Thank you, Alex," Ryker said gratefully.

"We are ready to assist whenever you are ready," Schreiber said. "But I cannot give the order that could doom my men to become spirits of the Wild Hunt. The risks are too great."

"I won't ask you to, General." The king looked back at his friends. "And I won't ask any of you to either. There are dangerous—"

"It's like you don't even know us, Your Majesty," Ken said, grinning. "I'm ready when you are."

"So am I," Ryker said quietly.

"All opposed?" Zoe called out, and silence was her answer.

Alex's mouth moved, and Tala knew he was planning on joining them. But Tristan was already glaring daggers at the king, already anticipating what his answer was, and in the end, Alex only sighed.

"Assemble before the courtyard in the next five minutes. The Germans will have a port ready and waiting for you there. I want you all to stay in contact with Avalon command. We'll keep all the other artifacts here but the lantern. We've come too far, and I expect you all back as soon as you find the bone."

Tala took a step closer to Tristan while the king issued more orders to his officers. It felt like this was the only chance she was going to get for a while to get her own answers from him. "Thank you for looking after Alex," she said quietly.

"Thank you for suggesting to him that I'm not as bad as he thinks I am. Though I'm not quite sure he's wrong with his assumptions."

"I was surprised you even came to Avalon."

He understood the unspoken question she was asking. "You thought I would choose not to speak up again. I understand. That's what I've always done before. Trying to pretend I'm what my parents think I am—both with Alex and with Zoe." His eyes strayed back to Alex, a softer expression stealing across his face. "It's different now. If he dies, then there's not much of a life left for me to pretend for. He doesn't like that I'm too assertive this time. But I should have been doing that from the beginning. I—I don't intend to hurt Alex again. I want you to know that too."

Tala nodded, satisfied. "I'll cut your balls off if you do."

Strangely enough, Tristan grinned. "I'd let you."

Despite Schreiber's assertion, several of the soldiers offered to guide them into the woods or at least part of the way into Wild Hunt territory. One handed Zoe a large case the size of a pet carrier. It was light enough for Zoe to accept without difficulty.

They had to travel alone after that, and it was easy to see why the Germans had refused to come any farther. While the rest of the forest had been teeming with flora and fauna, the decay here was palpable, from the yellowing, browned leaves of sickly looking trees to the ground itself.

"The soldiers believe it's because of the dead flesh that's accumulated here over the centuries," Nya whispered.

"That doesn't sound right," Loki said. "Macabre as it sounds, bodies mean more soil nutrients."

"Yeah, but they believe the bodies have been corrupted. Like there's poison inside them." Nya pointed at something half-hidden behind a sparsely leaved bush. With a shudder, Tala recognized it as a skull, brown from age and cracked in several places.

And then Nya gasped, much louder this time, and Tala saw a body stretched out some distance behind it, limbs stiffened in rigor mortis, the remains of a tongue lolling out.

"Seven bodies now," Cole said grimly.

"Hear anything, West?" Ken asked from atop Horse. The rest were riding horses at the moment—steeds specifically bred by the German fighters in the region to be fast. They were disciplined; not a one shied away from Cole, who always tended to make horses nervous. Tala's mount was named Lightning, a surefooted chestnut stallion that didn't need her guidance to follow the others.

Kelpies weren't comfortable in woods, Tala knew, but Horse

showed no signs of nervousness, only lifting its ear eagerly, ready to ride into battle if its owner would let it.

West had assumed hound form, sitting beside both Horse and its rider. He pointed his muzzle toward the east and let out a low affirming growl. His assertion was confirmed by the adarna, who let out a soft coo.

"I think something's approaching," Tala said.

"This is going to be a little different from our other missions," Zoe said briskly. "The Germans offered some strategies when dealing with the Wild Hunt, and it all boils down to being fast enough to keep out of their range and avoiding a direct confrontation. They say that once you're close enough to see the hunt, you're as good as dead, so they keep an ear out for the sounds of a stampede or yelling."

"That's not a very good strategy for us, Zoe," Ken pointed out. "We're not here just to run away."

"They did share one specific tactic. They occasionally capture a few shades out here." Zoe lifted the carrying case. "The Wild Hunt lives to run down nightwalkers, so we can use them as bait. Cole can stab them through with his sword to keep them obedient."

"There's a shade inside that?"

"You were too busy admiring the horses when they were giving the rest of us instructions."

"Did he give us any advice to, I dunno, bloody convince the Horned One or whoever that's supposed to be to turn over the singing bone?"

"They have no idea either. Lord Suddene couldn't find so much as a hint about it. We'll have to see the hunt for ourselves to make that assessment—and get out quick if we can't find some other alternative."

Tala was starting to hear things. The once quiet woods were slowly coming to life, but not with the sounds of nature. She could hear a faint rumbling from a distance—an approaching herd of horses. She could hear shouts too, but not in a language that she recognized as either English or German.

"Do we release the shades now?" Loki asked tersely.

Zoe shook her head, her gaze focused on where the sounds were originating from, which was growing louder with every heartbeat. "Wait for it," she said.

The thundering grew. Now the cries were more distinct. There was a faint underlying echo behind each one, an unearthly effect that gave the impression of a chorus despite the rough, cacophonous noise.

"Zoe?" Alex's voice returned.

"Tala?" Lumina's question followed his. "I can hear them. Alex, there's enough time for me to port over there and help—"

"I need you here right now, Auntie. I know Lord Keer's defenses are holding, but we can't let them through, and I want you ready to move in the next five minutes to nullify any looking glass—"

"Excuse me?" Tala asked. "What's happened since we left?"

"Just another attack," Alex said hastily. "Nothing more serious than before—"

"A bunch of mercenaries have ported near Avalon," Tristan's voice broke in. "American, only this time trained and disciplined, unlike the first batch. They're still not faring very well against the Avalon wards the Gallaghers have reinforced."

"Tristan!" Alex snarled.

"Alex!" Tala snapped.

"Like I said, there's nothing to worry about. We're keeping an eye on things. I've instructed Mairead to port in at the Löwenberg boundary should things get hairy." Alex's voice rose. "Tristan, if you're going to undermine every command that I—" He shut off communication abruptly.

Tala scowled and turned her attention back to her present surroundings. The firebird let out a long sigh on Loki's shoulder.

"Sounds like they're getting serious," Ryker said.

"We all should be," Tala said. "Allegedly, no one's ever survived to see the Wild Hunt, so even with Ken here, it's—"

"No, I mean Alex and Tristan. Alex gets that little hitch in his voice sometimes when he's trying to pretend nothing's wrong, when in reality all he wants to do is strangle someone."

"You still know his tells?"

"Hey, I was around the both of you long enough to notice. Like you." He reached out and squeezed her hand. "You always sound the most indifferent when you're at your most worried. I could tell inside Hamelin. Even when I wasn't myself there. Never thanked you yet for seeing me safe."

"Don't even think about it."

"See? Indifferent." Ryker turned and eyed Loki, who'd drifted closer. "Can't you give us some private time for once?" he muttered.

"Just staying close. Dangerous territory all around."

"If you've been around me long enough," Tala said, "then you also know that I do care about you. Even though it sometimes feels like you don't care about yourself at all."

She saw Loki's shoulders stiffen, but Ryker ignored them, the small smile on his face fading. "About the Ryugu-jo. I'm sorry. I wasn't trying to hide anything from you. I know that your feelings for me have changed, and that's all right. That doesn't mean mine have, but that shouldn't matter. When I looked in the mirror, I saw—"

"Get ready!" Zoe's voice rang out.

West's fur was literally rising on his back. His body was arched, tensed to spring.

Ryker snapped back to attention, and so did Tala, despite her burning curiosity about what he was about to say.

All her wondering disappeared the instant the Wild Hunt came into view.

Tala had seen those old English foxhunts in movies sometimes, and she'd been disgusted by them. But this was not a band of rich people decked out in riding gear and pedigree horses. This hunt was composed of the strangest bunch of riffraff she'd ever seen.

Every clothing style from every walk of life from the last five hundred years or so, possibly more, was represented within that mob, from bedraggled, dead-eyed men that belied their dated but luxurious-looking hunting clothes to highwaymen and robbers dressed in bandannas and rough linen. There were knights wearing dented armor and sporting lances, riding beside soldiers with bayonets strapped to their backs and wielding crossbows. There were fighters who looked like they had been born in the latter half of the century, equipped with rifles. There were others who were weapon-less, likely unlucky travelers from the distant past who'd been caught up, doomed to spend eternity chasing a purpose they never wanted.

There were far too many of them. The riders stretched out behind the pack for miles, and it was alarming to Tala that they hadn't heard them approach earlier. Their forms were faded and indistinct like ghosts. And leading the pack was—

Now she understood why people believed a demon led the Wild Hunt. Its leader was a monster. It had no human face but a skull reminiscent of some wild buffalo or moose, with a terrifying set of horns curling atop its gleaming head. The bone of its jaw widened, and blackness was all its mouth was made of. Its gaze was a sunken pair of eyeholes with a strange fire burning within their depths, like it carried flames within itself. In one hand, it carried the largest sword she'd ever seen, easily twice as tall as she was. It appeared to be con-structed entirely of bone, though she had no idea what kind of terri-fying creature it could have been made out of. It sat astride a destrier that was just as much a skeleton as it was.

It turned those blank, burning eyes their way, and at some invisi-ble signal, the rest of the pack changed course to bear down on them.

"Now!" Zoe shouted and flung open the case.

16

IN WHICH THE HORNED ONE HAS STUNT DOUBLES

The two shades within had none of the human corpse limbs that Tala and the others had to fight last time. They knew enough to spot the Wild Hunt gunning for them and flee, though they were not faster than Cole. Gravekeeper cut into them quickly, and they resumed their flight, though this time under Nottingham control.

Both shadows dodged to the left, away from where Tala and the others stood. The Horned One was close at their heels, and the rest of the riders followed.

It would have been impossible to trail behind the hunt; given its size, it would take days for the pack's stragglers to pass. Their faces were carefully blank, devoid of fear or anger or any other emotion, though they were likely prisoners themselves, bound to their leader out of misfortune.

Cole's steed broke into a hard gallop, pushing the shades to move faster before the Horned One could catch up. All it took was a nudge from Ken for Horse to follow, never one to be second. Tala didn't have as much experience with horseback riding—her last stint had been back at the Avalon frost, when the Earl of Tintagel had kindly lent them mounts for their journey to Maidenkeep—but her stallion needed no instructions, simply racing in step with the rest of the herd as they ran after Horse.

The Horned One was slowly but surely catching up. Cole gritted his teeth and sent his horse moving faster. The shades split up, one turning left while the other dashed to the right.

The firebird was practically on top of the creature, breathing fire onto it to no effect. Its angry bleating at the failure to burn it could be heard for miles around.

The Horned One blurred and split into two versions of itself, each racing after a shade. The firebird paused, confused, trying to figure out which to pursue.

"What the bloody hell is going on?" Tala heard Ken shout.

The magic their leader wielded didn't seem to apply to the rest of the hunt's riders. Some simply turned to join one of the Horned Ones while others rode after the other.

"This bastard can split into a million copies of itself if it wants, just to make sure there'll be no survivors," Ryker growled, his horse keeping pace beside Tala's.

If it caught the shades, the Horned One was likely to turn on them again. "Where's the singing bone?" Nya cried out. "The only bone I can see is the damned thing itself."

The adarna attempted to warble a few more notes, but it sounded like something was caught in its throat instead.

Loki hefted the lantern. For once, no light shone from its depths. "Feels like there's a strange barrier that can't be broken by this or the adarna's music."

A chunk of sharp-edged ice manifested against Ryker's fingers, and he lobbed it hard against the creature. It hit it squarely on its back, the attack shattering against the bone, but the monster didn't even pause.

"What are you doing?" Tala hissed. "Don't antagonize it!"

"We can't keep riding forever. It takes a lot of strength for Nottingham to keep those shades under his control."

"Tala!" Alex was back. "We're still not getting any visuals on our end, and the spells around the woods are strong enough that we can't port in."

"The Wild Hunt's not registering in any of our scans!" That was Dexter, sounding more frantic than usual. "I see that there's a couple of shades out there, but other than that, our equipment can't detect the Horned One or any of the riders, much less—"

"How's that possible? It's right in front of us!"

"Let's try some other means of persuasion, then." Ken urged Horse even faster so that he was beside the Horned One. "Hey, you!" the boy yelled, swinging Kusanagi at it. "Hey, we just wanna talk to you for a hot sec!"

Not even the presence of the Nameless Sword slowed it down. Ken swiped at it with the blade; there was a loud clang when he found his target.

It was fortunate that Horse wasn't just any ordinary horse, because Tala could feel the electric jolt that sizzled out from the contact between blade and bone. It was enough to send Ken nearly flying off Horse's back, and some quick footwork by his kelpie was the only reason he hadn't been blasted into a nearby tree.

Tala was already thinking hard. "We made a mistake," she said.

"Coming here?" It was hard for Ryker not to sound wry. "That's what I'm starting to think."

"No, I mean that we didn't bring with us the one artifact that might actually work. Alex, do you have the Pied Piper's flute with you?"

"It hasn't left my sight since you all entered the woods."

"Good, because we need it as soon as possible."

"The woods are closed to all outside looking glasses. Maybe we can get the prime minister to lower their barriers long enough to—"

"That'll put everyone within the vicinity in danger, and they're not going to do that," Tristan said gruffly. "Hand it over to me. I'll port into the nearest mirror the Germans have available and rush it over to them."

"What? But—"

"Weren't you furious at the thought of me sticking to you like a shadow? I thought you'd appreciate the break. Neither Lola Urduja nor Aunt Lumina can leave their posts, and there's no way I want you leaving yours. I'm the most expendable you have here. They need the flute now."

"All right," Alex said reluctantly. "Get it to Zoe as soon as you can."

"Roger that!" the brunette called over her own comm link. Her horse was matching Cole's stride for stride.

It was only a matter of time. Tala heard Cole swear, saw the Horned One lift its heavy sword and lean forward from its mount's back, swinging the sword. It cleaved into a tree as it rode past, sending it toppling onto the path before them. It was enough for Cole's concentration to break as the Horned One swung again, slicing one shade clean through. The air turned fuzzy, and then the two Horned Ones were one again.

The remaining shadow spun, bolting in the opposite direction, but the skeletal figure simply spun its undead horse around, continuing the pursuit.

"I'm on the ground," came Tristan's breathless report. "I've got a lock on your location. I should be there in five minutes, as long as you all stop moving around."

"It's not like we have a choice, Locksley!" Ken growled, still swinging. "Hey! It's me you should be fighting!"

The creature ignored him. Another fatal strike lopped the final shade's head clean off its shoulders. The shadow dissipated, and for the first time since it broke through the clearing, the Horned One slowed down and stopped, and its unholy companions halted along with it. It turned to regard the rest of them with its empty eye sockets, the flames within sparking higher than before. Tala could have sworn it was smiling.

It blurred again.

Now there were eight Horned Ones staring them down, their horses pawing with glee at the ground. Eight, Tala realized, horrified, one for each of them.

Only two things ever happened to those who encountered the Wild Hunt: they were either slain on the spot if caught or forced to join its leader on its endless, vengeful ride into eternity.

"Fuck," Loki said, quite loudly and with heavy emphasis, perfectly encapsulating what everyone was already thinking.

All eight horned horsemen kicked at their horses' sides, and the beasts broke into a run.

The Banders scattered. "The border!" Tala heard Nya shout. "Ride back to the boundary! They're bound to the forest, and they shouldn't be able to cross that!"

What Nya wasn't saying was that no one had ever made it that far, but Tala obeyed nonetheless, aware of Ryker nearby on his own stallion and the two horned riders chasing them. Their horses may have been bred for speed with the Wild Hunt in mind, but it was one thing to get away when they heard the sound of hooves approaching and another to already be within sight of the creatures. Tala knew they would be overtaken before they reached safety.

Ken seemed to realize this. With a bloodthirsty yell, he wheeled Horse around and leaped forward to meet one of the horned demons head-on instead of attempting to escape. With an exasperated shout, Nya spun her horse around to chase after him, and the Horned One on her tail followed suit. She dug into her pouch and threw something behind her that solidified briefly against the air long enough for the creature's horse to ride straight into it.

It neighed angrily, rising up and kicking with its front legs, and the Horned One struggled to keep it under control, snarling as it reached down to try and wipe the sticky goop now plastered to its steed's eyes.

The firebird was swooping down and unleashing its fire. More riders were dropping, but the skeletal leaders remained unaffected.

The two Horned Ones were gaining on Tala and Ryker. A trail of ice started from behind Ryker, covering the ground behind them, but it didn't help. Both undead horses ran smoothly across it like the lack of friction made no difference. They were now close enough that a swipe of one of the Horned One's swords barely missed Tala by a few inches.

The adarna had briefly flown off Tala's head. There were heavy spatters as poop rained down on some of the riders, toppling them off their steeds' backs. Some even hit a Horned One, though to no effect.

Tala stopped abruptly, spun. The blade that came crashing toward her head stilled in midair as her agimat took hold. It took Tala everything she had to keep the sword from moving down any farther, but there was no sign of any similar weakness on the Horned One's part. Its expressionless gaze met hers as the sword started to slowly sink down.

There was a loud crash as Ken and his horned pursuer locked swords again. The other riders accompanying that incarnation had surrounded the two, watching the fight silently but without interfering themselves.

"So now you pay attention," Ken snarled. Despite the heavier, larger weapon he was facing, his Kusanagi suffered no damage, able to withstand the terrible blows the Horned One was raining down. The boy attacked again, and this time his blade managed to land a slash across the Horned One's forearm.

All seven versions of the Horned One flickered, and this time Tala was sure it wasn't deliberate. It was as if Kusanagi had affected them all instead of just the one that Ken was fighting.

One of the ghostly onlookers stiffened without warning, tumbled off its horse. It began shriveling up the instant it hit the ground, its body rapidly decaying and shrinking until there was nothing of it left.

"That's why it can't be killed!" Loki shouted. Ruyi Jingu Bang was making a valiant effort at fighting off the attacks of their version of the Horned One. "It's powered by the life force of all the other riders it's taken prisoner!"

"Damn coward is what that is." Ken swung again and was met this time with a decisive block. As if realizing they had ferreted out its weakness, the creature redoubled its efforts, and its seven counterparts did the same.

The horse that Nya had slung one of her potions at could still not completely get the sticky substance out of its eyes. Its mobility was reduced to a confused canter, but the Horned One showed no indication of dismounting. Already the girl had flung more of the concoction at both Cole's and Zoe's opponents with the same results.

Nya's triumphant smile faded when her pursuer blurred again, this time of its own volition. Another ghostly companion fell to the ground and was made dust, and the undead horse was now whinnying with glee, able to see again.

West had shifted into a sparrow and alighted on one of the branches, out of reach from his attacker and its blade.

"Leave us and find help!" Nya shouted at him.

But Ken was shaking his head, even as he matched the Horned One's blow with one of his own. "And create, like, a thousand more copies of this bastard? Just give me another minute—"

"We don't have a minute!" Zoe shouted. The Horned Ones chasing both her and Cole were already blurring and reconstituting again, two more ghostly figures toppling off their horses. "You'll have to finish off all these riders to actually kill him. Where the hell is Tris—"

A very human-sounding cough interrupted her. It was loud enough to give even the Horned Ones pause.

A black shadow lounged on one of the upper tree branches. Its relaxed stance gave every indication that if it had a face, it would be smirking at them. Tala recognized it.

The eight Horned Ones were already moving, blurring back into the one main Horned One as it found a more important target. The shade leaped immediately and tore through the forest away from them.

"Is it actually helping us?" This from West, who had changed from his sparrow form long enough to pose the question.

Nya was already urging her mount forward, glowering and riding after the shade, oblivious to Ken's yells. With a grunt, the boy urged Horse faster to overtake them.

"I'm here!" Tristan panted, bursting into the scene atop his own horse. "You all kept moving around. I couldn't—"

"Tristan!" Zoe roared, and he obeyed, making for her with the flute already in his hand.

"We tried playing it," he panted as he neared her. "I'm a bit rusty but I can still carry a tune, and Dexter is surprisingly good at it, but none of it worked, even when we turned up the comm link's volume. Either it now answers only to you, or—"

Zoe reached over and swiped the instrument out of his hands. "Talk later," she growled and then took off after Ken, Nya, and the Horned One.

The shade led the Wild Hunt on a merry chase, agile enough to stay ahead of the Horned One. Ken was coming up fast behind it as well, slicing at the creature again. More of its companions fell, but just as before, the Horned One only had eyes for the shadow.

Zoe lifted the flute to her lips.

The music didn't quite stop the Horned One or its companions completely in their tracks, but it was enough. The creature staggered, wheeling its horse every which way as if confused by the music.

It gave Cole time to retaliate, and Tristan moved to aid him. Tristan's arrows made solid thunking noises as they hit the center of the Horned One's back. Cole made quick slashes against the Horned One's arms.

Tala's vision cleared, and she was finally seeing its terrifying form in stark detail instead of the blurred shape she'd been stuck with previously, and with the discovery came another burst of clarity. "It's warded!" she cried out to the others. "It's why I couldn't see it as well before! It's surrounded by spells! That's why the adarna's songs couldn't affect it either!"

She pushed her agimat toward the Horned One. As if reading her mind, the adarna began to sing in accompaniment to Zoe's flute. The firebird sent more flames down again, this time at the ground surrounding the skeletal figures.

"Do not stop playing," came a guttural voice that emanated from within the Horned One, from its unmoving jaw. It was like how the earth might have sounded if it could speak. "Do not stop singing, and keep your curses on me."

Zoe and the adarna, though briefly stunned, understood. So did Tala, who kept her agimat stretched around him, trying to envelop as much of its massive frame as it could.

The Horned One slowed down at a sudden blast of notes from Zoe, stopped right before its blade could swipe down at Cole. It lowered its weapon slowly.

And then it stepped down from its horse.

"Can it do that?" West asked from somewhere behind her, back to human form and quietly freaking out. "Didn't the legends say it'll crumble into dust itself if it ever sets foot on the ground?"

"I think that's what the combined spells of the flute, the adarna, and Tala's agimat is preventing," Loki said quietly.

"Sword keeper," the Horned One said. "The blade rises. The time has come."

Ken was still wary, Kusanagi raised just in case he needed to do more swinging the creature's way. "You were ready to add us to your spectral band of merry men only seconds ago. Why the sudden change of heart?"

"The curse upon me spares no other thought beyond the pursuit of the hunt, abated only briefly by the enchantments of your companions. I ride to eternity, bound to slay all nightwalkers until the end of time. To recruit both willing and unwilling to my cause."

"Why would the Snow Queen curse you to hunt her own nightwalkers?"

Something shifted and clicked within its ossified mouth. "It is not the Snow Queen's curse but Arthur of Avalon's."

"*What?*" Alex had been silent for most of the chase, but his disbelieving yelp startled Tala.

"I was once a general of Buyan. Once, I delighted in the killing. At Lord Koschei's death, I took a piece of his soul for safekeeping and fled. The Avalon king could not wrest the soul from me nor destroy it, so instead he cast a curse on me with his Maidens. For this, I was doomed to wander. Now I regret my part in Koschei's plan. Only after every nightwalker has fallen can I know peace. Until then, my blade is pledged to one who is worthy of Avalon's sword, as the King of Avalon demands."

"Me?" Ken asked, astounded. "What do I even do with you?"

"The bone is yours to guard. When the time comes, the dark sword is to call us, command us as you would an army." The Horned One lifted its head, bared its chest.

"You want me to kill you?"

"When Koschei is destroyed beyond any means of resurrection shall the curse lift and I find solace."

Ken shrugged. "Good enough for me," he said and promptly stabbed the Horned One through the chest.

There was no display of light like there had been with the flute, nor the glow that had been associated with the lotus lantern. The Horned One simply stood there one second, and then no longer was in the next. And with it, the rest of its companions disappeared until only Ken was left, looking both stunned and exhilarated, now holding a piece of bone in his hand.

17

In Which the Snow Queen Returns to Avalon

I n my defense," Alex said. "I didn't know how to break the news. You were all busy being chased by something straight out of a horror movie."

"I'm sure you could have inserted a 'By the way, the private mercenary group OzCorp used for security has been pardoned by King John and is now attacking Maidenkeep together with the rest of the nightwalkers in there.' In fact, 'Maidenkeep is being attacked' is so much shorter and gets enough of the point across too."

"Didn't want to worry you. If the Royal States is coordinating with the Snow Queen, they made one huge mistake at least. They shouldn't have sent in amateurs to blow up the Burn and short out our defenses that first time, because now we know what to expect, even if these are professionals now."

The Avalon rangers were slowly adjusting to the constant attacks. The hybrid shades had a certain monotony to their tactics that made their moves much more predictable. The private mercenaries, on the other hand, had since retreated from the city, instead busying themselves by sending spelltech-powered rocket launchers their way. The barrier spells were holding steady, so those could be ignored for now.

None of this was in the Royal States news, though no one was surprised.

"You did well back there," Tristan said quietly to Cole. Surprisingly, both were standing side by side, as if they'd never been enemies. "Don't always get to see Gravekeeper in action. You always did trounce me when it came to swordfights."

"Could never beat you in archery," the other boy conceded. "You hit your mark every time."

Zoe was off to one side, eyeing them warily. "Somehow," she muttered to Tala, "seeing them like this makes me nervous."

"You do look a bit apprehensive," Tala agreed teasingly.

"It hasn't been a good day. I can't even find my sleeping needle." Zoe rubbed at both sides of her neck with a wince. "And we still have two more artifacts to go."

Ken had tried to turn over the bone to the Gallaghers for analysis, only for it to disappear right before it dropped onto Lord Gallagher's hand.

"What?" Ken raised his hand and blinked when he saw that he was still holding the bone. He tried to pass it on again, only for the exact same thing to happen, the bone once more reappearing on his palm.

"Fascinating," Severon Gallagher said. "There appears to be some limitations. The Horned One was being quite specific when it said only you could summon it to battle."

"Still not entirely sure how to go about that, honestly," Ken said, apprehensive. "Does that mean I'm the only one able to use it? I don't even know how. It's not like this comes with a damn instruction manual."

"It has only been used once that we know of," Lord Suddene admitted. "It's said that a shepherd came upon the bone while his sheep grazed and inadvertently summoned a wraith who led him to the burial grounds of one Dmitry Ivanovich, the youngest son of Ivan the Terrible. The bone sang of Boris Godunov, Ivan's advisor who had orchestrated the murder, and the latter was executed as a result."

"Well, I'm not sure how playing detective to murder mysteries is going to help against the Snow Queen. Dude said we could call on it for assistance, right?" Ken waved Kusanagi over the bone. "Hey," he said. "You up?"

Nothing happened.

"See?"

"Let us find the next artifact before anything else." Lord Suddene brought up a new display. A strange-looking plant popped into view, its leaves curled in a way that each end resembled a question mark's shape. "The raskovnik, to my knowledge, has been harvested many times before. While the lotus lantern can reveal hidden paths, the raskovnik can unlock any door or route hindered by spells, or revert someone inflicted by a curse to their natural state."

"Like the Deathless?" Ryker asked quietly.

"No one has ever made the attempt. My apologies, Lord Cadfael, but I would rather not get anyone's hopes up until we know for certain."

"World's End is located near Nibheis." Alex raised an eyebrow at Cole. "Any information you can offer regarding that?"

"It's a wasteland teeming with dangerous magic," the other

boy confirmed. "My father has banned everyone from entering its borders."

"The Snow Queen herself doesn't travel there—not that I know of anyway," Alex said. "She didn't when I was still with her."

"But why wouldn't she try to find the plant when it's so close to her realm?"

"Because she told me once that the place was barren of raskovniks now. I think she visited it in the past but came up empty-handed. It's not like anyone's found any in recent years either. Think of all the possible bank robberies they could get away with. Museum thefts. House break-ins."

"You're saying that the raskovnik doesn't exist anymore?" Alex said.

"I'm saying that she couldn't find it," Ryker said, "and I'm not sure we'd be any luckier."

"That's a lot to risk," Tala murmured, trying to approach the problem the way Zoe would. "If the raskovnik no longer grows there, then it just ups our chances of getting caught while gaining nothing, which is a con. And then there's the added likelihood that she already knows that we'll be coming and is going to set up a trap to get the plant if we do find it. Another con."

"Or maybe she found it already but didn't tell Ryker," West added. "One more con."

"Could we leave it be, then?" Loki asked.

"Lord Keer?" Lumina asked.

The Wake approached them and bowed to Tala's mother.

"Are Zoe and Nya at Ikpe?"

"They are." The man turned to Dexter, who promptly switched the screen to that of a worried-looking woman. Behind her was a room devoid of any furnishings, with heavy padding lining the walls and a thick wall of glass separating her from it. And inside the room...

Tala had seen enough Deathless to know those who'd been inflicted with its curse. Several men and a young girl were inside the padded room, standing motionless and staring listlessly back at them. None of them appeared violent—yet—but there was no mistaking the unnatural, glassy white eyes looking back at them, evidence of their possession.

"Dr. Gren," the Wake said. "Thank you for your time."

"If there is a way to revert them, you may have all the time you require from me," the woman responded. Zoe and Nya were already beside her.

"We still don't know if it'll work, Doctor," Alex said.

"It cannot hurt to try. We are out of options at this point." The woman nodded to Zoe, who began to play the flute.

It was another beautiful melody. Either Zoe was much more capable than she had admitted, or she had practiced since returning with it, because it was a complex sound, a difficult tune to play. The music was all the more dazzling because of it.

But it did nothing to the male Deathless. Their heads turned toward the sound; the men regarded it calmly, then turned away, the flute having had no effect.

But not the girl. Laughing gleefully now, the Deathless pressed herself against the glass, her eyes burning into Zoe. Nya moved instinctively before the brunette, a vial already clasped in one hand, ready to use if it became necessary. "Iniko," she warned but received only a mocking laugh in response.

"There is no Iniko here," the girl snarled. "Only death and suffering live in this house. We answer to no music but to Her Majesty alone. No song is our barrier. Only the burning we fear. She will triumph, witchling. She will triumph, and Avalon will fall to the fires!" She began to scream, but a push of a button from the doctor's end cut her off abruptly.

"I'm sorry," Alex said, his shoulders slumping.

"Nothing has been gained, but nothing has been lost in the attempt," the doctor said sadly. "Thank you for all that you do to help us, Your Majesty. You and your team."

"So that's a wash, then," Ken said quietly after Lumina ended the call.

"One of the legends about the raskovnik," the Duke of Suddene said, "is that it can revert spells and bring one back to their original state. But it seems that the Deathless curse is resistant to the myth."

"Any examples of other successes?" Tala asked.

"Some Russian ones—not surprising, as World's End can be traveled to easily from their nation. Their heroes have taken the raskovnik, but none have successfully used it for its supposed healing properties. Many opted to wear it in battle as good luck charms instead. More often, they wind up finding animals who've located the raskovnik—moles, hedgehogs, snakes."

"So it's not even magical?" West asked.

But Ryker was shaking his head slowly. "The Snow Queen

wanted to find it. There has to be something there, even if we don't know how to unlock it yet."

"What do you think we should do, then?" Ken asked. "Do we go for it, or don't we?"

"I think you're forgetting something very important," Tala said quietly. "Don't you remember what the Dame of Tintagel said? Or the Baba Yaga? *Eight will stand at the end of the world. Only seven shall return.* One of us might die there."

The group fell silent.

"We could ask the Dame for an explanation," Ken finally said.

"She would have told us by now if she'd been willing to." This from Cole.

"Then all the better that we delay this attempt or skip it altogether, yeah? Or we can circumvent the prophecy by showing up there with a battalion of soldiers. Can't have seven returning if there weren't eight there to begin with."

"None of you will be going at all," Alex said firmly. "We have most of the other artifacts. As long as we can keep them away, the Snow Queen won't be able to revive her father."

"But what about the Deathless?" Lumina asked. "Your Majesty, what about you? Buyan may be the only way to lift your curse. We can't just—"

"This is my decision, Aunt Lumina," Alex said quietly. "And it's my final one."

"Alex!"

The protest died on Tala's lips when the young king turned to her. The regret was clear on Alex's face, but so was his determination. "I'm doing what's best for Avalon, Tala," he said. "You know it's the right decision. I can't let any of you go there knowing it's likely a trap. And I'm sorry. I know you want it for your father's sake. But I can't. Not yet."

Tala nodded, albeit reluctantly. "But this isn't going to be our last conversation about this."

Alex turned to Tristan. "And what's this? No protest from you?"

"None," the boy replied. "I think I understand better now, how much being king takes out of you. I...I'm sorry."

"Uh, Sir Locksley?" Dexter's voice rose uncertainly. "Your, um, parents are on the line."

Tristan's solemn expression disappeared, and outraged exasperation took its place. "Why?"

"They said they have important information about the Snow Queen but insisted they needed to speak to you first. I can always tell them you're busy if you're—"

"Put them on the line," Alex interrupted.

"Alex," Tristan said urgently. "I haven't talked to them since the engagement was announced."

"Are you going to hide us from them?"

"No. You can throw it in their faces, and I'll happily oblige. But I'm not sure you want to do this here with..." Tristan glanced around at the others' curious gazes and actually blushed.

"If they have any information on the Snow Queen like they claim, then everyone here deserves to know."

The display switched to the worried, angry faces of Tristan's parents. Nathan Locksley looked the same as he had when they'd visited Avalon several months ago, with the same arrogant bearing, though with more furrow to his brows. Valentina Locksley looked slightly more discomfited, the dark circles under her eyes still discernible underneath her makeup.

"Your Majesty," the elder Locksley said crisply. "Thank you for looking after our wayward son. I apologize for any attempts he might have made to meddle in royal business. We would like to retrieve him as soon as possible and—"

"No," Tristan broke in angrily, moving so that his parents could see him standing beside Alex. "I have no intention of returning with you or keeping to an engagement I didn't agree to."

"Tristan," his mother spoke up. "Surely you see the absurdity of all this. This is a private matter. Surely we can talk about this in a less public—"

"I've talked to the both of you about this, and neither of you wanted to listen. You're not actually concerned about what I want. You just don't want it sullying our reputation."

"You are being impossible, Tristan," his father said angrily. "Your Majesty, I beg your pardon. We are here to collect Tristan and leave as soon as—"

"I love Alex Tsarevich. Not Esmeralda. And I'm not going to marry her, no matter what arrangements you've made."

Tala wasn't quite sure if Tristan had done it deliberately or if he'd blurted it out in the heat of the moment. Alex turned pale and then a deep red.

Lord Locksley actually laughed. "And you expect us to believe that? It's not like you to be stubborn, Tristan, to the point where you would lie to us."

Tristan said nothing.

The humor died from Lord Locksley's eyes as his gaze moved from Tristan's stone-faced expression to Alex's blushing one. "You cannot be serious. First your brother and his Bluebeard bride, and now this. I will *not* permit you to—"

"I'm of age now, Father. You can no longer prevent me from doing anything I want, and what I want is to stay here by His Majesty's side. If you weren't lying about having information about the Snow Queen, then you'd best tell us now, because this is all you're getting from me."

"I could disown you," the man threatened.

"If that's what you feel you have to do, then that's what you should do."

Father and son glared at each other. "We'll talk later," Lord Locksley said with the confident air of one convinced he could still sway Tristan over to his way of thinking. "Your Majesty, the Snow Queen is on the move. My sources in Luxembourg have confirmed that she left her lair at Beira and was sighted along the borders near Germany."

Alex's face hardened. "Is she still there? Or has she left? How are the Germans faring?"

"She engaged no one in battle, though several legions were sent to defy her. She and her ice maidens simply disappeared into the Löwenberg woods and were seen leaving less than an hour later without returning fire."

"So that's it, then," Loki said quietly. "She knows we have it."

"And do you know of her current whereabouts?" Alex asked.

"No, Your Majesty," Tristan's father responded. "It's best that you reach out to the German authorities for more, but I thought you ought to know immediately."

"Thank you, Lord Locksley."

"I know my duty, Your Majesty. Unlike others that come to mind." And the man's gaze swept back toward his son, anger once more taking hold. "This is not over, Tristan," he said, and the screen winked out.

"I'm sorry about my parents," Tristan said.

"That's not what's concerning me at the moment." Alex had abandoned all pretense at maintaining his royal demeanor and was back to blushing.

"You are under no obligation to say anything to me," Tristan said brusquely. "I wasn't intending to be so candid, but then I thought— fuck that. I'm tired of hiding, and this was the only chance I had to tell that to my parents' faces. I don't care who else knows. I'm going to let the comms team know that my father is no longer allowed to use the private channels to contact me."

"Well," Tala murmured when Tristan stepped away to tell Dexter just that. "I thought this was what you wanted him to do?"

"I'm not sure doing it in front of Aunt Lumina and Lord Keer, among others, would have been the best way." The king, however, was glowing just a little.

"Congratulations, Your Majesty," Ken chimed in, grinning. "You know, he's actually given me a pretty good idea about how to—"

"Don't even think about it, Ken," Nya warned.

The warning bell took them by surprise. Tala shot to her feet.

Alex turned back toward the command center, where Dexter and his father were furiously scanning their consoles, a startled Tristan still beside them. "What's happened?"

Severon Gallagher looked up, face ashen. "Another unauthorized port has opened up just south of the city, Your Majesty," he said. "And from the newest reports filtering in, it looks like it's the Snow Queen herself."

Ken was already halfway out the door before Alex called on him to stop. "She's here, Your Majesty," Ken said bluntly. "You can't tell me to stay behind this time. She's literally at our gates, and if my sword's gonna be one of the things that can end her for good, then you know I'm going to go out there and do my damned best to."

"He's right, Your Majesty." Both Nya and Zoe had returned, looking grim. "We just heard," Zoe said. "If she decides she's going to take the battle to our door, then we have to stop her now. You've heard some of the prophecies the seeresses and the Baba Yaga predicted. They said Maidenkeep could burn."

"When did you suddenly become so concerned about prophecies, Zoe?"

"I'm trying to be practical, Alex. She knows we've gathered most of the artifacts. That's why she's here. All our efforts will be for nothing if we can't stop her now."

"Your Majesty," Lord Gallagher continued raggedly. "Reports are coming in that Kay Warnock has also been sighted with the Snow Queen."

"Your Majesty," Lumina said promptly, "permission to go on the battlefield to engage."

Alex rubbed at his eyes. "Do nothing reckless," he said. "She's up to something, and until we know what that is, I want you all to maintain your distance. She's going to use Uncle Kay to bait you, and I don't want you falling for it. Lord Gallagher, how many nightwalkers does she have with her?"

"In the thousands at last count, Your Majesty. We'll need to bring in more regiments stationed in other parts of Avalon to shore up our numbers."

"Lord Keer?"

"I wouldn't advise that for the moment, Your Majesty. My people know how to fight nightwalkers well enough, and those numbers won't turn the tide against us yet. It could be a ploy to divert more of our rangers away from the Burn, as that was where her armies were focused previously. I would, however, recommend bringing in some of our fighters from the outer territories and both redirecting them here and shoring up our numbers at the Burn. Call it a hunch, but…"

"I'd take your hunches over most people's advice, Wake. Make it so."

"And what about us?" Ken asked.

Alex hesitated, then nodded. "Fine. Don't take any unnecessary risks, and you know that's you I'm talking about, Ken."

"How secure are the defenses here in Maidenkeep?" Tristan asked.

"Enough to repel anything the Snow Queen can throw at us, I'm pretty sure."

"Then I'm going with them."

"What?"

"They'll need all the help they can get. I told you I would do my best to be useful, and I'll be able to do more fighting with them than I can here."

Alex inhaled. "All right. But I don't want you doing anything to—"

Tristan sank down on one knee. He took Alex's hand and kissed it. "Nothing will keep me from returning to you," he said.

Zoe sighed and cast a longing look Cole's way. The latter raised an eyebrow.

"Of course you don't have to do it like that," Zoe said. "But still."

"Alex," Tala said. "If anything takes a turn for the worse out there, I don't want you using the Nine Maidens again."

Alex smiled sadly. "Can you promise me that all of you will be returning here unharmed?" he asked.

"No, but…"

"Then I can't make any promises either. Lord Keer, I want the Third and Seventh Honors forming up along the castle walls. The Bandersnatchers will be joining them shortly."

The Snow Queen wasn't making any moves to attack them. Not head-on, at least, which was suspicious because she'd always done it that way before. From where they were waiting, it was hard to even make out where she was. Her legion of nightwalkers had retreated, and none showed signs of resuming the offensive. Even the Royal States mercenaries had stopped firing.

Winter had come earlier than the weather forecast had predicted, though Tala wasn't sure if that could be attributed to the

Snow Queen's presence. A light snow had fallen overnight, and it was enough to blanket the world outside.

"Why isn't she attacking?" Ken burst out, never one to wait. "I've half a mind to take Horse out from the garrison and just ride out to—"

"Half a mind is all you're going to have left if you face her out there!" Nya hissed.

"She can't wait forever, can she? And neither can we. I wasn't expecting to go out of my mind from boredom out here."

The Third and Seventh Honors of the Fianna accompanying them had spread themselves out, always on guard, though their frustration at seeing no movement from the enemy mirrored Ken's.

"His Majesty's orders," Tala said sternly. She gave an experimental stamp on the ground with her foot. The ice there had thickened, making everything slippery, which was another hindrance they would have to deal with should any fighting actually take place. "We'll wait for as long as we need to."

Ken sulked, but Tala was adamant. They waited. The adarna sang quiet songs to itself on Tala's head.

"Anything yet?" Lumina asked from Tala's earpiece. Her mother had joined the other rangers who were fighting off the nightwalker stragglers not with the Snow Queen, and Avalon was gaining ground quickly. The firebird was with them, having a field day burning down anything it could get at, to Ken's envy.

In another ten minutes, according to Lola Urduja's report from the other end of the battlefield, all the Beiran ruler's minions would be eradicated and the area cleared. Which was why this was all bothering Tala. There was no advantage to the Snow Queen to wait.

"I could go and scout," West suggested.

"They already have eyes on the queen's location," Zoe objected. "Going in alone would only put you in danger. Loki, what would you suggest?"

"Remain where we are," the ranger said promptly. "Monitor not just the Snow Queen's camp but every other strategic point within Avalon. No telling if this is a ruse for her to start something up elsewhere."

"I agree with Loki," Nya said.

"And what are you fiddling with inside your pouch, Rapunzel?" Tala caught the glint of scarlet from within at the same time as Ken did. "You brought the tamatebako with you?"

"Grandma said I should have it on my person at all times."

"What for?" Ken leaned in closer, and his eyes widened. "It's stopped glowing. Didn't it used to glow?"

"Didn't the stories say that it'll only stop glowing if it's been used?" Zoe asked. "Just like what happened with Tala's?"

"Mine's still with the Gallaghers for safekeeping," Tala said, worried. "Was I supposed to have brought it too?"

"That's all beside the point," Ken said. "Rapunzel, what's inside the box?"

Nya cleared her throat. "This is one of the things I'm not supposed to be telling you."

"You figured out how to open it, and you haven't told the others?"

"I couldn't. Otherwise, they'd tell you."

Ken's eyes narrowed. "Rapunzel, you ought to at least let me know what—"

The ground below them glowed.

Tala fell, the startled shouts of her friends as they, too, tumbled down with her lost against the sudden rushing sound of wind. Darkness assailed her on every side, and she flailed out anyway, trying to hold on to something, anything, that would slow her descent.

She heard a squawk, and then something seized her by the shoulders. The adarna flew up, flapping hard against the currents, and Tala heard another *oof* as it grabbed hold of Ryker.

The boy angled his hands downward, ice balling up against them. He let it go, and it spread out in the air and hardened to form a spiral slide. The adarna let go, and both he and Tala dropped down on top of the slide. The ice burned against Tala's skin, but the surface was smooth and frictionless, a better option than their previous free fall. She heard exclamations above her again as her friends—some grabbed by the adarna like she and Ryker had been, others finding the icy ledge on their own—slid after them as they spun toward… what, exactly? Tala couldn't see anything.

The darkness gave way to a cold night sky, but Ryker's concentration never wavered. He continued to generate sheets of ice before them, ensuring they could reach the ground safely. Tala flew out of the makeshift slide and landed lightly on her feet, heard Ryker grunt as he did the same. Soon the rest of the Banders were back on solid footing, though the landscape before them had changed.

They were no longer in Avalon. Instead, they stood on a wide expanse of barren nothingness. Before them stood a heavy granite wall made of shifting magic, the energies of which were so immense that it made Tala's hair stand on its end.

She counted them. Her, Ryker, Loki, Cole, Zoe, Ken, Nya, and West—eight in all, if one didn't include the adarna.

It was Cole who finally spoke, sounding like he'd known where they would turn up all along.

"World's End," he said.

"And she opened a portal underneath us to lead here," Loki said.

They weren't the only ones who'd been ported. There was another chorus of cries, followed by a series of thuds as more people tumbled out of the looking glass above them—two dozen men all in all. Without Ryker's abilities, they hit the ground hard but soon scrambled back to their feet quickly, guns drawn. West growled low in his throat, and the other Banders raised their weapons. Tala's heart redoubled its beating.

They were the private mercenaries who'd worked with OzCorp and now with the Snow Queen.

18

IN WHICH CLIMBING WALLS IS HARMFUL TO YOUR HEALTH

The mercenaries' weapons were out and trained on them, though for once, none seemed inclined to fire.

"We're gonna ask you real nicely," one of them said. "Get us back to Avalon, or some of you are going to be missing heads by the time we're through."

"We didn't port you here," Zoe said. "Unauthorized looking glasses are your queen's specialty, not Avalon's."

"She ain't our queen, lady. She just pays us well enough to do the job."

"Shut up, Longrin," one of the other men hissed. "I recognize this place. This is the one they call World's End. Wasn't the queen looking for some plant out here? Promised us a cool million each if we could find it. May as well look for that while we're here."

That seemed to energize the rest of the men. "None of you move," their leader ordered Tala and the others. "I'm calling in Brecker to send a port out for us."

"Why not just gun them all down?" another soldier asked with a cruel grin. "They're of no use to us anyway."

"Are you a fool? Do you see that sword? Don't you know what that is?"

"It's called Kusanagi," Ken said. "And I guaran-fucking-tee that none of you will be making it out of here if you start shooting."

The mercenaries eyed the sword. "There ain't even anything growing around here," another man said, kicking at the ground in disgust. "Nothing even remotely green in this fucking place!"

"What do we do now?" Ken muttered.

"Keep eyes on them," Zoe advised. "And for another way out. We're out of Avalon's comm radius, so I doubt Alex knows where we are. And I think something's leaching out all the magic from our spelltech, because my phone isn't working."

Tala reached into her pocket and watched the screen of her own phone light up. "Mine still works," she said. "I'm going to try and call him."

"So we took every precaution we had to avoid this place," Nya said, "and wound up here anyway?"

"Technically speaking," Loki said, "if we find the raskovnik and it's supposed to unlock every door and exit as they claim, then we could use it to find our way out of here."

"Look around you. There's nothing here." Ken gestured, indicating the rock-hard ground.

Tala knew he was right. It didn't look like plants were capable of growing in these parts. Nothing here resembled the question-mark plant that Lord Suddene had shown them. There was nothing else in this tundra save for the terrible wall before them, still teeming with the otherworldly spells that marked Avalon's war with Koschei.

Tala could feel waves of energy emanating from it, though they were about fifty feet away. It stretched on for miles on either side as far as they could see, with no seeming end to it. It was also completely made of ice, and every fiber of her being told her it was dangerous. From the way Loki's teeth whistled when they inhaled sharply, she knew they sensed it too.

"I have an idea of where it might be," Ryker said slowly. "But none of us are going to like it."

"Scanning," one of the mercenaries confirmed, having latched on to the same conclusion. He had a strange device in his hands that he was waving about. "Nothing of note in the area—except the wall. Holy fuck, energies are off the scales. Looks like that's where we ought to start looking, boys."

Still keeping their guns trained on them, the mercenaries began to edge toward the massive wall. Tala's eyes flicked briefly to Zoe, and the girl shook her head slowly. Her meaning was clear: *Let them.*

"Not as tall as what we had to scale during training," one of the men said with a grin as he set his foot on one of the stones jutting out from the wall. "You sure there's magic behind this shit?"

"Can't see any end to it," one of them marveled. "It looks like it just stretches on into the horizon. What now?"

"Only one way to find out," said their leader. "Keep climbing, Benk."

The man obeyed. He was up the wall in no time at all, hauling himself over the edge to look curiously at the other side.

"Well?" their leader called up to him. "What do you see?"

Benk turned to look back at them, opened his mouth—and

began to laugh. It was a loud braying sound, with tinges of hysteria behind it, and growing more maniacal with every second.

Benk swung his legs over the top of the wall and, still laughing, jumped down to the other side.

"Benk!" the leader shouted. "What the hell are you doing? Benk!"

There was no reply. The laughter had been quickly cut off the instant Benk disappeared from view. His body should have made a sound when he hit the ground on the other side, Tala thought. Yet they heard nothing but the whistling of the wind.

"Is he playing with us? Hey, Benk!"

No answer.

The leader scowled. "Markoff, see what happened to him."

The man obediently scaled the wall after his comrade, pausing at the top to look down gingerly over the other side like the other man had.

"Well?" the leader prompted when the soldier took too long. "Where is he?"

Markoff turned and broke into wild gales of uncontrollable laughter. Still hollering, he turned and jumped down, just as Benk had done.

"What the fuck is going on?" the leader barked.

"There's a chance that the raskovnik is growing over the wall, isn't there?" West asked nervously. "But how are we going to find out if it's going to drive us nuts like they are?"

"Jem, you're up next," the mercenary leader said.

But the soldier was wiser than his other two companions, shaking his head and backing away. "You're not gonna get me over that wall, Briggs. That's a death trap."

"If we don't find a way out of here, then this whole tundra is gonna be our fucking death trap."

"We can use them for ransom," another mercenary suggested tentatively. "They might know the way out."

"If we knew the way out, we'd have been gone ten minutes ago, you absolute wombat," Ken said.

"And how will anyone know if we can't even open up a line back into HQ? That fucking plant's gotta be somewhere over the wall somehow. Close your eyes."

"Why don't you do it, then?" Jem snapped back. "Sounds like you've got all the ideas. You test them out."

"You're all fucking useless. Once I get the plant, I'm collecting the reward for myself." Briggs slid his night vision goggles over his eyes and turned them on. Still grumbling, he began to scale the icy structure.

A loud sound echoed across the icy landscape, but it did not come from behind the wall.

Tala turned and saw the ice wolves lumbering toward them, because *sure*, this was what they absolutely needed right now.

The tundra must be their home base, because the packs of wolves that were coming from over the horizon, heading toward them, were numbering in the hundreds. Likely thousands.

"Crap," Ken said.

If the mercenaries viewed the creatures as their allies, none of them showed it. With loud curses, they turned their weapons away from the Banders and toward the approaching nightwalkers. "Briggs, you better find it soon!" Jem roared.

"Oh, so now *you're* telling *me* to hurry up?" Briggs was nearly at the top of the wall, turning his head so he wouldn't have to look beyond it. "I'm setting my body cam to record this shit, and then I'm coming down."

"Record the damn thing faster! Fuck!"

The mercenaries were unraveling. At least three had flamethrowers and were already spraying at the wolves within range.

"They're going to burn everything down if they keep this up!" Loki muttered.

Ryker was kneeling on the ground, hand pressed against the frozen soil. Ice barriers popped up all around them, keeping the ice wolves from coming too close and preventing the mercenaries' fire from hitting them. "If any of you know how to get a hold of Alex, you better do it now," he said grimly. "This is the ice wolves' turf. They can keep coming for days if we let them, and we're going to run out of strength before the day's even out."

"It's not like an agimat can travel wirelessly though comm links!" Tala tried anyway, but to no avail. She diverted her shield instead right into the body of an ice wolf about to leap, causing it to break apart.

Zoe's Ogmios sizzled in a straight line, taking out several rows of wolves. Cole had already taken control of three or four of the creatures, who were now spread in a circle around him and Zoe, keeping the others from getting too near.

"Can't find anything." Briggs had successfully made it back down the wall. He looked down at the camcorder on his hand, where Tala presumed he'd taken a recording of the other side of the wall.

And then, with a sudden burst of hysterical laughing, he tossed the camera onto the ground and began to climb back up again.

"What the hell are you doing, man?" One of the soldiers made a grab for him, but Briggs kicked him loose and kept climbing, still chortling uncontrollably with mad glee, until he'd scaled the wall once more. Without a pause, he threw himself over the edge.

One of the mercenaries had bent down and picked up the camera, looking at the screen Briggs had been watching with a frown. His face changed swiftly into one of horror, and then a grin broke through.

With a howl, he, too, began to scamper up the wall while his comrades looked on in terror.

"Okay," Ken said, "so I guess cameras can't be a safety precaution either."

"So either we scale up the wall to look for the raskovnik and face certain madness," Tala said, "or we take the risk with a never-ending stream of ice wolves, hoping Alex and the others can pick up on where we are through the power of telepathy?"

"I'll climb the wall," Ryker said suddenly, and a chorus of horrified gasps was the response.

"What makes you think *you'll* be invulnerable?" Tala snapped.

"Do we have any other choice? They say one of us isn't going to make it, right? What if that means the raskovnik *is* on the other side of the wall and someone has to get it before we can all make it out?"

"You told me you saw your own death in the mirror. Is this what you saw?" Tala grabbed his sleeve. "No, you know what? I don't care what it told you. We're not letting you go."

"We were eight when we came here," Ken added, "and we're gonna be eight when we… Wait, where's West? Oh bloody hell, West!"

The boy was already halfway up the wall. Tala only saw him shift for a second from human into some kind of animal before he disappeared completely from view.

"What's he doing?" Nya burst out, horrified. "I don't think his animal form is going to protect him!"

"I'm gonna retrieve him," Ken said, setting one foot on the wall himself.

"Your sword isn't going to protect you either, Ken!"

"I'm the only one out of all of us with any kind of chance! And I'm not leaving West on his own!"

There was a high-pitched squeal and more guttural sounds, and something pitched itself from over the wall and straight onto Ken's face. The boy staggered back, now juggling a sword and a ball of warm fur that slowly raised its head and poked him in the cheek with its nose.

"West?"

"Clever," Loki said with a grin, even as they fended off an ice wolf. "Moles are blind."

The mole squeaked again and raised its paw. Clenched in its tiny fist was something soft and green and curled at its ends.

"And he sniffed the raskovnik out with his nose!"

"How did he even know what it smelled like?"

The mole squeaked importantly.

"He knows what plants smell like," Loki translated.

"Good job, West!" Zoe electrocuted a few more of the wolves. "But how do we activate it?"

The adarna was knocked off Tala's head before anyone could answer. She only felt the weight suddenly lift, and then the poor bird was on the ground, completely covered in ice.

"You need not know," came the cold, triumphant voice behind them.

Alex had suspected a trap, and he was right. A sheet of ice even colder than the tundra around them swept toward the group. Tala saw the incoming wave and thrust her agimat at it, but she couldn't mitigate it completely.

She was on the ground, legs and arms frozen, and the others were in the same condition. Even the mercenaries hadn't been spared; Tala could hear them swearing as the ice hardened around their limbs, effectively immobilizing them in place. She couldn't turn her head to look around, could only focus on the woman in white now walking effortlessly toward them, her bare feet leaving no footsteps behind her as she stepped through the snow.

The Snow Queen looked the same as always: ageless, beautiful, cruel. She glided to where they lay trapped, and the ice wolves retreated. She picked up the sphere now encasing the adarna. "You have been thorns in my side at every step," she said. "But even you have your uses."

"I knew it," Zoe hissed. Ogmios sparked around her, trying in vain to break her free from their icy prison. "You couldn't find the raskovnik yourself, and you wanted to trick us into finding it for you."

"What the hell are you doing, you bitch?" one of the mercenaries barked. "We're working *for* you! Get us out of here!"

"Are you truly working for me? Or is this another of your leader's schemes to take the artifacts away from my control?"

"We only do what we're paid to do, lady. We're not involved in any of that political shit."

"On the contrary. You are." Vivien Fey stepped out from behind the Snow Queen, smiling widely. A console display lit up from her hands. "Your master tried to hide his finances, but I knew where to look. You're no different from OzCorp. You always hide it with the same methods, with off-shore bank accounts. Her Majesty paid you to retrieve the raskovnik. You told King John of her interest and accepted his payment for the same thing. An attempt to swindle the ruler of Beira does not bode well for you."

"I'm sure you're confused as to how a contract actually works," the mercenary said condescendingly. "Call our boss so you can have him explain things better to you. We can't deliver on our promise if you have us frozen like this."

"Oh, but I must assure you," the Snow Queen said in a brittle voice with an even brittler smile, "that I understand your leader's attempts to mislead me perfectly. I no longer have need of your services, save for one final task." She turned to Vivien. "I told you that I will require an oath from you, a pledge of your loyalty to me. Give me your hand."

Vivien did and cried out when ice briefly enveloped her fingers at the Snow Queen's touch. It disappeared as quickly as it came, but she doubled over, face ashen, clutching at her wrist. Tala saw it; a shard of a mirror had dissolved into Vivien's hand, slowly infiltrating her body, accompanied by the telltale swirl of spells as it began to take hold of her—the same type of magic Tala had always sensed with ice maidens.

"Here is your final test," the Snow Queen said. "You know what you must do."

"No," Ryker said, redoubling his efforts to wrest himself free. "No, don't do it!"

Trembling, Vivien stared down at her hand and then at the mercenaries, who had gone silent and pale at the realization. She took a deep breath, clenched her fist. "You're right, Cadfael," she said. "There is no going back after all."

Ice crackled at the tips of her fingers, the surge of magic growing more powerful with every spark. She turned toward the soldiers and raised her arm.

None of the men had time to cry out. The frost that overtook them was swift and deadly. In a moment, they were all encased in ice, barely visible underneath the thick, hardened crust. Vivien had summoned a spell much like the one Ryker himself had unleashed on the ICE agents two years ago. The look of cruel satisfaction on her face was similar to the one he had worn then, and the look of anguish on Ryker's face told Tala he knew that all too well.

"Do it," the Snow Queen rasped.

Vivien brought her hands together, and the ice blocks shattered violently.

Tala saw the change climbing from where the girl's hands were clasped together, the tinge of blue traveling up her shoulders and spreading up to her face, down to the rest of her body. She saw Vivien's features take on a glassier sheen, smoothing out any imperfections on her face but at the same time leaving them starker and sterile, like she was now carved from ice. And when the magic was done transforming her, she stood, no longer Vivien Fey but every inch an ice maiden. She turned her suddenly sky-blue eyes toward them and smiled.

"All your efforts for nothing." The Snow Queen turned to Zoe and plunged a hand into her side.

Zoe's eyes bulged out, a scream leaving her. Tala could hear Cole curse, struggling to free himself.

The Snow Queen lifted her hand. The flute was in her grasp. "Did you think the artifacts would sit quietly inside your Avalon vaults? You are all their conduits now, tied irrevocably to your fates."

The Snow Queen moved toward the still-struggling Ken next. Kusanagi had been driven into the ice, preventing him from drawing it out. She reached into his pocket and, despite his efforts, drew out the small bone with a victorious cry.

"We have no use for any of you now," Vivien said. She stepped toward them next, ice fractals building up on her hands.

"Wait," the Snow Queen said. "Where is the raskovnik?"

Tala couldn't completely turn her head to see, but she knew then that West had not been imprisoned in ice like the rest of them had and that he was nowhere to be seen.

"Where is it?" The Snow Queen was working herself up to a rage. She stalked past them, searching in vain for any sign of the plant among their persons. "I cannot sense it among any of you. Where have you hidden it?" She moved toward Tala, hands curled with the promise of more violence. "I shall freeze the blood in your veins and draw it out from you, every drop *agony*—"

Sudden laughter from Ryker stopped her in her tracks. "All that display of power, killing those mercenaries to strike fear into their hearts, and in the end, you never even thought to see if they had it?" he asked mockingly. "All that hard work for nothing."

The Snow Queen slapped him. Ryker's head snapped back hard from the force of it, and when he turned back, Tala saw blood on his lower lip.

"They refused your bait, so you had to come all the way to Avalon and lure them here," Ryker continued, undaunted. "You thought you could get rid of some of them by having them scale the wall. You thought you could get me out of the way as well. How's that working for you now, *Mother*?"

The Snow Queen hit him again. "You were always so ungrateful," she hissed. "Always so confident that you knew better than everyone. As if I never found you dying underneath a bridge. Always a disappointment."

"You're mad because Avalon betrayed you. But you've only ever been at war with Arthur and Merlin, and they've been dead for centuries. Your war with everyone else is because you turned out to be exactly like them."

"You talk far too much for one who's about to die." With a smile, Vivien drew the small transmitter from inside Tala's pocket. "You didn't think I wouldn't recognize one of my own creations around your neck?" she asked. "I figured the little Makiling was likely to have the controls to keep you on your toes, Cadfael, and I was right. How fitting. And how ironic." She pushed the button.

A jolt of pain rocked Ryker's body, and he couldn't bite back his cry. Tala struggled frantically, but her agimat couldn't reach him.

"That—all—you—got?" Ryker panted once his trembling had ceased.

"What is he doing?" Tala heard Nya ask softly, sounding horrified.

"He's distracting them," came Loki's lower whisper.

Tala finally saw what the ranger had already known. A mole was worrying at the ice that had trapped them all, hiding itself from view of both the Snow Queen and Vivien, with a piece of something green still in its tiny grip. West!

A sudden glow sprang up around the little critter. The Snow Queen turned with a growl at the surge of magic. She leaped for West, but she was too late.

The ice shattered, and Tala and the others were free. Tala lashed out immediately to grab Vivien's arm and deactivate the thrall collar, which slipped off Ryker's neck and landed on the queen's hand.

Ken was already moving. Kusanagi broke through the Snow Queen's barrier, and the woman leapt back before the sword could cut her.

"Break's over," Ken said grimly. "You want the raskovnik, you're gonna have to go through us."

Ice formed up again, but Ken broke it apart with little effort. His next swing drove his blade onto the Snow Queen's shoulder. Tala had been expecting water to gush out, the way it did when ice maidens were cut, but blood poured out from the wound instead. The woman clapped a hand to the injury. Steam rose from her fingers as she froze it. "You little bastard," she snarled.

"How did you do that?" Nya exclaimed, scooping up the mole in her arms. The little creature responded with a series of squeaks and rattles.

"He's gonna try again," Loki said. "But he's not sure if he should?"

"What? Why?"

The mole held up the raskovnik. It was now missing one of its four leaves.

"You're saying we can only use it another three times?"

The mole squeaked.

"Use it anyway, West," Zoe said. "If that's our only way out, then that's not a waste."

The Snow Queen spread her arms, angling her face up to the sky. The ground before her broke apart as a sudden earthquake hit, nearly knocking them all off their feet.

It was another ice dragon, clawing its way to the surface. It shook its head once, then lifted its head and brayed noisily.

Ever fearless, Ken was rushing forward. But his blade clanged harmlessly off the icy surface, not even breaking through the scales.

"A parting gift from Nome and his ilk," the Snow Queen said. "Did you think that all their experimentations with dragons would come to naught with his death?"

"Back away, Ken!" Tala could see something moving within the dragon—something black and round, beating against its rib cage like it had a heart of its own, but it was emanating with the most powerful magic she had ever felt. It made her knees buckle, just feeling the waves of spells coming from it.

"The Alatyr," Nya whispered. "A piece of it. A part of her mirror is lodged inside that beast."

More high-pitched yelping from West. The raskovnik in his hands was glowing with a dazzling light. Something even brighter leapt out of it and solidified a good four hundred or so meters away, widening slowly to become a golden blazing doorway.

"And that's how we leave!" Zoe shouted. "Let's go!"

Tala scrambled for the adarna. The bird had been partially thawed but did nothing to escape the rest of its confines. It hissed when she approached.

"Not now," Tala panted. "We have to get you out of h—"

The adarna screamed. A wave of dizziness washed over Tala, forcing her to stumble back.

"What are you doing?"

The adarna shook its head, resolute.

Tala stared at it. "You know what's going to happen, don't you?" she whispered. "That's why you intend to stay."

The adarna raised its colorful head, regal and solemn in its bearing, and nodded.

She had no other choice. "We're going to get you back!" Tala promised as she ran for the portal.

The ice wolves' attacks were increasing; hundreds were blocking their path to their destination, and it was difficult to fight through them all. Tala's agimat was all that was keeping the creatures from jumping them, and her strength was close to giving out.

Despite his own exhaustion, Ken was giving as good as he got, killing ice wolves every time he swung with his sword. It was enough for them to cover the remaining distance into—

"No!" Tala heard the Snow Queen shout, and Ryker fell back to the ground in agony as she shattered another of his ice barriers. Cole hauled him up, even as his ice wolves took their final stand, their former companions quick to tear them to bits, sparing them a few more precious minutes to escape. Tala felt the ground around them shift as magic bubbled up from within, and she knew instinctively what was coming.

She shoved her hands on the ground and channeled everything she could into it, just as stalagmites punctured up at them from below, skewering everything not within her circle of protection.

The ice was never-ending, constantly striking up at the surface only to melt when it came into contact with Tala's agimat, and each unsuccessful attempt nevertheless felt like she was being punched relentlessly in the gut.

The scream above them was a final warning. The ice dragon swooped down on them, mouth bared, ready to swallow them whole.

Ken swung upward with Kusanagi. So did Loki with their staff and Zoe with her Ogmios.

The world broke. Tala heard a sharp crack as their weapons made multiple points of contact with the dragon. The winter that came streaming out from the great creature's mouth had no barrier to overcome, and Tala felt the chill taking over, wrapping around her body.

Desperately, she angled her agimat upward to counter, feeling the cold melt away.

Another sharp crack jutted out from underneath their feet.

The dragon wheeled back up to the sky. There was a scream, and this time it came from Zoe.

Another stalagmite had erupted out from where Zoe had been

standing. She'd been shoved backward out of its reach where she lay sprawled, staring with horror at Cole.

The boy lay on the ground on his stomach, eyes closed. They flickered open when Zoe scrambled toward him.

"No," the girl choked, clasping his face between her hands. "*No.* Nya, can you—Tala—"

Tala had already reached Cole's side, running her hands down the length of the stalagmite, skirting the spot where it had driven itself through him. Desperately, she willed her agimat into the ice, knowing it would be fatal if she melted the area around his injury and caused him to bleed. She saw Ryker fighting to cut the stalagmite out of the ground, but the look of hopelessness on his face told her everything she needed to know. Nya and Loki were fighting the rest of the ice wolves, trying to give them time, but their window of escape was growing smaller, and the ice dragon was already beginning to circle back, prepared for another round.

"Leave me," Cole gritted out.

"No!" Zoe choked. "We're not leaving anyone here, much less—"

"Only seven return." Cole's hand closed over hers. "If it has to be this way, then at least let it be me."

Zoe's eyes widened. "You knew. You *knew.* This was what you refused to tell me. But *I don't care.* I'm not leaving you. Ryker and Tala will get you out. I can—"

She broke off in surprise, staring down at where their hands were joined together. And then her eyes glazed over, and she toppled forward.

Cole held on a few seconds longer before finally letting go. Tala saw the glint of silver in his palm. "Her sleeping needle," she gasped.

"Knew this was the only way I could get her to leave me," Cole said gruffly. "Don't make me use it on the rest of you."

"No." Ken crouched down beside him, anguish on his face. "We can't—we can heal this wound. I know we can."

"I know enough about getting stabbed to know you won't have the time you need to. I'm not making it out of here, even if you find a way to dislodge the ice." With some difficulty, Cole pushed Gravekeeper into Ken's hands. "Bring this back to my family. They'll know what to do next."

"Cole—I—"

The boy smiled, an absolutely un-Cole-like, reckless grin. "Take care of her. Tell her I'm sorry I couldn't do more. That doorway isn't going to hold up for long."

He was right. The gateway was shrinking slowly.

"Cole," Tala sobbed. "I—I'm sorry—"

"Make it up to me by defeating that bitch." Cole's hand dug into the ground. The ice wolves still under his control began fighting back even more aggressively than before. "Now go."

"Thank you for everything, Nottingham," Ken said quietly. He rose, carrying Zoe, and a crying Nya followed him to the doorway. Loki saluted him silently, the mole in their grip bawling as much as a mole was capable of weeping. Ryker tugged Tala back to her feet, pulling her toward the gateway.

The last Tala saw of Cole before the portal closed behind them was the boy turning grimly back to the armies of ice wolves closing in on him, the adarna settling beside him, keeping him company until the end, and the ice dragon swooping down on them both.

19

IN WHICH MAIDENKEEP
IS ON FIRE

They reappeared at the same position where they'd vanished. The rangers leveled their weapons, then eased their grip once they realized who they were.

"You're back!" came Alex's familiar, relieved voice over their comm link. "We had no idea where you were. We were so worried."

Ken turned, the unconscious Zoe still in his arms. His sword was glowing, a strange mix of dark and light. Gently, he turned the sleeping girl over to Ryker and then raised Kusanagi.

A large blast shot forward from the weapon in a straight line, a strange mix of light and dark, promptly eradicating everything within its range.

"He's never done that before," West whispered, sounding stunned.

With an angry snarl, Ken turned back toward Maidenkeep.

"Ken? What's happened? We're finally getting a visual on you. Is Zoe all right? Where's—" Alex's voice faltered. "Where's Cole?"

None of them answered. None of them could.

A loud explosion rocked the grounds. Tala's jaw set as she took in the new gleaming portal from a distance and watched as the cold, smiling visage of the ice maiden that had once been Vivien Fey emerged from the looking glass. The roar that bellowed out from behind the woman confirmed her worst fears.

"We have an ice dragon on the way," Loki confirmed grimly. "Dex, send someone down here to see to Zoe."

Another portal fizzled open, and a dragon's head poked out. Another looking glass activated, and then *another* dragon emerged.

"She's sending in her full army," Loki said as even more portals dotted open. "She's been waiting for this. Alex, I don't think we have enough to defend ourselves."

Alex only needed a few seconds to survey the dozen ice dragons now on Avalon territory to make a quick decision. "Lord Keer, I want everyone inside Maidenkeep. All the citizens, all the soldiers."

"But, milord—"

"This is an order, Wake."

A grunt from the Wake. "You heard him. Retreat!"

Most of the rangers were still on the front lines. Ken had realized this; he'd turned back toward the battlefield, Kusanagi already in hand.

"Ken—" Nya began.

"I've got the sword, Rapunzel. I'm not going to hide inside the castle as long as there are soldiers still out there. Get everyone inside. I think I know what Alex is going to do, and I'm going to help him do it faster. You understand, right?" The look he shot her way was pleading. "I can't run away."

Nya took a deep breath. "I know. And I understand. I love you."

Ken blinked, reddening. "Where'd that come from all of a sudden?"

"I just wanted to say it again. I love every infuriating, exasperating part of you, and I needed you to know that."

A wide smile broke over Ken's face. He hauled Nya closer and kissed her. "Wait for me," he said. "This shouldn't take long."

"We have our own weapons," Loki said calmly. They patted at their coat pocket, where West had taken up residence, still in mole form. "We're going to help you too."

"We're not going to let you be the sole hero even if you do have the damned sword," Tristan said and nocked an arrow onto his own segen, the crossbow taking on a fiery tinge.

Ken grinned. "Whoever takes down the most dragons wins?"

"Wins what?" Loki asked, puzzled, but there was the sound of neighing as Horse raced toward them. Ken swung himself up on its back without pause, and the two galloped furiously toward the dragons. Tala could see small portals blinking into view around them, this time Avalon gateways for the rangers to escape through.

Another bolt of light sizzled out from the tip of Ken's sword, aiming at a dragon's eyes. The massive beast shook its head back and forth, disoriented, and Ken swiped low, cutting through its left foreleg. The dragon crashed onto the ground. Ken angled his blade a second time and cleaved clear through its right wing. The limb crashed onto the ground and broke into millions of tiny pieces of shattered ice.

Loki and Tristan had teamed up to take on a second dragon. The Locksley boy's fire arrows were tearing holes through one of its wings, while Loki's staff battered at the creature's face, literally breaking it apart.

Tala concentrated on defense; whenever the creatures drew too close for comfort, her agimat extended to prevent a grotesque clawed foot from trampling on Ken and his kelpie or stopped the bursts of icy breath from overcoming Loki and Tristan. Ryker remained by her side, using ice to counter ice. Adapting the Snow Queen's own strategy, he was sending large columns of sharp icicles bursting from the ground to impale them.

The last of the soldiers made it through the looking glass, and soon they were the only ones left.

"Avast, ye laddies!"

The *Jolly Roger* ported in with a heavy thump just outside the city walls; Tala could hear the sound despite the distance. She didn't need to look back to see what Captain Mairead and her pirates were doing; she could already feel the strength of the magic prickling at her skin, the loud thrum of power as a cannon was being loaded up.

"We've got a few more regiments still out of radius," Tala heard one of the techmages report from Alex's end. "Another five minutes."

"That's good enough for me," the king responded. "Ken, Tala! Get your asses back to Maidenkeep now!"

Obediently, they retreated, giving grudging ground as they made their way back. Tala's strength was about ready to give out, and it was getting harder and harder to put up shields.

"Get out of the way, you Banders!" Captain Mairead had a powerful set of lungs, needing no megaphone or spell to let her voice carry to them. "We're blasting in five…four…three…!"

The resulting sound of cannon fire nearly deafened Tala. She saw the arc of the blast blazing up in the sky above her like a vengeful comet, hurtling toward two of the dragons with startling accuracy. Massive as they were, the beasts never stood a chance.

But the Snow Queen was countering them. The dragons brought their heads together and screamed. The ice accumulated around them, blasted back with a powerful concussive force.

The *Jolly Roger*'s fireball promptly incinerated them where they stood. Two other dragons were caught in the explosion, staggering away as their wings caught fire, rapidly melting their bodies.

The ice blast hit Mairead's ship. Tala saw the captain and the crew leaping off before the ice firmed up, transforming it into another icy block.

That was their cue to run. Tala dropped her agimat and took off, Ryker running beside her, the rest not too far behind.

A five-foot ice projectile swooped in front of her, narrowly missing her face. The Snow Queen had materialized near the port, blocking their path. Vivien Fey stood beside her, smoothly marbled face smiling cruelly.

Loki swung Ruyi Jingu Bang, and Vivien blocked it with one hand, ripples of ice enveloping part of the staff. "That no longer works on me, Sun-Wagner," she taunted.

The ice cracked, and the staff emerged from underneath it unscathed. Loki attacked again, and the woman dodged.

Tala saw Horse gallop past, carrying several injured soldiers on its back—Ken must have sent his kelpie ahead to bring some of the injured inside. The boy was already engaging the Snow Queen, and she was matching him blow for blow. "You cannot think to escape," she said. "You know as well as I that you will die here before Avalon for all the world to see."

"So what I'm hearing is that you were intimidated enough by me to actually look me up." There was something odd to Ken's grin; there was a touch more recklessness there, his attitude even more devil-may-care than what Tala was used to from him. He showed no inclination to move closer to the portal, more focused on fighting the Snow Queen.

"Ken!" Tala shouted over the din. "We have to move now!"

"Right behind you!" Ken said and continued fighting.

The dragons that had survived the *Jolly Roger*'s blast were already approaching, their teeth snapping. An icy wind from their combined howls tore toward them, and Tala gritted her teeth and warded off the incoming blow, though it felt like her head was about to split in half.

There was a look on Ken's face she hadn't seen on him before. It looked similar to the one Cole had worn before he was killed. The Snow Queen knew. Her triumphant smile said it all.

Tala started toward the boy, but Ryker held her back. "What are you doing?"

"Everything I can to make sure his vision doesn't come true," Tala said, now sure of it more than ever. She weathered the next round of dragons' breath, ignoring the cold that had penetrated through part of her agimat and numbed her right arm. She couldn't. Surely Ken didn't expect to—

Ken's gaze flicked to Tala. "Sorry, Tala," he shouted hoarsely, "but you can't change this, and I'm not going to let you. Tell Nya I love her and that I trust whatever the hell it is she's supposed to do next."

"Ken!" Tala screamed.

Another hard blast from the dragons sent an opaque fog over her vision, one she barely deflected. And when it cleared, Ken was stumbling back, his hand clasped against his chest, which was already blooming red, blood spilling out. The Snow Queen stood, laughing. She raised her icicle sword over him, tip pointed downward.

Something knocked the weapon out of the way, and now the Cheshire stood between her and Ken, a wooden staff leveled her way.

The Snow Queen's smile was triumphant. "You're too late."

"It's never too late." The Cheshire swiped at her, and the woman parried.

Ryker was by Ken's side in minutes, another ice barrier placed in between them and the Snow Queen as he dragged the injured boy away. Loki retreated quickly to join him.

Gathering everything else she had, Tala shoved her agimat at the Snow Queen. Something else cracked in the air before them, and the woman actually took a step back, like she'd encountered some invisible but physical resistance.

The distraction was enough; the boys pulled Ken through the Avalon gateway. Tala and the Cheshire dove in after them.

And just as she did, she saw Ken smile, saw him raise his hand. The bone that the Snow Queen had taken from him at World's End lay nestled in his palm.

The Snow Queen let out a cry of rage and started forward. But the portal was already closing up behind Tala, sealing itself completely before the woman could take another step.

They were now at one of the great halls within Maidenkeep set up for the wounded. Lord Keer was also there, arm and leg wrapped in heavy gauze and stained red, still giving orders as a team of techmages patched up a link back to Avalon's main command. All around them, screen displays showed parts of Maidenkeep at every conceivable angle. Tala saw the Katipuneros still by the castle gates on the east end, still fighting, as were Lola Corazon's team of Filipino soldiers.

The castle shuddered again. Tala saw the remaining fleet of ice dragons heading for them. The Katipuneros were an elite fighting force, but faced with six or seven of the flying beasts, they had little chance. She saw another looking glass opening beside them, saw General Luna shoving Titas Teejay and Chedeng, both sisters clearly wounded, into the portal. Some of the Filipino delegates and other soldiers nearby weren't as lucky; the dragons' breath came upon them quickly, turning them into sheets of ice.

"We ain't down yet!" Tala heard Captain Mairead shout through their comm link. She saw the *Jolly Roger* powering up again, melting the ice spells keeping it immobile.

The ground underneath her turned white with cold and then started to splinter. Tala scrambled away from the edges as they broke apart. "The queen's hitting us from underneath!" she heard someone yell. "Shift the shields below us, or she's going to tear Maidenkeep apart!"

She saw her mother, and then she saw her father. The Banders had guarded the west side of Maidenkeep, and they'd been unaware of how the fighting was going elsewhere. Her mother had led the northern defenses; Kay Warnock had shown up there, and she was matching him blow for blow, neither of them relenting, neither of them retreating.

Tala saw Vivien Fey bearing down on the Katipuneros with several projectiles while they were still busy fighting off the dragons, and she found herself screaming at the top of her lungs, yelling at them to look, to move, even though she knew they couldn't hear.

She saw General Luna go down. She saw Lola Corazon leap forward, pushing a startled Lola Urduja out of the way, and take a blow for her.

She saw her mother shove at her father with her agimat, then raise her hands as if pleading. And then she saw her father stop—just for a second or so—before he stepped forward once more to attack.

The Snow Queen arrived at his side. Kay Warnock turned at her call, moved to stand obediently beside her. Tala watched as the Snow Queen reached up to caress her father's face, saw the look of anger on Lumina's. But her mother was wise enough not to rise to the bait. She said something—not to the Snow Queen but likely to Alex through her earpiece. She took a step back, right into the portal that appeared behind her.

"Get ready!" Lord Keer roared. "Confirming that we have everyone inside, citizens and soldiers alike. Do what you have to, Your Majesty!"

"Out of the way!" Captain Mairead roared. "We're powering up. Move out of the way!"

"Hold on," Loki panted, pressing down against the wound on Ken's chest, trying to stem the flow. But there was too much blood. Far too much.

"Had to do it," Ken gurgled. "Needed…the damn bone. That's what I saw. She's the…only one who could take it from me. If she'd kept the bone…we'd all…"

"For once in your life, Ken," Loki said hoarsely, "shut up and let them help you." A team of medics was already rushing over to where he lay.

Ken smiled bloodily at them. "Worth it," he whispered. And then his eyes widened, and his whole body seized up, arching painfully over the ground. The doctors set briskly to work.

Tala stood there and felt helpless, her hands over her mouth as she fought to keep back her sobs. Loki slipped their hand behind her shoulder. "He'll be all right," they whispered. "Inoue's a fighter."

"No," Tala said as Ryker stood with them. "He's not going to be all right. He'd been hiding something this whole time. Ever since the Ryugu-jo."

Don't worry. With me in charge, you're all going to be all right. The odd look in Ken's eyes when he said that, using *you* instead of *we*. The way he'd talked constantly about doing his part as the sword wielder. His lack of curiosity regarding Nya's refusal to tell him her secret, when he'd previously been so angry over her decision to hide her mermaid ancestry from him.

Tala turned. Nya stood there, her whole body trembling. Her hands were clenched together so tightly Tala could see blood from the marks her nails were making against her skin slowly trickling down her fist. She didn't move toward her dying boyfriend. She didn't even cry.

And then the castle shuddered again, and Tala realized that it wasn't her imagination.

The Wake hollered out another command, and one of the screens flickered to the young king. He was standing at the center of the Nine Maidens.

"Alex!" Tala was scrambling toward the display, even though she knew Alex wasn't likely to hear. "Don't you dare use it! Alex!"

The king was using the spelltech like he'd never done so before. Bits of asphalt and dirt rained down on them from the ceiling, and Tala wasn't sure if this was a side effect of whatever spell the Avalon king was using at the moment or if the ice dragons were increasing their attacks—likely a combination of both.

Another loud roar confirmed her suspicions, and Tala saw part of the roof give way, a large portion of it crashing down onto them. It met a thick ceiling of ice that Ryker summoned to act as a shield, saving them for the moment.

Wild magic surrounded Alex. The king gritted his teeth, and one of the Nine Maiden's spellstone columns flared brightly, spells sizzling around it like it was a lightning conduit.

"I need to go to Alex," Tristan said, his face pale. He was already running toward the doors. "I have to—"

He lurched to the side when another jolt shook the castle. Looking up, Tala saw one of the ice dragons leering down at them from a hole in the roof, cold steam rising out from its nostrils. It opened its mouth, and Tala struggled one last time to force her agimat to meet the hailstorm she knew was coming.

The dragon's head snapped back, part of its snout suddenly melted. "Keep it steady above us, Ryker," Lumina instructed. Her mother lashed out again with her own agimat, and the dragon's face caved in abruptly, sending it crashing to one side of the palace wall.

"Fire!" Tala heard Captain Mairead shout.

Tala heard a victorious scream. The *Jolly Roger* had not aimed its great cannons at the dragons but rather at the firebird, whose fires now filled the sky as if the blast had only strengthened it a hundred-fold. Now it zipped through the air, tearing easily through the ice dragons as if they were wet paper, its brightness like a second sun.

Tala could hear the other creatures' death cries as the firebird attacked, obliterated them. The castle was now surrounded by fire— exactly like her dream in Tintagel Castle all those months before.

There was a loud snap. For several moments, Tala felt like she was suspended in time, with everything else moving in slow motion— the medics still working on Ken, Nya clasping his hand tightly, West slowly shifting back into his human form, still holding tightly to the raskovnik with its two remaining leaves. Ryker and Loki stood beside her, both trying to shield her from whatever blow might come next.

She could feel magic rippling around them, far too strong to be contained, and it reverberated throughout Maidenkeep like a whirl-wind. It felt like it was spinning them around even though they all remained upright and unmoving, like the laws of both physics and magic no longer existed.

And then, just as quickly, it was all over.

The palace no longer lurched and spun like it was about to break apart. Only silence reigned.

On the screen, Alex lay sprawled on his back, the shallow breaths leaving his mouth the only indication he was still alive. Tristan was already there, feeling for his pulse, cradling his body, calling desperately out to him. The ground around them lay in ruins, and the roof had been completely pulverized, sand pouring down from somewhere above.

The young king opened his eyes and smiled up at the other boy. He said something, and Tristan lowered his head.

Alex took him by the collar, pulled him all the way down to kiss. Then his hand dropped listlessly to his side, heedless of Tristan's panicked calls to wake him.

The medical personnel had stopped working on Ken. The boy lay on his side, his eyes closed. His chest no longer rose and fell.

One of the medics let out a harsh, pained sound. "Time of death, 2:25 p.m."

Nya reached out and gently moved Ken so that his head was on her lap, the way she'd done many times before.

"I love you." Nya didn't cry. She stroked his hair, the sides of his face. "And now I'm going to prove it."

20

IN WHICH THERE IS A TIME TO MOURN

They were no longer in Avalon. The winter here was harsher, more unforgiving. and yet far better than the destruction they'd left behind. Loki had gone off to scout and soon returned, their eyes still red-rimmed from crying. "I don't know how Alex did it," they said heavily, "but he ported not just the castle but the whole city of Lyonesse right to Nibheis. He even managed to port in the *Jolly Roger* along with it, and that's no small feat."

Nibheis. Cole's ancestral home. Another friend they hadn't been able to save. Tala forced her mouth to move, ignoring the dryness to her lips, the starchiness of her tongue. "Do they—does his family know about—"

"I don't know how, but I think they do. They're asking for Gravekeeper. Tristan has it, but he's with Alex right now."

Tala couldn't bear it. Cole's death and Ken's. How many more?

It felt strange not to have the adarna's familiar weight on her head. Her only consolation was that she knew the Snow Queen needed it alive for the moment to carry out her plans of opening Buyan. She should have tried to rescue it, even though it had spurned her offer. It had saved her life. She should have—

Should have, could have, would have. The worst words in the world.

Loki was right. Tristan was with Alex. The king was strapped to a medical bed, an IV line hooked to his arm. His breathing was deep but even. He was all right physically, the doctor in charge told her, but they didn't know when he would wake up.

The firebird was in no better shape than its owner, collapsing at the same time as Alex. The doctor couldn't say what was wrong with it any more than he could the Avalon king. The firebird had often been an indicator of Alex's health in the past, so it had been wheeled beside his bed, placed in a small nest there, and carefully monitored.

Avalon's command center had caved in just before Alex successfully ported them away; the Snow Queen had known where to target, and she had nearly succeeded. Heavy injuries had been reported among the personnel there and at least two fatalities. Tala's heart nearly stopped inside her chest when she was informed that Dexter was among those seriously wounded. Parts of the roof had landed on him, and they had had to amputate part of his leg to save his life. *The brave little tailor will lose his leg for you*, Tala thought, remembering the Dame of Tintagel's warning. It took all she had not to cry.

She'd been prevented from visiting. The boy was doing well and was expected to recover despite everything, but the doctor's orders limited anyone but family from seeing him, and Severon Gallagher was already there.

She'd been granted leave to visit Alex. Tristan was sitting at his bedside, face stricken. "I shouldn't have left him," he said, looking down at Alex's hand, which was clasped against his. "He kissed me," he added disbelievingly. "And I…I didn't turn into a frog."

"In shifting ice a prince you'll kiss, and the first shall be forgiven." Tala said. It was the first evidence of his doom being proven right, though she wasn't sure what that signified yet. After all, what use would Alex's ability to kiss be if he could not be roused? "The whole place was shifting, all right. He always thought his true love was tied to whoever he'd kiss if that could break the curse."

"Ha," Tristan said bitterly. "I don't know if he'd told you this, but we'd already kissed, before he ever told me about his spell. It took hours before I learned how to stop catching flies with my tongue once I turned back into human form. I'm not his true love."

"Maybe it just meant that you weren't worthy enough to be with him then."

"And I am now? Doesn't feel like it. I should have known he would push himself. If I'd been there with him, maybe I could've…"

"If you'd been able to stop him," Tala said, "Maidenkeep would have been overrun, and the Snow Queen likely would have destroyed the city. He saved all our lives."

"I know." His grip on Alex's hand tightened. "But still…I should have found another way."

I should have found another way. The words followed Tala back down the hallway and back to the medical center. Nya was still with Ken, in a separate area to give them privacy; she had refused to leave his side ever since they'd brought him there. Ken's parents had been secretly ported into Nibheis hours ago, soon after news of Avalon's defeat had circulated in the media. Ken's mother had thrown herself on top of her son's body, and her wails were the most heartbreaking sound Tala had ever heard.

Horse had gone mad. It had taken nearly a dozen soldiers to tranquilize the poor beast, and the castle veterinarian had told them she intended to keep Horse incapacitated for the meantime for everyone else's safety.

The Katipuneros crowded around the body of General Luna in quiet mourning. The man looked like he could have been sleeping. Tala wished he was.

"Paalam, Heneral," Tita Baby said, weeping. "Magkita tayo muli."

Lola Urduja was two beds over, staring down at Lola Corazon. The latter was so heavily wrapped in bandages that it was almost difficult to recognize her. Tala neared, her heart breaking. She didn't know her grandmother well, but she knew how much the old woman had done for her sake even if she disagreed with how.

"Why?" Lola Urduja asked heavily. "Why did you save me, Corazon? We were never friends to begin with. Foolish as your life has been, why choose to waste it on me?"

The old woman's eyes fluttered open at the sound of her archrival's voice; her eyes were warm, far from the sometimes condescending way she looked at Lola Urduja in the past. "We fight together in battle," she whispered, so low and so soft that it was hard to make out the scratch of her words. "That is enough. I do not like you, Urduja, but it was an honor to fight *with* you all the same."

"Bilisan mong gumaling, Corazon. We have many more battles to fight together."

The injured woman's gaze stole back to Tala, and her fingers twitched.

Understanding, Tala moved to the other side of the bed and gently took her frail hand in her own.

"Nay," Lumina said softly from the door, hesitating to enter.

Lola Corazon's eyes twinkled. "Ah, there she is. My favorite child."

"I'm your only child," Tala's mother said, taking up position beside Tala, reaching out to fold her hand over both Lola Corazon's and Tala's.

"I do not want to say that I regret," Lola Corazon said weakly. "I know that we have not always seen eye to eye, anak. But I am proud of you. Proud of how you fight. Proud of how beautiful you are now and of how Tala takes after you. I wish…" She let out a long, soft sigh, and her eyes closed. Her breathing slowed down, then stilled.

Urduja clutched at Corazon's arm in disbelief, pain across her austere features. Lumina gathered her daughter and her mother close to her, and Tala cried.

Kusanagi had disappeared. So had the singing bone. Lumina had the whole city searched, only for her soldiers to come up empty-handed. No one had seen either of them disappear from Ken's body. But Juuchi Yosamu and Yawarakai-Te had been found in Lord Inoue's room when he'd returned for a change of clothing, both leaning against the wall like someone had left them there for him.

Tala rejected the idea that the singing bone had come into the Snow Queen's possession. She had seen how badly Ken had fought to regain the bone, literally at the cost of his own life. He had not wanted the woman to have it. He had seen a vision in one of the mirrors at the Ryugu-jo that had predicted his death. He'd died knowing he'd succeeded.

Tala didn't care where any of the artifacts were at the moment. Their other losses had cost more.

There were wolves waiting together with the Nottinghams when they approached—not the Snow Queen's ice wolves but much like the ones that had greeted Cole near Ikpe when they'd still been stuck at the frost, or the wolves he and Zoe looked after at the sanctuary. They seemed to know what had happened, and the air was filled with quiet, mournful howls.

The Nottinghams accepted Gravekeeper in silence. Cole's grandfather stood in heavy black, looking older than Tala remembered, with more white in his hair and a grayer cast to his chin. Cole's mother stood like an alabaster statue, pale as the snow around them and only a slight tremble to her hands as she folded them before her. Her husband stood quietly beside her, a dark sentinel. The Dowager Nottingham was a small form beside her and even stiller. Only Adelaide Nottingham, Cole's young sister, gave them all away. Her slim form shook, and her eyes were bright with tears.

They knew. The Dowager Nottingham was one of the great seers. She herself had foretold Cole's doom.

"I am sorry," Tristan Locksley said. A lifetime ago, he and the Nottinghams would have been enemies, split by politics and old history. Now Tristan held the sword carefully, like it was the most precious thing he'd ever had to touch. Meeting Cole's family was the only reason he had left Alex's bedside.

He held Gravekeeper out to Lord Nottingham. The old man shook his head. "I am no longer the bearer of the sword," he said, lifting his arm. "I can no longer hold it."

Tala saw the deep webbed scars, the overlapping crisscrosses of raised white lines and red splotches that ran up his wrist and disappeared underneath his sleeve, knew that they would reach all the way to his shoulder, like Cole's did. Cole's mother and grandmother had borne similar marks the way every wielder of the sword had. Only Cole's father bore no injuries, without the shared blood capable of wielding it.

Tristan hesitated. Adelaide stepped forward, but her voice was strong. "Thank you for bringing Gravekeeper back to me, Sir Locksley," she said in a soft commanding tone that Tala knew would have made Cole proud. "I'll take it now."

Tristan stared at her. "I—you can't," he said, his tone incredulous. "Surely you know what it—"

"I am a Nottingham just as much as my brother, Sir Locksley. Just as my great-grandmother, my grandfather, and my mother. Let me carry out my duty, like you carry out your duties to the king."

Tristan bowed. He held Gravekeeper out to Adelaide. She seized the sword and lifted it easily, like she'd wielded it before. Her arm was smooth and unlined, and Tala knew it was only a matter of time before she, too, would be made to suffer the family legacy.

"I wish I could wield it for them," Cole's father said quietly. He had been estranged from the family, Tala knew, and had only recently reconciled. Cole had been sparse with the details, only that the man had been opposed to the family segen, the grief it brought to the family line. He was correct in his assessment, but there was no anger or accusations in his gaze now, only loss.

"We have ample room in our castle should anyone prefer to stay there while we find a way to repair parts of Maidenkeep," Lord Nottingham said. "Our home is open to whomever asks, Sir Locksley."

The lord's voice was stern and intimidating as always, but there was no mistaking the olive branch being extended. Tristan accepted by bowing low again.

"Wait," Nya said. She, too, had left Ken's side only to insist on meeting with the Nottinghams. "I hope I am not speaking out of turn, milord, but I have a request to ask of you."

"Anything, milady."

"I want you to bury Sir Inoue in your graveyard."

The Nottinghams were silent, studying her. "Do his parents give you leave?" Lord Nottingham finally asked.

"They do. I am speaking on their behalf as well. They have agreed to sign any necessary papers to make it possible."

"You know that our graveyard is not an ordinary one. It is for sinners." The Nottinghams were, according to their own customs, buried there as well, but Lord Nottingham didn't mention that.

"I know that, sir." Nya was perfectly composed now, though her expression was carefully and deliberately neutral, like she was stopping herself from showing any more emotion than desired.

Lord Nottingham let out a slow, drawn-out exhale. It carried into the early morning air. "I will make the preparations," he said. "I am sorry for your loss as well."

Tala thought about how they couldn't even bring Cole's body back to bury.

Nya had insisted on speed. Tala didn't know if it was her way to mourn, but the Nottinghams didn't question it. Surprisingly, neither did Ken's parents.

They gathered an hour later to watch the gravediggers bury Ken. The villagers at Ikpe who'd stayed at Maidenkeep to fight also attended the event. Nya's grandmother greeted the Dowager Nottingham; they stood apart from the rest, talking in low, quiet tones.

It hurt to see them lower Ken into the hard snow-covered ground. Nya was dry-eyed, hugging her pouch like it was the most precious thing she had left. Ken's mother made up for them both, her face buried against her husband's chest while he stared ahead, unable to tear his eyes away from the shroud that held his son's body.

It hurt to see the Nottinghams bury Ken while Cole was still at World's End. Loki was silent and Tala held fast to their hand. West had shifted into hound form and had refused to shift back, as if he could take grief better in this shape.

The last pile of dirt was heaped onto the grave, adding Ken to the tens of thousands within the graveyard, without even a marker to his name. Adelaide walked toward it, stopping beside the fresh mound to draw out her sword. Another feature of the Nottinghams' graveyard—as doomed sinners, anyone who bore Gravekeeper was to fight the demons that would inevitably come, seeking to claim the deceased's souls. It was their duty to keep them safe within whatever peace these burial grounds offered.

Adelaide waited. They all did, but no shades appeared. No demons came to fight for Ken's soul.

"He was worthy," Adelaide said and, finally, could not hold back a sob.

"He was," Nya said softly and traced the outline of something that lay inside her pouch.

Zoe had gone missing from her hospital bed. Lumina had wanted to call for a search, but Tala had asked her mother to let her find the girl first. She knew where Zoe was likely to be.

She was right. They hadn't used the secret room within Maidenkeep's gardens for some time now, the meeting place they'd used to test the Gallaghers' more advanced looking glass. Alex's abilities were such that he had brought the whole estate grounds with him when he had transported the city to safety. The last time they'd been inside was during Zoe and Cole's escape from the Royal States, unsuccessful at preventing Abigail Fey from casting her terrible curse. Tala suspected that the room had held bad memories for Zoe ever since. No one protested when she had stopped using it as their meeting place.

The room was nearly bare, save for a whiteboard that stood against one wall. It was where Zoe was most likely to be back then, forever writing out ideas and plans, pros and cons lists.

The girl was there, just as Tala had thought. But the room looked like it had been taken over by a conspiracy theorist. Manila paper had been put up on nearly every inch of wall, and theories filled every surface. "By winter, by fire, by madness" headlined most tracts, followed by scenarios and hypotheses listed underneath.

The prophecies regarding both Cole and Zoe had been written out on the whiteboard itself. "You will save her," it read, "once from frogs and once from fire and once from winter, and she will save you, once from poison and once from sword and once from madness."

Zoe was staring at it, a marker still in her hand.

With any other person, this would have looked like the ramblings of some madman, some afflicted brain. But even surrounded by the chaos, Zoe remained precise, methodical. Her neat handwriting listed the pros and cons of every possible situation, arguing whether it fit the part of the prophecy she had highlighted to compare it to or why it didn't.

Structured, orderly, and methodical. Zoe could have been a university professor working through a complex mathematical formula. But the crumpled balls of paper on the floor that showed she had been at this for a while had discarded even more theories than what was already on the walls. That and the cold blank look in Zoe's eyes—

Tala felt tears prickling at her own once she realized what the other girl was trying to do.

"I'm missing something," Zoe said. Her tone was crisp as always, like everything was normal. "I've been going about this all wrong. There has to be a reason why Cole's doom would have given such precise instructions. There has to be a reason why I was a part of his prophecies. Why would it go through all that trouble instructing us how to avoid death when the end result would be simply to leave him at World's End to die?"

The cool inflection, the calm tone. It was like Cole's death had no immediate bearing on the current riddle she was trying to solve.

Zoe lifted her hand as if to write something else down on the board. She let it hover in the air for a few seconds, then dropped it instead.

"If these prophecies are real," she said, "then I've left something out. He saved me from frogs and fire and winter. That's the marsh king, and then the harpoon, and then World's End. And I saved *him*—from letting his wounds fester while we were stuck in the frost, and then from the ice maiden's sword, and then from joining the Horned One's hunt. Why would the prophecy list them all down in such detail if it ends with him at World's End? What would have changed? Adelaide would have received Gravekeeper no matter how he died. Why did he have to die *specifically* at World's End, then? I don't understand it. We did everything right." She shook her head and then spun to a nearby wall, reaching out to tear down more paper. "I'll figure it out."

"Zoe, no." Tala grabbed at her wrist. "You're going to drive yourself mad doing this. We just—" Her voice broke over the words. "Zoe, we just buried Ken. We can't let this destroy us. We have to find a way—"

"Tala." Zoe found her hand and patted it, like *she* was the one giving *her* comfort. "Please let me solve this," she said, and the kind, mellow way she said it made Tala know that Zoe was not all right.

But there was nothing she could do but to wait for the other girl to process Cole's death her way.

It was the singing that called out to her soon after leaving Zoe, and it sounded so much like the adarna that Tala was convinced for a moment that it had somehow escaped the Snow Queen and had returned to her. She followed the music back toward the courtyard, where a cleanup crew was already moving some of the fallen trees and doing their best to clean up the rest of the ruins. Several of the Filipino delegates were on hand to help, as were some of the staff from Simeli Mountain. None seemed to hear the melody.

The anvil had survived both the carnage and the transport. It lay untouched among the broken pavement and the fallen trees. But the barrier spells Lumina had placed to keep it at arm's length from curious visitors fizzled out at a touch from Tala's fingers.

The sword was once again embedded in the anvil like it had never left. It had not been there the last time they looked.

The Cheshire stood beside her. Tala didn't even need to look to know it was him, his presence a quiet comfort. "And how are you holding up?"

"Badly," Tala said and stared at the Nameless Sword. It felt like every problem and every heartbreak she'd ever had to go through in her young life could be tied back to this sword and all the miseries that followed in its wake. "I wish you could disappear forever," she whispered. "I wish that no one else would ever have to raise you."

"So many times have I stood before this sword and said the same thing," the Cheshire said. "But in the end, the fates move as they always have. Sometimes it is hard not to feel insignificant."

"We lost Ken," Tala said. "And it should have been me. I was supposed to take up the sword, and I was the one who was supposed to die. Maybe things would have changed. Maybe my father wouldn't have become Deathless. Maybe we wouldn't have to lose Cole or Ken or Lola Corazon or General Luna or anyone else. Maybe we could have saved more people. Maybe—maybe there could have been something—"

"That's always been the case, isn't it? Always thinking you could do better. Thinking you could *be* better, like hindsight in itself is a magical spell you can but master."

It was the old woman from Simeli who'd spoken up, the one who had ferried Tala so many times out of the mountain, who always had encouraging words to say when she failed. She was sweeping up the debris around the anvil.

She looked at the sword, sniffed. "You never would have thought it could break kingdoms in half."

"It didn't do anything for Ken," Tala said, suddenly angry. "It didn't protect him. It didn't protect Alice Liddell. It didn't protect anyone else who wielded it. It's all about protecting itself and its legacy. Anyone else using it is only a vessel to further its ends and nothing else. In many ways, it's almost as bad as Koschei. At least you know he was in it for himself. This sword only ever pretends to be on your side."

"My goodness. I have never heard the sword talked about in such a manner. But perhaps you are right."

The Cheshire was staring hard at the woman. "And why are you so curious about it, milady?"

"You can say that I made a bet on it, once upon a time."

"And did you win?"

"It is far too early to say. It's only been eighteen or so years ago since I made it."

There was no spark of magic at all that Tala could sense within the woman, unlike the Cheshire, who was a heat signature composed of spells. But something about the nice old lady standing before her now made her think of old curses and prophecies.

The Baba Yaga entered the courtyard. Their eyes widened as they took in Tala and the Cheshire and the cleaning woman beside them. "I knew it," they said. "I thought I was imagining it at first, but it really is you."

"I?" the Cheshire asked. "I have been spending my time pulling in favors from the other kingdoms, though they have still been reluctant to voice their support so openly. I have made progress, only to return back here to find ice dragons breathing at Maidenkeep's—"

"I'm not talking about you, you dolt." The Baba Yaga turned to the old lady. "You were gone for so long," they said. "We all thought you'd croaked, Messinda. And then to find you out of the blue, cleaning Avalon's courtyard of all places!"

Tala knew then, long before the elderly lady turned back to her, smiling.

"I wanted to see if this was all worth giving up my foresight," the old woman from Simeli, the former Baba Yaga, said. "How nice to see you again, young Makiling Warnock. And thankfully no longer in the fowl form you were so accustomed to taking back when you were running the mountain gauntlet."

21

IN WHICH TALA MAKES ANOTHER CHOICE

W hy didn't you tell us?" Tala asked.

"A worried need to ensure that I do not change the course of history any more than I already have," the former seeress said. "And also, just a little bit, shame and embarrassment. It is difficult to be known as the Baba Yaga who had so shirked her duties to change the very future she had sworn to preserve."

"What would have happened if you'd left Alex to die back then?" Tala asked.

Baba Yaga paused. "Would you have hated me for it, child?"

Tala swallowed hard. "How could I? Alex is alive against the odds because of you."

"I was a good-for-nothing layabout before I received the curse of prophecy," the younger, *current* Baba Yaga admitted. "A drifter just swinging from place to place without a care in the world. When the foresight fell upon me, I learned to make a better person of myself—at first because I had to and then because I wanted to. Do you know what I've learned since then, Tala? Prophecy isn't as important as the choice."

Choice. Tala had chosen not to wield Avalon's sword, and Ken had paid the price for it.

"Surely now is the time to tell us what the future brings next," the Cheshire said. "Maidenkeep is not out of danger yet. The young king you tried to save is still in peril, still burdened by the weight of his ancestors' legacy. And the same goes for you, Ilyena. You cannot be this cold to hide it from us now."

"My visions have been murky ever since the attack on the city," Ilyena said. "I wish I *had* something to tell you. The Nine Maidens or the Snow Queen, or possibly both, have broken my visions. All I can see is fog. What comes next is as unclear to me as it is to you."

"So that's it, then? We all simply give up? Everything we fought for has come down to nothing?"

"It's not like you to be so downtrodden, Cheshire. You've survived centuries on nothing but spite before."

"I took a gamble on what today might hold. And now the scoreboard is missing, and I don't know how much we've won or lost." The Cheshire strode forward and tried to lift the sword from its stone. It refused to budge. "I promised Alice," he said. "I told her I would protect the Avalon line. I've used prophecies to guide me toward that goal. But every one of them regards this strike at Maidenkeep as the decisive battle, and they offer little of what comes after. What else can I prepare for? Do we hide and wait another two decades while the Snow Queen gains a stronger foothold over the rest of the world? A world largely indifferent to our cause because it has never concerned them? Did the prophecies intend for her to rule and for Avalon to fall into obscurity?"

"This is why the sword chose Alice Liddell instead, you old sourpuss," the elderly woman, Messinda, said with alarming frankness.

"Milady!"

"There are two things we cannot predict, no matter how much we try. One is the negating spells such as those of the young Makiling Warnock here. The other is the Nameless Sword's wielder. Alice Liddell had not been in any of our visions until the moment she raised it. As Ilyena says, it is not the prophecy but the choice."

It is not the prophecy but the choice.

Tala moved before any of them could react, grasping the sword herself.

It slid easily out of the anvil. It felt familiar in her hands.

The intrusive thoughts that stole their way back into her head were familiar as well.

She could *kill* with this sword. She could level kingdoms. She could turn its point on the Snow Queen, King John, on all the ICE agents and Royal States soldiers who tried to murder them, kill them all so quickly. So easily. They would be powerless—

She wanted to put the sword back. But the Baba Yagas were looking at her, surprised and at the same time oddly not. Nor was the Cheshire, whose gaze was both understanding and sad.

"Maybe none of you could predict what's to come next," Tala said, hoping to sound as confident as she didn't feel, "because I tend to have that effect on a lot of magic."

The former Baba Yaga was staring at her. "I see now," she said. "Now I know what compelled me to defy fate. What made me choose to save the young Tsarevich's life."

"Yes." Ilyena, the current Baba Yaga, couldn't take their eyes away from Tala either. "As soon as you drew it out, the fog lifted…yes. Everything is clearer. Two will destroy Koschei—one his body, the other his soul. Only when you walk through the everlasting fires will you find what you seek."

"Are you still going to be speaking in all these riddles," Tala asked a bit irritably, "or are you finally going to tell us?"

The younger seer shook their head, looking slightly awed. "We don't have to. You'll know what to do soon enough."

"Tala?" Lumina looked exhausted, her eyes falling on the sword her daughter now wielded.

Tala felt a pang of regret, knowing what she was going to put her mother through.

"Tala." Her mother fell to her knees before her. "I—" Lumina began, paused to wet her lips. "Are you sure?"

They had likely lost her father. They had just lost her grand-mother. And now her mother was steeling herself to possibly lose her daughter as well. "I'm sorry, Mom," Tala whispered, forcing the tears away. "But I have to do this."

"I know," Lumina said. "If I could take it up for you, I would. Just—please. You have to be safe."

"Well, Ilyena?" the Cheshire asked.

"Fire," the Baba Yaga said. "Nothing else but fire from above."

"Maidenkeep must burn before Maidenkeep can rise," Tala said. "That's done, and we've survived. And now I think I know where to go next." She raised the blade, swung it experimentally. The perfect size, the perfect weight—it felt like it had been made for her. From somewhere within it, she fancied she could hear the adarna sing.

"We're going to the Burn," she said.

There had been a complete ban on porting in and out of Nibheis in the wake of the attack on Maidenkeep, Ken's parents notwithstanding, but Lord Nottingham had understood the importance of her request. Reports were coming in that the Snow Queen had abandoned Avalon after Maidenkeep disappeared, and no one knew for sure yet where the whole city had vanished to.

There were other reports, too, of King John proclaiming martial law, though it was up in the air as to whether he actually had the right to declare such a thing. There was more news of other extremist factions from other kingdoms attempting revolutions. It was like the whole world had been waiting for a signal from the Snow Queen to create chaos under the guise of patriotism.

Tala couldn't think about that now. She was thinking of Alex, whose vital signs were holding steady. Of Dexter and everyone else who'd been injured in the fallout. Of Ken and Cole, and of Lola Corazon and her father and General Luna and everyone else who didn't make it. So she concentrated on the raging fires before her, refusing to think about what would happen should this fail too.

Only Lumina and the rest of the Banders were with them, as was the Cheshire and, strangely enough, one of the Filipinos who had come with Lola Corazon's contingent, who insisted that he be there. "What are you doing here, John Lloyd?" Lola Urduja asked, glaring suspiciously at the man.

John Lloyd raised his hands. "I understand your disdain for us, Urduja, but I am here on Corazon's behalf, simply because she is no longer able to. If anything, I wish to see her theories confirmed with my own eyes."

"She is far too interested in the Burn than she should be. Was," Lola Urduja corrected herself, a shadow of what was almost sorrow briefly crossing her face. "What does—what *did*—she know of this place?"

"She believed that there are more creatures lying in wait here than even Avalonians know. The Burn was thought to be the consequence of the fight between Hook and Pan, but she had always argued that it made no sense. Esopia is far enough from World's End that the concentration of magic here would not have been of this potency. She was an expert in the study of magical barriers, given our own agimat, and she thought that the Burn had all the makings of a barricade— one deliberately created to keep everyone out of Esopia."

Lola Urduja pursed her lips. "I suppose she had a point," she muttered. "But she would have been better off sharing her knowledge with us instead of keeping it to herself like she always did."

"Lola Corazon had always been a proud woman. It was difficult for her to admit she was in the wrong, and her hostility toward you stemmed from the belief that you had encouraged her daughter to drift apart from her, to wed the Scourge. But whatever your disagreements with her, she always thought you wise and kind."

Lola Urduja looked away. "If it means anything, I thought the same of her, for all her irrationalities. Did she provide you with any more ideas as to how we are to break this barrier, then?"

"Unfortunately, no. All she said was that it would require immense willpower to do so."

"That's why she was trying to punch holes in the wall of flames," Tala said quietly. "And why she was encouraging me to do the same."

They had all agreed that more soldiers in the area would attract interest and would cause the Snow Queen to return. Ryker and Loki had taken up their usual spots on either side of her. Ryker remained stoic upon seeing Tala and the Nameless Sword, though she could still sense his worry. Loki's emotions were harder to disguise, their anxiety over her plain to see.

"It'll all work out," Tala murmured to them, hoping to inject more confidence into the words.

"I am going to glue myself to your side from now on," the ranger said stubbornly. "I'm not going to let anything happen to you, Tala. I can't. We've lost so much already."

"As will I," Ryker said.

"I can protect her well enough on my own."

"Even after everything that's happened?"

Loki hesitated. "You're just as easily a danger to Tala as the queen. She wants your head now."

"I know." Ryker flashed them a brief, terse grin. "You'll protect me too, won't you?"

"I'm more than capable of protecting myself," Tala said irritably. "I'd rather not have you two breathing down my neck if you're both going to be weird about this. You two will be better off protecting the others."

"No," both said at the same time, then glared at each other.

Tala sighed and directed her attention back to Nya. "I'm not entirely sure it works, honestly. But the logic should hold."

"I think you might have something there," the other girl said cautiously. She was bearing Ken's death easier than Tala had thought, though there was something now blank and quiet about her, like she was only going through the motions. "But can West repeat it a third time?"

"I think I can," West said soberly, the raskovnik in his hands. Only two of the four leaves remained healthy and evergreen. "Except I, um, I'm not entirely sure how I did it the first two times either." He held out the plant toward the wall of fire and concentrated. "Do you see anything?" he asked after a few minutes. "Is it working?"

"Not a thing, unfortunately," the Cheshire said. He had shunned his human form and was now back to his cat shape so as not to add to the plethora of spells already running rampant within the area.

"Do you remember anything you did leading up to the moment you were able to use it?" Loki asked.

"I was scared," West said. "And worried that we wouldn't be able to find a way out. I remember just squeezing my eyes shut and trying to think about how to break you all out of the ice, and then I felt the raskovnik grow warm. Before I knew it, you were all free. And then I thought that it would be useless anyway, because we didn't know the way out, and then it turned hot to the touch, and the doorway was there all of a sudden. Was it because I felt desperate?"

"I think it's because you wanted to believe so badly in an escape that it was able to turn your desires into reality," Lord Suddene said in his low burr through their earpieces. "The Serbian stories I have read dealing with the raskovnik often dealt with those who'd been backed into a corner and knew it was escape, fight, or die."

"What I want is for Ken to be alive, and Cole and General Luna and everyone else," West said with a low sob. "It's—it's hard. And I know that's not what the raskovnik is for, but I can't help thinking that maybe if I wasn't so weak—maybe if I could do more than just shift, that I could have done something to..."

"West," Nya said, placing her hands on both West's shoulders, forcing the shorter boy to look up at her. "I think it's okay to grieve," the young mermaid said quietly, a sudden quick spasm that flitted across her face the only evidence that she was also in pain. "But we can't let their deaths be in vain. We have to do this for their sakes. Otherwise, if we give up now, then everything we've done to this point has been for nothing. Do you want to face them and tell them you've given up when they fought so hard to get us here?"

"West," Tala added, placing her own hand on his arm. "You and your animal forms are literally what saved us from freezing at World's End. You were the one to find the raskovnik when none of us could. I don't want you ever belittling yourself again when you are the reason we're still here."

West wiped at his face. "Thanks. It's just—it's still hard."

"West," Nya said again, voice raw. "I don't want to give you any false hopes, but I think there's still a way. You have to trust me on this. But we need to find a way past the Burn."

"And we have to do it quickly," Zoe said in her quiet, emotionless tone. Normally one to offer suggestions and plans of attack, she had remained unnaturally silent until then.

West looked at her, straightened his back. "I'll do it," he said firmly, then clasped his hands before him as if in prayer, the raskovnik still in between his fingers.

They were silent for several minutes, watching West concentrate. Lumina brought her hand up to her earpiece, a startled look crossing her features. "What did you say?" she asked into the receiver on another communication channel that Tala wasn't privy to.

A loud crackling sound came from the wall of fire—and then the flames began to part.

Astonished, Tala stared at the slowly widening pathway as the Burn shifted itself to offer them a way inside. She had not even known that was possible.

"Fascinating," she heard Lord Suddene say.

"Did I do it?" West asked giddily, looking down at his hand. Sure enough, three-fourths of the raskovnik had curled up, wizened and unusable, leaving only the one last healthy leaf.

"How did you do it?" Ryker asked.

The shifter reddened. "I—I thought about how much I love you all. How much I want us to be together again. And that if finding a way into the fire is how that's gonna happen, then that's how it's gonna happen."

One last chance at doing this right. One last chance to protect Avalon.

The path that the plant had opened up led straight into darkness. It was as if no light existed beyond the burning wall, like everything beyond it existed within a cave.

Loki aimed the lotus lantern at the entrance. A ray of light shot out of its center, shooting unerringly into the penumbra.

Tala raised her sword. She had not thought to name it yet. In her mind, as ridiculous as it was, it felt like it was still Ken's sword and that she was only borrowing it for his sake, to finish what he had started. "Let's go," she said.

Despite the light of the lotus lantern, darkness continued to loom before them. There were no pathways beyond the Burn. There were no cities. Tala wasn't even sure if it was ground they were walking on or if anything above them contained sky. Not even the stars were visible. It was like the night had consumed everything in this place and nothing else could exist alongside it.

The gateway behind them had disappeared before any of the Katipuneros could enter. Only the Banders and the Cheshire had managed to make it through with Tala before their only way back winked out of existence. But the lotus lantern never wavered, only continued to shine a road ahead of them. "Nowhere to go but forward," the Cheshire said. "I doubt they would take all the trouble to allow us entry if they were only going to eat us."

"To *eat* us?" West asked apprehensively. "Who's going to eat us?"

"If the legends are right, they wouldn't. I hope they don't."

"This is a really good time for you to tell us if there might be cannibals here, milord," Tala said. Holding the sword seemed to have gained her some of Ken's usual levity, as if she was trying to be a poor imitation of him. Nya realized that, too, and smiled sadly at her.

"Not cannibals, technically. If I am right, we will not have long to wait."

"I hope so," Tala said, gripping her sword tightly. "Doesn't look like there's been anything else living here since the fires went up."

She was, as it turned out, wrong about that.

Fire blazed before them again—first singly and then in pairs. All too suddenly, the light burst forth, and the fearsome faces of strange creatures loomed down on them from hundreds of feet above, both familiar and strange at the same time.

Dragons, Tala thought, stricken. These were dragons, but unlike the Snow Queen's creations, these were not made of ice. They had scales that rippled when they moved, leather wings that expanded on either side of them, and small streaks of fire that drifted up from their nostrils. Real dragons, like the stuff old legends were made of.

"Oh," Nya said. "Crap."

22

In Which You Are Crunchy and Will Taste Good with Ketchup

W ho dares enter?" one of the dragons asked. Or perhaps it was all the dragons asking at once. The words came from all around, booming like thunder.

"The raskovnik thought us worthy to enter your domain," the Cheshire said calmly. "We have come asking for a guarantee of safety and an alliance with Avalon that may be to your liking."

One of the creatures huffed out a laugh, and it felt like the earth moving. "It was Avalon that forced us into exile to save our kind," it said. "It was Avalon that killed us for their jousts and for their rewards, the reason we have shunned the outside world and dream our endless sleep. And yet you are here asking an alliance? We sense Koschei's touch among you—one gifted with Buyan magic. What other purpose does he have but to come here and destroy us once more?"

The dragon's snout leaped forward, straight toward Ryker. Tala didn't even remember moving, only that she'd gotten in front of the boy before the creature could reach him, swinging her sword at the same time.

The blade met the spiral of fire that came streaming out of the dragon's mouth. The Nameless Sword glowed fiery hot, but she felt none of the heat or the pain that should have caused. The flames sizzled into smoke the instant they touched the steel, rising steam the only thing the dragon had to show for its efforts.

The dragon dipped its head back. There was a loud chuckle from one of its brethren. "You have always been too impulsive, brother. Koschei would have led an army through our doors rather than rely on these younglings, capable as they seem."

"Your sibling has good reason to doubt me, milord," Ryker said. He took a step forward, despite Tala's hissed command for him to stop. "If you believe this is all a trick, then do to me what you must."

"Can you please stop asking people to kill you as a peace offering, Ryker?" Nya groaned.

But that elicited more laughter among the dragons. "We can smell your intentions, and they are sincere," said a yellow-hued dragon with wings like a summer cape wrapped around its body. "A defector from Koschei's ranks. You have piqued our curiosity. Say what needs be said. Our time is precious."

"Much has changed in the centuries you have dwelt here, milords," the Cheshire said. "Avalon has changed. No longer do they seek out the innocent for their quests of glory. Our king is kinder and wishes for peace."

"The same as it ever was, and the same as it ever will be. Peace for the interim, until you grow dissatisfied with your lives and seek more amusements at our expense. Only one of humankind has ever been our friend, and now she, too, dreams that dreamless sleep."

"But your alliance goes beyond just Queen Talia of Avalon. Your alliance with her is manifested in the sword she carried. A sword you forged on her behalf as testament to your friendship with her. Her descendants now share her cause, and it is they who suffer Koschei and his daughter."

Tala realized what the Cheshire meant and stepped forward. The sword didn't look all that different from when she'd drawn it out—it was still on the rusty side, still brittle-looking. It had not changed its appearance for her the way it had for Ken. But there was a rustling of scales and the flapping of heavy wings as the dragons drew nearer for a closer look.

"It is ours," one confirmed. "We recognize its fires within its blade."

"You created it on her behalf, knowing she would eventually give her life for both your causes. And you let her, because it was your greatest weapon against Koschei and Buyan."

Low growls met the Cheshire's accusation. "Buyan enslaved us. Sought to cage us and glean our knowledge to wage war on the world. Your species have hunted us for eons, our heads for trophies, our wings for spells. You use our hearts to destroy your own kind in battles we never wanted. We had no choice. Talia Briar-Rose knew that. Not all sacrifices are willing. Some are made out of duty.

"Pledge your love to the blackest flag," the blue dragon added. "It was what Koschei would demand of the human sacrifices made to his dreaded Alatyr—that corrupted magic, his affront and mockery to us. He took the purity of our magic and turned it into fields of blood."

"Pledge your love to the blackest flag," Tala echoed, stunned, as the third part of the Avalon king's doom was finally made clear to them. "That was Alex's prophecy."

"It may come to pass that your king shall be asked to make that ultimate sacrifice, young wielder. And should that happen, then there is nothing you and your Nameless Sword can do to prevent it."

"Did you not remember the oaths you both made upon its forging?" the Cheshire asked. "For as long as one who is worthy enough can hold the blade, you fight with us. *From winter's darkness, till dawn of light, do man and dragons battle night. Our swords are yours.*"

"The Earl of Tintagel's oath," Zoe murmured.

"Koschei was slain," said one of the dragons.

"Koschei's daughter seeks to revive her father for the purpose of regaining entry into Buyan."

Angrier snarls. "Impossible."

"It is possible. We have staved her off for as long as we can, but she has attacked Maidenkeep. Our king lies unconscious. She has cursed the kingdom in frost before, in her rage."

"I am the sword wielder," Tala said before she could lose her courage. "I have been for close to two hours now. The one who fought with this sword before me gave his life opposing the Snow Queen. Her ice dragons savage the land, and all other kingdoms are under threat of being attacked in the same way. She is enraged and will stop at nothing to open Buyan once more. I understand now that Avalon has not been kind to you in the past, and I want to ask what it would take as compensation for you to help us."

One dragon lowered its head so that its bright golden eye was looking right at her. "You are different," it said. "You are more than just a sword bearer."

"I am a Makiling," Tala said, not really knowing if they would recognize the name but feeling compelled to say it all the same.

"You come from a people who have fought with us since war grew inevitable. Humans once hunted our dragon hearts because of their capability to negate magic. This, however, we shared with your ancestors, whom we trusted."

Tala's eyes widened. "Our agimat?"

"As they named it, yes. You carry within you the quietness of old magic not unlike our own. We remember the oaths we swore on this sword. We will listen to your request. Compensation can be discussed later."

"The Snow Queen seeks to revive her father, and we have been doing our best to stop her. Alex— our king—used the Nine Maidens to save us, but he cannot be woken. Kensington Inoue, the previous bearer, gave his life to bring us the singing bone along with other artifacts the Snow Queen requires to resurrect Koschei and open Buyan."

"We see the pathfinder and the great key." The crimson dragon swiveled its head to regard the lotus lantern Loki carried and then West's raskovnik before turning to Nya. "We see the soul carriers, three of them—one bearing that tainted, revolting shadow. We see our fledgling adarna and the shard of bone. But we do not see the music maker."

"You can see what?" Tala spun, hoping to see the adarna somewhere within the darkness, only to be disappointed. "The Snow

Queen took the adarna when we were escaping. And the singing bone disappeared when Ken died."

"A child of wondrous magic within you, and yet you cannot sense it? You cannot feel it reverberating across your being? Does not the sword you hold show you the truth?"

Tala glanced down at the Nameless Sword and thought she could once again hear the adarna's song. "But I saw the Snow Queen—"

"Koschei's daughter took its physical form, true. But the adarna's soul remains with you. You bear with you your own soul carrier, its essence saved within."

The tamatebako that the lady from the Ryugu-jo had given her. *It is rare enough for an owner to be chosen*, the woman had said. *It opened for you and will no longer do so for another.*

Tala had almost forgotten about the strange turquoise box she carried with her. She brought it out, its shine a soft gleam in the dark. "This one?"

"The adarna's soul resides within. Was it not a guarantee of its safety that you chose to place its essence within?"

"I didn't even know that's what I'd done!" She remembered opening the box, felt like she was being pulled into it. But the adarna had thrown itself forward as if to protect her from—

"The tamatebako," said the silver-colored dragon. "I have not seen my treasures in such a long time."

It bent its head toward Tala. Understanding, she held it out for it to sniff at.

"I built a palace once, under the sea," it said, "and constructed such jewels to share with the people who dwelled near my home. I took among them the most loyal of my priestesses to guard it forevermore, intended it to house memories for people to remember loved ones long after they were gone. But humans are an innovative species. They learned to contain souls within the tamatebako, to stave off death. But they cannot use such powerful spells in their pure forms the way we can. An equivalent exchange is required, and such magic always comes at a heavy price."

"The humans have legends about a man named Urashima Taro," the Cheshire confirmed. "His life was said to have been kept within one such tamatebako, and it rendered him nearly immortal."

"Not a life," the dragon said. "Life cannot be hidden within, only lived. Not a life but a soul's shadow."

Tala gasped.

"You claim to fight against Koschei's daughter, and yet you do not understand the weapons you use to oppose her," the blue dragon said accusingly.

"Do not be so harsh on them," the jade dragon admonished. "We have chosen exile exactly so that the humans will forget our magic and prevent their own eventual destruction."

"You really think we'll destroy ourselves one day?" Loki asked.

The dragon fastened its golden-eyed gaze on them. "Yes," it said. "We know this with certainty. There is a peculiar selfishness within the lesser among you that will be the downfall of the greatest among you. We are prepared to sleep for as many centuries as it will take before the last of you are gone and only we remain. But we are not completely heartless. We shall help you against Koschei's daughter. But it is necessary for you to understand the weapons you wield if you are to succeed. Open the tamatebako, sword wielder."

Tala felt her way across the box with shaking hands. She'd searched many times before. There was no hidden crevice to uncover, no keyhole to unlock.

"Concentrate, youngling. Remember not the box but what lies within it."

The adarna. The cheerful, infuriating, good-natured adarna, who had made her head a nesting place because it was comfortable, so that it was on hand to protect her when her agimat had still been weak and useless. The adarna, who would sing to ease her spirits, sometimes at the expense of its own strength. The adarna, who had been a strange companion, who had saved her so many times before—

There was a click.

The box opened.

It wasn't quite the adarna but a dark shadow of it. But its presence washed over her immediately like a warm, soothing glow, the familiarity of it sending fresh tears to her eyes. It looked like a shade but with none of the Snow Queen's influence corrupting it.

It dipped its head to Tala and piped out a soft melody the way the adarna always did.

"Close the box."

Tala did, and the shadow disappeared as soon as the lid was shut.

"The adarna that Koschei's daughter has taken," the jade dragon said, "it will not sing for her. For as long as you keep its soul with you, it will not die. Use this to breathe life into its corporeal form."

It moved its head and regarded Nya. "And what of you?" it asked. "Whose soul do you guard with such fidelity?"

"Nya," Loki said, understanding dawning in their eyes. "Did you—are you—"

"I couldn't tell any of you," Nya said. "That's what I saw in my vision. I had to keep it a secret. I couldn't take that chance." She hugged her tamatebako tightly to her chest. "I couldn't do that to Ken."

"The shade that was following us, helping us," Tala said. "And Ken—back at OzCorp, he lost his shadow when he tried to infiltrate the building. Nya, are you saying—"

"—that there might still be a way to save Ken? I don't know. The visions didn't tell me if I would be successful, only what would happen if I failed. But I have to try."

"There is something else," the Cheshire said. "You say you sense the singing bone among us. That was lost when the previous sword bearer passed away."

"You have lived far longer than most humans, and yet you cannot taste the magic yourself?" The blue dragon huffed. "Must we show you how everything is done?"

The Cheshire's brows creased. He stalked toward Tala, circling around her, deep in thought.

"You're right," he said. "How silly of me not to have noticed. My old age is catching up to me."

"Where is it?" West asked.

The Cheshire held out his arm, opened his hand. The bone lay at the center of his palm. No sooner had he done it than it winked out of existence again.

"Don't fret," he said. "I picked Tala's pocket for it, and it is simply once again returning to its owner. Didn't the Horned One say that it answers to Nameless Sword wielders? Hadn't this same thing happened to Ken when he tried to hand it over to the Avalon techmages?"

Startled, Tala reached into her pocket and felt the telltale smoothness of bone.

"The singing bone was taken from the skull of a man who was once doomed to eternal suffering," one of the dragons said. "A young human who possessed innate magic showed him compassion at his wake and unintentionally brought the wretched man back to life long enough to repay his kindness. The young human's descendants continue to watch over such sinners, believing that one day the dead they guard will be resurrected long enough to do the same and gain merit in their next lives."

Zoe had been quiet this whole time as well, but now she raised her head, eyes wide, staring at the dragon. "Gravekeeper," she said. "It wasn't the *Nameless* Sword; it was Gravekeeper it meant when it said to call for its army. The *dark sword*."

"Perhaps you lot are not so clueless after all," the yellow dragon noted with satisfaction.

"Now what remains is the hidden spot in Wonderland where the portal to Buyan can be accessed," the Cheshire said. "The last of the artifacts—the Wonderland Tree."

"That is easy," the crimson dragon said. "We shall show you the way, for a price."

"Name it."

"The first: that after you find what you are looking for in Buyan, you destroy all connections linking it to this world for good. It was in Buyan that the darkness of the human heart was rekindled by spells none of you were meant to possess. Let them fade from existence as we have strived to fade from human memory."

The Cheshire nodded. "That goes without saying. We know far too well the damage that magic run amok could do."

"The second: that you allow us to return to our sleep and speak to no one of the means by which you were able to gain entry to our domain. Whatever foibles you humans seek to create next are no longer of our concern."

"A concession, if I may: we pledge never to tell anyone else, but in the far-off future, should anyone be able to pass through the Burn using their own resourcefulness and knowledge, I ask that you do not turn them away until you have at least listened to what they have to say."

"And why should we do that?" the yellow dragon asked haughtily.

"You agreed to help us because you oppose Koschei as much as we do. You are just as much invested in the world as we are. You cannot look that far into the future and say with any certainty that such problems would not arise again."

The dragons lowered their heads toward one another in silent communication. "Very well," the yellow dragon said. "Our third and final demand: that the artifacts you have gathered remain in our keeping once the threat of Koschei has passed. Let no one else seek to resurrect the ghoul, no matter what their intentions shall be."

"Other kingdoms have claimed ownership of many of these items, and they cannot be surrendered without their agreement," the

Cheshire told the dragons. "But I think they can be persuaded if the requests come directly from you. We can vouchsafe, at the very least, turning over the singing bone. I suspect the Germans would be happier without the Wild Hunt in their woods."

"Wait," Tala said. "Are we supposed to turn over the adarna to them once we've recovered it too?" The thought of the cheerful bird stuck in this strange limbo with the dragons did not sit well with her.

"And why not?" the blue dragon asked. "We are, after all, its ancestors."

They all stared at it. "The adarna is a *dragon*?" West quavered.

This time, the laughter emanating from the dragons was louder. "Firebirds are our descendants, so to speak," the jade dragon said. "They share in our essence and are the closest to us that still exist in your world. It is why Koschei and his ilk seek them out."

"The firebird shall find the consort's child, but she shall find it twice," the silver dragon said. "The sword shall seek her out, yet she shall seek it twice. Twice she chooses and twice she falls and twice she rises. She is fire. And all shall burn. Rare as it is for a Makiling, you bear a prophecy because we are a part of it. The adarna is not the artifact in question. The final artifact necessary is us. Koschei took a part of our magic into him, and we shall take it back soon enough."

"Buyan was once a peaceful place," said the blue dragon. "We taught humans to harness the old magic. It was our greatest mistake. We have seen parts of the future, murky as they may be. We know our place in its destiny."

The crimson dragon approached and pressed its nose against

one side of Tala's sword. Drops of red fell upon the blade, glittered for a few moments, and then disappeared.

"Here we seal our bargain," it said. "When the time comes, you need only raise it and call. But there are dangers to our assistance, for our fires can burn you. A weaker bearer may not survive our storm. Hold strong and rise to the occasion, young Makiling. And then the world shall hear our answer."

There was an advantage to having one's ancestral home situated in the middle of nowhere, surrounded by graveyards to prevent the superstitious from trespassing. It meant there was no one around when the dragons materialized right outside the Nottingham castle. Even Lord Nottingham, not one to express much emotion even during worst-case scenarios, had not been indifferent to the sight.

"There are dragons," he actually sputtered. "*Fire* dragons. Milord, where in this hell's earth did you find—"

"I've given my word not to divulge their origins," the Cheshire said primly. "You only need to know that they have pledged to assist us against the Snow Queen. Secrecy is paramount."

"It's a real dragon," Adelaide gasped. "You're bigger than what the history textbooks portray, milord—uh, sir, um—"

The crimson dragon lowered its head so that its snout was within touching distance of the girl and then looked impressed when she didn't back away. "What a polite young thing. How can someone so gently reared be in possession of such a sword?"

Adelaide's face fell slightly. She gripped Gravekeeper harder in her hand. "It was—it was my brother's. He died yesterday. I've only just—just—"

"It is a heavy burden for one so young, but I am afraid we will be needing your strength soon enough. Let us make haste to the graveyard and heed my instructions, little one. I shall teach you a great trick, one that had been forgotten even by your ancestors. Would you like to hear it?"

Adelaide looked up at it. "Will it help us defeat the Snow Queen?"

"Indubitably. But I must warn you that such a spell will take its toll on Gravekeeper's owner, though I am convinced you will rise to the occasion admirably."

The girl nodded. "Then lead the way, kind sir."

As always, the harsh winds and the snow covered most of the burial grounds; no one would have thought there were thousands of bodies lying buried beneath the soil. Tala turned to the spot where Ken lay buried and saw Nya doing the same, fear and anticipation stark across her features.

Tala didn't know what she was expecting. Certainly not the bone in her pocket suddenly trembling when Adelaide, still wielding Gravekeeper, approached her uncertainly. She could hear a murmur of voices within the bone, though none of the words were distinct. From the look on Adelaide's face, Tala knew she heard it too.

The crimson dragon's orders had been specific. Slowly, Tala took out the singing bone and held it aloft. Adelaide raised her sword in response.

It happened quickly, because suddenly Tala wasn't holding the bone anymore. A coil of darkness was once more whipping itself into a frenzy around Gravekeeper, despite the absence of nightwalkers. Something solid grew out from within it, wrapping itself around the blade, the thorns flattening down and turning white until a fresh carving of bone was inlaid against a hilt now shining a bright ivory, the first spot of light she had ever seen the sword possess.

Adelaide took a deep breath and held it higher.

Nothing moved for a few minutes, and Tala nearly thought they'd made a mistake somewhere. That doubt disappeared when she saw the ground move.

It was like watching a horror movie. A hand burst out from the ground, bits of dirt raining down its arm, as one of the previously undead struggled to climb out of its grave. The whole burial ground had been transformed into masses of corpses pulling themselves out of their resting places.

The Nottinghams had told them that Nibheis housed tens, perhaps even hundreds of thousands of bodies throughout the centuries they had tended the graveyard, and they didn't lie; they outnumbered any army Avalon could bring. The only consolation Tala could find here was that none of the corpses were visibly rotting; whatever magic it was that bound them to the burial grounds, they had preserved at least that.

There was a sharp intake of breath from Lumina. Tala heard the sharp bark of Lola Urduja's orders as the rangers readied their weapons.

But none of the corpses mounted an offense. They all remained silent, their heads turned to Adelaide, sensing who their mistress was.

None of the other Nottinghams looked surprised. How many of the undead were their own ancestors, buried to honor an oath older than any of them?

Poor Adelaide was shaking. Tala, who had not left her side, drew out the Nameless Sword. She wasn't entirely sure if the sight of the blade would affect any of the undead, but that wasn't her priority. The younger Nottingham smiled gratefully at her, appreciating the support.

And then West followed suit, standing beside Adelaide, and then Zoe and Loki and Nya. The young girl raised her head as if finding strength from their closeness.

"Come to me," Adelaide said in a loud voice that echoed across the open air, "and honor your pledge to those who came before me, who lived and fought for your sake."

The undead masses faced her.

It was a frightening, exhilarating sight, to see so many bow to Adelaide within that terrifying silence. The Dowager Nottingham moved forward, unafraid, and laid her hand on Adelaide's shoulder.

"You did well, love," she said softly. "He would be so proud of you."

Adelaide's lower lip wobbled. "I know." She looked at Tala. "This is your army more than it's ever been ours," she said. "We've always been the graveyard's guardians, but the end goal has always been to aid whoever wields the Nameless Sword."

"The Nottinghams have pledged themselves in blood to Avalon as penance for our own sins," Lord Nottingham confirmed, stepping up to them with Cole's parents. "Our swords are yours to direct as you see fit."

Tala took a deep breath and nodded. A part of her still wished that Ken was here instead, because he would know how to take charge better than she ever could. She also wished that Cole was here, taking the burden away from his sister.

She looked down at her sword, which glowed in tandem with the shine of Gravekeeper's new hilt. "Agimat," she said. "My sword is called Agimat. And we will take this battle to the Snow Queen and have it done once and for all."

The earth moved again, and she realized that despite the many corpses that had climbed out of their graves to pledge their vows, one had remained untouched.

The earth shifted and broke apart as the latecomer lifted itself out of the ground to add to the number of undead. The freshness was still apparent in its clothes, the gleam on its buttons evidence that it had not been buried long.

It did not join the ranks of other undead who were lining up beside their respective mounds, waiting for their liege's next orders. Instead, it shuffled up toward where Tala and the others stood, oblivious to the gasps from those who were watching.

Adelaide let out a soft whimper, and Loki shakily whispered something under their breath, almost a prayer.

Only Nya stepped forward to meet the corpse. Her face was frozen in the expression of one who'd gotten what she'd wished for, though not in the way she wanted.

The figure stopped before her. A hand, both gray as stone and yet also bleached by the winter frost, reached out to tuck a curl of stray hair behind her ear.

"Rapunzel," it said.

23

IN WHICH TALA SEEKS TO MAKE AMENDS FOR PAST CHOICES

The news they received upon returning to Maidenkeep remained bleak. There were no changes to Alex's condition, and the firebird was the same. Mainstream media was finally starting to talk about the attack but was leaning hard on the worst possible take from it.

"Are they actually saying we deserved to be invaded?" Tita Baby asked in disgust, watching one particularly vile pundit state confidently that the fight had been nothing but a hoax engineered to make the Royal States look bad, and after what had been done to them after the Abigail Fey incident, they had all deserved it.

"It doesn't look good for the rest of the world either," Lola Urduja said briskly. "There is an insurgency problem happening within the Royal States, and many other terrorist factions in other kingdoms are using it as their rallying cry. There are many Americans on the ground who are fighting back against these nationalists, but it does not bode well when King John remains in power, with no clear way to remove him from his position."

"The Snow Queen has *my* flute," Zoe said through gritted teeth. "That's what's inciting them."

"The guillotine could help pursue...peruse...change the American king's mind," West spoke up. "Jasper's been managing Three Wishes while we were busy. She says that's been a popular sentiment among a lot of his subjects recently."

"It's not like you to be baying for blood, hijo," Tita Baby said.

"There are limits to being nice. And there are limits to it if the other side doesn't want to be. Otherwise, they'll just walk all over you and still say you're the one being mean."

"Wise words, Lord Eddings." Lola Urduja riffled through the reports that were coming in, brow furrowed. "We need to reach out to the grassroots, the ones who are familiar with their own localities. We need to coordinate with them, offer what spelltech they can use."

"Now?" Loki asked. "We're literally still in hiding."

"All the better. No one quite knows where we are, but their guard is down. We do not need to divest Maidenkeep of manpower to aid when we have cargoes of spelltech waiting to be used and the logistics needed to bring them to where they're needed most. If the resisters within the Royal States are willing to accept our assistance, then the old coot will be too busy frothing at the mouth to do much. It'll take the heat off us at any rate. Let us not limit ourselves to just the Royal States either. They do not have the monopoly on greed." She looked up crabbily. "Do we have all the contacts we've gathered from the Three Wishes?"

"Zoe transferred all the necessary information you'll be needing to my console," Dexter said. "I am already reaching out to some trusted sources she says will keep our secret for as long as we need."

"Dexter!" Tala cried, turning. The boy's face grinned back at her from a secondary screen. He was still in his hospital bed, but his laptop was out and he was already typing furiously.

"Before you say anything," Dexter said hastily, "I got the doctor's permission to do this. Dad's not happy, but he understands. I'm not even doing a quarter of the workload that I'm used to doing inside the command center. I have all the details I can access just fine here."

"You're not supposed to be doing any work at all!"

"I was the one who worked with Zoe for these contacts. They trust me too," Dexter said pleadingly. "Please let me help. I'm not good with weapons, but I am good at this one, so let me be useful. I deserve a crack at the queen, too, in my own way. Plus I'm going bonkers sitting here doing nothing."

Lumina sighed. "At the first signs of fatigue, I'm going to ask someone else to take over, understand?"

The face on the screen brightened. "Yes, ma'am! I've already got a few replies, and they want to help. Zoe and I had set up a system where we can drop off the wares and have them picked up without needing a physical meeting. They say they want anything that can break through walls as quickly and as quietly as possible, and also something to bypass ICE's security like we did when we infiltrated their detention facilities."

"ICE?"

"They've been using the prisons there to hold more than just the asylum seekers. They're bypassing local enforcement laws and keeping a lot of activists under arrest without reading them their Miranda rights or even saying what the charges are."

"I think I can help out with that one," West said. "Lemme talk to some of them."

"What are you planning, West?" Loki asked suspiciously.

West flashed them a wide beaming smile. "Trust me. Besides, Dex is on hand to keep the reins on me, right?"

A low, resigned sigh came through the speaker.

"What about Alex?" Tala asked. "Sword wielder or not, I don't want to make any big decisions while he can't give the final say." She looked down at her sword. She hadn't tested it out yet, but its main purpose seemed to amplify the abilities of her agimat. She looked down at her tamatebako next, which she still kept in a sling around her waist. She'd somehow taken the adarna's shadow into the box, and it might have potentially saved its life, whatever the Snow Queen might intend while its physical body remained the woman's prisoner. "I'm going to Alex," she said. "I want to test something."

Tristan was by the king's bedside as always, and he looked up, puzzled, when they all arrived.

"I have no guarantees about what happens next," Tala warned him before he could say a word. "But I know Alex would have wanted me to at least try. Don't freak out just yet."

"Somehow you telling me not to freak out is making me do exactly that," Tristan said, but he managed not to look too anxious when Tala set down the tamatebako on the sheets, then focused the flat of the sword against Alex's chest.

It was, in many ways, like using her usual agimat, only this time, she was using the sword instead of just the incorporeal shield she was used to all her life. Having something physical to hold on to made her

340

feel stronger somehow, and not just because the sword was amplifying her abilities.

She'd never really known how Ken had managed to be so intuitive when it came to working out what his sword could do. It had also been an extension of his twin swords, Yawarakai-Te and Juuchi Yosamu, but he'd done more than both swords were capable of, like its blinding bursts of light or the sudden strength to cut twenty-foot ice dragons effortlessly in half.

She was starting to realize how.

Visions flooded her mind—not of the future but of images of her, showcasing the many ways in which she could use Agimat to wake Alex. It was like she was staring at multiple parallel-universe versions of herself, each one making a possible choice that the sword was suggesting to her.

There were three options this time, and not all good. In the first, she was delving into Alex's mind, fighting her way through the demons that kept him bound to his sleep; her mirror alternate's strength visibly waned, even as Tala looked on. In another, she had— much to her horror—let Alex die, usurping his powers from the Nine Maidens as his life waned and taking control of it to fight the Snow Queen herself. And the last had been to give up again. Tala saw herself relinquishing the sword, sticking it back into the stone like she had done months before.

She was beginning to understand why the seeresses had difficulty in predicting the future when the Nameless Sword was involved.

Had Ken seen these parallel visions each time he'd had to use Kusanagi? Tala finally understood what the Cheshire meant when he described the fear he had felt when he rejected the sword. She hadn't known that rejecting it would be a constant battle she would have to fight.

But Ken had done it. Every time he had wielded Kusanagi, he had done so with a witty quip and the determination to do his best despite the odds stacked against them. And what would actually be unworthy of her was not being able to honor him and do the same.

"What are you planning to do?" Tristan asked worriedly.

"Everything I can," Tala said and focused on Agimat.

And just like that, she knew what she needed to do. The spell that surrounded Alex and tied him by fate to the Nine Maidens was just that—magic that she and her agimat could *technically* circumvent, though the power required was much more than one person had on their own.

Without the sword, it would have been impossible. A vortex of silence surrounded the sleeping king, and it negated the healing spells the medics attempted on Alex, keeping him imprisoned in his own mind. If she could just get past those barriers and find a way to reach out...

It felt like a black hole, where any attempts to be in command of her own mind were sucked away into the void, like the barrier the Nine Maidens had put up was doing its best to vacuum up her will. It was like diving into molasses without a bottom to reach.

The thoughts in her own head turned ugly, putrid. What right did she have to hold the sword? What right did she have to change fate? Every king and queen who wielded the Nine Maidens was meant to die as a warning—a reminder that even those who tried to wield its power for what they believed to be true and good could not escape the consequences of its spells. Alex had already defied destiny before. What right did *he* have to receive another chance? She couldn't even save Ken. She couldn't save Cole or her father.

They *sounded* like her own thoughts, sounded like every single insignificant insecurity about herself manifesting all at once. The Nine Maidens used your own insecurities against you, took a truth you'd always thought about yourself and threw it back at you like images in a funhouse mirror, reflecting the bad things you'd ever believed yourself to be, even if they weren't the truth. That was the legacy of the Alatyr, for all the good some of its rulers had tried to do with it.

"Fuck you," Tala hissed under her breath.

It wasn't easy. Somewhere within this thick syrup of magic was Alex, and she knew he was battling to get out just as hard as she was trying to find him. And while she had never been good at fighting for herself, she'd always been better when it came to fighting for someone else. She had a sword in her hands and a promise to keep.

In her mind's eye, she was raising that sword, using it to cut through the darkness to reveal what lay beyond. She was sick and tired of being told she wasn't good enough, that she wasn't worthy enough. With Agimat's own abilities surging through her, giving her what she needed to repel the rest of those intrusive thoughts, she was tired of believing all that too.

She slashed through the void, but the abyss fought back. The twilight stuck to her sword, threatening to pull her in with it, and Tala realized this was the real threat. If she hesitated, she could likely be sent into unconsciousness in the same way Alex had.

Not gonna happen, she thought.

Tala thought of Ken again and his sword—Kusanagi's ability to cut through all nonliving things using Yawarakai-Te as one of its dual cores. An agimat was supposed to do the same with spells.

The trick is to find the point where the magic can be cut off from its source, to do with as you wish, Lola Corazon had said.

Tala cut up more of the darkness, and it gave way, solidifying enough that she could start carving out chunks from it, revealing a low but steady light beyond. Emboldened, she renewed her assault until she had cut away enough of the night to hear a soft, dearly familiar voice echoing from somewhere behind it.

Tala?

Tala bolted awake, and Tristan jumped back. "You were out of it for a while," he said warily, watching as she finally registered that she was back at the hospital room. "It was like you were in a trance. I didn't want to wake you just in case, but I was about ready to call a nurse when it woke." He gestured at the firebird, who had nested itself at Alex's shoulder, cooing anxiously and stroking the boy's face with a wing as if it hadn't been comatose alongside him. "I wasn't sure what was going on…"

His words trailed off when Alex stirred and grunted, opening his eyes.

"Alex?" Tristan was by the king's side in an instant.

"Tala," the young ruler croaked. "It could have caught you, too, you jerk." And then he cracked them both a weak smile—easily the best thing she'd seen today. "Thank you."

Nobody really knew what to do with Ken, if the apparition before them could still be called by his name. All the undead were keeping their distance, perhaps sensing that the sight of them brought the living discomfort. They stuck to the Nottinghams' burial grounds for the most part, content to stand around aimlessly and do nothing until Adelaide or another Nottingham could give them their marching orders. None were willing to leave the boundaries of their former resting place, and it seemed like an unwillingness rather than any actual magical restrictions keeping them in place.

Nya showed no fear. She strode into the graveyard, and no one thought to stop her. Tala saw her sit quietly beside Ken's form. Beyond his initial greeting, the former sword wielder had said nothing, choosing to remain with his fellow departed, but the boy's unnatural quietness did not perturb Nya. Some of the wolves approached them, lying meekly by their feet like they were domesticated dogs.

"Am I the only one who thinks this might not be the healthiest way for her to process her grief?" Loki whispered. They and Ryker stood beside Tala, keeping a watchful eye on the girl with her.

"I don't know if this is grief that I'm seeing," Tala said slowly. Nya was in surprisingly good spirits. Tala couldn't quite hear the one-sided conversation that was taking place, but Nya was talking and gesturing animatedly while Ken kept an aloof if respectful silence, and it looked so wrong, when it was Ken who had always been the garrulous, charming talker and Nya the exasperated listener. "Nya's not at liberty to tell us what her plan is. Still, I can't help but hope."

She looked down at her Agimat. The sword had changed when

she used it to heal Alex. It felt coarse and wooden underneath her fingertips despite its now sleek and shiny appearance, almost like the arnis sticks she was fond of using. She swung it experimentally, and despite their fresh bond, it was a familiar feeling. "We can do this," she said quietly. "We will."

24

IN WHICH THRALL COLLARS HAVE A NEW PURPOSE

Y ou never told us you were a dragon," Tala said reprovingly to the firebird.

It shrugged, stuck its beak in the air, and sniffed arrogantly.

"Oh, don't you be condescending to me now."

Alex was finally up, grudgingly acquiescing to being pushed around in a wheelchair so he could once again take charge. The awe that the rest of the team at Maidenkeep had greeted Tala with, no doubt spurred on by Tristan's embellished recounting of what had happened, had been mildly embarrassing.

"Fortunately, the groups are not as large as the ones in the Royal States are," Tala heard one of the techmages reporting. "But it looks to be coordinated. I'm tracking down websites and forums showing that they've planned this across kingdoms and countries, have been for months."

"How long?"

"Much longer than we thought. The first real proof that many of them had been planning an invasion was right after the frost. The Snow Queen's become something of a symbol to most of them."

Tala could practically hear Alex's wince. "Have any succeeded so far?"

"None. Germany, Norway, and New Zealand have been arresting the major players. Spain and France has been having difficulty, but I don't think we're going to see anyone successfully storm the Bastille a second time. People in Asia are rising up, but their main contention is against the Middle Kingdom and not from any coordinated attacks with other groups in the west."

"It might get worse," Lord Suddene said.

"Thanks, milord."

"Only trying to tell it like it is, Your Majesty. There's reason to suspect that the Snow Queen has been using the flute to rile up more people than would have ordinarily participated. There are reports of armed insurgents in several states, and King John is using it as a reason to encourage more riots."

"Swell," Loki said. "Creating your own violence and then claiming you're the solution to the very violence you're sowing."

"Let's not be too quick to blame a flute for something they would have wanted to do in the first place," Alex said with a scowl. "Claiming they were compelled is just another tired excuse. Remember when they tried to use that against me? Monitor what's going on within the Asian kingdoms. Has anyone else pinpointed our location yet?"

"Nothing on the news, just a lot of speculation. Aleena and a few of the other techmages have found a few calls from allies trying to find out where we are, but I advised not answering and giving out that information until we decide what to do next."

"And that's the crux of the whole matter, right? Deciding what to do." Alex rubbed at his eyes. "I've been sleeping for over a day, and I still feel tired."

"I'm not sure I would describe what you've been doing as sleeping," Tala pointed out dryly.

"Maybe, but I've wasted enough time trying to fight my way out of that, and I still haven't thanked you enough for it. The Snow Queen may have the flute, but we still have most of the artifacts."

"You forget, Your Majesty," Lord Suddene said soberly, "that the Snow Queen likely already knows the location within Wonderland where the portal to Buyan lies."

"She wants the singing bone, too, though I'm not sure why yet," Tala said. "Ken sacrificed himself to make sure she didn't have it." Her eyes fell back on the display screen, which had been trained on the Nottinghams' graveyard. Through it, she could see Ken, who had not moved from his position, and Nya still chattering away. Ken's parents were beside them both, though neither seemed inclined to talk, only gazing back at their son with quiet grief in their gazes.

Tala's mind flitted back to everyone else they'd lost. Lola Corazon saving Lola Urduja because she had known Lola Urduja would be important for the battle ahead. She had also known there was something important about the Burn, which was why Tala had focused on the location. Cole giving up Gravekeeper. He had also—

Tala stood up a little straighter, her mind furiously working. "Lord Gallagher, when you modified the thrall collar that was used on Ryker, didn't you also add a tracking device to it?"

"Well, er, yes. I thought it would be much more useful than

the, um, barbaric shock features that Sir Cadfael insisted on keeping for it."

"Can you track it now?"

"I believe Sir Cadfael is right beside you."

"Yes, I am." Ryker's eyes were bright, realizing what Tala already had. "But I don't have the collar anymore."

"Dexter," Severon Gallagher said, sounding more excited, but Dexter was already interrupting his father.

"I'm running the tracker right now," the boy reported. "Shouldn't take more than a few seconds if the cold didn't get to its—no, wait. It's still activated and—and it's *moving*!"

"Show it to us!" Tala practically shouted, and the display swiveled around so they could see—a red blinking dot on a map that Dexter had drawn up. Tala was no expert on geography, but she knew it was no longer at World's End. The blip on the screen told her instead that it was somewhere in Washington, DC.

"What's it doing in the Royal States?" Loki asked.

"And if the Snow Queen discovered it, why keep it with her?" Tala asked.

"This tracker's currently in the kingdom's capital, where King John resides." Zoe's eyes were bright, some of her old fire returning. "If the Snow Queen intended this as a lure, I doubt she would be at a place with the highest security in the country."

"She isn't there to attack them," Tala said, catching on. "She's there to uphold whatever secret alliance she has with King John. She doesn't know about the tracking device on the collar."

"She doesn't even need it," Zoe continued. "She could control people even without the collar on. She's only using it out of spite. As a way to flaunt him in our faces when we meet her again. To mock us."

"Zoe," West said. "Are you also saying that—that—"

"It's only speculation, West." It was a wonder, how steady Zoe's voice sounded. "But it could explain everything. Why his doom was written that way. Why he had to be at World's End to—"

And then, just like that, the dam broke. Tears began to stream down Zoe's face, even though her tone remained quietly aloof, relentlessly logical.

"The whole reason for his prophecy was to make sure we learned the location of the portal into Buyan, which is the only thing we still don't know. It wasn't just about him or me. It was this all along. I..." She trailed off, blinked, and raised a hand to her face. "Am I crying?" she asked, and only then did her voice break for the first time. "Why am I...?"

"Zoe," Tala said softly.

"Your Majesty," one of the techmages called out as West drew close to Zoe for a hug when she finally began to weep in earnest. "I think we have some people trying to get our attention."

Alex whipped around to her. "Someone knows where we are?"

"Not exactly, Your Majesty." The screen switched to several social media accounts, highlighting posts made by a number of organizations. Photos showed them on the streets, rallying and waving the flag of the Royal States—and also of Avalon.

We are standing in solidarity with the kingdom of Avalon, one post read. We march for Avalon now as much as we are marching for every person the king has denied justice to, from our Black siblings to the families he has and is still separating to other kingdoms and countries who have had to suffer from the Royal States' policies in their quest for profit. We will not forget. We cannot forget!

"They're from the Fight for Kids Project," Dexter said. "We helped them out earlier this year, handed them spelltech to provide instructional materials to low-income neighborhoods."

A video showed a group of police officers converging on the rally, weapons already drawn. A few began firing into the crowd, only to hit an invisible shield of air as the group began activating what Tala recognized as Avalon spelltech, rendering themselves impenetrable to the police bullets.

"They're providing instructional materials of a different sort now," Loki said with satisfaction.

More posts popped up. Organizations they'd helped in the past. Organizations they hadn't. Groups that spanned multiple countries. And the calls were growing as more became emboldened to voice their support, heading to the streets despite the threats of violence from the authorities. They were taking to the streets to defend both their own freedom and Avalon's.

Alex took a deep breath. Tala could tell he was fighting the urge to cry. "They'll still need our help," he said hoarsely. "What we gave them may not be enough."

"There's still the problem of the Snow Queen," Lord Suddene reminded him.

"And that could work in our favor," Lumina said. "We already know the Snow Queen is allied with King John, and that it's likely he'll use both his royal army and private mercenaries to cause more trouble. We can't fight this battle on several fronts, but we can count on allies like these to take the load off us."

"And we already have the networks necessary for it," Tala said, looking to Zoe. West was holding her carefully as the girl wept.

"I agree," Lola Urduja said. "They think they face protesters with little defenses to their name. Let us even the odds. And there is the chance that the Snow Queen, too, might use the ongoing chaos to distract us as she seeks out the Buyan portal."

"She doesn't have the raskovnik yet," West pointed out, clutching the plant close to his chest.

"No, but she has the flute. If I were her, I'd keep close to the place, waiting for Avalon to show up so I could wrest it away. We need to use the thrall collar's tracking device to find which part of Wonderland she'll be gallivanting over to, and then we'll know where Buyan is ourselves."

"While we're waiting," Dexter said, "would you like to hear the conversation between the Snow Queen and King John yourselves?"

They all stared at the boy, who was grinning back at them.

"You're going to want to hear this," he said. "I remembered that the thrall device had a listening device originally integrated into it. OzCorp might have been too greedy, but they were smart. They knew it would be excellent at ferreting out compromising material on their targets. I just activated it."

"Dexter," Alex said. "If I survive this, I am making you our national treasure and decorating you with as many civilian awards as I can. Do it. Show us what they're saying."

The boy hit a button on his laptop, and the sounds of the news reports still going on around them faded, replaced by an angry male voice.

"I lost men at World's End thanks to you. And it's still my ass on the line. I'll need triple the money you promised to carry the rest of this out. Enough to buy my own kingdom if I have to."

"That doesn't sound like King John," Tala said, startled.

"You will be compensated well for your efforts," came the familiar cold tones of the Snow Queen. "You do not have to worry on that score."

"I'm putting my men in danger just so *you* can revive your dead father and claim territory. I'd like at least half for an advance, plus your help in annexing our own territories in the future. You know I'm the only one who can get King John to see things my way. He pardoned my soldiers on my fucking recommendation. It was my idea to ally with you and OzCorp. He doesn't trust you, but he still trusts me."

"You flatter and fawn over him. That is not trust."

"But it gets the job done, and that's all that matters. King John's a narcissist. He'd betray his own country to stay in power. You could say that he already has after having his other goons kill off most of the contenders for the crown. Ask me how I know."

Zoe gasped softly into the silence that had fallen over the command center at the words.

The Snow Queen didn't ask. "Your king will be rewarded by ridding his kingdom of his most vocal and most persistent enemies. You will be rewarded with as much wealth as your heart desires. Unlike those around you, I do not break my vows."

"Let me and my men accompany you back to Wonderland when you raise the portal. You really think those shadow skeletons and some wolves are enough protection?"

"You care little about me." The smile was clear in the woman's voice, and it likely looked as cruel as it sounded. "The riches of this world are not enough for you. You want the power lying within Buyan."

"Can you blame me, lady? After all, isn't that what you're trying to do?"

A laugh. "You are free to accompany me if you'd like, Creller. You and as many of your men as you wish to take. See if you can handle the magic as well as you think you can. Where is the king?"

"Sleeping off a conniption. He's not liking the sudden surge of riots all over the kingdom."

"I leave for Buyan in two hours."

"A warning, though. If you think you're gonna control me like you do the Scourge of Buyan and that lad over there, then think again."

"If you wish to join me, then have your men ready."

A grunt from Creller, and then his footsteps faded away.

Dexter hastily switched off the listening device. "Can't keep it on for long," he explained. "Without a distraction, she might sense it."

"Creller is the name of the man who leads the private mercenaries we encountered at World's End," Loki said. "The same ones hunting for the jabberwock with OzCorp."

"She plans to go to Wonderland in two hours," Tala said. "She might not have the raskovnik, but she might have something else she can use. Do we have enough time to mobilize?"

"We'll have to," Alex said. "But we'll be at a disadvantage. Many of the rangers are in no shape to fight so soon."

"We shall make the time for it, Your Majesty," Lord Keer said fiercely.

"So will we," Captain Mairead said, stepping forward. "We've repaired the *Jolly Roger*. It won't be up to capacity as before, but it can still deliver a solid punch."

"What do I do with this recording?" Dexter asked.

Alex leaned forward. "Leak it to as many of the press as you can."

"Your Majesty!" Lord Keer said, startled.

"They'll find out where we are sooner or later. Their viewers have the right to know about this, don't you think?"

"So many in power have let him get away with it for so long. What makes you think that releasing a recording will change that?"

"Because I have to believe that there are many good people out there who still believe it can. That's what I'm trying to fight for too."

Slowly, Lumina nodded. "We lose nothing by releasing it," she said. "Whatever atrocities he's already committed, this would at least provide them more proof." She glanced at Lola Urduja.

The old woman inclined her head as well. "Set it so that they receive the recording in an hour and a half's time," she said. "It will give us the element of surprise when we ambush the woman."

"Here we go," Dexter said and typed rapidly. They all watched him for several minutes before he finally leaned back with a sigh. "Made it so they'll automatically get a packet less than two hours from now," he said. "They'll be able to pinpoint our location, though."

"Assemble all the soldiers we can spare," Alex instructed. "I want to be at Wonderland to greet the queen when she arrives. What do you think, Tala?"

All other eyes were trained her way, and the weight of Agimat rested against her. "I keep forgetting you're all asking about my opinions more because I have the sword," Tala muttered.

"Tala?" Lumina asked softly.

She knew her mother was not all right. She remembered their conversation back at the café Titas Chedeng and Teejay ran, talking to her father about turning himself over to the authorities. She'd only just told her mother then that she'd already drawn the Nameless Sword, guilty that she had convinced her father not to say anything. She had felt her mother's disappointment, the fear that she had come so close to being yet another victim of the sword. And now she was doing it a second time.

"Mom," she said. "I'm sorry. I don't know what's going to happen after this, but I'm tired of running and saying I'm not good enough. Because I am. I know that now. And I'm going to make you proud of me."

"I have always been proud of you, love," Lumina said, drawing Tala close. "And nothing will ever change that."

"We have the undead, and we have the dragons. We can count on the latter, but we need to make sure that the former will be with us when the time comes."

"Are you going to officially *ask* the undead to join us?" West asked apprehensively.

"Not just the undead," Tala said, steeling herself for the task ahead. "I'm going to ask Ken."

The graveyard was still as cold as ever, but Nya didn't look like she was bothered by it. She had stopped talking some time ago, content with the silence. To Tala's surprise, Lady Adelaide was sitting with her and Ken's parents. Even more strangely, so were both Baba Yagas, former and current. All looked up when Tala approached.

"We leave for Wonderland in less than two hours," Tala said. "Lady Adelaide, I wanted to ask if you will be accompanying us for it."

"I will," Adelaide said. "The rest of my family are. I have the sword. It would be cowardly of me not to." Her grip on Gravekeeper tightened. "My brother wouldn't forgive me if I didn't."

"I didn't know Cole as well as I should, but I think Cole would forgive you anything if it would keep you safe."

The younger girl nodded. "He knew about this. Did he tell you that? I don't think he even told Zoe. Great-Grandma tried, but every prophecy she saw told her that he was going to die. He'd been preparing for that for so long...but it still feels unreal." She sniffled. "I was convinced that we would find a way."

That doesn't mean you have to force yourself to fight if you don't want to."

"I want to. I really do. I might not be as good as Cole yet, but..." Adelaide made a few practice swings with her sword. "I'll figure it out," she said more confidently. "I'll fight for him as much as I'm fighting for Avalon."

"How sure are we that these undead will fight?"

Adelaide cast a nervous glance at where most of the corpses were still standing, motionless, despite the heavier winds picking up and the snow falling around them. "Do you think I should ask them? Baba Yaga?"

"There's a reason they tell people to respect the dead," the current Baba Yaga, Ilyena, said. They squinted at the row of unmoving shapes and shuddered. "I can see why."

"Any more prophecies that you feel like sharing with us before shit hits the fan?" Tala asked dryly.

"You are a lot more assertive now that you have the sword."

"Or maybe it's because I have run out of fucks to give, and Agimat is helping me enunciate that better."

The seer nodded approvingly. "I am not at liberty to tell you what I've seen. But even now, so many things remain murky that it would be useless to make a much more concise prediction, even if I could. I can tell you one of them. You will know what to do when you hear three songs intertwine." They turned to their mentor. "You said you saw it too. I thought you can no longer tell the future."

"I cannot. But it was the last vision I saw before my gift left me. Perhaps that was a consolation, a final parting gift for years of service." The older Baba Yaga smiled at them. "But I do not need to see into the future to trust in you young folk, whatever it might bring us all. Perhaps the undead have something to say themselves."

"Why not?" Nya asked calmly. "Ken, Tala and Adelaide want to ask you something."

The boy said nothing. Tala wasn't even sure if he'd heard, but Nya continued regardless.

"We're keeping track of the Snow Queen's whereabouts. She's heading to Wonderland, to Buyan. We plan on ambushing her there."

Still nothing. Ken had never been so quiet before. It was heart-wrenching.

"We'll need all the help we can get. You're sworn to fight with the Nottinghams. Will you fight for Avalon's cause just as much as you'll fight with Lady Adelaide?"

Ken finally moved. His eyes trailed down, toward the sword Tala held. Something that could have been a smile appeared on his face. "Kusanagi," he said, and despite his unchanging expression, a little bit of the Ken she'd known returned in his voice. "Agimat now. We fight for Avalon. For the sword. Always."

The other undead shuffled closer. "We fight for the sword," one of them said. "We honor our vows."

"We fight for the sword," another echoed. His corpse appeared to be older than many of the others. His clothing was more fur than linen, but the others moved to give him room as if in respect. "We honor our vows. We fight for Gravekeeper's wielder. We fight for the sword bearer. We will follow. When those that were missing shall fly again. When those who were dead shall rise again. When that which was cold offers warmth again."

"Alex's prophecy," Tala said. "And—and—"

"And yours, despite yourself. Once, I rose for a young lad no older than you. And now, we rise again. We hear. We obey."

Tala's earpiece chirped. "Tala," Alex said, "get your butt up here as soon as possible."

"Another attack?" Tala asked worriedly.

"No. Strangely enough, quite the opposite."

"Lord Nottingham reports that he's still receiving messages, Your Majesty," Lord Severon Gallagher said. "Specifically from Lady Felicity of France, among other kingdoms, all asking for information regarding Maidenkeep's disappearance."

"Mom's trying to find us?" Zoe asked.

The woman appeared promptly on screen. "I knew you were still out there," she said, almost scoldingly. "Where is my Zoe? Is she all right?"

"I'm here, Mom," Zoe said, inching closer toward the screen. "What's going on?"

"I am happy to see you unhurt, my poppet. It has been an agonizing day, trying to search for you. Your father says hi."

Jonathan Carlisle peered into the screen beside her, looking sheepish. "Hi, honey. Are you okay?"

"I am. Dad, I'm so sorry—"

"Never apologize for what you're not responsible for, Zoe. I'm doing well. I'll be staying temporarily with your mother until everything blows over, just in case."

"I told you before that we cannot officially aid Avalon due to other foreign policies in place that we must uphold," Lady Felicity said, taking over. "But after the attack on Avalon, His Majesty believes that we cannot sit by and do nothing. We have already done that once before, when the Snow Queen came after His Majesty's parents. We cannot have it so again." A pause, and then Felicity cleared her throat. "That is, of course, the official statement that I am to make to Avalon once communication can be established," she said. "But the reality of the situation is that His Majesty understands that the insurrections taking place all over the world are likely a direct result of King John and his foolishness, and that the Snow Queen's support has convinced him of his invincibility. It is enabling other extremists in France. It would be to our advantage to stop this nonsense once and for all. I hope you do not mind if I am being too forthright, Your Majesty."

"I appreciate the frankness, Lady Felicity."

"We also have several regiments on hand ready to fight with you, Your Majesty. This has gone on long enough."

"Your Majesty," a techmage called out. "We have a few more on the line. A diplomat from Spain, several officials from Germany and Sweden, more from Japan, Hong Kong, Canada, Vietnam…"

Tala sat back and watched as more kingdoms began pledging their support, offering use of their military forces to fight the Snow Queen at King Alex's decision.

"Some of them just want to save their own asses, you know," Loki said darkly right after Alex ended a call with the Belgian government. "You know they're not fighting for him really but fighting because they find it beneficial to their own policies."

"I know," Tala said, watching Alex's face carefully. "But Alex hasn't had anything even close to an alliance with many countries for so long. It's at least something that they're pledging their assistance now, even if they never bothered before."

Not every supporter was an official kingdom representative. Alex grew more emotional as he accepted calls from other organizations also pledging support. Tala stood by his side each time and slowly squeezed his hand whenever he sounded too choked up. Tristan was on Alex's other side, and she knew he was doing the same.

At one point, one organizer politely asked for Zoe. The girl responded, cautious.

The young man on their screen coughed. "I hope you don't mind," he said, "but I, well, me and my wife. We couldn't get pregnant. But we are now. And I know that wasn't the reason, but I—I just want to thank you. To let you know that there are a lot more like us who are grateful, even though we came about it at a different method than others."

"Oh," Zoe said, her tears welling up—the third time she'd shed them since her curse seemed to have been broken. And just like that, the waterworks couldn't stop. "I understand, and I appreciate it."

"We have everything ready and waiting," Lord Gallagher reported. "As soon as we get the coordinates from the Snow Queen's location, we can disseminate them quickly to the other waiting kingdoms. It's her move at this point."

"Are we ready?" Alex asked, turning to the rest of them. The rangers were, and so were the Bandersnatchers. The Neverland pirates already had cuirasses and other sharp weapons drawn, and the Katipuneros had followed suit with their abanicos. Rather than admonish her team, Lola Urduja herself already had her fan in one hand and General Luna's shiv in the other.

Somewhere within the Nottinghams' graveyard, Tala knew Adelaide and Nya were waiting with Ken and the rest of the undead.

"We'll do it, Alex," Tala whispered. She didn't need to yell at him not to risk his life by using the Nine Maidens. Not when she was holding Agimat herself. This was their last chance. If they couldn't defeat the Snow Queen now, then Avalon was lost.

Ryker and Loki were quiet, reassuring presences beside her. On a whim, she took their hands in both her own and squeezed, receiving similar responses in turn.

Beside her, Lumina took a deep breath, then let it out. "If you see your father," she said, "you must leave him to me again."

"The Snow Queen's porting out," Tala heard Dexter say; then she saw in her own visor that the red dot vanished.

And then it reappeared—this time right at the heart of the Wonderland ruins.

"Now!" Alex shouted.

25

In Which the Battle Begins

They'd never been this deep inside the Wonderland ruins before; not even the rangers were permitted to explore here. Wild magic had run thick through these parts in the years since it had been destroyed. Whatever remained had since been reclaimed by the forests, rendered irrelevant by the passage of time, and made even more dangerous by the lingering spells that still survived against all odds. Tala could sense them the instant she emerged from the Avalon portal. Her whole body ached from it. Loki growled as well and shielded their eyes as if from some glare.

The Avalon forces had ported in half a mile away from where the Snow Queen had been detected, an added precaution. The very air was steeped in wild magic; any spell they cast could potentially trigger an explosion. Lumina, Tala, and the other Makilings got to work as soon as their feet touched ground, their agimats popping up as shields while the group stealthily made their way to, Tala hoped, wherever Buyan lay hidden.

The ruler of Beiran stood before a small clearing, her back toward them. There was no sign of the adarna anywhere. Tala felt sick with dread at the thought of what she had done to the gentle bird.

Several people stood with the Snow Queen. Vivien Fey was easy to recognize, and she was accompanied by other ice maidens. Tala's heart clenched at the sight of her father standing beside the Snow Queen, heard the soft hiss from her mother when she spotted the same.

The woman stood before a twisted, withered tree, one of the largest in the area. There was nothing about it that would have attracted her curiosity, nothing to tell her that it hid the way back into Buyan.

"The last artifact," Zoe breathed from somewhere behind Tala. "The Wonderland Tree."

But West made a whimpering sound. "What is it doing?" he whispered. "I didn't do anything to—"

The raskovnik in his pocket was shining, and something within that blackened tree was glowing in response—a soft swirl of sparks and color, like a tiny galaxy was contained within it.

It was the beginnings of a portal.

With the Snow Queen and Tala's father was another familiar figure, the thrall collar they'd left behind encircling his neck. Though she had already guessed, it didn't stop Zoe from choking back a gasp at her first sight of him.

"So you've finally arrived," the Snow Queen said pleasantly without turning around. "Is this sorry lot you've brought all that survived my previous attack, Alexei?"

"Give yourself up," Alex ordered. Lumina and Lola Urduja had agreed to let him take part in this battle with great reluctance, and Lord Keer was part of the compromise, surrounding the young king with the best of his Fianna. Tristan, as always, was by his boyfriend's side. Even Lord Suddene had joined the battle, hefting a great war ax. The firebird was a blazing wrath of fury above their heads. "You know this won't end well."

Kay Warnock turned to face them. His glassy white eyes were as cold and as blank as ever. He drew out his fearsome battle-ax.

Cole Nottingham turned too. His eyes were just as pale as the older man's. He clutched a sword that looked to be made entirely of ice.

"See how easy it is to be betrayed," the Snow Queen said. "I asked you before to leave me in peace. You would not. And now your reckoning is at hand."

"Your peace came at the expense of the peace of others," Alex said grimly. "There is a reason why other nations stand against you now. Whatever you and King John have hatched between yourselves, we will not allow it to pass."

Ice thickened the ground before her, grew higher until it crystallized into another great dragon, larger than those they'd encountered before. Three others began to take root in the soil beside it.

"Don't let them manifest!" Tala shouted, hefting Agimat into the air. "Now, Dexter!"

More portals blinked into existence. But this time, more armies came pouring out from kingdoms all around the world, answering Avalon's call to defend them.

Many of the Banders' parents were there, taking up the fight along with their children. Lady Felicity was in her element, directing the French forces, and Lord Inoue was on hand fighting grimly alongside his undead son, as quick with the sword as Ken was. Anthony and Shawn Sun-Wagner were at Loki's side, wielding a bo staff and a short sword respectively as they helped them fend off more shades.

Lord Nottingham had joined the battle himself, wielding a rapier elegantly with his unscarred arm, and Cole's mother had fallen in with the archers, her arrows swift and true as they felled shades heading their way. There were more snarls as the Nibheis wolves followed closely behind, lunging at the ice wolves that cowered at the sight of them.

Nya's whole village had shown up to participate, though many were serving as healers and support, quick to pinpoint those wounded in the field and bring them away to safety, while others tossed potions at nearby nightwalkers and inhibited their movements. West was joined by a pack of hounds, and soon the Eddings family was howling for blood.

At the same time, Adelaide raised Gravekeeper, and another portal behind her opened up. Now it was the undead who came thundering out—no longer listless and grave but bloodthirsty and spiteful. They attacked the first row of nightwalkers, falling on them like ravening dogs.

The battle had begun.

The Makilings had joined their agimats to expand their shield around more of their allies, even as guns fired and spells were exchanged. Most of the other kingdoms had been cautioned against bringing spelltech weapons into battle. Many came armed instead with as many spell negaters as they could wield.

Some of the ice maidens and most of the nightwalkers had not thought of such restrictions, and the results were terrifying. One ice maiden lobbed bursts of pure concussive forces of ice at those charging to meet her and hit on an unexpected patch of volatile spells nearby. She burst, loudly and violently, into pieces, and the combined efforts of Lumina and the Makilings protected her opponents from the same fate.

At one point, Tala found herself fighting side by side with the rest of the Bandersnatchers in a circle as they took on anything that came flying or rushing into their radius. "I need to get my flute back," Zoe growled. She couldn't stop looking at Cole, who was vicious with his new ice sword and was slashing at soldiers unfortunate enough to engage him. Tala's father with his ax was doing just as much damage.

"We need to find a way to get them both back," Loki said grimly. "We can't reach the Snow Queen while they're defending her."

Zoe changed direction, fighting her way toward the ice maidens, and Tala followed after her, knowing Ryker, Loki, and West were close by. She could see Vivien, ruthless as she sent waves of ice toward several groups of Avalon allies focused on defending and maintaining their shields rather than fighting back. Even in the thick of battle, Tala could sense powerful magic emanating from somewhere in Vivien and knew she had the flute.

"If you're here to try and change my mind again, Makiling," Vivien hissed, "then you are once again wasting your breath."

"We're no longer here to argue with you," Ryker said, and Loki proved it when they snagged their staff out of the air and delivered a series of stunning blows, battering at the hastily erected shield Vivien had created at the last minute to protect herself from their attack.

The hound that was West growled. Something was shining against his side.

"There's nothing you can do for now, hijo," Lola Urduja shouted at him. "The Wonderland magic activates it even if you do not wish it to! Keep it safe for as long as you can instead!"

"You will die just as quickly as the sword's previous bearer did," the ice maiden predicted mockingly, and ice grew around Tala, quickly climbing up to encase her in a ball.

Gritting her teeth, Tala slashed, and the ice shattered into pieces around her. She dodged when heavy icicles jutted up from the ground attempting to impale her. Ryker slammed his fist through one of them, and they broke on impact. He threw a powerful ice bomb back at them, only to have it explode loudly before it could reach the ice maidens. A series of powerful explosions stuttered through the air in its wake, like his magic had triggered invisible traps.

"Be careful!" Zoe shouted. "We're outside the Makilings' shields!"

The ice maidens didn't seem to care. Heedless of the danger to themselves, they continued to blast magic their way, a couple of them falling as Wonderland's wild magic countered, overwhelmed them. The rest hit and bounced harmlessly off Tala's agimat as she surrounded the rest of the Banders with her shield.

West and his family were biting their way through several ice wolves, joined soon enough by their Nibheis counterparts. Ryker was sticking close to Tala, taking down any nightwalkers that came within range.

"Do you really think this can stop me?" One of the ice maidens laughed when Ogmios wrapped itself around her wrist.

Zoe only smiled wider, and the electric currents that jolted their way into the ice maiden produced loud and painful results. The ice maiden staggered, part of her features dissolving and melting away as she collapsed.

Tala switched to offense and swung Agimat toward the nearest ice maidens as she advanced. The women hit the shield surrounding the sword and shrieked as it began to leach the magic out of them.

Tala swung her Agimat again, and another ice maiden shattered against it.

Why stop there, though? She could do more damage if she extended her Agimat's reach. She was strong enough to do it now. She could end this fight in a single, decisive blow. It didn't matter that it could destroy the negating shields protecting their other allies, leave them open to physical attacks. She could end it—

No!

Tala forced the thoughts out and switched targets, feeling for any more hidden, dangerous Wonderland magic and finding some a few meters away. She stepped toward it, luring the rest of the ice maidens to follow.

"Tala?" Ryker asked warily, keeping pace with her as she inched toward the trap she was setting up.

"When I give the word," Tala said, "throw more ice at them."

Ryker didn't even ask for an explanation. "Just say when."

"Is this the vaunted courage of Avalon's wielder?" one of the women taunted. "So quick to run and hide? As weak and as spineless as their king, who—"

"Shut up," Tala said and then added, "Now!"

The ice maidens were all but dissolved on the spot as the frightful spells did their work, steam rising from what little ice remained.

"We can't stay here for long," Ryker panted, looking down at the remains. "Sooner or later, someone is going to make a mistake, and then it's gonna be Pan and Hook all over again."

"I'm on it." Zoe had joined Loki in fighting Vivien, but unlike her ice maiden sisters, the woman was smarter, refusing to be cornered while using the myriad of ice wolves and shades at her disposal to keep them from coming closer. She reached into her robe and pulled out the flute. "Shit," Zoe said and redoubled her efforts. Ogmios came whipping through the air, but Vivien deftly avoided the lash, jerking the flute out of reach just in time. She raised it to her lips—

—and Tala felt like she was falling out of her body, even though she knew she was standing still. The woman must have been practicing since she'd acquired the flute; Tala saw Loki, his parents, and Zoe immobilized, as was every other soldier within hearing range of the strange music Vivien was playing. There was a squawk of anger from above as the firebird, who had been bombing the ice maidens with fire, struggled to push back against the spell.

Tala was screaming at herself to move, but her body refused to comply. She was moving without her own consent, turning to walk toward the ice maiden.

Vivien's eyes were on the Nameless Sword even as she continued to play. If the music carried far enough, it would halt their forces, and all would be lost.

Agimat was hot to the touch in Tala's hand. She stopped fighting and brought all her focus to bear on the sword instead, channeling every vestige of her willpower into the blade.

One of the other ice maidens held out her hand for the sword. She touched the hilt and froze, literally, as Agimat did its work. The salamanca spells Tala created accelerated the Snow Queen's magic quicker than even the ice maiden's body could allow for, keeping her as immobile as a block of ice.

And then the woman was on fire, screaming though she was still unable to move, as the ruthless firebird breathed flames onto her.

The fog lifted from Tala's mind. Her grip on Agimat tightened, and she whirled, putting everything she had into one powerful blow.

And then it was Vivien's turn to scream. Her severed arm dropped to the ground, the hand still holding on to the flute.

Zoe wrested the instrument away and raised it to her lips.

Vivien's eyes widened and she stilled as Zoe began a new melody. The song carried despite the sounds of fighting, and the ice wolves within range halted, ears raised as if listening. It made it easier for the other soldiers to move in, their swords busy, meeting with little resistance.

Avalon and its allies surged forward. Tala saw Alex and Tristan, still surrounded by rangers, still in the thick of the fight. She saw more and more nightwalkers succumbing to Zoe's song, allowing them to gain ground quicker. The undead were at the forefront, barreling through anything else that tried to put up a defense, slaying everything that remained spellbound to the flute's music.

But the Snow Queen was smiling. "You are too late," she said.

Ken stepped out from within the masses of undead. He held a

sword in his hands—no longer that of Avalon but the twin swords he carried before he had become the kingdom's sword bearer, given to him by his father before they stepped through the portal. The Snow Queen's gaze flicked toward him, and her smile grew knowing.

An icicle of immense length formed along her hand, and she struck at Ken with it. Ken parried neatly, his face registering no change of expression. In life, he would have responded with some witty banter. Now he was silent as he matched the queen blow for blow.

But the music was not enough to completely free Cole or Tala's father. They both hesitated briefly as the melody reached them but continued to defend their mistress. Lumina was fighting them both, and Zoe was moving to join her, facing off against her boyfriend. The other Deathless that surrounded them were proving to be just as invulnerable.

"So the flute really can't revert them back?" Tristan asked, trying not to sound as despairing as Tala felt.

Laughter from Vivien. She stood up, the stump at her shoulder reforming as she grew another arm from it. "You fools," she said. "That was only a distraction."

Tala saw the Snow Queen raise her hands. And then the earth beneath them rocked furiously, throwing her to the ground.

"This was what she was planning," Ryker said grimly. "This was why she was so smug and unsurprised about us finding her here. It's another trap."

"What kind of trap?"

A mighty roar answered Loki's question. An ice dragon's head loomed up before them from behind the thicket of trees above. It was followed by at least four more heads as they all brayed at the sky, wisps of deadly ice emanating from their nostrils.

And then there were more. As Tala looked on, horrified, a dozen more ice dragons made their appearance until the air was rife with the sounds of their bellowing.

"Your Majesty!" Dexter's voice over the comm link was just as terrified. "You have to get out of there! None of them are registering over our scanners, but we are counting at least fifty of these things through our visual displays."

"Did you say *fifty*?" Tala heard Alex say, aghast.

"Alex." This from Tristan. "You need to get out of here. Let us stay and cover your—"

"I am not leaving again!"

All the dragons brayed noisily and then, all together opened their mouths.

"Shields up and at maximum!" Lord Keer shouted. "Brace yourselves!"

Tala could not even begin to describe the winds that tore through them as the dragons breathed their worst down on the Avalon forces. She had put everything she had into her Agimat, pushing it out as a shield over her, Ryker, Zoe, Loki, West, and everyone else she could reach as the blizzard tore through their ranks. Without it, they would have frozen in seconds.

And then more detonations as the dragons' icy breath set off more hidden magic within the area. Tala felt a burst of pain but kept her Agimat steady, refusing to relinquish it until she felt the gale recede, until the noises finally faded away.

Everything was blanketed in white. Many of their own forces had not had shields to weather both attacks, and she saw that many soldiers had been frozen, so thickly and thoroughly that their shapes within the ice they were trapped in only looked vaguely human.

Lola Urduja was swearing long before the shield protecting her fizzled out. Tita Teejay was frantically digging through the rest of the snow, her face tearstained. "Chedeng's underneath the snow," she choked out. "She wasn't completely within the shield's protection when she…"

The dragons had risen off the ground, circling above. Several swooped down to the ground, and there were more screams as they went through a platoon of soldiers unable to defend themselves.

One made for Tala, and she threw herself to one side just in time as it barreled past, narrowly missing her. She hit the ground, and something jabbed hard at her stomach.

She reached down and fished out the tamatebako.

"Tala?" Ryker crawled over to where she was, where she was still staring down at the box.

"We thought it was the flute that mattered," Tala said. "But we keep forgetting that it's not the only artifact that can produce song. Three songs intertwined, the Baba Yaga said. That means it isn't just the flute. It's the flute and the adarna and the dragons."

Her fingers ran through the box, still finding no keyhole, no means to open the lid. *Please*, she thought desperately. *We need you now. Please, please, please.*

There was a click. The lid lifted.

The sweet song that carried out from within buoyed her spirits.

Every shade stood still, listening raptly to the melodies. Tala saw her father shake his head slightly, as if the music was finally starting to affect him, only to snarl and resume the fight.

"Zoe!" Tala shouted. "Keep playing!"

She couldn't see where Zoe was at the moment, but from across the field came the answering strains of a flute playing. This time, the telltale pause among the Deathless was much more discernible.

Tala lifted her sword above her head and closed her eyes.

"Tala." A hand encircled her wrist. "You know what the dragons said," Ryker said desperately. "They said you could die summoning them."

"I know," Tala said, strangely at peace with that. "Tell me you're not going to stop me, Ryker. If I don't, we die all the same."

A pause, and his hand withdrew.

It was heat unlike any she'd ever known when she lifted the sword a second time. It felt like the fires were baking her blood, the agonizing pain that suddenly consumed her being from the inside out. This was what it must feel, she thought, to die from burning.

"From winter's darkness, till dawn of light, do man and dragons battle night." She didn't know how she was still able to shout the words, even as she continued to endure the flames. "Honor your vows!"

She had not known how loud her voice could be until the overwhelming silence met her cry. Even the Snow Queen had turned to her, the outrage in her face plain to see.

But her call was rewarded.

More dragons graced the sky, but these creatures were made of scales and bone, and from their mouths came deadly fire rather than brittle ice. Their roars, loud as they were, blended in with the adarna's singing and Zoe's playing, the magic stronger for their accompaniment. They swooped down on the Snow Queen's dragons, and the beasts of ice shrieked in agony as claws dug deep into their glassy flesh, which broke easily underneath their talons. The dragons were unyielding; their teeth snapped and their mouths opened. More fire blazed out, melting their ice opponents as they fell back to earth. Tala saw the firebird among them, puffing up its chest like it was one of the majestic creatures before unleashing its own smaller yet powerful flames on the enemies below.

Tala sank down. Ryker caught her. "You're not burned," he said with relief, inspecting her quickly.

"No!" the Snow Queen exclaimed as she saw her advantage disappear.

Lumina saw their dragon allies approaching and ducked out of the way. Tala's father, still unafraid, turned to face the incoming beast. Zoe turned back to Cole in a panic, as if she wanted to yank him out of the way with her.

And Cole was seizing on her hesitation to make the final blow. A shove sent her stumbling to the ground, the music from her flute ceasing. He moved forward, sword raised.

The dragon's jaw unhinged.

Kay Warnock, Cole Nottingham, and two scores of Deathless immediately disappeared in a sudden conflagration, and despite knowing it had to happen, Tala cried out despite herself. Zoe had avoided the searing blast but remained on the ground, staring in horror above her at where Cole had stood, now obscured by flames.

But the fire died as quickly as it had arrived. And when the smoke cleared, Cole remained with barely any of his face and hair singed, his clothes still intact. But he had lowered his sword, and the eyes that had once been a transparent white had now returned to their gray color.

"Zoe?" he asked weakly, looking down at the girl sprawled on the ground before him and then at his icicle sword. For a moment, he stared uncomprehendingly at it.

And then he turned and swung it hard at an ice wolf that had been barreling toward Zoe, the sharp end driving deeply into its insides and coming out the other end. The beast roared in pain, cracks appearing along the wound as it disintegrated.

Cole sank to his knees, hands clasped over his head.

Zoe scrambled forward, weeping as she tugged Cole into her arms. The boy didn't even seem to notice, still hunched over with his breath leaving him in short bursts.

"He's in shock, Zoe. Bundle him up and get him out!" Lumina fared a little bit better with Kay; Tala's father had abandoned his ax and was standing dazedly around him, like he wasn't sure how he'd gotten there.

"Lumina?" he asked in a heavy brogue thicker than what Tala was used to from him but finally—finally—in the familiar warm voice that she knew and loved dearly.

She would have run to her father had she been close enough. As it was, Lumina had the clearer head of them both. She grabbed Kay's arm and dragged the dazed man toward where the other rangers had set up a line of defense. Zoe was doing the same with Cole.

The howl of outrage from the Snow Queen was loud and long; hundreds of meters of snow were immediately blanketed in ice, worse heaped onto stragglers as she unleashed her rage. The ice dragons, too, were turning away from their Esopian counterparts to focus on both Lumina and Kay, and Tala knew they wouldn't make it to safety in time.

And so she ran—toward the Snow Queen, toward the gathering of ice dragons.

One of the ferocious beasts swooped in her direction, as if the Snow Queen had sensed what her intentions were. It roared as it gained speed, claws lowering, but Tala ducked the attempt, rolling beneath its wings as it landed clumsily. She swung Agimat up, and the blade made a screeching sound like nails down a chalkboard as it sliced its way into the dragon's underbelly, water spilling out from the wound.

The dragon screamed and brought its head down to bite, but another of the Esopian dragons attacked. Distracted, the ice dragon turned to face the new threat, and Tala kept running. Behind her, she could hear more of the ice dragons rushing to the aid of their brethren and more of the Esopian creatures preventing them. More of Wonderland's wild magic was triggered, but the dragons kept fighting, heedless.

Though bereft of both her Deathless and her dragons, the Snow Queen had not left her post by the strange gnarled tree. The other undead were still approaching her, fighting their way through the rest of the ice maidens. Ken was still hammering at the shields that the Snow Queen had set up to protect herself. Numerous other smaller ice projectiles jutted out from his body, but none of them had slowed him down.

Tala didn't attack. She laid a hand on the protective barrier the Snow Queen had erected, felt parts of it melt away at her touch as Agimat flared against it.

"Did you not come all the way here to stop me, Makiling?" The Snow Queen looked tired and wan and just as sick of all this as Tala was. "What are you waiting for?"

Tala said nothing, only watched as the portal that the queen was creating grew bigger.

A smile crossed the older woman's face. "Your pathetic little king is dying. Do you still think gaining the Alatyr can cure him?"

"You thought he was dead years ago when you killed his whole family," Tala said. "You thought you could take my dad away. You thought you could kill Ken and the people I care about, that I would just roll over and let you. Well, guess what? Alex is still alive. Being Deathless didn't make my dad love you any better. And Ken isn't done with you just yet. You're still alone, and that's what you'll always be."

The Snow Queen snarled. Her shield shimmered and formed sharp icicles that shot out at Tala.

They melted before they could get within reach of Agimat. And then Ken was there beside her, slicing off the rest.

"Tala," Loki panted as they appeared beside her, Ryker seconds behind.

"You're both supposed to be retreating with everyone else!"

"And leave you here alone?" Loki demanded at the same time as Ryker said, "Do you really think I'm gonna obey that?"

An ice barrier grew, keeping the ice wolves and shades at bay. "Are you sure you want to let her do this?" Ryker asked, thickening the shield as Loki struck at those attempting to sneak past.

"Yes." As much as they would have wanted it otherwise, Tala knew she was going to die. But Alex had a chance. He'd already defied fate once before. She knew she could help him defy it again.

Loki's face fell. "Tala," they began, agonized.

With a loud ripping sound, like the very fabric of reality was being torn because of it, the portal fully opened.

The flute flew out of Zoe's hands. There was a startled yelp from Loki as the lotus lantern did the same. The raskovnik was plucked away from West's side. Dexter yelling in her ear told Tala that the black tamatebako that housed Koschei's soul was disappearing.

Something bright and crackling rose from the ground—a figure in rusting armor, a large steel sword. Tala had seen the man before, inside a mirror. "Koschei," she whispered.

The portal behind them grew, shining even more brightly.

Tala was flying through the air before she knew it, even as Ryker desperately tried to grab at her hand and failed. The winds were pulling her along, and she was powerless to stop them as she was yanked right into the Buyan portal.

26

IN WHICH THE ALATYR IS A TRAP

There was only darkness. At first she thought she was back at Esopia, but there were no other dragons looming before her here.

Instead, she was standing at a crossroads. Above her head, multiple signposts pointed in all directions, though there was nothing else to be seen on the horizon but the ever-present night.

Tala looked up at the signposts—all wooden and rotting, like they had been there for hundreds of years. She read the faded words on each.

GO EAST, AND FIND A PRINCE'S SOUL.
GO WEST, AND FIND A DRAGON'S CURE.
GO NORTH, AND FIND YOUR PUNISHMENT.
GO SOUTH, AND FIND A KINGDOM'S RUIN.

"What is all that supposed to mean?" Tala asked aloud, irritated. She was done with riddles. She was done with having to figure out what prophecies meant. Her Makiling abilities meant that she wasn't supposed to be beholden to any, and yet here she was.

Agimat felt reassuring in her hand. If she had lost her blade some-how, she wasn't sure what she would have done next.

A prince's soul. Surely that meant Alex?

And where did they even point to? There were no roads here, and the ground was so black that she couldn't see where she was treading. The vastness of Buyan stretched on for miles. *Was a curse placed on the land itself?* she wondered. The Snow Queen had cer-tainly thought her home would be as pristine as when she'd left, that it would at least be habitable.

Unless this wasn't Buyan at all.

She took a step toward the east.

A young boy lay huddled on the ground beside her before she could take another. His knees were drawn up to his face, and he was shivering rapidly. He also looked familiar.

"Are you okay?" Tala asked, reaching for him.

Her hand passed effortlessly through the boy's blond hair. The boy didn't notice her and continued to sob.

"You cannot stay here," another voice said. Tala turned, only to realize that the words weren't directed at her. A woman stepped out from the darkness, knelt down beside the sobbing child. A hood cov-ered her hair, and she looked younger, but there was no mistaking the old woman who worked at Simeli Mountain—Messinda, the former Baba Yaga.

The young boy—it *was* Alex—shrank back at the sight of her.

The woman shook her head. "I'm not the Snow Queen, boy. And if you don't want to die at her hands, then you must hurry and come with me."

"She hurt Father," Alex whispered.

"I know, darling. And we shall make sure she doesn't hurt anyone in your family again, least of all you." The woman pulled the boy along, and Tala followed. She'd hardly taken two steps before the scenery around them changed again, and they were now back at Maidenkeep, this time standing before the Nine Maidens. "Follow my instructions carefully," the old woman said, guiding Alex up the platform and into the center of the towering spelltech. "Think of winter, boy. Think of the frost, of everything in Avalon swallowed up by it. Imagine it spreading across your kingdom."

"But why?" Alex asked, shivering. "Isn't that bad?"

"It sounds like it would be, but this is to protect your people."

"Won't they die?"

"Not if you use this." The woman rapped at the side of one of the Nine Maidens' columns. "It will protect everyone from the Snow Queen. She hates warmth, you see. She despises the sun. And once she sees that everything has been covered in frost, she will leave you and your people well alone. Can you try?"

The boy lifted his small shoulders. "I can," he said, and he sounded a lot more like the Alex Tala loved.

"In shifting ice a prince you'll kiss," the Baba Yaga said, "and the first shall be forgiven. The sword rises twice from palace stone, and the second shall be forgiven. Pledge your love to the blackest flag, and the third shall be forgiven. And then, my dear, and only then, shall you lift that which was forbidden. Remember these words, boy, for they shall save your life one day. Now, go and think of the frost, and save your people."

And then the boy and the old woman were gone, and in their place stood Alex as he was now, with the Nine Maidens surrounding him, imbuing him with their magic—far too much magic, far more spells than he could possibly hold on his own. And as Tala looked on, terrified, she saw the magic warping him, withering his bones as if determined to suck the very life out of him until there was nothing left but a husk.

"No!" She leaped, passed through his form like she was the ghost, like he was the one real thing in this place and not her. She tried again but with the same results. Alex burned before her, and she could do nothing but sob as he was rendered into ash.

And then she was back, staring blankly back up at the signposts like she hadn't taken that first step.

"No," she said again and then took a step in the opposite direction, toward the sign that talked of a dragon's cure. There was another shift, and this time the dragons they had encountered in Esopia lay dying, mutilated, their chests torn.

A version of her stood over them, weeping, distressed, with a bloody heart clutched in her hands, and Tala realized what she had done.

Your species have hunted us for eons, our heads for trophies, our wings for spells. You use our hearts to destroy your own kind in battles we never wanted.

She took a step back in horror, and the vision around her dimmed and disappeared, leaving her alone with the signposts once more.

"This isn't real," she said aloud and took a step southbound.

Now she was in Avalon, but at the same time, she wasn't. Nothing remained of the castle or of the surrounding city. What lay before her were smoking ruins—nothing she could identify as the kingdom she'd grown to love.

But she knew the Snow Queen's mark. The cold wind that blew over the now-desolate landscape carried with it faint sounds of the woman's laughter. Whatever Buyan magic powered this spell, she knew it was showing her what it would look like if they lost.

She planted her feet north.

Here was another version of herself, weak and bleeding, fighting the Snow Queen. Through the haze of battle, she watched as she finally cut the woman down with Agimat, only to fall over herself moments later, breathing her last mere seconds after her opponent did.

She forced herself to move to where her body lay, kneeling down beside it. Even in death, grief and anger were still evident on her doppelgänger's face.

She reached out tentatively with one hand. This time, her fingers connected with flesh. Her body was still warm, her wounds still damp with blood, still trickling out of her.

"Is that it?" Tala asked aloud, to herself and to no one at all. "Are these the only options I have left? Sacrifice myself, or sacrifice everything else?"

Her corpse faded, and the signpost that remained provided her with no other answers. The winds had gone.

But with their absence came a bird's song. It was loud in the vastness of all this empty space, and Tala spun, trying to figure out where it came from. It echoed around her, its melody sad yet hopeful all at once.

Tala took out her tamatebako, now gleaming with a soft shimmery light, as if whatever was inside was bright enough to pulse through the wood.

It opened easily in her hands, this time without any urging from her.

The music burst forth from the box; within it, a shadow spread its wings and chirped. Tala felt something heavy and familiar settle on her head, though there was nothing she could see. "I missed you," she said, and the adarna cooed again.

The tamatebako tucks a part of your soul away, the lady of the Ryugu-jo had said, *to bring out when all else seems lost.*

Dexter talking. *Schlemihl's theory about the tamatebako was that it's possible to use it to house part of a person's soul to revive them after death, but only Buyan technology has ever been successful at it.*

The adarna's music continued, and Agimat responded. As Tala watched, it began to split into two distinct weapons—arnis sticks. Both lengthened and took on the solidness of hammered steel, designs flaring out on one side of each that soon resembled bird's wings similar to the adarna's but with a tinge of gold.

She felt stronger. The constant jostling of thoughts in her head that whispered and cajoled her to wield the sword against Avalon's will whenever she tried to use it had finally fallen silent.

Wonderingly, Tala studied her new Agimat and then turned to the signpost, now knowing what she should do.

The sticks cleaved effortlessly through the post, the wood splintering from the force. The darkness around her shattered as if she had been standing within a mirror, and this time it was a very different spelltech that stood a few meters away.

It looked so very different from the Nine Maidens. Where the Nine Maidens' columns had been slender and smooth, this was an asymmetrical mishmash of obsidian spikes and protrusions that turned it into no known shape, only vaguely cylindrical. Magic was crackling all around it, as if it had already been activated, so Tala retreated to what she hoped was a safe distance.

It was taller as well, perhaps a hundred feet, and shot up into the sky above—

There *was* a sky above her now, just as blue as it was back in Avalon. She was in a forest again, though much more overgrown and denser than the one in Wonderland. The Alatyr—for surely this was the Alatyr—had not been well tended. Vines twisted along its irregular corners and grew over the platform it stood on. Moss grew along its base.

"Was this all a test?" Tala asked aloud and, as expected, received no answer.

She wondered where the old palace of Buyan was, where Koschei had once ruled. Save for the mirror and the Alatyr itself, there was no other indication that the place had ever been inhabited by humans. There was no stonework lying about that would have suggested the foundations of a castle. All she could see was the woods.

Yet even without other spelltech around, the Alatyr was dangerous on its own. The magic sparking off its surface was more than Tala had ever sensed from the Nine Maidens. Avalon had chosen restraint over unchecked magic when they had crafted their spelltech. They had feared a repeat of Buyan's folly. Tala could see why Avalon would not want the Alatyr unleashed on the world.

But if the Nine Maidens had been built in the Alatyr's image, then Buyan's spelltech, too, would have to be controlled and directed. Koschei had lost his humanity with every use, and that had eventually corrupted him. Tala wasn't sure she wanted to be the one to follow in his footsteps.

The shadow adarna on her head had fallen silent. Tala poked at it cautiously. Her hand passed through the shade like it wasn't even there. "We're going to have to hunt for your corporeal form once this is over," she muttered. It chirruped again. She'd never even noticed that the adarna had lost its shadow after the Ryugu-jo.

There was a mirror beside the Alatyr, easily the biggest she'd ever seen—twenty feet tall and ten feet wide. Most of the glass was missing, though there were no shards littering the ground. Mirrors often had a distinct feel to them, a taste of smoke and heat that told Tala they were used for portals, for traveling. This was different. It was hard to describe, but it was like sampling something that shouldn't have had that flavor, like bread suddenly tasting like fish for no reason.

It felt like the Deathless curse.

This was the mirror that the Snow Queen used to enthrall her victims. She had collected enough of its pieces to bring back with her before Buyan had disappeared, enough to have used it frequently over the centuries.

Tala returned to the problem of the Alatyr. The Nine Maidens had been configured in such a way that only those from the Tsarevich bloodline could use it, and she wasn't sure if the Alatyr had been set the same way, if only Koschei's descendants could control it.

But she didn't have a spell-negating agimat for nothing.

She could die. That had been very clear to see in the visions.

The adarna hopped off her head, but its shadow hovered close to Tala. Agimat gripped tightly in one hand, Tala began to circle the stone monument, probing for anything within its spell-riddled surface that could give her an opening, any weak point that could provide her with an idea of what to do next.

She dodged on instinct, avoided an icy projectile that swooped past her and shattered harmlessly against the obsidian. She raised her sword just in time to parry the Snow Queen's second blow, jumping back to put more space between her and her unexpected foe.

The Alatyr flared to life without warning. Tala saw something emerging from the remains of the mirror, heard the playing flute. She stepped back, horrified, as a figure in black stepped out, garbed in the same black armor and sword she'd seen inside the Ryugu-jo.

Koschei.

"You hate him," she choked out. "Why would you—"

"I needed him to complete the portal into Buyan," the Snow Queen said, triumphant. "I killed him before, and I can do it again. But none of you will leave here alive!"

Tala's arnis stick struck back at the Snow Queen's ice sword, and the other swung to catch her unaware by the knee. The Snow Queen was used to proper swordfights and seemed at first highly unequipped to deal with fighting against two weapons, though she soon rallied.

There was no one else to watch them fight. Ice climbed up the trees wherever the Snow Queen missed, bursts of unraveling magic suspended in the air causing small earthquakes when their weapons drew too near. There was a desperation to the Snow Queen's fighting now that Tala hadn't seen previously; she had lost her Deathless, and she was being painted into a corner as the Avalon forces gained ground. More importantly, the Snow Queen had lost Kay Warnock for good. The Alatyr was her last recourse.

"You could have been my daughter," the woman rasped, no longer cold and emotionless but anguished. "We could have made the world better together."

"Reviving your tyrant father is not my idea of making the world better."

"And you think your king, with his history of traitorous ancestors, can do any better?"

"Probably not," Tala said wearily. "You think my little corner of the world is unimportant. But we are all here, fighting for our right to have our own little corners because they matter to us."

Another ball of ice came hurtling toward them. It missed Tala completely and crashed into the Snow Queen, sending her skidding away.

Ryker was already channeling another sphere of ice to lob. "How did you get here?" Tala shouted at him, stunned.

"I was close enough to get sucked into Buyan without meaning to."

"I should have let you die that day," the Snow Queen told him, venomous.

"Not too long ago, I would have wished you had. But I've learned to like myself a little better since." Ryker dodged another icicle, moving away from Tala so that the Snow Queen was forced to defend herself on two opposing fronts. "Stop this, Mother. You know you can't win."

"You no longer have the right to call me Mother, ever again. And after all I've done for you, you ungrateful boy!"

Ryker moved again, and Tala saw that he was once again wearing the thrall collar. "I don't owe you anything," he said. "You never cared for me. I was only there to aid your plans. That's not what family does."

"How would you know what family does?" the Snow Queen shrieked. "My own father used me as an experiment! He kept me alive only because I could revive him if necessary! I gave you the world! I gave you power without demanding fealty like I had done with my other maidens! I looked at you as the son I never had, and you betrayed me just like all the others!"

"I never betrayed you, Mother," Ryker said, anguished. "I was trying to save you."

Tala saw then what Ryker was doing; he had angled himself far enough away so that the Snow Queen's ire was now fully focused on him, so that she would not notice the small portal that was steadily growing near where the Alatyr stood. Alex, she thought, using Ryker's collar to track them.

But the relief was short-lived. As if finally sensing the magical disturbance, the Snow Queen's eyes darted to the growing port, rage twisting her features. The now fully formed Koschei was already striding toward the opening, his great sword prepared to thrust through it.

Tala wasn't close enough to stop him, but she was close enough to the Alatyr to adopt a new strategy. She threw herself onto one of the columns and plunged Agimat right into the rock.

And then she was someplace else entirely again.

It felt like she was shuffling through several different lives in only a moment, all flashing before her eyes. She saw dragons there, teaching men the ways of magic. She saw them building the Alatyr. She saw them using the Alatyr to try and make the lives of those around them better, eventually giving up their own in the same way countless Avalon rulers had—their strength sapped and poisoned by magic beyond what their physical bodies could withstand. Some died abruptly; many succumbed after long, agonizing illnesses.

She saw noble leaders, frustrated by the constant sacrifices expected of them, using the Alatyr for other purposes—for immortality, for power—until in the end, those were the only things they remembered to want. She saw Koschei, the last of that line, falling under that same spell.

Not all sacrifices are willing, the dragon had said. Koschei had sacrificed others in his place. Tala watched as good men fell, many who opposed his reign, others even more innocent. She watched his daughter turn to Avalon in the hope of saving him still. She saw how the Snow Queen had killed her father herself, dooming Buyan forever even as she wept in Kay's arms. Tala could feel the woman's loss, her anguish and her guilt like they were her own.

Tala was not Koschei's descendant, but something in her Agimat had broken through, like a wrench had been thrown into the cogs to stop a machine from working, disrupting it long enough for the Alatyr to blaze into life before them all and—

Oh.

Was this how Alex felt every time he commanded the Nine Maidens? Like everything that was powerful and grand was right at his fingertips, like he could spin the world on a different axis if he wanted to? Tala was used to magic having little effect on her; to suddenly be its conduit, to be at the center of the most powerful thing in the universe, capable of doing anything within the realms of her own imagination—it was a stunning, exhilarating place to be.

Self-preservation took over then, and she pushed the magic away out of instinct.

"Look out!" she heard someone shout, and she turned just in time to hear a heavy, very sickening *thunk*, like a knife going through bone.

Ryker stumbled back, and Tala saw the icicle that had been shoved through him when he jumped in front of her, protecting her from the Snow Queen's strike.

27

In Which Love for the Blackest Flag Is Pledged

Tala didn't hear the roar Koschei made when it was Ken who stepped through the opening first, parrying the armor-clad man's attack. She didn't see her friends scrambling out after him to join the fight. All she could see at the moment was a pale-faced Ryker lying on the ground before her, his hands gripping at where the icicle remained lodged inside him.

"Don't take it out!" she ordered harshly, grabbing at his hand, knowing that, like Cole, he would lose far too much blood the moment he did. "Hold on!"

A weak laugh from Ryker. "When I first saw this in my vision, I thought it was showing me my past—the night I stumbled into Maidenkeep after the Snow Queen stabbed me that first time. Didn't realize till later that it was to be a repeat."

The other Bandersnatchers were quick to take in the scene. West and Loki were already springing forward, providing fresh cover for Alex and Tristan, who were circling over to where Tala was cradling Ryker in her arms. The firebird was overhead, raking the ground with fire as it dashed for the Snow Queen, avoiding the ice she was throwing its way. Nya was following them, already digging frantically into her pouch.

Zoe, Cole, and even Adelaide were there, the first lashing out with her whip and sending waves of electricity at the Snow Queen, preventing her from approaching. Tala's mother and the Cheshire were the next to jump out, and then Lola Urduja and the Katipuneros, and then Captain Mairead and her pirates, hollering for blood.

The weight of the undead army she was leading was catching up to Adelaide; she sagged down, breathing hard. Cole's face was still paper-white from his previous ordeal, though the stubborn set to his jaw showed that he had insisted on coming, that both Zoe and his sister had given up on convincing him otherwise. Gently, he reached out and took Gravekeeper from her, then spun to demolish a group of shades clambering after him. He tossed the sword and this time Lord Nottingham caught it, fighting his way through another horde before passing it on to Cole's mother, who was soon stabbing her way through another group, the Nottinghams switching the blade among themselves before one could grow tired, keeping control of their army.

"Don't move," Nya instructed tersely on reaching Tala and Ryker's side.

"Yes, ma'am," Ryker croaked.

The Snow Queen had lost interest in Tala and her former ward on catching sight of Alex. The hailstones that were unleashed in his direction were the size of small boulders. Tristan drew his arrow, sending a fresh wave of fire that melted most before they were halfway to them. The firebird was in fine fighting form, responding with its own version of a firestorm, turning the area around the Snow Queen into an inferno.

"We're in a forest!" Zoe called sharply. "Be careful!" She was disobeying her own advice; the white-hot flashes of electric currents were running through the ground toward the Snow Queen, determined to burn her if the fires wouldn't.

Alex had reached the Alatyr. Tala took her eyes off Ryker long enough to grab his arm. "Don't you even think about it."

"I'm the only one with the experience for this. Have you got any other bright ideas?"

"As a matter of fact, I do. I'm controlling the Alatyr."

Alex stared at her. No doubt he could feel the intense energies emanating out of her skin, making her feel like she was made of lightning. "Tala, I—"

"Being able to negate magic even at its purest form apparently means there are no laws when it comes to me. Don't you dare tell me I can't when you're just as willing to do it yourself."

"Do you even know how to work it?"

"I think so. Alex, how the hell could you endure this?"

"Painfully. We can compare traumas later. How do you start this up?"

Gently, Tala turned Ryker over to Nya, who was working on trying to stanch the wound and keep the icicle from melting, and reached for her Agimat, which was still stuck to the Alatyr's surface.

And the whole world opened up before her.

This must be what it feels like to be a god. This must be what Alex feels like whenever he uses the Nine Maidens, Tala thought, and it was a wonder to her that he had been able to stop himself from simply destroying everything he hated with it. It was like she could blast through the world if she wanted to. No wonder it had corrupted Koschei. No wonder the Snow Queen believed it would solve everything.

She and Alex could turn the full force of the Alatyr and the Nine Maidens on Koschei and the Snow Queen, ending them for good. But using it meant she would die. Using the Nine Maidens like this meant that Alex would die. Already the Alatyr's magic was pulling energy out of her even before she could channel anything through, eager for the bits and pieces of her that it could whittle away even before she could cast any spell.

She remembered the vision she'd just seen, of her prone form amid a forest that was very much like this one, surviving the Snow Queen only by a few minutes, the spells from the Alatyr dissipating around her as she fell.

"No," Ryker said and gently pushed Nya away. He grabbed Tala's arm and wouldn't let go.

"Ryker—"

"Zoe was right," Ryker said. "I didn't tell you everything I knew about the Alatyr and how it works. Not because I didn't want you to know but because I knew you would stop me if you did."

"What are you talking about?"

But it was too late. The adarna began to sing again, and Tala felt the familiar threads of its magic wrap around her and then extend toward Ryker. "What are you doing?" she cried, but the shadow bird refused to listen, continuing on until she could feel Ryker tapping into the Alatyr's magic as well.

"I have the Snow Queen's magic through me," he whispered. "It's not as strong as what you're capable of, but it's enough for me to tap into the Alatyr too. And since you're here to negate anything else that would have prevented me more access…"

The battle was still waging around them. Ken, his face blank and stark, was going head to head with the revived Koschei, unflinching. Any blows he delivered to his opponent were received with little consequence. Any wounds that he received from Koschei amounted to the same. The two undeads hammered at each other, neither refusing to give in.

"I'm dying," Ryker said. "You know this isn't going to come out of my stomach any time soon."

"Cole survived it. What makes you think you won't—"

"Because Cole was never tied by magic to the Snow Queen beyond the shards she used to make him her Deathless," Ryker said quietly. "I lied to you, Tala. When I told you that I was standing on that bridge after I escaped my last foster home, waiting to fall…I lied. I was so tired of everything and I…I didn't wait for anyone to catch me."

"Ryker," Tala said, stricken.

"The Snow Queen found me in time. She had a knife—apparently it was from a shard of the mirror, the same one she used to save your father's life centuries ago. She took pity on me, used it to save mine."

Tala remembered the vision she'd had of a young Kay Warnock. The dagger the Snow Queen had used on him to bring him back to life, binding him to her for the rest of her unnatural life.

"That's why I was with her for so long despite everything she did," Ryker whispered. "There's magic inside me still, keeping bits of me alive. It's why she didn't need to turn me like she did the other ice maidens. It's the same kind of magic she used to keep your father immortal all these years."

"You can't ask me to do this," Tala choked. "You can't ask me to doom you, my father, and Alex as well. You can't ask me to leave my mother alone."

"Yes, we can, love." Kay Warnock was there beside her, his large hand enveloping her small one. The adarna's song continued, and this time it wrapped around her father as well. "Your mother and I knew this was a long time coming. The only way to prevent Koschei from returning permanently is to kill the Snow Queen and end this."

Which meant everyone being kept alive by her magic would die as well. "You can't ask me to do this," Tala repeated desperately.

"The good news," Ryker said with a smile, "is that we don't need to ask you to."

The vision he'd seen in the mirrors of the Ryugu-jo, the reason he had refused to tell Tala exactly how he was going to die—

The Alatyr is a crueler spell than the Nine Maidens, said Lord Suddene. *The latter requires a sacrifice from a royal of the Avalon lineage, but the Alatyr consumed any sacrifice it found, used their life forces as batteries to power the next massacre—*

"No," Tala gasped as magic now fully surrounded Ryker, accepting his offering. "No!"

"Live long and well, Tala," Ryker said, "and for what it's worth, I love you." The blinding light hid him from sight.

And then he was gone.

"It's not enough," the Cheshire said. Before anyone could stop him, he too was moving toward the grotesque spell. He ducked Loki's frantic attempts to grab at him, then paused for a moment before the illuminated Alatyr, casting one final glance back at her. "No more regrets, Tala," he said, and then he, too, was gone.

A song from the adarna's shadow. The firebird roared out in agony, speeding frantically toward it, but another melody immobilized it midair, sent it crashing to the ground. The adarna sighed, gave the frozen bird a friendly peck with its beak in farewell. It, too, looked at Tala and sang her one last tune—an upbeat, lilting refrain. And then it turned and flew straight into the Alatyr after Ryker and the Cheshire. For a moment, it took on its original physical form, its splendid feathers and magnificent plume shining. And then it disappeared.

The Alatyr flared brighter, the magic too strong to hold back any longer. Tala gritted her teeth despite the tears falling from her eyes and redirected everything she had back toward the Alatyr.

"We don't need you," she wept. "We aren't ready. Leave us and go where no one else can use you for greed ever again." And then she brought her salamanca to bear and drove Agimat down on the obsidian once more.

For a moment, she wasn't sure it succeeded. The Alatyr stood there, still teeming with spells that warped the air.

And then there was an odd, satisfying crack.

The Alatyr split. From the top of its irregularly shaped cylinder down to its very base, it broke apart, the bits flying off it swiftly turning into ash that soon dissipated.

Tala felt her hold on the Alatyr abruptly cut off but then heard Alex gasp as his connection with the Nine Maidens, too, was unceremoniously severed. Tristan caught the king easily when the latter staggered back, suddenly weakened but still alive. "I can't sense it," he whispered. "I've shared a bond with it nearly all my life, and now it's—"

"Pledge your love to the blackest flag," Tala said, echoing Alex's prophecy that was now, at last, fulfilled. Alex had naturally assumed that it would be *his* love to pledge, but—

Was that what happened? Was this the result of Tala's choice to wield the Nameless Sword again, changing their destiny one more time?

"No!" the Snow Queen screamed, but the Alatyr continued to destroy itself, the massive column being broken apart by no other forces but its own, until not even its very foundations remained. The black obsidian monument was gone. All that remained was a strange black box—the tamatebako where the Snow Queen had kept Koschei's soul.

And it was opening.

Koschei fell back but had enough of his own magic to keep fighting, to attempt one last stand, one more trick. Ken was still fighting him, still showing no mercy. The Snow Queen ignored them both; already she was flying toward the box, her eyes alive with rage.

Tala righted herself. She reached the platform before the Snow Queen could, Agimat raised above her head. With one last move, she drove the blade down toward the box.

It shattered.

The Snow Queen's scream was now fearful. Mist rose from the box, which crumpled like it had been made of paper. Tala saw something writhe and recoil within that thin dark mist before it evaporated completely from view.

It was the Snow Queen's turn to fall. Kay caught her easily.

An inhuman roar from Koschei. Smoke rose from within his armor as he began to burn from inside. He screamed and clawed frantically at his visor, to no avail. Within seconds, he was ashes and soot, nothing of him remaining.

A loud cry rose from among the ice maidens. They began to melt as the magic that the Snow Queen once commanded and had now lost left their bodies, and they melted where they stood. Vivien Fey cried out, clutching at her heart. "No," she said, frightened. "No!"

She reached out blindly and found Loki, the nearest to be grabbed. The ranger held her, unable to do anything as she slowly began to dissipate. "I'm sorry," they said quietly, kind to a fault, even till the end.

"I did it for her," Vivien said. "All I ever wanted was revenge for her sake. Maybe I can find her this time." Her voice dipped. "You tried to save me, didn't you? No matter how badly I didn't want you to. But even so, even now, I regret nothing. I would do it all over again. I wish—"

And then she dissolved, a waterfall splashing at Loki's feet.

The Snow Queen opened her eyes, trained her gaze on Kay. "Kay," she whispered. "How did we ever go wrong?"

"Sleep now, Gerda," Tala's father said sadly. "You've fought for so long, and now it's time for you to rest."

The Snow Queen shuddered as the last of the spells that kept her alive, the magic that tied her inexorably to what had remained of Koschei's soul, slipped away from her. "I am sorry," she said and closed her eyes.

Gently, Kay set her down on the ground when she began to dissipate as well, and he looked down at his own hands. Particles of magic were rising from his body as if he, too, was in the process of being turned into light.

Tala dashed to his side, reaching him just as her mother did. His arms wrapped around them both, holding them dearly even as parts of him turned to ether. "Kay," Tala's mother wept.

"Been a bother to you two for a while, haven't I?" Kay said. "The both of you, always having to clean up after me, having to shoulder my sins like they were your own. Don't be sad, my loves. I had a good life with you both. The best life."

"Dad," Tala sobbed. "You can't—we have to find a way. I won't—I love you so much."

"Not as much as the depths of my love for you, my Tala." With a fading hand, her father drew her closer, kissed her softly on the forehead. Then he turned and kissed his wife. "I'll be here even if you both don't know it," he said. "I'll be here all your lives, and then I will see you both again one day."

And then all the rest of him trickled up into the sky above, blowing into the wind.

The undead were silent and waiting. Adelaide turned to address them.

"You have performed your service admirably," she said. "Rest well, and know that you have honored your vows to us and to Avalon, and that we shall honor you in turn."

The corpses said not a word, only inclined their heads low. And then they too began to disappear.

"No!" Nya shouted. "I claim surety on one Kensington Inoue and forbid him his rest."

A pause. Ken turned to her, expression cold and forbidding.

Nya took out the ruby-red tamatebako, held it out before her. "I captured your shadow," she said, "the same way Urashima Taro once bound his shadow into the jeweled boxes within the Ryugu-jo to save his life. Your shade rests within this box. For as long as it remains intact, your life is mine to protect. Return to life, and return to me."

The box opened. Something bright and glowing fluttered out of it, like the bright butterflies at Ikpe village they used for protection, and surrounded Ken. The boy looked down at Nya's determined face, at her tears. And then he took a deep breath, the first he'd had since rising from his grave.

"I trust you, Rapunzel," he said and smiled, and it was an arrestingly cheerful grin, one so much like the ones he often wore when he was alive. A sizzle of light went through him, and then he and the glowing light were gone.

Nya dropped to the ground, still hugging the empty box to her chest, and wept.

Alex sat up, his arm slung over Tristan's neck while the latter helped him stay upright. "Tala," he said.

The firebird walked toward Tala's feet and curled itself up there.

It folded its wings around Tala's knees and buried its face against her calf, and Tala clung desperately to its warmth, knowing nothing else would ever be the same.

The portal was still there, held up by the fading remnants of Buyan magic, slowly shrinking as it, too, began to fade.

"You know that we're not likely to open this port again without the Alatyr or the Nine Maidens," Captain Mairead pointed out.

"Who knows what sort of magic we could learn within, even without the Alatyr," Lord Keer agreed.

Tala and Alex looked at each other. "If we aren't able to use the resources we already have to make this world better," the young king said, "then Buyan spelltech changes nothing. Let's wait for a future wiser and kinder than our present, with spelltech we develop ourselves, to deserve another visit here."

Tala lifted Agimat. The sword cut swiftly through the portal. It swelled up for a few seconds as if in protest and then disappeared abruptly, like a candle snuffed out without warning, until it was like it had never existed at all.

EPILOGUE

In Which, A Village

The flowers would not stop coming. They arrived from all over the world, a show of solidarity for Avalon. All the graves were awash in them now, piled on top of one another. There had been far too many burials, far too many wakes.

The headstones all looked the same; her father's grave wasn't easy to spot at first glance. This was how he would have wanted it, her mother had said. He'd always wanted an ordinary grave to make up for a life that had been anything but.

Zoe got to work, sorting out the flowers in neat rows, Cole moving to work by her side without any prompting. Loki was quietly reading off the names that had been inscribed at a monument nearby, listing the lives of all those lost to the Snow Queen's war. Vivien Fey's name was on it as well, because Alex had always been magnanimous to a fault.

Lumina Makiling Warnock had brought roses—red ones, with the dew still fresh on their petals. They had been Kay's favorite, even if that didn't seem in keeping with the large hearty man he had been. That was what Tala had always loved about her father, that he was constantly defying what people expected of him, for the better and sometimes for the worse.

There had not been anything left of him to bring back home, so the grave was a memorial more than anything else. General Luna lay beside him, having been buried with full military honors. The Katipuneros had wept when he was lowered into the ground. Already Tito Boy and Tita Baby were talking about creating scholarships in his honor; the man had grown up in poverty and had struggled to earn himself an education, succeeding despite the odds.

Tita Chedeng and Tita Teejay were polishing his stone, intending for it to be the shiniest in the lot. Tita Chedeng was still injured from the mild concussion she'd suffered from being knocked into the snow, but she'd insisted on attending.

"He always said it was an honor to fight by your side and for the king," Tita Baby told Tala, already on her third handkerchief. She honked noisily into it. "I think this will make him very happy."

That the Katipuneros had chosen to bury one of their most visible members beside her father, Tala knew, was a statement on its own; General Luna would not have wanted it any other way.

Lola Corazon's body had been brought back to the Philippines. Tala and her mother had already made plans to visit her grave there, to meet the rest of the Makiling clan. Tala knew her mother still felt guilty about their estrangement, knew the what-ifs that were going through her head. But the other Makilings were eager for them to come, and Tala couldn't help but feel hopeful.

"That is good news, hija," Lola Urduja said. "It would be good to reconnect with them, learn more about that side of your family."

"Would you like to come with us? You said you missed living in Manila."

"I am not a Makiling. It would not be respectful to barge in on family affairs that you would need to—"

Tala reached over and took the old woman's hand. "You're family," she said sincerely. "Whether you're a Makiling doesn't matter. Please?"

Lola Urduja looked at her for a moment, and a slow, warm smile filled up her normally acerbic face. "If you insist, mahal," she said. "I would be glad to."

While Lumina mourned over her husband and the Katipuneros paid silent tribute to their fallen comrade, Tala turned to the grave to the left of her father's.

There were several kids standing before the stone marker. No longer Deathless, they were quiet and melancholy. A few were openly weeping. All stood to attention when they saw Tala step toward them.

"Lady Makiling Warnock," one of them warbled. "I—we don't know how we can possibly thank you and…" He trailed off with a sniff.

"He knows," Tala said, smiling sadly. "And he's happy to see you all visiting him still." She knelt down and placed her own bouquet of roses and a small stuffed puppy dog before Ryker's tombstone. The grave was already overflowing with flowers—the kids had been paying their respects religiously over the last few months. She could see other stuffed animals were propped against the stone, gifts from them.

"Wherever you are," she whispered to the grave, "I hope you're watching over us and that you're happy. And maybe one day, I'll get to see you again. I hope I'll get to see everyone I love again."

Three months since, and everything had changed. The Royal States was currently going through a revolution of their own. Attempts to depose King John were making better progress, and Tala wished them all the luck.

Officially, Alex maintained his neutrality, knowing his attempts to help would be seen as foreign intervention. He had gotten most of their Avalon spelltech patents back and announced that they would not bring litigation against anyone replicating them for altruistic ends. His lawyer, Mr. Peets, was having a field day gleefully sending out cease and desist letters to companies that made the attempt, while protesters used them to hand out food and protect the poor like Three Wishes had done with nary a lawsuit.

"They've always been fighting," Alex had said. "Just because King John's had control for so long doesn't mean there was never resistance, that there aren't good people there fighting the assholes in charge since—well, all of history. And I know they're going to succeed and save themselves, the same way we did. I just can't be *too* vocal about it while I'm still Avalon's king."

"We're still figuring out a way to make sure everyone gets the health care they need," Zoe had added with a sigh. "But I know enough about being American to know it could take a while. I want Abigail Fey's legacy to be a good one, even if it didn't start out that way. And I hope wherever she is, she's with her older sister now."

"Cute dog," Alex said now from behind Tala. He and Tristan were inseparable at this point, and Lord Locksley's outrage had soon been drowned out by the mostly approving photos of the two constantly being snapped by the local paparazzi. The idea of a royal and his bodyguard protector getting together apparently appealed to the romantics of the world.

The firebird was on his head. It had been quieter in the months after the battle, more inclined to sit and listen rather than fly into trouble. With the Nine Maidens no longer functioning, it was the only thing Alex had left of their legacy, and it brought him comfort. It chirped at Tala in greeting as the other kids bowed low to the king.

Tala wasn't even sure if Alex was going to remain king for much longer. He was in the process of investing most of the Tsarevich royal fortunes in further development of the kingdom, and his titles were the next thing he was likely to renounce. It was hard for Tala to imagine him as a president or a prime minister instead—or even stepping down completely and letting someone else take over—yet at the same time, she felt that whatever role Alex opted for next would suit him admirably.

"His name is Picard," she said, adjusting the toy dog so it wouldn't topple over. "He said he'd always wanted one."

For a moment, neither of them said a word, content to watch over the tombstone of their fallen friend, his death one of the reasons they'd survived.

Tala wished she could have found a way. The problem with an agimat is that it's easy to think you were above the rules. Tala could see why even her ancestress, Maria Makiling, had called it a curse.

It was hard to accept that she was not the only one capable of changing prophecy, the only one capable of making sacrifices.

She felt Loki's presence, waited until they knelt on the ground beside her. She leaned into their shoulder, liking their warmth, waiting while they, too, paid their respects.

"I was wrong about him," Loki said. "I wish I'd been able to tell him that."

Alex sighed. He laid a hand on the headstone as if somewhere out there, Ryker could feel his touch. "Sleep well, bro," he said. "And thank you."

The place before them was called Sakangea, which meant "a widely held belief" in old Avalonian according to Lord Suddene. It was a fairly new village, even by the kingdom's standards. There was a limit to the cures and medicines the people of Ikpe could make in a day without sacrificing quality, Nya's grandmother had said, and so they had begun teaching their potion-making skills and building trade schools outside Ikpe, including in Sakangea, in a bid to create a bigger export industry for Avalon.

The old woman had not had any visions since the day Tala and Alex had killed the Snow Queen and closed the portal to Buyan for good, or so she claimed, despite what Nya tried to pry out of her. Tala could understand the other girl's frustration. The Dowager Nottingham and the Dame of Tintagel had said the same thing. So did the current Baba Yaga, who nowadays was more inclined to spend their days with Captain Mairead than tell fortunes, much less confirm what they were going to find in the village that day.

Despite the lack of visions, Tala hoped she wouldn't have to wait any longer.

They had arrived there shortly after visiting the Lyonesse graveyard, still in a somber mood despite their optimism. Nya was clearly trying not to panic; her face was tense with hope and stricken with fear at the same time. "What if I did it wrong?" she asked. "What if they're wrong, and they found someone else who they mistook for him? Why won't Aunt Lumina let us inside the village and have us see for ourselves?"

"Because you are very important people, hija," Lola Urduja reminded her, "and the Snow Queen's demise does not mean there are not others who would fake amnesia or use a disguising spell to harm any of you. We must be thorough in our confirmation, and it will only take a few minutes more."

Loki looked down at the village, their face pensive.

"Penny for your thoughts," Tala said.

They flashed her a brief smile. "Just thinking."

"Anything you want to share with me?"

"A museum curator offered to put my staff in a museum Alex was talking about setting up. But I have a feeling it would be bored out of its mind there."

"I don't think it would be selfish to keep it."

They smiled at her. "It feels like it's not done with me yet, and I'm not done with it either. There are still more adventures out there to find together." And then they snorted. "You're one to talk, when you gave back your Agimat."

The Nameless Sword had been back at the Maidenkeep court-yard for over two months now, stuck deep within the same anvil it had always been in. It had reverted back to its rusted appearance. Tala had chosen not to take it out again to see if she still could. She didn't need that kind of validation anymore.

The Nameless Sword was always the one that garnered the most attention, she thought. Its plain stone anvil was overlooked. And that was a shame. If the Nameless Sword represented power, then the anvil represented wisdom, knowing when to sheathe it to do the least amount of harm.

There was another sword of the Damoclean variety still hovering over her head—the threat every wielder had to bear, of the curse that claimed every wielder of the Nameless Sword would die.

But strangely enough, Tala was no longer afraid. It wasn't because her agimat could potentially negate such a prophecy. It was just that for the first time, that no longer mattered to her. She wanted to live without regrets.

"Do you still feel guilty about Vivien?" she asked.

Loki shook their head. "She made her decision. She was willing to hurt people to do it. It is what it is."

"I think you're just too much of a good person at heart." And here she started to stumble. "Were you interested in—was she someone that you—"

Loki stared blankly at her, and then their expression cleared—and then reddened. It wasn't often that Tala got to see Loki blush. She found that cute. "What? No! I was concerned of course, but I actually wasn't thinking about—Tala, there is no way I was. I was, uh, I was more interested in someone else."

"Oh," Tala said, feeling a lot better and not quite knowing why, but at the same time feeling a little despondent. "So there's another person you like?"

"Yes!" The ranger was turning crimson with every second. "I

mean, it's not something you should be worried about. After everything, I figured it wasn't right yet, but I've been trying to find the right way to—I was thinking of maybe traveling with the Neverland pirates."

"Why?" Tala asked, surprised by the abrupt change of subject.

"What the Dame of Tintagel said about me didn't come true. What scepter was I supposed to deliver to Neverland's mercy? They've been able to fix their *Jolly Roger*, but I don't think it was that. Was the scepter my staff somehow?" They looked away. "Lord Keer was open to it. He was thinking of making the pirates a more permanent agency in Avalon—help patrol our waters, things like that. I could serve as a temporary liaison, and I could figure out what that prophecy means. I don't believe it's actually going to happen, but maybe there's some adventure out there waiting for me still."

"I don't want you to leave." The words came out before she thought about stopping them. It was selfish, and she knew they would have to part ways eventually, but Loki—she wasn't ready to say goodbye to Loki the most out of everyone here.

The ranger hesitated. "You could go with me," they said quickly. "We'll only be gone for one, maybe two months tops. Just enough time to get an idea of how things will work out with the pirates. We can do anything else after that."

Tala's spirits lifted. It would be good to go somewhere. Not to forget but to have all the time to remember. And two months wouldn't be all that long. Alex would be too busy to hang out with, but she'd be with Loki. "I do. I want to go. But would Lord Keer be okay with that?"

Loki coughed. "I might have already asked him. He might have already agreed."

"How did you know I was going to say yes?"

"I didn't. I was just hoping you would."

Tala watched them for a few moments. Loki wasn't always one to show emotion, but their ears were still very red at the moment. She slipped a hand through theirs. "I'll need to ask Mom, but I don't think she'll protest. I would love to go travel on a ship with you," she said and was rewarded with a wide, broad smile on Loki's end.

"Hmm," Alex said from nearby, watching them with a smile.

"What?" Tala asked defensively, not sure why she was turning red herself.

"Nothing," the king said cheerily. "Nothing at all."

"I feel cheated," West spoke up. "You all had most of your prophecies fullfelt—falafelled—*done* at this point, but mine hasn't happened. And that was the ordinariest one of the lot."

"Are you saying you want to get married now?" Zoe asked him with a grin.

"Of course not! It's just—that's all anyone ever predicted for me. Getting married. Not fighting the Snow Queen, helping to take down the Alatyr, getting elephantized in the news—"

"West, I think you mean *lionized*."

"Why? Elephants are bigger and more impressive. Anyway, the prophecy didn't say anything about that with me."

"Could mean you'll be having the wedding of the century," Cole offered. The boy was much more prone to speaking now as opposed to remaining silent and letting the conversation flow without him.

According to Zoe, he had been making very good headway with his therapist despite not remembering his time during the short while he'd been under the queen's thrall.

It was a common trait among most of the other recovered Deathless, Tala's mother said—common among most survivors in general, even—as a way of self-preservation. "Sometimes the memories come back," she explained, "and sometimes they don't. But what's important is that they recover at their own pace and we give them as long as it takes to do so."

Cole himself had mentioned that the Nottingham segen was on a rotating basis between him and his sister, his family not wanting him to take on its duties while still on the mend but also understanding that his sister deserved her spotlight with it.

Zoe grinned adoringly at him and squeezed his hand. West rolled his eyes at the couple, though he was also smiling.

It had been a hard three months, and it was good to see everyone finally remembering how to smile, how to laugh.

"I think your prophecy is the best one out of all of ours, West," Tala said. "It says you've got a good future ahead of you, and I think that's what we all want too."

It didn't matter if West's doom hadn't come true. It didn't matter if Loki's never would. It wasn't the prophecy but the choice.

"A good marriage," Tita Teejay said with a sigh. "Sana all."

Lola Urduja had returned to where they were waiting. "I have good news," she said. "He doesn't have most of his memory back yet, but the physicians believe it's temporary. He's already recalling bits and pieces. I've sent word to his parents."

"Lola Urduja," Nya said. The tears were already falling down her face, unable to help herself. "Tell me—is he—did I—"

"He's back." Tala's mother's smile was blinding. "I don't know how you did it, Nya, or why he showed up there of all places, but it's him."

He looked exactly how Tala remembered—the same dark hair and brown eyes, the same infuriatingly infectious grin, the same set to his shoulders like he could handle any burden he was given. He was playing with some of the children, hopping onto the numbered chalk markings on the ground and groaning when he stepped on the line. The adults gathered there were looking at him with awe, though the kids were far less impressed by his jumping skills.

He had a shadow now. It bobbed and moved whenever he skipped down the ground, like it had always been there.

Horse was already waiting. Lola Urduja had told them to bring the kelpie to the village as another means to help identify him. It was standing placidly to one side, its eyes never leaving its master. It nickered and tossed its head happily.

The boy turned when he heard them approach and smiled. "Hey," he said. The same mischievous glint to his eyes, the same British accent that he somehow hadn't forgotten despite losing everything else. Like the last three months had been a dream, and he had not fallen to the ground before Tala, bleeding from the Snow Queen's strike.

"You guys look awfully familiar," he added.

Nya couldn't wait. With a low sob, she rushed toward him, throwing her arms around his waist and staying there.

He held her, looking down at her in surprise. "Not every day I have beautiful girls crying over me," he said. "Was it something I said, Rapunzel?" Almost without conscious thought, his arms closed over Nya in turn, holding her in the many ways he'd done so before. And then he blinked. "Rapunzel," he said again, every syllable in her name softer and more drawn out as he spoke it, like he was recalling the word from memory. "Your name is Rapunzel, right?"

The firebird began to sing, snatches of song that the adarna had been fond of.

Tala looked up briefly at the sky and blinked, trying not to cry herself. *Thank you,* she thought. *Thank you.*

Then she took a deep breath and stepped toward them. "Ken," she said, "you're not gonna believe any of this."

CHECK OUT A CHILLING HORROR FROM RIN CHUPECO

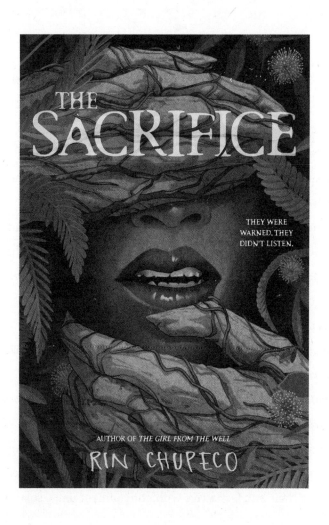

ONE

THE CAVE

Nobody tells Hollywood about the screaming.

Nobody tells Hollywood about the curse. Or the way things walk across the sands here like they are alive enough to breathe. Nobody tells them of the odd ways the night moves around these parts when it thinks no one sees.

Nobody gives them permission to visit, and it's all the incentive Hollywood needs to permit themselves.

The people who live in the provinces nearest the island don't talk. Not at first. But money is the universal language, and the years have been lean enough, desperate enough. Tongues loosen. The words come reluctantly.

Yes, they say. *There is a curse. Yes; at least five people dead.*

No, they say. *We will not step foot on that island with you, not even if you gave us a million dollars.*

Hollywood crashes into the island, anyway; it's a new breed of conquistadors trading technology for cannons. First their scouts: marking territory, measuring miles of ground, surveying land. Next their specialists: setting camp, clearing brush, arguing over schematics. Then their builders arrive with containment units, solar panels, and hardwood. In the space of a few days, they construct four small bungalows with an efficiency I'm not accustomed to seeing.

The noise is loud enough that they don't hear the silence how I've always heard it.

They scare the fishes away most days, and so I've gotten accustomed to idling, to watching them from my boat instead of hunting for my next meal. Hollywood does terrible things with machinery. They whirl and slam and punch the ground, and the earth shakes in retaliation. They dig perfect circles, add pipelines to connect to local supplies, and install water tanks. They set up large generators and test the lighting. They cut down more trees to widen the clearing to place more cabins.

None of them step inside the cave. The one at the center of the island, where the roots begin.

They don't talk about the roots that ring the island, half-hidden among white sand so fine it's like powder to the touch, so that they trip when they least expect it. But they talk about the balete. "I came here expecting palm trees," one of the crew says with a shudder. He stares up fearfully at one of the larger balete trees, with their numerous snake-like gnarls that twist together to pass as trunks, and at the spindly, outstretched branches above. "If trees could *look* haunted, then it would be these."

Soon they notice me standing by the shore, only several meters away.

"Hey, you there!" one calls out. He wears a Hawaiian shirt and dark shorts. A pair of sunglasses are slicked up his head. "You live nearby?"

I nod.

"Oh, thank God, you can understand us. We'd been having a hell of a time trying to translate."

"Most of the people here understand English," I say. "They probably don't want to talk to you."

"Ouch. Big ouch. Well, you're still the only local I've seen this close to the island. Even the fishermen stay clear. You're not afraid of the curse?"

I shake my head. Askal peers cautiously from around my legs, watching the foreigners curiously. "You?" I ask.

He guffaws. "I'm more afraid of my bosses docking my pay if we don't get this right." He peers back at Askal. "Cute dog. I've never seen the locals bring pets on their boats."

"He's used to the water."

Askal wags his tail, sensing he is being praised.

"Want to make some money, kid? We need someone who knows their way around the place. Everyone we've asked on the mainland has turned us down."

I row closer to where they stand, hopping out and dragging the boat through the last few feet of water. Askal scampers out after me.

"Not scared like everyone else, eh?" Hawaiian Shirt's companion asks, a guy with a goatee and bad haircut. Clouds of smoke rise from the little device he's puffing away at, and it smells of both cigarettes and overly sweet fruit. A half-empty beer bottle is tucked under his arm. His eyes are bloodshot, and I've seen enough drunks on the mainland to know what that means. "You hang around this place a lot?"

"You shouldn't be here."

Hawaiian Shirt scowls. "That's what the officials here have been telling us the past few months while we've been negotiating, but it's not gonna stop us. We have all the necessary permits. It's hypocritical, don't you think, telling us to leave when you've obviously been poking around here as much as we have?"

"I didn't ask you to leave. I said you shouldn't be here."

"Semantics. Look—we need someone to point out the mystery spots, maybe tell us about cursed areas on this damn island. Besides the Godseye. We've heard about that. We're on a deadline, and we need to get things moving before the rest of the crew arrive."

"The Godseye?"

"The cave on this island. The one where all those deaths happened. The locals didn't have a name for it, but we needed one for the show and that's what Cortes called it. You know why we're here, right? You must have heard the news by now."

Goatee blows rings in the air. "How are we gonna build three seasons around one fricking cave?"

"We'll figure it out, Karl. They say there's gold hidden in the cave that Cortes stole. Viewers love hearing about buried treasure. I'm sure Ethan's storyboarded more ideas." Hawaiian Shirt scratches his head. "You ever been inside the Godseye?"

"Yes."

Both stare at me. "All this time," Goatee mutters, "and he's been here all along. Kid, if you're who we think you are, then you're famous among the locals. You're like a ghost whisperer, they said. You're the only one brave enough to come here. We're hoping you could help us."

I look about pointedly and gesture at their building. "Do you even need permission anymore?"

"We signed off with the authorities. Well, we offered them a ton of money and they took it, so I guess that's permission. But we need more information, and that's the one thing they ain't selling."

"I'll give you five thousand dollars to come on board with us," Hawaiian Shirt says eagerly. "And another five if you stay the whole season, but that means you'll have to go on camera to talk about any creepy stories you have about the island. All the highlights of this place." He eyes my empty net. "That's gotta be more than you make fishing in at least a decade, right? I'll have a contract drawn up for you in an hour. You can look it over and tell me what you—" He stops. "You can read, right?"

I frown. "Yes."

"No offense, just checking. Get a lawyer to look it over for you if you want. It's got some terms and clauses you might not be familiar with—saves a lot of headaches later. So you'll help?"

I take my time, coiling my nets, making sure the boat's beached properly. Askal lingers near me, keeping a careful eye on the two men. "Have *you* been inside?"

"Well, no. Not till our legal department clears us to proceed. Or the exploration team gets a crack at it. Standard precautions."

Without another word, I head up the path, Askal keeping easy pace beside me. I can hear them scrambling to follow me.

No one can miss the cave entrance at the center of the island. It's two hundred feet high, built for giants to walk through. Limestone stains mar the walls. Something glitters in their cavities.

It doesn't take long for Hawaiian Shirt and Goatee to catch up, both looking annoyed.

"Ask it permission," I tell them, and they guffaw.

"The hell I'm asking some ghost," Goatee says with a snort.

"We can't go in until we get the all clear," Hawaiian Shirt repeats.

"A few steps in won't make a difference." I place my hand on the stone, which is cool to the touch. "Tabi po," I murmur, and enter.

The ground is softer here, and my sandals sink down slightly wherever I trod, leaving prints in my wake. Though reluctant at first, I hear them following, Hawaiian Shirt grumbling about all the trouble they could get into should R&D find out. Askal pads along, ears pricked as if he already senses something we cannot.

It's not a long walk. A stone altar lies a hundred feet in. Part of the ceiling above it caved in at some point, revealing a view of the sky. It's late afternoon, and the moon is already visible and silhouetted against a sea of blue.

The altar is more yellowing limestone bedrock, chiseled from ancient tools and carved with purpose. I look down at the ground and see, running along the sides, withered tree roots so old they've grown into the cave wall, stamped so deeply into the stones as to be a part of its foundation.

The passageway branches out, circles around to another tunnel that lies just behind the altar, leading deeper into rock.

"You said something before we came in," Goatee says. "'Tabi po'? That's how we're supposed to ask permission to enter?"

"It's a sign of respect," I say.

But the two men are no longer listening. They're too busy staring

427

at the stonework, and then at the sky where the moon stands at the center of the hole above—a giant eye gazing down at them.

Askal whimpers softly. I lean down and stroke his fur.

"They weren't kidding about the Godseye," Goatee says, impressed. "How'd you have the balls to come here all by yourself, kid? Seen any of the so-called ghosts? See Cortes himself?"

I pause, debating what to tell them. "I've heard the screaming."

"No one's told us about any screaming."

I approach the altar but do not touch it. I hear a soft, rasping sound, and look down to see small makahiya leaves writhing quietly on the ground. From the corner of my eye, I catch the tree roots on the walls curling, stilling only when Goatee, sensing their movements, steps nearer.

I have spent enough time on this island to recognize when it's distressed.

"You all shouldn't be here," I say again.

Goatee snorts. "Let's wait until the cameras start rolling before you get all creepy, kid."

"The Diwata knows me. But outsiders are another matter. You can't stay here."

The smile Goatee shoots my way is patronizing. "Kid," he says, as the sounds of digging outside resume, "we're just filming a TV show. We have *permission*."

"Better drag Melissa here to do some initial shots," Hawaiian Shirt says happily. "This is gonna look beautiful in our promos."

"We'll still need to hook viewers for a second season," Goatee says. "Maybe something's haunting the mangroves on the eastern side of the island—a spirit that pulls people underwater. Or maybe a dead woman. Dead women are always hits."

He laughs. Hawaiian Shirt laughs along with him.

From somewhere within the cave, something mimics their laughter.

They stop, tearing their gazes from the eye above them to into the cavern's depths. But all I hear now are the faint reverberations of their voices.

"Easy to see why people think this place is haunted," Goatee says, with a nervous, quieter chuckle. "Makes you start imagining things." He raises his hand, which trembles slightly, and downs the rest of his beer in one noisy gulp.

They do not linger long. Askal nuzzles at my hand, lets out a soft whimper. "We're leaving, too," I assure him. Before I follow the men out, I look back at the tunnel stretching farther into the cave, waiting for a shift in the darkness beyond—but find nothing.

There's only the altar, which has borne witness to old horrors, blessed with the moon's quiet, unrelenting light.

ACKNOWLEDGMENTS

Growing up, I was an avid reader of fairy tales and folklore. I was fascinated by the tales of knights and dragons, witches and wizards, and enchanted forests and magical realms. I devoured every story I could get my hands on, and I spent countless hours lost in the pages of books that transported me to worlds beyond my wildest imaginings. I was an introvert and frequently alone by choice, but when surrounded by these stories I never felt lonely.

It was this love of fairy tales and folklore that led me to create my own hodgepodge of stories where fairy tales shared one weird multiverse; a place where the tales and myths of different cultures could come together to form a rich tapestry of magic and wonder. I wanted to explore the many facets of these tales, to delve into their themes and motifs, and to create a world that was both familiar and new, timeless and contemporary. I wanted humor and tragedy, subversions and resolve in the face of adversity. I especially wanted to showcase the Filipino concept of the barkada: a group of close friends ready to ride and die for each other. I wanted to write about found families, of people who look out for one other through the good times and the bad.

I stand on the shoulders of giants. I am deeply indebted to the many authors, storytellers, and artists who have come before me, who have crafted the stories that have shaped my imagination and inspired my creativity. From the Brothers Grimm to Hans Christian Andersen to Lihui Yang, these writers have given me the tools and inspiration I needed to create my own stories.

I am also grateful to the many people who have supported me on this journey. To my family and friends, who have always believed in me and encouraged me to pursue my dreams, I cannot thank you enough. Your love and support have been my rock, and I am deeply grateful for all that you have done for me. Shoutout to my dad especially, who weaned me on ghost stories and fairy tales as a child and stirred in me a hunger for them that has never been satisfied since.

All my gratitude to my agent, Rebecca Podos, who has always been a source of comfort and cheer throughout the years we've been working together, and here's to many more!

I am also indebted to my editor, Annie Berger, whose keen eye and insightful feedback helped me to shape this book into the best version of itself. Her patience, guidance, and encouragement were invaluable to me throughout the writing process, and I am deeply grateful for her help. I am also grateful for the Sourcebooks team: Sabrina Baskey, Gabbi Calabrese, Thea Voutiritsas, Erin Fitzsimmons, Laura Boren. From the cover design to the marketing strategy, from the copyediting to the typesetting, you have all played an important role in bringing this book to life, and I am deeply grateful for all that you have done.

Finally, I want to thank the readers who have taken the time to journey with me through this story, especially through the ups and downs the last few years had brought. Your support and enthusiasm have been a constant source of inspiration to me, and I hope that this book brings you as much joy as it has brought me.

About the Author

Rin Chupeco is a nonbinary Chinese Filipino writer born and raised in the Philippines. They are the author of several speculative young adult series, including The Bone Witch, The Girl from the Well, The Never-Tilting World, and Wicked as You Wish, as well as *The Curse of the Gravemother* from the Are You Afraid of the Dark series. They are also the author of the vampire adult fantasy *Silver Under Nightfall* and its sequel, *Court of Wanderers*. Formerly a graphic designer and technical writer, they now write fiction full-time and live with their partner and two children in Manila.

sourcebooks fire

Home of the hottest trends in YA!

Visit us online and
sign up for our newsletter at
FIREreads.com

. . . .

Follow
@sourcebooksfire
online